LOVING THE PLAYBOY

S.L. SCOTT

S.L. SCOTT

You're the sky.
I'm the Earth.
Together we make our own universe.

1

EVAN

"Evan?" Mallory is staring at me, but her face is expressionless.

"Hi there." I wait for any reaction *other than shock*—happy, mad, maybe even confusion. *No*, I don't want her to be mad or confused.

While I wait for what feels like minutes, I notice how much she's changed in the last month. Somehow, she's managed to become more beautiful than I remember and video chat definitely doesn't do her justice.

She has no make-up on and her hair isn't styled, but the best part is, she's practically naked with her robe exposing the top of her pale pink bra and it makes me curious if her panties match. My ring is on her finger—exactly where it should be, but this weird feeling builds in my chest and I start to wonder why she's coming to the door undressed like this if she didn't know it was me.

Easily distracted, her breasts are rounded at the top of her bra, which makes me want to fucking attack her. I hold back though. A—because I'm holding flowers that are heavy as hell and B—because her roommate is standing to the side of us, forming an obtuse triangle of awkwardness since Mallory hasn't said anything other than 'Evan.'

I look at Sarah, who helped me set up this surprise after Sunny gave me her number. Mallory looks at Sarah, and Sarah says, "I'm going to head over to Josh's place and stay over there this weekend. We're going to that party if you guys want to join us." We both look quickly back at each other, knowing we're not going to any party. We glance back to Sarah, who puts her hands up, and laughs. "Guess not. Okay, sooo..." she walks over to Mallory and hugs her. "Happy birthday."

After setting the large vase of flowers down on their dining table, I get Sarah's attention before she rushes out the door, "Hey, thanks for helping me surprise her."

She giggles. "No problem and it was nice to finally meet you. I've heard a lot of great things about you, and Mal's shown me pictures from summer. Hawaii is beautiful." She grabs a bag near the door. "She's a great girl. Take care of her." As she walks out, she sings, "Have fun, you two."

Mallory hasn't moved from her spot or said anything. But when she does, my heart starts racing. "What are you doing here?" As if she doesn't trust her own eyes, she blinks hard. When she opens them again, I'm smiling because she's just so damn cute. "You're here," she says.

"For your birthday. I came to make your birthday wish come true. I'll give you anything you want."

"You. I only wished for you." Her expression changes, the reality of me being here, standing in front of her, sinking in. Tears fill her eyes then one slips down her cheek.

Not able to stand the distance any longer, I move to her, taking her in my arms and hold her tightly to me. "That's why I'm here. How could I not grant your *only* wish?"

"I can't believe you're here." Her voice shakes in obvious

resistance to crying. I feel her body tremble against mine as she hugs me, embracing me fully. "You did this for me?"

Stroking the back of her head, I wind my fingers into her hair, and try to calm her, "I didn't mean to upset you."

"You didn't upset me. It's just... you're here..." She presses her cheek against my chest, fists my tee, and says, "... you're the best birthday present I ever got."

I chuckle. "I love you."

She looks up at me, disbelief still residing in her eyes. "I love you, too. I love you so much, Evan. I can't believe you're really here. Like *here* here."

I kiss the lips I've so desperately missed and she kisses me back just as eager. Everything in the world seems to be right in this moment. I've got my girl back in my arms and life is perfect again.

When our lips part, I quirk an eyebrow, and ask, "So tell me, do you always answer the door in your underwear?" I'm half joking, but half not.

The right side of her mouth goes up and I prepare myself for a smartass remark that she's so good at delivering. Instead, she pulls her robe closed and says, "If you don't like what you see, I can always cover up."

"Whoa, whoa, whoa. Don't misunderstand. I like what I see," I say, taking the robe lapels in hand and slowly pulling them apart to reveal her sexy collarbone and the tops of her breasts. "As a matter of fact, I want to see more. But I don't want other guys to see."

She lifts up on her tiptoes and kisses me, commanding my lips apart. I give in and our tongues embrace. It's been too long, my body reacting and responding. She's the only one who does this to me.

Rational thoughts cloud my dirtier ones of what I want to do to her. I push those sensible ones aside because we have time for reasonable and respectable another day. I need her too much. Walking her backwards through the living room and down the short hall, I stop. With my lips pressed against hers, my eyes search for signs of which open door leads to her bedroom, or more importantly—to her bed.

She giggles. Leaning back, looking me in the eyes, she nods her head to the left. "It's this one."

I spin her around, pulling her into the room by the sash of her robe, and kick the door closed. That makes her laugh and seeing that beautiful smile and her happy eyes make all the planning that went into this trip worth it.

Standing next to the bed, we look at each other in the soft light from the bedside lamp. Removing the hideously obstructive robe from her body, I drop it to the floor.

Our smiles disappear and that familiar intensity that formed our bond back in Hawaii exists again. It's comforting, but engulfing, making my chest ache in the most painfully acute way and my heart feels grounded in her. This is right. This is us, and I can finally breathe again.

Whispering, she questions my stalling. "Evan?"

Cupping her face, I kiss the tip of her nose. "We can wait... if you want."

"I don't want to wait."

There's a confidence to her response that convinces me to move forward, but I know what I want, but I'm not sure what she wants—to make love or fuck. She sits on the end of the bed and takes off her bra.

I've experienced a myriad of emotions since I met Mallory, but nervous was never one of them until now. I can tell she's a little nervous too by the shy smile she gives me when she stands to take off her underwear.

When she sits back down, she tugs me by my belt loops.

I'm hard and can't hide the fact, so when I look down at her lying beneath me, her eyes meet mine, and she says, "I want to be with you."

"*Oh, thank God.* I don't think I can go another day without you." Reaching into my pocket, I produce a condom and toss it on the bed. I strip my clothes off in a hurry. They all fly off and we move to the top of the bed where I lay above her, so ready to be inside her, but I slow everything back down, wanting to appreciate the act of reuniting with my girlfriend.

I start by kissing her neck and when I reach that spot just below her ear, the one that makes her giggle every time, she lets a small laugh out and rolls her head to the side allowing me to reach every inch of her. Using my tongue and lips together, I gently suck, but not enough to leave a mark. She moans and that's when gentle flies out the window. My hips drop down and I press my cock against her, needing the feel of her.

With a slow blink of her eyes, she licks her lips. She fucking licks her lips, driving me wild. "You're a tease."

"It's not teasing if I plan on following through."

"So you have a plan?"

"Lots of them," she says, her voice raspy as I rub against her, making her breaths come harder, building her desire.

"Nothing like when a plan comes together," I say, waggling my eyebrows.

"Yep, nothing like coming together." She runs her fingers through my hair and pulls me by the back of the head down to kiss her. "Less talking and more coming."

"You sound like me, bossy pants."

"No pants on here."

Lifting up, I scan down her naked body and then back up. "You're right. Less talking and more coming."

The emerald of her eyes draws me in, and it's so easy to see why I fell in love with her—all her emotions lie there. I run my hand over her cheek and into her hair, admiring everything I've missed so much. Mallory's tan has faded, her hair seems darker, and I suspect she has lost some weight. But the look in her eyes still sets my soul on fire every damn time.

She wiggles under me and with a shy smile, says, "Are you okay, babe?"

"Yeah, I just missed you." I lean down to kiss her quickly and reach for the condom to rip it open.

"Let me." She takes the packet from my hand.

Leaning up on my elbows, I watch her fingers carefully roll the condom over my hardened length. She glances up at me once, timidly, but then returns her focus downward. My erection twitches in response to her loving attention as she drags her finger along the underside, from base to tip.

She lies back and I lower myself down, pressing my hips against her heated center. I kiss her as she wraps her arms around my neck, then push into her, slow and careful.

She feels incredible, more than incredible. An overwhelming sensation drags me under when my hips meet hers. I stop even though all I want to do is go, but I give her time to adjust. In all honesty, I stop because I've lost my mind and control of my body. All I feel is her—beneath me, arms holding me, legs as they twist around my middle—Mallory consuming me.

I drop my head to the side, next to hers, and swear, "Fuck, I'm never gonna leave."

"You're never leaving my apartment?" Her whisper has an edge of a moan surrounding it.

She starts wriggling and I halt her movements, her reactions speeding up my own. I'll fucking come instantly if I can't get my mind in order, and she definitely deserves more than a one-minute reunion fuck. "I'm never leaving your pussy." I pull back and push in again. Her eyes close and I can tell she's right there with me.

"Mmmm, I missed you so much," she says. "You feel so good."

Bliss builds deep within, coiling inside. I lean forward, rubbing the base of my cock against where I know she needs it.

She sighs her pleasure and softly demands, "Yes, right there, Evan, don't stop, just like that."

"Oh, fuck!" I slam into her twice, causing her to squeeze me into oblivion, both of us giving into our orgasms.

When our bodies subside from the tremors, I roll off of her, and collapse onto the mattress. Dragging her against my side, I wipe away the stray strands of hair that are stuck to her face. I kiss her on the sweat-dampened forehead and stick the tip of my tongue out, touching it against her just enough taste her. I'm starting to feel like a psycho, but I need to taste her.

"Did you just lick my forehead?" she asks, quietly and skeptically.

"*Um, might've.*"

"Okay," she says, treating me like what I just did is normal. I appreciate the lack of judgment.

After a few minutes of cuddling, we get up. I go into the bathroom to dispose of the condom and take care of business before returning. Climbing back under the covers, I wait for her to come back to bed. She walks in, but detours to the bathroom. I notice how cold the bed feels without her.

She returns with a small smile, crawling back into bed, and right into my arms. "My memories don't do you justice,"

I say, "and yet in my memories, you're the most beautiful girl in the world."

Resting her head on my chest, her hand rubs my side. "Stop or you're gonna make me cry again."

"As long as they're happy tears, cry away. I love you, Mallory." I sound serious even to me.

"I don't think it's possible to ever love anyone as much as I love you." Her head tilts and I can tell her gaze is on me. "I hope that doesn't scare you."

"It does quite the opposite."

Her fingers tinker across my abs as she confesses, "This is... *we're* more than I expected to find. Does that make any sense?" Her voice is soft like her skin.

We're starting to talk in a roundabout way, touching on our true feelings, but not saying anything too direct. I'm just going to say what I really want to. "This may be too soon to admit, but being away from you this past month has confirmed what I was feeling back in Hawaii."

"And what is that?"

"That one day you're going to marry me. There's just no other option for us."

Her head lifts quickly, her beautiful eyes meeting mine as she sits up to face me. "Evan, do you really feel that way?"

"Yes." My voice is not as strong as my feelings. "Did I say too much?" I hope I don't scare her. "You just always seem to be on my mind—a factor in all my decisions."

She gulps, her gaze roaming the features of my face. "This has happened so fast and been so crazy since we met. I thought we were being playful, even a little idealistic. I don't want you to feel any pressure from me."

Looking at her sitting naked beside me, she's so comfortable in herself and her surroundings— so comfortable with me as I stroke her cheek. Sliding my hands around her, I pull her onto my lap, leaving nothing between us. "I don't feel pressured. I'm saying what I feel."

I shift and my hand reaches up to find the comfort zone of my hair, but her hand catches mine and she brings it to her mouth to kiss my palm. Her eyes don't leave mine as her tongue slips out to press a wetter kiss against my skin.

She's mesmerizing and stunning, breathtaking. I think I momentarily stop breathing, but I'm not sure. My heart beats heavily waiting to hear what she says next.

"There will never be anyone else," she states, firm and confident.

"No one, Mallory. You own my every thought, my heart, and my soul," I respond without letting my own insecurities stand in the way of telling her everything I feel. The confession almost makes me want to drop down on bended knee or something. "Shit, this is intense. I might need a cigarette."

"No cigarette will change what we feel. It's intense because we're admitting our deepest thoughts and fears, babe. This will make us stronger when we're apart."

"After this semester, nothing will ever come between us again. I promise you that," I say, assured in every one of my words.

Her voice is low, a bit husky, and completely fucking sexy when she says, "You once told me you only believed in the *'right now'* kind of girl.

Flipping her onto her back while holding my weight above her, I lightly tickle her ribs, and say, "I just hadn't met the *right* girl yet."

She's giggling when she asks, "So you think you've found her, do you?"

I grin, knowing she's fishing for more. After a sweet kiss to the forehead, I press my lips against her ear and whisper, "I don't think. I *know* I have."

2

EVAN

She's quiet in contemplation. I can tell by the creases formed between her eyebrows. They give her away every time. "How long can you stay?" Mallory asks, slipping out from under the covers and standing at the end of the bed. The low light in the room accentuates her soft curves and my body stirs in response.

Resting my arms behind my head, I keep my voice low like the moment seems to call for. "Tell me how you feel."

She glances beside me and I know she's looking at the clock. "I'm a little tired, but feel good."

"About what I said. About marrying me one day."

The bed dips where she sits and she pulls her robe onto her lap, keeping her bare back exposed to me. Looking back at me over her shoulder, she says, "I like what you said."

"You like what you said," I repeat, trying to figure out if that's enough of an answer to tide me over. It's not, so I sit up and move closer, kissing her back several times. "I meant it, Mallory. It's been a month and I've been going crazy without you. I've never cared about anyone the way I do about you. This is real for me."

She turns with an intensity in her eyes, and says, "You don't seem to understand how easily you can destroy my heart and yet I've handed it over to you on a silver platter. I feel nuts sometimes, like I should protect myself, but I can't because I love you too much, so don't doubt my sincerity or my feelings for you."

"It's not too much if I feel the same for you. C'mere." I take her hand in mine and bring it to my lips, kissing it three times. "We're young, but we're not dumb. We know what we're getting into. I want this with you. I want everything with you. I'm not talking about tomorrow. I'm talking about a commitment that I can make right now."

Her hand settles on my cheek and a soft smile appears. "My sweet surfer. What a change a month makes."

"It's not the month that changed me. It's the girl." I turn and kiss her palm. "You make me want more than I feel I deserve."

"You deserve everything your heart desires."

"My heart only desires you."

"Then I'm yours. All yours. Always." She kisses my cheek then stands up, slipping the robe back on.

"Don't bother getting dressed because I plan on having you naked until I leave on Sunday."

"Three nights? Sounds like the perfect birthday present to me," she says, walking into the bathroom all sassy and sexy.

"You're perfect." When she returns, she drops the robe carelessly to the floor and climbs back in, snuggling against me. "Are you hungry?"

A sly grin graces her lips. "I'm starved, but I want to stay in bed with you. We can order something or I can make you eggs, or cereal, or a sandwich? We haven't stocked up on groceries."

"Let's order food and then I want the grand tour."

"A tour of this apartment will take about thirty seconds."

I maneuver on top of her, look her in the eyes, and smirk. "I meant of your body."

She giggles and says, "You, sir, are a very naughty boy and I like it."

"I've really missed you, baby."

"I've missed you, hot stuff."

I grab her, dragging her further down the mattress and flip the sheet over our heads. She squeals in delight and I get busy making her squeal in other ways.

An hour later, I'm sitting across from her at the table eating pizza. Her smile fades and she takes another bite. Worry invades her thoughts and those pesky lines reappear. "I'm supposed to go home for my birthday. I promised my parents."

"You still can if you want." I'm trying to be supportive, but I want her all to myself.

"No. You're here and I want to spend time with you. I'll call and cancel. They'll understand."

I don't know what I'm thinking, but I blurt a thought out that I question the moment I say it. "We can go see them together if you like? I mean if you think you're ready for me to meet your parents." Deep down I'm hoping she doesn't pick this option because that will put the kibosh on everything I plan to do for her and *to her* this weekend.

"We won't be relaxed or be able to... you know... sleep together or anything if we stay at their house."

That's my girl.

"I'll just call them," she says, picking up her cell.

I move to the couch and watch as she fidgets with her phone while waiting for them to pick up.

"Mom, hi." She pauses. "It's been a good day. A very

good day. I know I said I'd come home in the morning, but..."

Looking around the small apartment, I see a new side to the girl I thought I knew in Hawaii. There she was surrounded by Sunny's belongings. Here, I wonder what is hers and what stuff is Sarah's. As she talks with her mother, I start analyzing. There's a short bookcase in the corner filled with books, some stacked on the floor in front of it too. A four seat dinette set is in the small space by the kitchen which is also pretty damn small. I look at the couch and it's a loveseat. Everything is so... *small.*

I don't know the housing market here, but I've had bigger places in Manhattan and the rent there is outrageous. Taking in her standard of living makes me curious if this is by choice or because she has to budget? And I didn't have to have sex with her to tell she's lost weight. Can she afford to eat? *Shit,* maybe I should buy this girl some groceries before I leave.

"It's all settled," she says, her eyes sparkling with joy. "They're gonna drive up tomorrow and take us out for dinner. And they're really excited about meeting you. We just need to figure out where we want to eat." She takes a large breath and then exclaims, "I know where I want to go! Palace Arms I've always wanted to eat there...oh, but that will probably be too expensive. I hear it's quite pricey." She angles her head down in thought, gnawing the inside of her cheek. "No, we shouldn't go there. It will definitely be too pricey. I don't want them to spend that much money on me just because it's my birthday."

"If cost wasn't an issue, is that where you'd want to eat?" I watch her reaction carefully. She may say no to spare her parents shelling out that kind of money, but I can never say no to her.

"Yes."

"That's where we're going then. I'll buy dinner."

"No, Evan. It's really expensive, like $30 an entrée or maybe more." Her tone gets all hushed like she's telling me a secret. "I don't even think that includes a side."

I chuckle because she's cute, but also because she really seems to be clueless to how much money my family has even though she's been to my parent's house and seen my car in Hawaii. Actually, I don't even know how much money my family has, but I know I don't ever have to worry about it either. "I think I can manage. If that's where you want to celebrate your birthday, that's where we'll go."

"*Really?*"

"If you want to eat at the Palace Arms then we'll eat at the Palace Arms. I'll do anything to make you happy."

"I know you will and I will for you. I just wish I knew how I could do that." I love the way she speaks from the heart.

After we finish our dinner, I go to the fridge where Sarah hid a cake I ordered from a local bakery. I set the box on the counter and open the lid. The candle they packed is there and I stick it in the top. I take the cake from the box and with my lighter, light the candle. "Turn out the light and close your eyes," I call to her in the living room.

"What are you up to?" I can hear the happiness through her words.

I sing her Happy Birthday as I walk in and crouch in front of her. Her eyelids pop open and she gasps, covering her mouth. After setting the cake on the table in front of her, I say, "And I hope you have many more. Make a wish, baby."

"It already came true."

"I think you stole that line."

She smirks. "A *Sixteen Candles* fan? Ya learn something new every day."

"Eh, I know the girls get all mushy over that movie. Figured I should investigate."

"Investigate, huh? Kind of like how you and Zach watched *Titanic* together?" She levels her eyes on me. "Don't even try to lie. Kate told me all about it."

I sit down next to her. "Fine. I watched *Titanic*. So has most of the world. As for *Sixteen Candles*, it was on TV one time when I was sick. I blame the fever for making me watch it."

"The real question is," she says with her hand on my knee, "did you like it?"

"I'll never confess."

She laughs then leans forward and blows out the candle. Falling back on the couch, she says, "You didn't have to do that, you know?"

"A cake? Pfft. Of course, I did. What's a birthday without cake?"

"Good point." She swipes her finger through the frosting and brings it to her mouth, savoring the chocolate.

Irresistible. She's completely irresistible.

Just as my tongue tastes the frosting on her lips, there's a knock at the door. I get more comfortable on the couch, irritated by the interruption, knowing that one taste was going to lead to so much more before that knock . "You expecting company?"

"No." She stands and walks to the door.

"Mallory? You in there?" some guy shouts from outside the door. "Sarah said you stayed home."

"Let me guess... *ummmm* Ryan?" My sarcasm is not lost on her. Smart girl.

"He's just a friend," she whispers, grabbing her robe and

tightening the belt. "I promise." Before she opens the door, she looks back at me and I can see her nerves developing in her expression. "I'm sure he just wants to talk about our project or something. I'll get rid of him and we can pick up from where we left off."

As much as I'd love to open that door and come face-to-face with this guy, I remain on the couch, sitting in only my black boxer briefs, the ones I know she likes on me. I'm not worried about this creep seeing me. It'll be good for him to see me like this in Mallory's apartment. I gulp down the jealousy I have toward this guy who is spending more time with my girlfriend than I am these days, and try to play it cool.

As soon as Mallory opens the door, this Ryan guy presents her with a cupcake and a candle sticking out the top. "Like I said on campus today, everyone should have cake on their—" he says, Mr. Smiling Smooth until he sees me staring back at him. He shakes his head, putting two and two together as he looks between us. I think the lack of attire clued him in. I inwardly laugh as he scrambles to play off that he showed up at his current obsession's place to find that she's just had sex with her boyfriend. "Hey man," he says, "you must be Evan?"

My chest heats inside, feeling a lot like heartburn, but I know the difference these days. This jerk-off actually believes I'm not onto him. What is he expecting? Are we supposed to be besties because we both surprised *my* girlfriend with cake? Yeah, right, fucker. I stand up when Ryan strides across the living room with an outstretched arm, offering a handshake.

"Yeah, and you are?" I play dumb.

"I'm Ryan. I brought Mallory a cupcake. I thought she might be down since she didn't come to the party. You know how that is," he says as if that justifies his presence in my girlfriends' apartment.

I take his hand because it's the right thing to do, but I'm not happy about it. "How do you know Mallory?" It's best for him to think she's never mentioned him before, ultimately showing his unimportance in her life. But then another thought occurs and I get pissed wondering if this guy *is* important to her.

"I'm one of Mallory's friends from school," he explains, a little too flagrantly for my liking.

"We're assigned to the same group in English class. Yeah..." he says not finishing whatever he was going to say and shoves his hands into his pant pockets. I think I make him nervous, which is good. He should be nervous.

"We're working on a project together," Mallory says, interrupting, obviously hoping to water down their relationship and the situation.

It's not working because I saw the disappointment in his eyes as soon as he saw me sitting here. We stand in silence, an uncomfortable tension filling in the room and I begin to gloat because I'm back. The boyfriend is back in the picture and he'll have to try to fuck someone else's girlfriend. But something he said stands out and I call him on it. "You said, 'You know how that is.' How *what* is?"

"You know. No one should be alone on their birthday. I thought maybe she was sad or something and I wanted to cheer her up." He shrugs as if this conversation is mere chitchat.

"Why would you assume she's sad?" I ask, tilting my head and crossing my arms over my chest, so I don't punch him right the fuck out for acting like he knows my Mallory on such an intimate level.

"I guess I've interrupted," he says with his hands

momentarily in surrender before he drops them and faces Mallory, fishing for an invitation out of this situation. Yeah, you scurry along and fuck off now.

He turns back to me and I say, not mincing words, "Yes, I have lots of big plans for my girlfriend tonight and they really don't include anyone else... *You know how that is.*" I throw his words back at him. He gets the message loud and clear and walks back to the door that was never closed—another good hint for him to take-off. "Good meeting you, Ryan," I add just to mess with him a little more because I'm immature like that.

I sit down while Mallory walks him to the doorway, thanking him for stopping by and for the cupcake. I don't hear it all because I'm too caught in my own swirling emotions regarding his presence in my girlfriend's life. But then I swear I hear a whispered apology though I don't know what she would be apologizing for.

As soon as she closes the door, I can tell she's pissed. *Majorly pissed.* She turns to face me, hands on hips, looking incredibly sexy, and demands, "What was that all about?"

And she says I'm the one who gets all protective and shit. "Need I remind you of your own jealous nature, *Mrs. Ashford*?" Yeah, it's a low blow, reminding her of her jealous antics in Kauai, but she's cute as hell when she's like this and I just like calling her that.

She huffs. "Fine! I get it."

"I thought you'd see it my way, baby. Now, come over here."

Two deadbolts are locked and then she turns, narrowing her eyes at me. She may be pissed at my behavior, but I know she'll forgive me or I have other ways of distracting her and making her forget. Which reminds me of what I tucked into the cushion earlier... "You want your birthday present?"

She straddles my lap, with her arms around my neck and a big smile on her face. "You already bought me the laptop and then flew out here. There's nothing more I want."

Slipping my arms around her waist, I say, "I wanted to buy it for you."

"Was it expensive?"

I know what she's doing. She going to justify not accepting it based on money like she always does. A gold-digger—she is not. "It doesn't matter if it was expensive or not, I bought you what I wanted to give you. Everything else is irrelevant."

"Because you're being evasive about it, I can tell you spent too much. You don't have to do that."

"I know I don't, but I like to. And if you're so against pricey presents, I'll just add it to *my* collection instead."

"Wait! *Collection?*" she asks as if it all dawns on her all at once. "Is this a book, Evan?"

"Yes," I say, nodding.

She takes the present and carefully opens the wrapping. While she stares at the spine, stunned, I clarify, "It's only a 3rd edition. I couldn't find a first or second edition in my price range."

"Your price range? A third edition shouldn't be in your price range either, babe. You spent too much," she says, handing the book back to me.

"You love 'Great Expectations' and I wanted to give you something you love," I state, pushing the book toward her.

She runs her fingertips over the leather embossed cover and spine, appreciating the artistry in the detail. "How'd you know I love this book so much?"

"Sunny."

"Mmmm." She's shaking her head and then looks at me. "I can't..." she starts with tears in her eyes.

"Yes, you can. It's done. Please accept it."

She sets it on the couch beside us and leans down to kiss me, her lips lingering a moment against mine. "Thank you for the book. It was very thoughtful of you, Evan." She sighs and leans her forehead against mine. "You've given me the best birthday ever. Not because of the amazing gift but because you're here when I needed you most."

3

EVAN

"Stop worrying about it. They're very normal," Mallory says, looking at me over her shoulder from the closet.

I watch as she sets her dress on the bed, and I say, "Your dad works for the government. If you didn't realize it in Hawaii, I don't usually get along well with authority figures."

"He doesn't work for the CIA," she replies, rolling her eyes. Picking the dress up she slips it on.

"But Mallory, I break a lot of laws—"

"You drive a Maserati. Breaking a speed limit every now and again is kind of expected, but you're not exactly on the FBI's Most Wanted list, Evan, so don't worry." She puts her hands on my chest and rubs gently. "They're going to love you, I promise. You know I've already told my mom about you, and as for my dad, he's more a meet and judge for himself kind of guy. He trusts his first impressions, so with him, that's your key to success."

She turns away to spray perfume on her neck and watching her tilt her head back like that does things to me, serious things down in my pants.

She claps her hands and says, "Okay, I'm ready."

"I'm not."

"I've never seen you like this. It will be fine. I won't let my big bad parents hurt wittle Evan."

"Okay, *really*," I say, shaking my head. "And no baby talk."

She hits me on the back and says, "Then buck up and let's go."

We take a cab to the restaurant because I plan on having a drink or five to get me through this dinner. When we arrive, I begin sweating as I pay the driver. The taxi leaves and I stand there, gathering my nerve and try to relax. I tug at the tie I bought today when Mallory was in class, and sheepishly ask, "What's his Achilles heel?"

She looks at me with a raised eyebrow. "I'm not giving you ammo against my dad. This will be just like meeting any other girls' parents. I'm sure you've done this a million times, Romeo."

"No, I haven't."

"Okay, so I exaggerated. But I'm sure it went smoother than you expected when you did meet them."

"I've never met a girl's parents before."

She turns abruptly, staring at me. "Never?"

"No, never. My family was usually already friends with their families or they were just... a thing... you know, not important enough for that."

A devious grin slides across her mouth, and she says, "In that case...he loves bird-watching and a good lager."

Okay, this I can work with. "I knew I loved you."

Too perky and snarky for her own good, she says, "Because I give you inside information to win my dad over? Not because I'm smart, beautiful, and tenacious?"

"You being smart and beautiful is obvious, but you

saving my ass was unexpected." I smile, feeling more confident going into this dinner.

"My dad has nothing on the shit your mother put me through, so I'm gonna need a proper thank you later."

"You don't even have to ask. I have lots of plans to thank you properly when we get back to your place." I smack her ass making her yelp, and add, "And I'll be testing that tenacity later tonight."

I open the door to the Palace Arms restaurant and the cool air hits my face and in a blur of commotion, Mallory is grabbed from my side. A man, I assume is her dad, hugs her so tight she can't escape, but with his eyes narrowed on me trying to intimidate. "How is my baby girl?"

She grabs at his arms and hoarsely says, "I'm good, dad. I mean, I can't breathe so I might not be good for long."

"Oh, sorry. I'm happy to see you," he says, still staring me down while talking over her shoulder.

"Happy birthday, honey," her mom says with open arms.

As Mallory hugs her mom, her dad stands there, arms crossed, staring at me.

After their greeting, her mother steps around Mallory. "Evan, I'm Elise, it's so nice to meet you. I've heard a lot of wonderful things about you." I stick my hand out, but she comes in and says, "Sorry, I'm a hugger."

I return the hug, politely and a little caught off guard, but in a good way.

Her dad watches the interaction, then says, "You must be the *new* boyfriend."

"Hopefully better than the old boyfriend." I inwardly roll my eyes at how stupid that was, my nerves taking over. Mallory elbows me, keeping a smile on her face for the family.

"Guess that remains to be seen." He glares, but I know

he can't be that bad. Mallory has always talked about how great her parents are.

But I'm not winning any points here, so I formally introduce myself. Stepping forward, I reach my hand out to greet him. "I'm Evan Ashford. It's very nice to meet you, Sir. Mallory has told me lots of good things about you."

"I'm not a hugger." He shakes my hand—firm and domineering—trying to control who's boss around here. "I've heard the cliff notes version about you, so I'm curious what parts have been left out. Should make for an interesting dinner."

"Stop it. You're scaring him," her mother says, hitting her husband on the chest, which reminds me a lot of Mallory.

"Elise, that's the point." She gives him a look that I wouldn't want to be on the receiving end of. He clears his throat, and says, "I'm Clay Wray. Nice to meet you."

Clay Wray?

My eyes meet Mallory's and she shakes her head once, meaning don't even go there. She knows I want to laugh over that name, but I'll restrain myself... for now.

Mallory squeezes between us with her hands up like she's breaking up a fight. "I think we're late for our reservation. We should check in. Dad?"

Her mother says, "Our table is ready, and please call me Elise."

"You can call me Mr. Wray."

The ladies laugh and I gulp. Mallory hits me on the chest, and says, "He's kidding, Evan."

"Yeah... I'm kidding, Evan. You can call me Clay." I note his dry humor. Tonight is gonna be a long night.

As we follow the maître d', Mallory giggles. "See. No big deal." Taking me by the hand, she pulls me behind her parents.

We're seated at a booth in the corner and as Mallory and Elise *ooh* and *ahh* over the restaurant, I slip the maitre d' a tip before he leaves.

Everything about her and her parents at dinner is fascinating. The way Mallory and her parents interact, their appreciation over little things like when Elise is offered a taste of the wine for approval, and that the food is presented instead of delivered to our table. They're very endearing and refreshing, grateful and kind, compared to what I'm used to in Manhattan. They're real. They share their feelings and thoughts openly not worried about being judged or having that used against them. They have a zest for life that isn't manufactured.

When we finish our entrees, I rest my hand on Mallory's thigh. She's engrossed in a conversation with her mother about a book she just finished reading. I take a sip of my beer, which I ordered to match her father's taste since I'm seeking his approval. When my eyes meet Clay's, his eyes dart from mine to the table in front of Mallory, giving a clear warning to remove my hand from his daughter. I do, immediately, and he gives me a half-hearted smile.

Her parents ask about my family and my time in New York and how I'm liking it. I'm honest with them. I miss their daughter and it's been hard to be apart. Elise smiles while taking her daughter's hand and giving it a little squeeze. Her father grumbles.

Mallory tells them about the places I took her sight-seeing back in Hawaii, saying she wants to return one day. Maybe even to earn her master's degree. I catalog that tidbit to talk about later, in private.

After sharing Mallory's chocolate dessert, the bill arrives. I know with drinks and food that the bill will be close to $400. I quickly reach across the table and take the little black folder out from under Clay's hand before he has a chance to view it.

"If you wouldn't mind, I'd like to treat your family to dinner tonight in honor of Mallory's birthday. You were very kind to let me ruin your plans, so I'd like to make it up to you."

Elise reaches across the table and tries to take the folder. "That won't be necessary, Evan. It's a very nice gesture, but we're thrilled you flew here to celebrate with her and that we got to meet you. Right, Clay?"

Her father leans back in his chair and with both hands, rubs his stomach. "Elise, let the boy pay if he's so eager."

She whispers, "This is a very expensive restaurant. We should pay."

I take Mallory's hand and justify, "I can easily cover the bill and like I said, I'd be honored."

"See?" Clay says, pointing at me, "He'd be honored."

Mallory leans forward and says, "Evan told me last night he'd like to buy dinner as a gift to me, so no more arguing please."

As we stand outside waiting for the valet, her father has a toothpick in his mouth, and is eyeing me up. "Normally, I'd question where a young person such as yourself got a hold of that kind of money, but it sounds like you have your parents' permission to pay on their credit card, so I'm going to let that line of questioning drop." He looks between me and Mallory then adds, "For now."

After many thank you's, nice to meet you, and hugs, Elise elbows him. They look at each other and since he's doesn't understand what she wants, he asks, "What?"

"Goooo oonn," she says, expressing her displeasure with him.

"OH!" He turns to me and says, "It was good to meet you.

We'd like to invite you to our home sometime in the future since this," he points between me and Mallory, "is looking pretty serious. I can take you bird-watching and we can talk…"

It seems like he wanted to say more, but doesn't. "I'd like that very much, Sir."

"Okay, well, alright. That's settled."

Our cab pulls up to the curb, and after our goodbyes, we get in and go back to Mallory's small apartment.

"I'm glad we didn't drive. Now we can just relax," she says, snuggling into my side on the ride home.

"I'm glad we didn't drive either. I tried keeping up with your dad, but he out drank me by two beers."

"My mom kept topping off my wine. She loved it, by the way. Thank you for suggesting it."

"It's one my parent's like a lot. I was glad they had it there."

"It was expensive, wasn't it?"

I don't answer.

"Whatever. I don't really want to know anyway." She turns toward me and kisses me sweetly on the cheek. "Thank you for dinner and meeting my parents and all that. It means a lot that you've met them."

"I think they're pretty great, *even Clay Wray.*"

"Oh, don't even go there."

"How can I not? That's gold right there."

"It's old and worn out is what it is. I've had to hear people making fun of it my whole life."

I pull her closer and kiss the top of her head. As much as I want to push that joke further, I'll respect her wishes.

"You're laughing, aren't you?" she asks, looking up at me.

"Only on the inside."

She hasn't entirely lost her sense of humor on the subject, and laughs.

Too tired to mess around once we're back in Boulder, we kiss for a few minutes, but end it before it gets too heated.

Just as I'm starting to doze off, I hear her mumble, "Wish come true."

I smile, opening my eyes once again to look at the stunning girl next to me. She's asleep, falling fast tonight. After sneaking a kiss onto her forehead, careful not to wake her, I whisper, "Wish come true indeed." All my wishes and future are wrapped up in the beauty sleeping next to me.

4

MALLORY

I'm hot and smothered, but I like it. Lying in my dark room with my surfer wrapped around me, holding me so tight that it wakes me up. But when I peek over my shoulder, he seems at peace in his sleep.

Evan wiggles and his erection presses against my hip. I find it remarkable how hard a guy can get in his sleep. I wiggle back and his breathing changes as he stirs, pushing himself further against me, if that's even possible.

Hot breath covers my neck and he whispers, "Baby, you do things to me."

"Correction," I whisper. "I *want* to do things to you."

"Well, mission accomplished. This," he says, moving his cock against me again, "is getting painful."

Making love to him is never a chore and I love sex in the middle of the night in this dreamy state—it's freeing from my daily worries and is easy to focus on the good sensations.

He wraps his arm around me and we spoon before falling back asleep, tired from the middle of the night sexcapades.

I like to think morning brings bluebirds singing, the

smell of fresh coffee brewing, and sleeping in since Evan is here and it *is* Saturday. But, to my disappointment, it doesn't. My alarm blares, startling both of us awake.

Evan reaches over me and slams down on the clock so hard that it falls off the nightstand and bounces across the floor. "Remind me to get you a new alarm clock," he mumbles, snuggling his face into the pillow.

The sun peeks through the cracks of the curtains and I huff knowing I have to leave this safe, cozy haven to meet my parents.

I try to slide out from his secure grip. Without opening his eyes, he squeezes me tighter, and states, "No."

"I have to get up. I promised them."

"No, I'm not ready for you to leave."

"A planned weekend turned into only a dinner. I can at least have breakfast with them. I'll only be a few hours. You'll probably still be asleep when I get back anyway."

His arms loosen, still keeping his eyes closed, and I slip out of bed. Making my way to the bathroom, I quietly shut the door and start the shower. I walk back out and pull my standard jeans and school sweatshirt from the closet shelf.

I close the door behind me when I return to the bathroom and grab a towel from the rack. Reaching into the shower to check the temperature of the water, I turn around and jump when I see Evan standing there—all sleepy-eyed, mussed hair, and bare chest. He's perfection come to life—naked and smirking.

"You didn't say you were going to take a shower," he says, a sly grin playing on his lips.

Feigning coy, I put my hand under the warming water, and reply, "I figured I should probably not meet my parents for breakfast smelling like I've been doing naughty things all night."

"Can I come?"

"You did. Twice since you've been here." I laugh at my joke.

With light amusement, he says, "Ha ha."

"Do you really want to come to breakfast with my folks?"

"Yeah."

I'm weak to him. "Then you can join us."

He walks past me and steps into the basin. I grab another towel and hang both on the hook outside the shower before I enter. His hair is already wet and seeing him like this reminds me of when I'd watch him surf—wet and sexy as all get out.

Taking me by the pinky, he tugs me closer until I'm under the water with him. I let the warm water cascade from the top of my head and down to my feet. With a light touch, Evan chases a trail of droplets the length of my body. Kneeling in front of me, he rests his cheek against my stomach then places soft, sweet kisses on my inner thigh.

When he stands, he pushes my hair away from my face and kisses my mouth. Moving me back against the wall, his lips trail down my neck, one of his fingers tracing across my chest while his other hand holds my head in place. I can't help but tilt my head accompanied by a moan when I'm immersed into everything that is Evan.

"Babe," I plead, not meaning to, but unable to stop myself. "Three more months is too long to be without you. I need you so much."

His hand skims over my skin, stopping between my legs as he murmurs against my neck, "*Mallory*. I need you more than you know, not just your body. I need to possess you in ways that scare me." He slides two fingers inside of me and we both sigh in unison.

"I'm lost without you," I say, my head swimming in an

ocean of overwhelming emotion and lust. "I was made for you... only you. I only want you."

His fingers leave me and coldness invades my empty body. Before I have time to ask for more, he lifts me up and pushes inside, filling me as his chest presses against mine, pinning me against the tiled wall.

"Tell me how this feels, baby. Tell me how *I* feel."

I rock my head back and forth a couple of times unable to get a grasp on my thoughts. My eyes suddenly pop open. "You're not wearing a condom!"

"You feel fucking amazing," he says, whispering in my ear and calming me down. "You're still on the pill?"

He continues moving up and down my body, in and out, turning my world upside down. In my incoherent mind, I grasp the one word that makes everything alright. "Yes."

Taking that as a sign to go for it, he thrusts. Through whispering breaths, he utters words of love and ownership, destiny, and a forever together. He speaks of his dreams then comes while staring into my eyes.

Without relenting, he brings me to my own peak, sending me blazing into my own spinning orgasm. I'm not afraid to tell him, commit to him wholly. As he holds me in his arms, both of us breathless, I realize he is my purpose in life. Evan Ashford owns me and nothing compares to the love I have for this man. Nothing and no one will stop me from being with him in every imaginable and possible way.

And all is right in the world knowing he feels the same when he says, "*Fuck*, I can't go back to New York without you."

"Good. Because I'm not letting you leave." I press my lips against his chest, letting them linger as the taste of his skin, salty and soapy, graces my tongue. I push his wet hair off his face. "I've got to get ready. You still want to come with me?"

"I just did," he chuckles.

"Stop it," I chide, enjoying our lightened moods after the intensity of the activity.

"You need the time with your parents and I actually have some business on campus."

Surprised, I ask, "What? *A meeting?* It's Saturday. I thought the offices were closed on Saturday?"

He pours shampoo into my cupped hand and some into his. As we start washing each others' hair like we've done so many times before, he says, "They are, but this is when the last name Ashford *and* my school record come in handy."

"So they're giving you special treatment because of your name?"

"*And* my school record. I'm not just a hot body here." He smiles.

"Does everything in life come easy because of your name?" I ask, rinsing my hair under the water.

He watches me with focused intensity, looking deep into my eyes. "No, not *everything* has come easily." Just by his emphasis on the words, I know he's referring to us, but what he still fails to recognize is that he always had me. We both foolishly thought we could walk away, but it wasn't meant to be as clean or easy as that. He breaks my train of thought by adding, "It's a fact I've used my name to my advantage over the years, but like in Lani's case, sometimes it can cause more harm than good. The press loved smearing me in the papers."

Turning off the shower, I reach for the towels, handing him one and we dry off. As I brush through the tangles in my wet hair, he sits on the edge of the tub and watches me. "I think you look really pretty without make-up."

In the reflection of the mirror, I smile when I see the sincerity in his eyes. "My mother still says that too." I revert my eyes back to my face, and ask, "Don't you think I should cover these dark circles though?"

"I don't see any dark circles."

My sweet boyfriend has always seen the best in me.

Thirty minutes and many complaints about my slow driving later, I drop him off on campus. "Do you need directions?" I offer. "The campus is really big."

"No. I looked it up yesterday when I called about my application. I think I head south from the quad. It's four buildings down on the right."

"Who are you meeting with anyway?"

"Um, I think the name is Lawrence."

"Dr. Lawrence, *The Dean of Students*, is meeting you on a Saturday?"

"He's giving me a tour of the campus too." He nods, his expression all smug.

I try to keep my jaw from dropping open at the 'special treatment' he's receiving and instead focus on the positives. He's here having meetings and taking tours, which is amazing and I smile at the realization. "You're really gonna do it, aren't you?"

"What? Take a tour?"

"No, move here. You're really transferring for me, aren't you?"

He tilts his head to the side and smiles, "Yes, I am and honestly, it feels like the first right decision I've made in a long time." He opens the door and gets out. As he walks around the front of the car to my side, I roll down the window. It only goes down half way though since it started jamming a few weeks ago. He leans in through the opening the best he can and kisses me. "I'll see you back at your place. Have fun and send my best to the parents."

"I will. Good luck, babe," I reply, waving as I back up.

I arrive at the restaurant a few minutes late and rush toward my parents who are already sitting at a table. "Sorry, I'm late," I say, taking my hoodie off and sliding into the booth. We've been coming here since I was five. I love the gingerbread pancakes, so it's always my pick for my birthday breakfast.

"That's alright, honey," my mom says, smiling.

My dad sighs, letting me know he has something on his mind, and then he says, "I hope you're keeping your head on straight. Boys can be distracting. I don't want you screwing up in your last year of school."

While perusing the menu, I roll my eyes. "Good morning, Father." Yeah, I say it sarcastically, but whatever. "And Evan is not a distraction, so don't worry." He's my focus. *School's the distraction.* If I didn't have to go to school, I could spend all my time in bed with Evan. The thought makes me smile.

My dad is not amused this morning. Maybe breakfast was a bad idea. We order our food and my mother leans forward. "I think Evan is lovely. He's so polite, too polite. I hate that he paid for dinner. That was entirely too generous."

My dad straightens his back and clears his throat. "I may not have seen the bill, but I can guess how much it was and I'm just wondering why he has access to that kind of money. He's not a drug dealer, is he?"

"Don't be ridiculous. You know me better than that. You know I wouldn't date a drug dealer." I take my napkin, unfolding it slowly as if this is the most interesting thing in the world and doing my best not to get caught up in an Evan's financial means conversation, so I try to put it to rest. "I've told you, his family has a lot of money."

"The boy is in his twenties and still living off his parents—"

"Clay," my mom says, touching his arm. "I've told you he's working with his family this semester and transferring in Boulder next semester, so stop giving Mallory a hard time. She's with a nice guy who, from watching him last night, clearly is in love with her."

My dad furrows his brow. "I thought he seemed a bit obsessive hanging on her every word—"

Focused intensity. He's always like that with me. I smile... like a stupidly, giddy smile.

"Look, she's in love too. Let's just be happy for her," my mom says, smiling at my dad. She leans closer and kisses him on the cheek.

But when my dad is concerned about something, he fixates. "I hope you're using protection. Don't go messing up your life now."

"Oh my God, Dad. I'm, uh, so... just never going to talk about that with you," I stammer, throwing my hands up into the air.

"She's twenty-two, Clay, and as much as we're worried about her welfare, it's really none of our business."

"You had her two years younger than she is now, Elise. I'm sure you don't want her giving up her dreams—"

"Dad! I'm being careful. Can we just please end this embarrassing conversation says the-mistake-my-parents-made-at-twenty?"

"You were the best mistake we ever made, honey." *My mom, the eternal optimist.*

Thank God the food is delivered, ceasing this incredibly embarrassing topic of conversation. The rest of breakfast goes much smoother and I open my presents before we leave. I receive a new sweater, a gorgeous pair of pearl earrings, and they say they'll pay my phone bill for three months. I totally score.

They walk me to my car and my dad taps the hood, and says, "Let me know if your car gives you any trouble, okay?"

"The window's been jamming, but other than that, I don't drive much since I walk to most of the places I need to get to."

"I'll look at that window over Thanksgiving." My dad looks around the parking lot with narrowed eyes. He's got something on his mind. "Hey Mallory," he starts saying when he looks back at me and shoves his hands into his coat pockets. "I can tell this relationship with Evan is getting pretty serious." He steps closer and then hugs me.

Wrapping my arms tightly around him, I hug him. "I love him, Dad."

"I can tell, but if you're meant to be together, you will be. The distance won't matter."

"You sound like mom," I reply, enjoying the safety of my dad's arms.

"Yeah, well," he says, leaning back to look me in the eyes. "She might've started rubbing off on me after all these years."

"Break it up," my mom says, squeezing her way into a group hug. "I want to give my birthday girl one more hug before we leave."

Tears well in my eyes, but I try to keep them from falling, knowing if I cry, my mom will too. "I love you both."

"We love you too, honey."

"Make us proud, Mallory," my dad says, letting me go.

"I will."

When we part, I yell, hoping they'll hear me, "See you at Thanksgiving."

I drive back to the apartment to find Sarah packing a

bag. She looks up and smiles. "Just stopping by to grab clothes and then I'll be out of here again."

"No rush. It's only me. Evan's dealing with some stuff on campus and I just came from breakfast with my parents."

"It's good you got to do your breakfast tradition."

I follow her into her bedroom and sit on the end of the bed, crossing my legs. "Yeah, it was nice and they got to meet Evan last night."

"Uh oh, how'd your dad like him?"

"He likes him, but I think it's hard for him to accept I'm grown up. He got in a few of his little threats like if you hurt my daughter... blah blah blah. You know, the usual." We laugh. "Evan was definitely feeling the heat, worried about doing the wrong thing, stepping out of line or whatever, but he still had a good time."

"Are you worried about him getting out of line?" she asks, sitting down at her desk.

"Not anymore. These last few weeks and this visit have proven how much he loves me. I trust him."

"Oh Mallory, I'm happy for you." She gets up and hugs me. "After last year, I'm so glad you found Evan. He's so in love with you."

"My mom said the same thing."

"It's pretty obvious," she adds, going back to packing her bag.

My phone rings and I hurry to answer, hoping it's Evan. "Hello?" I answer without looking at the caller ID. *That is a mistake.*

"Mallory?"

My heart sinks. I would know that cold, elitist voice anywhere. I don't reply, not sure what to say.

"Hello? Mallory Wray, are you there?"

As if I still owe her some sort of respect, I respond, "Yes,

Mrs. Ashford, I'm here." I take a deep breath, stand up and retreat into my bedroom for privacy.

"I know this may seem odd to hear from me, but I just found out about my son's visit to Colorado. I hope he's doing well."

It isn't a question, but I feel the need to justify his happiness when he's with me. "He's very well."

"I don't understand what he was thinking. He missed two days of work for this visit, but I'm sure you're aware of that."

Like a trusting puppy, she lures me into revealing information that is really none of her business. "Evan surprised me for my birthday."

I don't know what I expected. Maybe I thought this would make sense to her as it would to anyone else in the world... anyone with a heart. But I forgot, Evan's mother doesn't have a heart.

"Oh," she says, her tone remains emotionless. "I didn't know it was your birthday. I would normally send my best wishes, but alas, this is not a social call, so we won't waste time with petty occurrences in your life."

I remain silent, forgetting that I have the ability to hang up as she continues her verbal assault.

"I'm going to be frank with you, Mallory. I want my son in New York permanently. He can finish his degree here and continue in the family business. Three generations have worked hard to make Ashford Holdings the success it is, and Evan will one day lead it to greater success." She sighs as if she's bored. But her words are stern, and I can tell she means every one of them. "With that success, Evan should marry an equal worthy of the Ashford name. Wray is sweet, but pedestrian. It's entirely unnecessary for him to attach himself to someone that can't uphold our family ideals. You live in a different world with different traditions and values. Your Mile High City charms won't work here. I don't know what he was thinking back in Hawaii, but he's back in New York now, a place where Evan Theodore Monroe Ashford is revered and respected. He's a catch not only amongst the best families in Manhattan, but across Europe as well. If you care for him at all, you will cut ties with him and let him live up to his potential. Don't ruin his destiny. He can own this city if he chooses. He's *that* talented."

"Mrs. Ashford—"

"This isn't a discussion or a request, Miss Wray. If you love him, you will put his needs before your own and won't hold him back any longer. It's going to be embarrassing and probably painful for you if you procrastinate any longer. Don't worry though, he'll most likely reflect fondly on the time you spent together."

I remember saying something similar to Evan the first time I met him at the airport about his past flings. The words strike my heart, making it hurt, that I'm relegated to a mere 'fling' status in her mind.

Her voice starts fading away, her message already received loud and clear. I stay quiet, my heart broken, as she says, "And let's be honest, I'm sure you're just as surprised as I am that it's lasted this long." She exhales as if she's relieved to get that off her chest, then concludes, sounding lighter. "Thank you and good luck with your studies."

She hangs up and I'm left there with a shattered soul, unable to think clearly.

5

MALLORY

"Mallory? Earth to *Malllllory?*" Sarah waves her hand in front of my face. "Hey there, welcome back. I'm off again. Josh is waiting down in the car for me." She hugs me tightly and I go through the motions, but sit quietly in shock as she carries on. "You have fun with your man and I'll see you tomorrow."

I nod, barely looking at her, still too caught up in the phone call, the threat, I just got from Evan's mother. "Okay, bye," I mumble.

When she opens the door, I hear Evan, which snaps me to the present. I was hoping for a few minutes to collect my thoughts, but I'm not that lucky. "Hey, don't rush off on my account." I hear them speaking in the other room.

I wipe at my eyes, where tears were starting to form.

Sarah's voice carries. "No, no. I was leaving already. You two have a good time. Hopefully I'll see you later."

"Thanks again for helping me surprise Mallory." I can hear the smile in his voice. He's genuine and honest and I weaken just a bit. "Is she here?"

"No problem, and yeah, she's in her room."

The door closes and I hear the faintest sound of footsteps coming closer. I put on a fake smile, hoping to cover the damage the Wicked Witch has caused. It may be surface, but I don't want to have any emotional conversations about his mother without processing her words first. I shouldn't give her even a second of my thoughts, but she comes from a place of protecting her son and I don't take that lightly. Even though my instant reaction is to prove her wrong, I don't want to make us about that. As soon as he rounds the corner, I put on a smile and say, "I gave you a key to use—"

"I didn't want to barge in, just in case Sarah was home."

I stand to greet him, wrapping my arms around his middle, and resting my cheek on his chest, effectively hiding my face. "How'd it go today?"

"Really well."

"Yeah?" Leaning back to look at him, I raise my eyebrows, hoping he opens up more. "You want to talk about it?"

He leads me to the bed and we both sit down, making ourselves comfortable. "I'm in."

I'm trying to decipher his quick, but casual response, but the two words seem too simple. It can't be that easy. Can it? "You mean you're *in* in?"

"As of January seventh I'm officially a Buffalo." He leans forward, taking my hands in his, and says, "Do you think you can handle me being around all the time?"

His mothers' words begin taunting me as they roll over in my head playing on repeat. I look away from what feels like his too direct of a stare and state, "Evan, please never doubt my intentions. I hope that you trust I'm being honest with you when I say that I want you here with me."

Two fingers grace my chin and he turns my head to face him again. His tone is soft and gentle as a smile toys with the sides of his mouth. "I do believe you. Thank you." I watch his lips, still not allowing myself to look into his eyes. He kisses the end of my nose.

Guilt sets in, rumbling my stomach. "You're making so many sacrifices. I wish I could do the same for you," I utter the words that are becoming the bane of our existence. With us, the imbalance of what we can give always tips the scales in his favor, making me feel bad.

He doesn't hesitate. The strong-willed, confident, surfer I met last summer emerges determined. "You've given me life, Mallory. What I've given you pales in comparison. I owe you everything." He pulls me over to sit on his lap. "I love you so much. Moving to be near you comes from a purely selfish place. Believe me when I say that, so don't go nominating me for sainthood just yet."

I relax, resting my head on his shoulder. "I can't wait for you to be here."

"It's gonna be tough going back to New York when my heart is here with you. Hey," he says, looking at the window. "It's still early. You want to go house hunting with me?"

"A house? You want to get a house?" I ask, sitting straight up, astonished once again by how he seems to have the world at his disposal.

"I'm not sure. I think I'd prefer an apartment, something close to you, but I'll look and see what I like."

"You're so sweet, and by the way, have I told you lately how much I love you?"

"No, tell me," he smirks.

"I love you, Evan Ashford." There's a definite neediness building inside of me, all signs of playfulness evaporated from my lowered voice. I need him to know how much I love him, to feel my love. I need that love to be strong enough to bring him back and fight for all that's good and honest in this crazy situation.

He takes my hand and kisses my knuckles and without needing *his* words, I feel his love for me.

We spend a good portion of the day driving around and stopping in on a few apartments. His long list of complexes quickly gets narrowed down to three options, all close to me.

After a nap and some fun at my place, we go out for dinner then I offer to introduce him to our local dive, The Sink. It's already bustling with co-eds when we arrive just after ten. Making our way through the crowded bar. I spot Sarah and Josh hanging out in the corner with a group of other people. We stop to get a beer at the bar before heading over to join them.

After introductions, Josh and Evan hit it off, discussing the current rankings of the Pac-12 Conference, which is a big relief because I've seen too many relationships strained because the friends didn't get along with the significant other. After a few more beers, Josh convinces Evan to throw a game of darts, betting the bar tab on it. I push him forward, but he playfully resists then gives in with a smile. "If you're sure," he says with a wink. *Why do I get the feeling that he's a really good dart player, maybe even a hustler?* Oh, yes, that's right, because he's good at everything and he kind of is a hustler.

Sarah and I plant ourselves on barstools out of the way and watch from a distance. I enjoy watching Evan in this environment, *in my environment*, a little too much I worry. His mother's words still haven't left my thoughts and dampen the fun for me a bit.

"He's really hot, Mallory. I can definitely see the attraction." She bites her lip as she checks him out. After looking around the bar, she adds, "I think every girl in here can too."

"You should see him when he's coming out of the ocean after surfing—all wet, sun hitting..." I sigh heavily wishing I'd taken more pictures.

Evan comes up and kisses me on the cheek. He slides his nose across my skin until his lips are pressed to my ear. "If I hit a bulls-eye, what do I win?"

His warm breath and amorous tone heats my face and warms my body. I turn until my cheek is against his and whisper, "What do you want to win?"

"Your undying devotion," he says, standing up.

I pat him on the shoulder and give my version of a romantic interlude. "That's so Romeo and Juliet of you. I, thee, my Romeo, henceforth cherish you with my undying devotion and ask for nothing, but a mere kiss in return."

"I'll give you more than a kiss any day of the week, my Juliet." He stops to kiss me on the cheek again.

Sarah rolls her eyes, and says, "Sunny was right about you two."

Josh walks up, taking a drink of his beer, then taps Evan on the chest and says, "Your turn."

"What'd Sunny say?" Evan asks, waiting with the darts in hand.

We all three wait for Sarah to continue. She looks at me, and says, "She said you guys were different."

I lean my elbows on the table and ask, "Different how?"

"It's real, your love for each other. I can see it. She's right."

My gaze drops from her and goes immediately to Evan, who's taking in her words. When he looks at me, he nods his head to the side, calling me to him. I get up and go, sliding my arm around his back, and lean my head on his chest. "They're both right, you know," he says, then kisses my temple.

"I know. I believe the same thing."

He swats me away and says, "Now back up, woman. I'm throwing darts for undying devotion and I'm hoping for some naughtiness when we get back to your place tonight." He raises the dart into the air, squints one eye, and aims.

Right when he throws, I smack his ass, and the dart goes flying, but because it's Evan, it still hits the dartboard. "Seriously, Evan, is there anything you're not good at?"

With a smirk plastered on his face, he says, "I'm not good at losing or sharing." After that statement, he finishes his off his beer.

"Damn it," Josh says, staring at the dartboard.

Sarah and I turn, surprised. Laughing, I say, "I think that's the first curse word I've ever heard you say. And if you're trying to keep up with Evan, you're gonna have to give a lot of fucks to compete with him."

"Eh, not competing. Just irritated at my crappy dart throwing tonight," Josh adds.

Sarah gets up to console him with a hug.

Evan saunters to me, and says, "About that undying devotion, Miss Wray."

"And here I thought you'd only be focused on the naughty you threw into the bet at the end there."

"You caught that, huh?"

I lean forward as if I'm going to tell him a secret, but don't bother whispering. "Hate to break it to you, but I had you all figured out at the airport and I still slept with you. I kind of expect some naughty when it comes to you, Mr. Ashford."

Grabbing me around the neck in a pretend headlock, he laughs. "This is why we make such a great team. We understand the dynamics of our relationship and have our priorities straight."

"Always the charmer when it comes to sex," I add, rolling my eyes, and patting my hair back into place.

"Worked on you." He smiles, taking my hand and kissing it. "Luckily for me."

"Why does it feel like you think you've won more than a dart game here? Like you charmed the pants right off of me when we've had this talk before? I'm the one who chose you."

He bursts out laughing, but reins it in quickly. With a smile that says he's lying out his ass, he says, "Yes, dear. You were in total control that day at the airport."

As much as I want to get all defensive and hide the fact that we started as a one-night stand, it's our story and look at us now. Anyway, he's too sexy to get mad at. Instead, I pull him by the hand and say, "I think I'll have to remind you exactly how that day played out, but later, after I kick your ass in darts."

Josh steps forward, and says, "I was hoping for a rematch."

Evan smiles. "I'm happy to take your pride twice, dude, but first my lovely girlfriend has challenged me to a game."

With a laugh, I offer, "You guys go ahead and play and I'll get another round of drinks."

"Thanks, Mal," Josh says.

Looking at Sarah, I smile. "I'll be right back."

"Need help?"

"No, I've got it." I walk to the bar and slip onto a stool. The place is busy and the bartender is running around trying to fill drink orders. Before I have a chance to order, I feel a body press against me from the side. I spin on the barstool and see Will with a smile on his face, staring back at me.

"Mallory, how are you this fine evening?" Adjusting to

squeeze in closer, he maneuvers between me and the next seat, which is currently occupied by a large guy. Will doesn't bother me as much since I had the revelation I did back in the cafeteria that day. It's not like he wants me back. It's more that he wants what he can't have, so he continues to flirt and I continue to blow him off. It's become a little game we play.

Leaning forward to get the bartender's attention, he waves his hand which makes his drink spill onto my chest.

The liquid is cold, making me jump. Up. "Shit!" I say, accidentally bumping him and causing him to stumble backward.

That's when I notice he's pretty drunk. He rushes me, hands out, all grabby. "Oh hey, Mallory, I'll get that for you," he says rubbing his hand across my chest, no napkin in them, just his hand over and over again.

Smacking his him away, I shout, "Get off of—"

Startled by the hit, Will trips on the leg of a stool, losing his balance, and begins to fall backwards. But as he falls, he grapples for anything to keep him upright. In haste, he grabs me and I fall with him.

My head scrapes across the edge of a nearby table before I land directly on top of him with a thud.

He doesn't miss a beat. "I knew you wanted me, Mal, but all you had to do was ask." He laughs, a bit drunk-dazed, a lot amused as he pulls me closer.

Trapped between his legs, I feel him growing harder against me. I fight against him, but my head throbs and he quickly rolls on top of me, pinning me underneath him. He has an apologetic expression, maybe even regret covering his face when he says, "I'm sorry for cheating on you. Give me another—"

"Get off me, you asshat," I say, angry. Pressing against his chest, I push hard to get him off. "You were such a mistake. There's no chance in Hell I'll make it again."

In an instant, he's gone when Evan yanks Will off of me, holding him high enough that his feet barely touch the ground. "What the fuck are you doing?"

With his hands up in surrender, Will stammers, "I, er, uh—"

"If you ever come near her again, I'll make you regret the day you laid eyes on her. Do you understand me?"

Obviously losing his sensibilities, he replies, "I understand that I fucked your girlfriend and she came back begging for more." Will laughs.

I cringe as I get up. Standing there in shock as I listen to Will, clearly unaware of who he's taking on.

Evan's glare is unwavering, not showing anything other than hatred toward Will. His biceps are strong and defined as he holds him up. When he releases him, he shoves him in the chest and says, "You apologize to her or you're gonna be the one begging, but for mercy."

"Fuck you," Will spews, his temper flaring.

"Fuck me?" Evan laughs. He grabs his arm, turning him toward the door, and pushes him. "Fuck you, dude."

Sarah's suddenly by my side, her eyes searching mine. "Are you alright?"

Frantic, I say, "We can't let them fight. I don't want Evan fighting."

From behind, I feel a hand on my shoulder. "Are you hurt, Mallory?" Ryan's there, worried and cups my cheek just as Evan and Will disappear outside.

My head is pounding and I'm uncomfortable by the intimacy of the touch, so I turn away and reply, "I'm fine—"

"You hit your head and there's blood. I can clean it and make sure you don't need stitches." He starts to pull me by the hand, insistent with his grip, and leads me toward the bathroom.

I pull my hand free and stop just as Evan appears, and says, "I'll take it from here." Taking my hand in his, he bends his elbow, which tugs me closer, and holds my hand against his chest, his eyes never leaving Ryan's.

Evan doesn't look like he's been in a fight to my relief. I follow his gaze back to Ryan, who remains close—protective in his stance. I'm not sure if he's on guard for himself or me though, which makes me nervous.

Stepping forward, my body is the only thing separating the two ego-puffed chests.

"Sure, man," Ryan says, "just making sure she gets taken care of *properly*."

A heavy sigh escapes me, knowing Ryan's words are meant to incite, insinuating everything, and that they will set Evan off again. There's no fear in Ryan's eyes, though I think there should be. He confidently stakes his claim to the spot where he stands... maybe even of me. *Fuck!*

When I look from Ryan back to Evan, I freeze. I've only seen Evan truly mad once before. It was the night he fought with Noah, the night we both fought with Noah at the luau, but his eyes were different. Evan's eyes back then showed hate, but also hurt, sadness, and confusion mixed in. The look in Evan's eyes right now sends a shiver down my spine while breaking my heart simultaneously. Taking a step back closer to Evan, I squeeze his hand and try to pull him away from this tense situation, but he doesn't budge. "Evan? C'mon. Let's go," I whisper.

Surprising me, he looks down. His face softens when his eyes look into mine. When he turns back to Ryan, his eyes harden with a narrowed glare.

"You say you're her friend," Evan says, his voice calm—

maybe too calm. "But it seems to me that you..." he pulls me closer, against his side and wraps his arm around me, "...want more from her."

Ryan is quick, dangerously so, stupid for fighting for something he'll never have. "Are you afraid of the competition?"

The gauntlet has been thrown down, and knowing Evan can't resist a challenge, I instantly pipe up hoping to put an end to this ridiculous fight. "Ryan, there is no competition and there never will be. I've told you repeatedly how I feel about Evan. So despite what you seem to think, I'm with Evan because I want to be, because I love him."

Evan kisses the side of my head then straightens back up, and says, "I think you've gotten your answer. If you really care about her, you'll respect her decision."

Ryan glances between the two of us several times before he shifts, looking down at his feet. "I am her friend." His gaze returns to me, and he says, "I'll see you around, Mallory."

The pain I've caused him is written on his face, which makes me feel awful. I try to step forward, but Evan holds me firmly in place. Glancing at Evan, I see the plea in his eyes to stay. I do, but I say, "I'm sorry, Ryan," while he's still within earshot.

He stops, looking over his shoulder, a small smile crossing his face when his eyes connect with mine. "I understand." He turns and leaves the bar.

"Go to the bathroom and I'll check out that cut," Evan says, breathing into my hair while directing me toward the small hall where the restrooms are located. Inside, I lean forward over the sink and look at the scrape in the mirror. Evan gets a paper towel and wets it then dabs my skin. He hands me the towels, but continues rubbing his finger close to the cut. He rests against the counter, not bothered at all that he's in the women's restroom. "That's the same place you hurt your head in Oahu. Are you okay?" His concern is evident. "I don't think you'll need stitches."

"I'll be fine." My heart hurts just looking at him. He shouldn't be dealing with my past and here it is hitting him square in the face with insults everywhere he turns.

There's no humor in his tone when he asks, "Is your life always this exciting?"

"I was about to ask you the same thing," I reply, taking a long look at him. "You're upset. You have every right to be. I'm sorry." The atmosphere feels thick with tension, an argument of what we both want to say brewing beneath the surface.

"I don't want you to apologize. I want to understand what's going on with those assholes out there. Are you close to them?"

"No, not like you're thinking. I'm working on a project for one of my classes with them. Sarah does too. I've hung out with Ryan but you knew every time. He knows we're together."

There's silence as he watches me continue to pat the small cut, but then he says, "Guys only wanna fuck you. If Noah didn't prove that point back in Hawaii, tonight should."

The door opens and a girl walks in, but when we turn to look at her, she backs out and says, "I'll use the men's."

The interruption gives a much needed reprieve from the tension.

I try to temper the fight I feel looming between us. "Evan, because a guy flirts with me doesn't mean I'll fall for it. You don't have to fight the world to protect me."

"That asshole had his hands all over you and you what?

Expect me to let him get away with it? Did you hear the shit he was saying?"

When I reach over and touch his chest, his body is hard, heavy with the burdens of our long-distance relationship before he slips away from me. "You can't be friends with every guy you meet, Mallory. You think you're being nice, but it's gonna fuck us up." Pacing, his agitation is obvious in his every movement.

My hands grip the counter behind my back as I lean against it watching him. "Are you telling me I can't be friends with men?"

"No." He stops in front of me. "I'm not threatening you. You can be friends with who you choose to be, but the reality is this whole night could've been avoided if your *friends* respected your boundaries. But they don't. They're disrespecting you, me, and our relationship."

Tamping down the emotions I have built up from the earlier phone call with his mother, I say, "They know where I stand. They've just chosen to ignore the facts."

He stops with space between us, leaning his back against the wall. "I'll be honest. Seeing these guys hanging around you is fucking with my head. You say they know where you stand, but I need to know. I need to know when I'm in New York and you're here, where do you stand then?"

I move in front of him, pressing my hips against his. Taking his face between my hands, I make him look me in the eyes. "I'm right here. I'm right here standing by you, only you. Always." I kiss him—slow and light, cautiously, as I try to calm him.

"I miss you, baby."

"I miss you like crazy," I say, and hug him.

His heart thunders in his chest, beating against mine as his arms wrap around me.

When he leans back, a small smile tugs at the sides of his mouth when he says, "This doesn't change the fact that your Ex is a real asshole."

I laugh, loving the humor he can find in the moment. "You're right, but he always was and probably always will be. You're not though, so I don't want you getting upset over jerks like him. Anyway, not every guy wants to sleep with me. Case in point, the manager of the third property we looked at today. He didn't even notice me."

Amused, he laughs. "Because he was gay and you know it."

"That would explain why he lingered on your every word. But what you're really saying is that I can be friends with certain guys because they *don't* want to sleep with me, but not all guys because they *do* want to sleep with me. This is kind of ridiculous, you know."

"I never said they wanted to *sleep*." He pulls me closer and holds me. "Come here." He kisses me again—hard this time with no reluctance and all the passion we had in Hawaii is back, making me whole.

Our lips part and I watch him as his eyes slowly open, and he says, "I don't want to fight with you, but this…" He rubs his hands over my hips. "…Is all mine. This…" Continuing, his fingers slide across my mouth. "…Is mine. And this…" He strokes between my legs, firing every nerve into a frenzy of sexual hypertension. "…Will never be touched by anyone other than me again. I told you, I'm not good at losing or sharing. You remember that when I'm back in New York."

Another girl opens the bathroom door and stops, startled when she sees us.

I release a heavy breath, my heart beating fast and my body turned on by his claim to me.

Evan steps forward, taking me by the hand. "We're leaving," he says to her with no apology for hogging the woman's restroom for so long.

When we walk out, Sarah and Josh are at the table, waiting for us. I thought Evan would want to go home, but he doesn't. He walks straight over and says, "You guys up for a game of pool. Teams. Me and Mallory against you two?"

Sarah hops off the stool with a big smile. "Yeah, we're game." She looks at me and asks, "You okay? Your face is all pink." Her hand goes to my cheek. "And you're hot. You feeling alright?"

I look at Evan and he has that damn, confident, sexy smirk on his face, and I reply, "Better than ever." I try to get my thoughts off of how good it feels when his hands are on me and back to the reality that I'm in the middle of a bar.

Evan gets the rack from the slot under the table and hands it to me. "Rack'em up, sexygirl."

With a smile on my face, feeling the liberation from weighing issues, I take the rack from him. "Anything for you," I reply with all the sexual intent I can muster.

He crosses his arms over his chest and asks, "Anything? I'll keep that in mind later."

I roll my eyes. "Okay, anything within reason."

"Damn," he says, snapping his fingers.

I collect the stray balls while walking to the other side of the table. After putting the balls in the rack, I lean forward to push it onto the mark and center it. He comes around and smacks my ass. "I'm liking this view."

Shaking my ass, I give him a little show. Then he leans against me from behind, bending with my body as his hands take the rack and pull it closer to us. "The balls have an order. Let me show you." He lifts the rack and sets it next to the triangle of balls then takes the one ball and places it at the top of the rack. "Now a stripe and a solid, a stripe and solid with the eight ball between them." He presses his middle harder against my ass with each ball he racks.

I grab a stripe and he tells me to place it in the bottom left corner and then a solid in the other corner. His hands rest on my waist as I rack the rest 'how I want.' Turning around, I slip a finger into a belt loop of his jeans and tug him even closer. When I kiss him, Sarah says, "You know you're in public, right?"

I laugh just as I'm about to kiss him again. Evan, looking over my shoulder at her, says, "A little PDA never hurt anyone."

Josh grabs Sarah, surprising her with a full on, knee-weakening kiss. When they finish, she's a bit dazed and has a goofy grin on her face. "Nope, never hurt anyone," she replies dreamily.

In the middle of the first game, I spy Will leaving the men's restroom while holding bloody paper towels to his nose. He looks pissed, so fortunately he never sees us. Seeing the damage on him, I immediately glance over at Evan and look for any marks. There are none on him. Our eyes meet while he chalks his stick, and then he smiles at me, not seeing Will walk out of the bar.

Josh gets his attention by nudging him. "Your go, man."

He looks down and sets up the shot before sinking two balls. We play two games, tying them when we decide to call it a night. It was hard for Evan to lose that second time because he sunk the eight ball and couldn't blame me for the loss. Not that he would, but it was a hit to his manly pool-playing ego. Tired from the day and all the emotional turmoil from earlier in the evening, we all four leave, parting ways with Sarah and Josh out on the sidewalk.

Once we're back at the apartment, he sits down on the

couch and kicks his feet up on the coffee table. "You're all goodness and trust. You know that? Two of the qualities I love most about you. Hell, I wouldn't be here right now if you weren't so kindhearted."

I walk to the couch and sit down next to him, needing to be close. Leaning my head on his shoulder, I enjoy his warmth. "Being with you like this is one of my favorite ways to be." I curl my legs under me, and add, "You're also made of goodness, Evan, inside and out."

Any other night and the old us would have made love, buried our feelings in sensations, moans, and ecstasy. Tonight, we don't. Instead, he kisses me on the top of the head and we cuddle in silence, appreciating the quiet of the world while listening to the other's soft breath.

Birds are singing. Go away, happy birds. I'm tired and worn down, physically and somewhat emotionally. Life with Evan has always been emotional but his mother's call yesterday is weighing heavy on my heart.

A shadow moves across my closed lids, causing my eyes to flutter open in the early hours of the morning. Evan is standing next to my desk in only his underwear. He's scanning the pictures on my corkboard—my collage of Evan and the ones of us. He's smiling, completely unaware that I'm watching him.

Sitting up on my elbows, the shuffle of the sheets alerts him and he looks over his shoulder, then points back at one of the pictures of him. It's one of my favorites though I'd find it hard to actually pick just *one* favorite of him.

"When did you take this?"

"I don't remember," I answer, trying to clear my scratchy morning voice away.

"Liar," he teases.

I smile, remembering exactly when I took the picture. I remember everything about Hawaii and the world we created there.

"I didn't know you took so many pictures. You're all ninja like with the camera."

I sit up all the way, not caring that the sheet slides down my chest, exposing my breasts in the dim light sneaking in from the outside.

He slowly exhales, walking to the side of the bed and sitting next to me. "Lie down," he instructs, stroking my hair behind my shoulder, his fingers caressing my skin.

When I lay down, he slides under the covers with me, cuddling against, his bare skin to mine. I feel him harden against my thigh I've so casually draped on top of him. He doesn't move. Like me, I can tell that this is enough for him.

We lay there until the clock clicks and the dreaded hour arrives. Ten a.m. His flight is at noon, so he needs to leave.

Showering together, actually showering—we wash our hair and clean our bodies. No time for antics or sex this morning. I'm kind of disappointed, but something today feels different. I want to say we feel more solid, but I won't allow myself to think those words as he's leaving because then it would make me think I didn't believe we were solid before.

By ten twenty-five, we're dressed and he's standing at my door, suitcase in hand. He pre-arranged a car to take him to the airport, not wanting to relive the torture of another goodbye as much as I don't. So we pretend this isn't happening and say our goodbye casually as if we'll see each other tomorrow... or the next day. After a kiss that quickly escalates into a few body grinds, he leaves, shutting the door behind him and leaving me standing there in the middle of my living room alone.

I stand there like a fool for at least five minutes trying to get my emotions in check. It doesn't work. I'm unsure what I'm supposed to do with myself. This apartment was starting to feel like home before Evan showed up. Now it feels empty without him, barren like my chest.

The door bursts open, startling me, and Evan runs in, grabbing me so hard that I'm squeezed against him with my feet off the ground. He kisses me with a passion that hasn't been necessary until this moment.

Setting me down abruptly, he grabs the sides of my face, looking deep into my eyes, and says, "I love you, Mallory. I need you to know that I will *always* love you. No matter what."

6

EVAN

November 1st.

November 1st.

November 1st.

37 days.

It's been 37 excruciating days since I last held her. It's been 37 days since I last kissed her. 38 days since I was a part of her and we were one. *Fuck!*

Jogging through Central Park isn't doing it for me anymore, but the pub across the street from the Ashford Holdings building is, so I veer off path and go straight there.

I'm working long days for my dad and still trying to stay in shape by jogging. But every part of me needs to *'get wet'*— fucking soaked to the core. Water has been my salvation for as long as I can remember. I feel lost without it. Mallory helped that need to be buried under water go away, but now I have neither—no ocean or Mallory to submerge myself in.

"You're too young to become a drunk. Go home." The bartender says this to me every time I come in here, which seems to be more frequent lately. He's right, but I need to bury reality into a haze of numbness. I miss her... we don't talk like we used to. She tries. I'll give her credit there, but I'm usually stuck in a meeting, and can't take it. It pisses me off.

I chase the whiskey with a beer and head home. Walking into my apartment, I toss the keys on the console and plop down on the couch, fully suited, and loosen my tie. Sitting in the dark and silence, I will myself not to go to my room. The computer's in there and if I walk through that door I'll want to logon and then I'll be disappointed because she's not home. She has midterms and she's studying crazy weird hours and the one thing I swore I wouldn't do is mess with her studies. That needs to be her priority right now, not me, even though I selfishly I want to come first.

Fuck, I need to get wet. I need to surf and feel that harmony with the ocean. I need to clear my head and getting lost in a wave never sounded so damn good.

The door opens and in walks Kate, along with Lacey, one of her high school friends. I can't say I'm happy to see Lacey. We have a past. We fucked once, which was a mistake, so I'm not in the mood to deal with her tonight.

With a smile, she comes. "Hi, Evan."

"I'd stay away from him. He's been a moody bastard lately," Kate warns, walking down the hall to her room.

"I'm right here, by the way," I yell, annoyed she's talking about me like I'm not even in the room.

"How's it going?" Lacey asks, sitting down on the couch.

"Fine," I grumble completely disinterested in having a conversation with her.

Her weight shifts on the couch and I look to find that she sat down while trying on a coy smile, which doesn't suit her. "Glad to see you're back in New York," she says.

I ignore her because Kate is right. I am a moody fucking bastard these days.

And she's persistent, but she always has been. "Do you want to come out with us tonight? We're going to see some of the old gang."

"I have a girlfriend," I state flatly, hoping to end this one-sided conversation. I know her too well. She doesn't make small talk unless she wants something and everything about her tells me that she's not looking to start an in-depth discussion.

"I thought you didn't *do* girlfriends?" She asks skeptically.

She's right, I used to not *do* them, but that was before I met someone worth having as a girlfriend. For her, my sarcastic side rears its ugly head, and I remark, "I'm moody because I'm not *doing* my girlfriend right now."

"I see. So this bad mood is about you not getting laid. You're horny?" she says, her hand suddenly on my thigh. "I can help you out in that department. I've learned a few new tricks since we were last together."

Scoffing, I say, "A few *new* tricks? It was so bad three years ago that if memory serves me right, there was only room for improvement. So thank God you learned some 'new tricks' because the old ones fucking sucked and not in a good way."

She stands, stomping down the hall to Kate's bedroom, but bothers to stop and yell, "You're an asshole, Evan Ashford. Go to hell!"

I'm still laughing when Kate walks out of her room, down the hall, and straight up to me flicking me really hard on the forehead. "Don't fuck with my friends, Evan, or should I call you Sourpuss?" She turns and goes back to her room where Lacey is probably waiting to bitch about me.

"You call me that again and you're gonna finally meet FootUpYourAss, Katherine." I threaten her even though I know that if she really wants to, Kate can put up a good fight. I lie back on the couch and laugh at how entertaining this has been.

With a much better disposition in place, I go to my room and turn on my laptop. I login to video chat and see Mallory is online, so I ping her.

She comes to life before my eyes. I recently installed a twenty-nine inch monitor, so she would be bigger for my personal enjoyment.

"Evan."

"Mallory."

She smiles, lighting up my whole heart, and I tell her, "You have an amazing smile."

Tilting her head, she smiles again, a pink creeping up her neck and onto her cheeks. "Stop, you're making me blush."

"I'll never stop and I hope you always blush for me."

She's embarrassed and changes the topic, her usual reaction when she feels she's getting too much attention. "How was your day?"

"I don't want to talk about that. Nothing matters but this call right now."

"Then what do you want to talk about?" she asks.

"I just want to look at you and hear your voice."

"You cut your hair. It's a lot shorter."

I ruffle my hand on the side of my head. "Yeah, I cut it yesterday. I was told it wasn't professional."

"I like it. You look... older, definitely more professional." Eyeing me, she adds, "You look like you've lost weight."

"I took up running. I couldn't stand sitting at that desk and not moving all day."

Shaking her head, she looks contemplative. "You didn't need to lose any."

"It's the running. How about you?" When I visited, she'd lost a few pounds and her face is looking even thinner now.

"I'm eating my veggies, if that's what you're asking," she says sarcastically.

"Mallory?"

"Yeah?"

"I just care about you."

Her expression softens and her sweet smile reappears. "I care about you, too, but what's with all the seriousness tonight?"

"We promised to talk every day," I point out, then bite the inside of my cheek.

"I had mid-terms. I told you I'd be busy in the evenings. I've called you every day though." She's not defensive but sounds remorseful.

"We didn't talk last Wednesday."

"You remember that?"

"Yeah, I remember and there have been other days we didn't talk." When she looks away, I can tell I'm making her defensive, which is not what I intended to do. "Know that I notice because I miss you."

"I mis—"

"Hey Evan, knock knock." Kate barges in. "We're leaving to go to the salon. The car will be downstairs at 7. I'm riding with Lacey. I'll see you there. Oh, is that Mallory?" Kate practically pushes me out of the way. "Hey there, how's it going?"

"Good, but crazy with mid-terms and stuff like that," Mallory replies, looking happy again. "Kate, you never got back to me about your plans for Thanksgiving."

"Murphy's flying in," Kate replies. "What about you?"

"I promised my parents I'd come home since I didn't for my birthday."

"That's too bad. Well, let's try to plan something soon. I hate to cut this short, but I've gotta run. We have a fundraiser tonight and I'm about to be late for my hair appointment. Good to see you. Call me, okay?"

"Yeah, yeah. Sure. Bye," Mallory says to her before my sister disappears out the door.

I slide my chair back in front of the monitor as Kate warns over her shoulder, "Evan, don't be late."

"I won't. Go!" I turn back to Mallory who's looking unsettled.

"What about you, Evan? You haven't answered my emails about Thanksgiving. I take it you can't come?" Her voice is detached from emotion. She's put up a wall. I don't blame her for wanting to protect herself.

Anyway, she's right. I've avoided this topic on purpose. "I can't come."

"I knew you probably wouldn't be able to make it," she says and sighs. "But why didn't you just tell me?"

"I tried to get the time off, baby, but there was an agreement I made when I took the time off to visit for your birthday."

"Dad, please let me go. I'll work every weekend in December if I have to," I say, running my hands carelessly through the hair that remains. This 'professional' hair doesn't give me the same satisfaction my longer hair did.

"No, Evan. I already granted you vacation days you hadn't earned and that was the deal you agreed to. You need to learn to live with your decisions. I'm sure Mallory would be happy to come here instead. Your mother is making a rack of lamb."

"You mean Jean-Luc is making a rack of lamb."

"Your rude comments are not welcome in my office," he says, finally looking up from his paperwork. *"I'm very busy, Evan. My decision is final."*

I turn, outwardly sighing and let my frustration be heard.

"That's fine," Mallory says.

"I tried to get out of work. I really did."

"I know you did, babe, and I appreciate it. I know your job and family are demanding." She looks down. "I miss you so much. I'm starting to feel disconnected. Some days you don't take my calls and others I don't see you on chat. Somehow I'm getting used to life without you and it scares me."

"It'll be okay. I promise. We'll see each other at Christmas. I'll be done with work and we'll be together again."

Her tone is harsh, not sounding like her at all, when she looks at the clock over her shoulder and says, "Kate said the car will be there in twenty minutes to pick you up. You should go."

"I've got some time still. What's wrong?"

"Nothing," she replies, messing with the keyboard in front of her.

"Something's wrong. Tell me."

She's looking down, twisting her lips. When she looks back up, she says, "I'm never gonna be enough, Evan. I'm two hundred count polyester blend and you're fifteen hundred Egyptian cotton. You can't put a fifteen hundred count top sheet on top of a two hundred count fitted sheet. If they mix, you lose the gloriousness of the Egyptian cotton. It's like they cancel each other out, blending together and pilling until neither one of them feels suitable anymore."

"Sheets? I don't—"

"Evan, go to your Save this-or-that event and we'll talk tomorrow. I think I'm tired or something. I've been studying too much and need sleep."

I squint my eyes at the screen, not comprehending what the fuck she's talking about. "Mallory—"

"Go. Just go. Like I said, I'm tired. These exams have worn me down. I think I'll go to bed."

"It's four o'clock in Colorado."

"*Oh*. Then, I'll take a nap."

"I have time for you. I'll be late. I don't care."

She smiles—softly, but it's a smile and I'll take it. "You will?"

"For you, I will."

"You're always such the charmer."

"You bring out the best in me. What can I say? You also bring out the other sides... maybe we can explore those," I say, waggling my eyebrows. "It's been a while, you know."

She grins—it's devious and suggestive. "It has been a while. Too long, in fact. So about those other sides that need exploring... tell me more."

I unbutton my shirt and pull off my undershirt, wadding them up and tossing them into the hamper in the corner. "It's your move."

"Geez, no warm-up. Just jump right in, why don't ya. I might have to take back that compliment about being charming."

"You're right. How about a little poetry to get you in the mood?"

She smiles, liking that offer. "Give it your best shot." She sits back and crosses her arms over her chest.

Thinking back to freshman year English, I have an idea. "You know I always give my best. Get ready. I'm about to charm the panties right off you." I grab a pad and pen from the desk and start writing, hoping I can remember how the quote goes. I look up and see her watching, waiting. "A few more seconds." I finish and hold the note in front of the camera.

Whispering as she reads, she says, "If I had a flower for

every time I thought of you... I could walk through my garden forever." I lower the paper and look at her. Her eyes are swoony looking and I think I've won this round. But when she says, "Awwww, you win. I'll get naked." I know I have.

She crosses her arms in front of her and takes her shirt by the hem. She lifts it up just enough to tease me with a glimpse of her stomach, but stops. "By the way," she asks, "Byron?"

"Tennyson. Now strip for me, woman." I give her the smile I know that works on her every time.

"Tennyson. I should've known. You play dirty. But sometimes I can play dirty too." Her shirt goes flying over her head and she stands there with her hands on her hips. "Your turn. Ante up, big boy."

Sexygirl is sexy, but it's time I take control of the situation. "Turn off your bedroom light and turn on the lamp by the bed." She listens to my commands and does as I say. "I want you naked. Strip for me, baby."

Back in front of the monitor, she slides her jeans down her legs. Her hands twist behind her back to unhook her bra and she slides it down her arms presenting herself to me. "Take a step back," I say, keeping my voice even and my orders direct. She does and I can finally see her face. She likes to believe she's the one in charge and sometimes I let her take the lead because she possesses an innocence mixed with a naughtier side—I love the combination.

I'm mesmerized as she hooks her fingers into the sides of her panties and pulls them down. My erection presses uncomfortably against my trousers, so I shift. When she stands back up, she won't look at me, her gaze aimed down... vulnerable.

To be fair, I take my pants off and let them fall to the

floor, and step out of them. Giving her a little peek-a-cock, I tease, then drop my boxers. My dick's hard for her and I need relief. "Lay down at the bottom of the bed." I sit on the end of my bed, matching her movements. I want the full show.

She settles onto the mattress, close enough to the end, so I can see all of her clearly. Her eyes are open and watching me while her hand rubs lazily over her stomach. "I remember what it feels like to have your hands on me," she says, turning her head so she can see me on the monitor.

"I'm right here with you. My hands are on you," I say, getting into the fantasy and moving my hand to where I need to feel her touch. I stroke my cock, but my attention is on her hand as she slides it between her legs.

Her breathing deepens. "How do you want me?" I close my eyes, but force them open when she asks, "Like this? Do you like to touch me like this, babe?" Her fingers move with a slickness and I know she's ready for me. Just like I'm ready for her.

My grip tightens, and I pick up the pace. "I fucking love touching you like that," I say, my breath becoming irregular. "But I don't rush. I like to tease you first."

"I remember how much you like to tease. How do I feel wrapped around you right now? Is it the way you like?"

The heaviness of her lids, mingling with the sexy voice and words, leaves me struggling to keep my own eyes open. Giving in, I drop my head down and start stroking hard, squeezing tighter, moving faster. "You always know how to make me feel good." I can't suppress my own moans. I want to take and give and fuck her senseless—all at once.

I lift my head and watch her on the screen. She's almost purring, her breath coming out jagged yet somehow smooth and melodious. Her fingers while her back arches up off the bed. She pleads, "I need more. I need all of you."

"I need you, too." I need to feel her wetness surrounding me, my hand is a poor substitute, but I try to lose myself in the images and the memories of us together. "Don't go easy. Fuck me. Give me everything."

"Evan." She moans. "Keep talking. Just keep going."

"You feel so good wrapped around me—tight and wet. Fuck, baby. Fuck me. I need to hear you. Let me know how you feel." I pump harder, getting close, but try to hold off until she comes first.

Her words mix with heavy breaths as she says, "It's all for you, only and always for you."

I look up grinning as I watch her getting herself off. She's so damn sexy. Watching her is carnal, raw, real, and so much better than doing it alone in the shower.

"Evan, I'm so close. I need to hear you, anything as long as it's you."

"Slow down, sexygirl. Use your other hand where you want to feel me."

She slides her hand up her stomach to her left breast, her nipples ready to receive their share of attention. Scanning her body from tilted head to bent knees, my gaze travels to her thrusting hips, and fan-fucking-tasic tits, and lands on her face. She's a goddess and she's mine. A rage of possessiveness fills my chest. "Tell me you're mine." I gasp, feeling my insides wanting to come out. "Tell me, Mallory... Fuck, I'm gonna come."

Facing the camera, she watches me with a look I would call her own form of ownership, her chest rising and falling with her heavy breaths. Staring into her eyes, I see the green that haunts my lonely days and star in my nightly dreams.

I bend forward, the muscles in my stomach constricting,

coaxing my climax out with a burst of unbridled want. "Aaaggghhh!"

Her back relaxes down onto the mattress and the tension in her face eases. I suddenly feel I'm invading a private moment, like maybe I shouldn't be privy to such an intimate recovery.

"God, I needed that!" she exclaims with her arms wide open and to the side. She giggles. She fucking giggles, making me smile.

Lying there, exhausted, I laugh—her laughter contagious. "I couldn't agree more."

When I look up again, she's rolled onto her side, her eyelids heavy and her sweet smile looking like it's planning to stay there a while. "I'm definitely going to need a nap now."

I sit up. "I wish I was there."

"I wish you were here too. My bed is lonely."

"Only your bed?"

She chuckles. "Maybe I'm a little lonely as well."

"Come New Years, you're gonna be sick of me."

"Impossible."

Now I chuckle. "So you say now."

She lifts up, resting her head on her hand, her elbow pressing into the mattress. Her legs are crossed at the ankles and she's beautiful like the first time I ever saw her... but without the defensive attitude. Okay, I wasn't thinking words like beautiful back then. I was thinking she was a hot piece of ass that I wanted to conquer. Yeah, I was a shallow prick. But now when I look at her, I know she's mine and her smile is comforting. I fucking love this girl.

7

EVAN

If my dad wasn't receiving an award from the mayor himself, I'd blow off this event. But I'm expected to be there with the family to represent the company, so I shower and shave, then return to my closet to put on the tuxedo that was delivered to my apartment yesterday— a perfectly tailored white jacket... I sigh, rolling my eyes. "So fucking pretentious."

My hair is dried, my teeth brushed, and I leave. Mallory was losing the battle with a nap when we disconnected earlier, but we both left the video chat on a high. The car is waiting for me when I walk out the building. The door is held open by the chauffeur and I slide across the cold leather as the driver resumes his position up front. I don't tell him where to go because all that information has been provided already.

I'm not in the car but for a few minutes when my phone rings. I answer quickly when I see it's Mallory calling. "I thought I wore you out?" I say, leaning back and getting comfortable, happy to hear from her again.

"I should have told you sooner, but your mothe..." she starts to say, but hesitates. "Evan?"

"Yes?" The world settles into a disheartening silence, but I can't fill it. My heart begins to race waiting for her to continue.

"If you meet someone... *someone that interests you*, you should—"

No. No. "No. No! Why are you talking about meeting other people? Why are you saying this?" She's giving me an out and I won't let her. "No! Mallory, it's you and me. Us. This is us. Remember? Please don't say it."

Her voice is quiet, hard to hear over the noisy Manhattan traffic. "You need to know that I love you enough to let you go if you meet a more suitable partner."

"A more suitable partner? *What the fuck?* No! That's like saying I don't love you as much because I *don't* want you to be with anyone else. I'm your suitable partner. You're mine. So what you're saying is bullshit because I love you more than I knew it was even possible to love someone. What brought this on? I just left. We were fine." I know she can hear the panic in my voice.

"I promised myself I wouldn't say anything, but as time passes, I keep wondering if she's right."

"Who?" I sit straight up, listening to my world begin to crumble. "And right about what?"

"Your mother. She only pointed out the obvious, Evan. You have so much to gain and achieve on top of the foundation your parents laid out for you and Kate. You deserve more than I can give—"

"Stop it! I'm fucking serious, Mallory. Don't say another fucking word." Anger swells inside. I've got to see my mother right now. I pull at my too-fucking-short-to-give-me-any-relief-hair, then bang on the privacy glass. "Hang on, baby. Please."

When the glass rolls down, the driver asks, "Yes, Sir?"

"How much further?"

"We have one more stop."

"What stop?"

"Another passenger, Sir."

Putting the phone back to my ear, I say, "I have to go, but this conversation is not over."

"Evan, just think about it. Think about what you really want in life."

The car pulls to the curb, and in one long breath, the words rush from my mouth, "I love you, Mallory. I need you to know that being with you earlier tonight was incredible. Really incredible."

"I love you, Evan. Please know that I do," she says right before she hangs up.

I pound the seat next to me. "Fuck!"

The door opens and a woman—dressed to kill—bends down to get inside the car. The chauffeur takes her hand and helps her. The slit of her dress is high enough to reveal she's not wearing anything underneath and apparently she's not shy about it.

She catches me staring and adjusts her dress as she smiles. "You must be Evan?" Her voice is friendly, but I'm still clueless to who she is and why we're riding together.

I offer a handshake. "Please accept my apologies, but I don't know your name. I didn't know there'd be anyone riding with me tonight."

"I'm Nina Devillier. Claire mentioned you've been busy with work and it might slip your mind."

Claire! *Mother!* Another fucking set-up. I should have known. I won't be rude since she's just a pawn in this game. "Of Devillier Industries in Lyon?"

She holds my hand, and says, "Yes, that's my grandfather's business. Your father handles his portfolio."

"I've heard a lot about the company. It's nice to meet you."

"Likewise." I watch as she eases back into the seat with grace, keeping her posture perfect, accentuating her long neck. The way she moves is quite elegant, obviously surrounded by the finest in her upbringing. But the way she crosses her legs is suggestive in a most sexual insinuation. "You're enjoying being back in Manhattan?"

"No," I say, shaking my head. "Not really."

"Oh, that's a shame. Business not going well?"

"My girlfriend lives in Colorado."

"Ahh, I was under the impression you didn't have a girlfriend."

I smile lightly. "My mother likes to ignore reality when it doesn't align with her own motives." My mother is definitely pulling out all the stops. She thinks she knows me, knows what I like, Nina fitting my old type to a tee: blonde, check; long legs, check; model body, check; polished, check; intelligent, check. I would say challenging, but there's no challenge. I can see it in her eyes. My old arrogant ways resurface, knowing if I wanted I could have her before the entrée is served. But she's no longer my type.

Nodding, she sighs, "Well, I can't say I'm not disappointed. You're just as handsome as she said you were."

Glancing over at her in the quiet of the car, I compare Nina to Mallory. They're opposites. And while stunning, the woman next to me is nothing more than a quick fuck in coat check while Mallory is everything.

"I'd like to hear about your girlfriend, if you want to share."

Taking a second look at Nina, she surprises me. She's not the typical, shallow socialite I thought she'd be. She seems genuinely interested. "It's complicated."

She looks out the window, and says, "We have a few more minutes before we get there."

I turn and look out my window. "Mallory is everything. She turns me on while turning my whole fucking life inside out. I'm frustrated, angry, and jealous of every guy who gets to see her every day. She makes me feel possessive and greedy," I say with a chuckle and a shrug. "But I try to disguise it as protecting her best interest. I'm in lust with her *and* I've been in love with her from the minute I laid eyes on her. She's gorgeous and so fucking smart. Mallory is my brand of beautiful."

When I look back at Nina, she's staring with her mouth wide open.

Suddenly a little embarrassed, I shake my head. "I sound nuts, but that's what she does to me."

"I, um..." she gulps. "That was beautiful, Evan. Does she know all that?"

"I tell her every chance I get."

She looks me straight in the eyes and says, "You should tell your mother because I wouldn't be sitting here if she understood how you really feel."

My mother's ploy to distract me from my girlfriend didn't work. I can't be tricked, tempted, threatened or lured because Mallory's my soul mate; the other half of my heart, the missing puzzle piece...

"Evan?"

"Huh?"

"We're here. Are you ready to go in?"

The car door opens, and I realize there's a red carpet lined with photographers. Nina's been too nice and it would be rude to make her walk it alone, so I decide to escort her inside. I pop out of the car right after her and offer her an arm. She smiles, taking hold of me, and we walk without stopping for photos.

When we enter the crowded lobby, I lift up on my feet to look for my family, but I don't see them.

Nina releases my arm and says, "So I guess this is it."

"Guess so."

She sticks her hand out. "Well, it was very nice to meet you, Evan."

I take her hand and shake it. "You too."

"Your girlfriend is a very lucky lady."

"Thank you," I reply, "but I'm the lucky one."

With a smile, she walks away, and I head straight into the banquet to find my family.

When I spot their table, I head over. Lacey sees me first and turns her head in disgust, which gets Kate's attention. She stands, hugs me tight, and whispers into my ear, "Play nice tonight, baby brother."

I don't bother whispering. "I came to play alright, but I won't be playing nice." I leave her standing there, her expression volleying between concern and curiosity.

I need to find my mother. Right. The. Fuck. Now.

When I turn around, I see her in the far corner near the bar surrounded by a group of women and stalk straight for her. I make my way through the crowded room ignoring the 'Hello's' and the 'Hey Evan's' I hear as I move across the room.

"Ashford? Over here."

I turn to see Landon and Hamilton with smug grins on their faces. "Why'd you pussy out that night?"

For guys that are supposedly considered sophisticated, they sure are a bunch of wankers. I flip'em off and keep walking.

My mother's eyes' flash to mine as she continues into

whatever story she's feeding the envious junior league socialites around her. Although her mouth is smiling, her eyes give her away. She knows something's wrong and I don't bother hiding the fact that I'm pissed as hell.

Without stopping, I take her by the elbow and pull her out through some nearby doors that lead to the large balcony.

"What are you doing, Evan? Let go of me right now!" she protests.

Releasing her, I say, "No more, Mother! No. More."

She sighs as if I'm throwing a childish temper tantrum. "What are you upset about?" She puts her hands on her hips.

"Nina Devillier. The others. Your persistent interference in my life. The list goes on—"

"*Well*," she says, huffing for added drama. "I'm so sorry that I have an interest in your future—"

"No, you have an obsession, but I'm not your puppet. You can't flash pretty women in front of me like a squeaky toy for a dog. I'm not that stupid. You've made it more than clear who you'd like me attached to. Well, it's not gonna happen. I'll choose Mallory every damn time and the sooner you come to accept that the sooner we might be able to have a relationship again. But you've damaged us and that will take time no matter what."

"Evan, please don't do this. Look at how well you've done since you've been back in New York and that was when you weren't even trying. You're a natural. You were born to lead this company and if you put your heart into Ashford Holdings, you could have anything and any*one* you want—"

"That's just it. My heart's not in this. Yes, I'll finish what I started and what I promised Dad, but I won't stay on. I'm moving to Colorado after Christmas. I'm finishing my degree in Psychology and I'm going to be with Mallory. I'm not asking for your permission or holding out for your blessing. If you want to cut me off, go ahead, but I won't let you control me any longer."

I've said all I need to say, all she deserves to hear, so I turn on my heel and leave her standing there in the cold calling my name.

As I mindlessly work my way back through this crowd I could care less about, I realize everything I knew is true. This city will destroy me if I let it. I've got to get the fuck outta here as fast as I can. I push open the double doors and keep walking.

"Evan? *Evan?* Stop!" Kate calls from somewhere behind me. I don't turn back and eventually her voice, like the music from the party, and the chatter of the crowd, fades away.

8

EVAN

Thanksgiving came and went, uneventful and somewhat depressing. I didn't feel thankful. I felt lonely. My resolve for Mallory was set. But the waiting to be with her again was wearing thin. I would've joined my family for dinner, but wasn't in the mood for another lecture on family duty and future potential. Kate brought me a plate and Helga brought me a piece of pie, which was nice, but that was the extent of my celebration.

Black Friday.

The weight of the name alone hunkers down on me, so I go into the office and put in a full work day when everyone else is off. It keeps my mind occupied for at least 9 hours, providing a mental reprieve from when I'm at home alone.

After work, I go for a run. It's become a normal part of my routine. It's a chilly fall day, which suits my mood better. But the unwanted and unsolicited attention of the women here in Manhattan is exhausting. In other words, it's hard to be faithful when opportunity is constantly presented to you on a silver platter. Even Central Park has become one giant pick-up joint.

Maybe it's all of the attention or maybe I just want to feel closer to Mallory, but I end up in a jewelry store scanning the cases. The ring is only a deterrent. The words ramble around my head as I try to convince myself it's not more than a preventative measure. But for some reason, I'm struggling to convince myself. I continue looking down at the rings on display, dragging my hand and leaving smudge marks across the sparkling clean glass.

"You look like you're in need of some assistance," a saleswoman whose nametag reads Becca says, leaning across the case a little too close for comfort or professionalism. "I would love to show you this new Tag Heuer Carrera watch. The leather is divine." She rests the tips of her fingers on my wrist, stroking last years' model Omega watch. "It would look incredible on your wrist, so manly and rugged."

I quickly pull my arm away and look into her eyes. "I'm here for a ring."

"Oh." She reacts surprised, but happy. "Let me show you our collection of men's rings in the case over there. We've got some lovely gentlemanly pieces—"

"No. I'm looking for a wedding band."

"Oh," she repeats, but not as chipper this time around as she buttons that pesky top button of her blouse that has apparently popped open of its own accord during our conversation. "Well, congratulations are in order then." There's no feeling behind her words.

"I'm not getting married. I just... well, it's kind of hard to explain."

"Oh," she says again. "Well, that's an odd request, but I do *aim to please*." She licks her lips not so subtly and slides her card across the top of the glass. Looking down, I see her cell number scribbled on it. "I would love to grab a drink sometime or maybe just get to the main event." She winks as if she needs to clarify her intentions. I knew what she wanted the second she walked up.

"Listen—"

"Becca."

"Okay," I start again, "listen, Becca, I know that this," I signal to her chest where the top button has miraculously popped open once again. "This must work well for you, but I have a girlfriend."

"Oh." And there she is with that damn *'Oh'* again. "I can promise my name will be rolling off your tongue in pure ecstasy."

"See, *'Becca'* doesn't roll off my tongue. It's actually taking a lot of effort to get it out right now. But you know what does? Mallory. *Mallory* rolls off my tongue and sometimes gets sandwiched between an *'Oh, God'* and a *'Fuck'* because she's that fucking good. So I need you to back off and find me a different salesperson."

She turns abruptly on her high heels and mumbles, "Asshole."

Thirty minutes later, I stroll out into the late autumn day with a new matte platinum band on my left ring finger. As I look at it reflecting in the low sun streaming through the gap of the buildings, I smile. Now this feels right.

A long, intense week of work later, I cross the street from Ashford Holdings and into the bar across the street. It's run down, so it's not crowded, which I prefer. Young, Wall Street types and tycoon wannabes wearing two-thousand dollar suits don't hang out here. That's why I'm here.

I order my usual two beers and a shot of whiskey, lining them up, then sip one at a time, pacing myself until I'm relaxed, the tension of the day disappearing.

It's Thursday. 6:48 p.m. The door opens and out of habit, I turn my head. I'm not the least bit interested in the woman who enters the dark cavern I've escaped to, so I turn back to the bar and finish the shot knowing I'm gonna need it.

She sits down on the barstool next to me even though there are ten other lined up against the bar that she could've chosen. "Two shots of what he's having," she orders comfortably.

The bartender sets them down in front of her. Pointing to me, she adds, "He's buying."

The bartender looks at me and I nod, accepting the charge.

"I take it one of those is for me?" I ask already knowing the answer.

She slides the shot of whiskey over and taps her glass against mine, and we both drink, finishing the shot in one gulp.

"So you want to talk about it?" she asks me, angling her body toward me as if we're going to share our inner demons. With a small hand gesture, she signals the bartender for another round.

"Not really," I reply, bothered my sanctuary has been disturbed.

"I'm guessing you're not coming to the Lancaster party tonight?"

"That would be a very good guess." I know her well enough to know she's going to start in on me if I don't say more. "Don't worry. I'll be at the Ashford Gala next Friday." I loosen my tie. "So, when did you start slumming it, *Mummy*?" I ask sarcastically.

Out of the corner of my eye, I see her picking some imaginary fluff from her jacket. "I wanted to talk to you and for some reason this is where you choose to spend your spare time."

"Then talk."

"How are you doing? I haven't seen much of you in the last few weeks."

"You know the reason for that. Plus, I've been busy doing my job. That's all that matters to you, right?" I turn to see her reaction, our eyes connecting for the first time since she arrived.

"No, your well being is important to me."

"Don't. Just... don't," I snap, trying to keep my voice down.

"Evan, I miss you. I'd like you to come tonight if you—"

"I'm not. I don't like going to those bullshit events. They're boring and the people even more so."

She slides the next shot toward me, tapping her glass against mine. Impressively, she shoots the second shot and slams the glass down. "Damn! I haven't done shots of cheap whiskey in a long time. That tastes better than I remember."

I smile, softly chuckling to myself. I kind of like my mom right now. I take the shot in my left hand, keeping my right firmly on the beer chaser. As soon as the glass touches my lips, I hear a loud gasp. I swallow the warm amber drink and look at my mother who now has her hand covering her mouth in horror.

"What?" I ask.

"Please tell me... Evan!" She takes a deep breath and starts again, "Dear Lord, please tell me that is not real." She swallows hard enough for me to hear.

Following her pointing finger to my platinum-ringed finger, I then smile. *Ah, the wedding band.* I wage a mini debate whether I should tell her the truth or not. As much as I want her to accept Mallory as an important part of my life, I won't lie about us, ever, even to piss off my mother.

"It's not what you think," I say.

Her stiff expression softens and she exhales. "Thank

God," slips from her mouth before she catches herself. "Why are you wearing a wedding ring?"

I explain, making it clear that I would wear it for real in a heartbeat. I still feel lost without Mallory, and yet I haven't seen her in almost three months. Fuck, look at the sap I've become because of her. "I love her. I'm *in* love with her."

"Do you think you've just magnified your feelings because of the memories? You've been apart for months now. Why haven't you seen her?"

I'm surprised by the sincerity in her voice. "I haven't had the time off or she had to study. Or there was always some other bullshit reason." I take a sip of beer. "Time hasn't intensified my feelings, Mother. Time's just made me recognize them."

"Does she feel the same about you?"

"Yes."

"You say that very confident."

"I am confident in her, in us."

She takes a deep breath and stands up. "I need to go. I've got to drag your father from the office to the party or we'll be late." She wraps an arm around my back and whispers in my ear, "I've always loved you, Evan." She walks off before I have a chance to respond.

I take my phone out and set it on the bar in front of me. After finishing the beer in one long drink, I call my girl.

9

MALLORY

September...

October...

November 23th.

Sixty-two days to the day since Evan showed up to surprise me for my birthday. Sixty days since I kissed him, since I held him. Sixty days since I felt whole.

I sign for the organic groceries that have shown up exactly on the 23rd for the last two months. Four bags sent full of food, specifically picked with me in mind: fresh produce, usually a full weeks' worth of prepared meals, and odds and ends to make more. I can't help but smile as I tip the delivery guy. I love that Evan does this for me. It's nurturing, romantic and makes me feel his love even though he's not here.

At this point, I've discounted his mother's opinion. Her speech about putting him first is bullshit. He's the most important person in my life. But putting him first doesn't mean I should give him up or that he'll be happier with someone else. I almost called to tell her what I really think about her 'opinions,' but decided I didn't want to start a war.

I'll fight that battle when I need to, but I love Evan and he loves me and the best revenge is us being happy and together forever.

Forever? Did I just think forever?

Lying back on my bed, I fall asleep to memories of him naked next to me, touching my body, and making me feel loved... *forever.*

"What are you doing after class?" Ryan asks, leaning forward in his chair.

"Studying."

"You want to study together?"

I think fast. "Um, I already promised Sarah I would go to the library with her." I lean back in my chair, hating that I just lied. Ryan has been really nice to me over the last two months, respecting my boundaries.

Sarah walks up, dropping her backpack on the floor next to me. "Did I miss anything?" she asks, whispering.

"No. He hasn't started yet," I answer, referring to the professor up front.

Ryan doesn't waste the opportunity and asks, "Hey Sarah, you mind if I tag along to study with you and Mallory at the library?"

She looks at me, eyebrows up. I will her to tell him not to come with my eyes, not wanting to get busted for lying.

"Ummm, sure. I guess. What time did you want to go again, Mallory?"

After a heavy sigh and a roll of my eyes, I say, "I was thinking after dinner. Let's meet at nine on the fifth floor."

Ryan whispers, "Cool. I have some great quotes I found that we can use for the project." He sits back.

Guess I need to work on that group project anyway. It's better to just get it over with.

Later that night, I'm flipping through the pages of "A Study of Classics for Undergrads" when from behind I hear, "That book's a cheat. You're smarter than a book that's basically an expanded version of Cliff Notes."

"Maybe I'm not. You shouldn't give me so much credit," I state, turning around.

Ryan leans against the bookshelf in front of me, and says, "I think you deserve more credit than you give yourself."

My eyes flick up to meet his smiling ones. Tucking the book neatly back onto the shelf, I walk past him and leave. He follows me back to the table where Will is sitting next to Sarah. She shrugs, and I roll my eyes again, something I tend to do a lot around these guys lately.

After divvying up the remaining research, we head out to find the books we need. Dragging my finger along the spines in a deserted corner section of the library, I appreciate the feel of the old cloth books mixed with the modern slicker spines.

When my phone buzzes, I pull it from my pocket, and answer. "Evan!" My heart begins to race, my excitement showing through my quickened breath. Even his voice makes me feel more alive.

"Hi, is this a bad time?"

I duck into a corner at the end of a row where a light bulb has burned out. "No, it's perfect timing. I'm at the library doing research. What are you doing?"

"I'm in bed thinking about you."

"That sounds ten times more interesting than what I'm doing."

"I miss you and your body," he says, his voice sounding even sexier than usual, which I didn't know was possible.

I lower mine in response, suddenly feeling more intimate, like we're the only two around. "I miss you and your body too, babe. I've become too familiar with myself lately. I'm ready for the real deal again."

"I love when you talk about sex." A low, breathy moan is released long and slow, for my ears alone.

Knowing what he wants, I close my eyes and encourage him. "Evan, I want you to remind me how you feel," I say, forgetting that I'm in the school library.

"I need you." A sigh of relief fills the air between us as his breath staggers from motion on his side. "But I want you to talk to me too. I need to hear you."

Leaning my shoulder against the wall, I rest my forehead against *Mémoire's de Saturnin*, which feels very apropos in the moment. Closing my eyes again, I block out the rest of the world and enjoy the sounds of him.

"I need to hear you, baby, please," he pleads this time.

My mind drifts back to a few days ago. "I was lonely on Wednesday and called you. I knew you must've been in a meeting, so I had to take care of things on my own. You know I'd much rather have you—"

"How'd you take care of things?"

I take a deep breath and lower my voice. "I sat in my chair in front of my mirror and looked at my body. Then I dragged my finger down my chest and pulled my tank top down to my waist. When I looked at my nipples, they hardened like they do under your touch, your hand, your mouth. Fuck, I like watching your mouth on me."

"*Mmmmm*, more." He moans and the sound of his hand quickening can be heard. My thighs involuntarily squeeze together and I cross my legs at the knees. "Tell me more."

"I took my panties off and sat in the chair facing the mirror, then spread my legs apart so I could see everything. I thought about you and how much I missed you and your mouth, your face, and the dirty words you say when you fuck me."

"Damn it. Fuck. Baby, I'm so close. Tell me you touched yourself. Tell me. Lie if you have to."

"I took my finger and touched my—"

"*Aghhh! Mallory.*"

Through his groans of pleasure my body aches for the same satisfaction. I open my mouth needing more air to calm my own needs down.

"Mallory?" My name sounds different this time.

"It felt just like that for me, Evan," I whisper into the phone.

"Fuck, gorgeous. I needed that." Evan breathes heavily as he settles on the other end of the call.

"Mallory? Are you okay?" I hear that strange voice in my head again. My eyes pop open and I find Ryan standing there, staring at me. "Ryan?"

"Ryan?" Evan repeats with a heaviness to his tone.

"Are you alright?" Ryan asks. "I heard you groan. Are you hurt?"

Evan becomes louder in the phone, the distance non-existent in hiding his anger. "What the fuck is he—"

My hands are forward, stopping Ryan from coming closer. "I'm fine. I, I, I just need a—"

"Mallory, get rid of that motherfuckinggirlfriendstealingfuck!"

Torn between Ryan in front of me and my boyfriend on the phone, I say, "Evan, hold on," holding a finger to the phone like he can actually see it. "I'll—"

Ryan's face contorts from concern to annoyance. "Oh,

you're talking to your boyfriend. I'll give you some privacy to finish whatever you were just doin—"

"No! No. We weren't doing anything. I'm in a library. That's like blasphemy or something—"

"Mallory, get on the fucking phone."

"I'm here," I reply, feeling my face heat from the awkwardness of the situation.

"What's the deal?" Evan asks. "Tell him to fuck off. I want to hear the end of your story."

I hold the phone against my chest, not wanting Ryan to hear what Evan said. "Let me finish this call and I'll be right over," I say to Ryan, totally humiliated as he looks at me like I'm a dirty whore... or maybe I just feel like a dirty whore because I was busted.

Ryan backs away. "Yeah, *sure*, no rush."

I lean against the wall, but this time I bang my head two times. "I should probably go—"

"Why? He can wait."

"Evan, the whole group is waiting on me."

"Mallory?"

"Yes?"

Then Evan says the unexpected, "Promise you'll tell me the rest of the story next time we talk."

I laugh. "Okay, I promise."

"Hey, baby?"

"Yes?"

"I love you."

Just when I expect him to go ballistic, he surprises me by controlling his anger. "I love you, too."

When I hang up, I grab a random book from the shelf, so I don't appear completely useless, and join the group, sitting at the table.

"*Lolita*? Why'd you bring *Lolita*?" Sarah asks, surprised by my book choice.

"I think it's fitting," Ryan responds. I'm not sure if he's joking since he doesn't laugh, which makes me uncomfortable from his implication.

But before I let that unease turn to anger like it wants to, I look at him, challenging him to explain more. "How so?"

"The older guy taking advantage of the young *nymphet*. If the shoe fits..."

My head jerks back in reaction as my mouth drops open. "I know you're not referring to me and Evan when you say that!"

"Listen," Sarah cuts in, "this is pointless and our project isn't. Can we just focus and get our work done?"

"No. I want to know what Ryan meant by that comment."Crossing my arms, I tap my fingers, waiting for him to justify his words.

Sarah sits back, huffing in annoyance.

Will leans forward completely engrossed like he's watching a suspenseful show on TV.

Ryan smiles, but it's smirky, and not in the sexy way Evan pulls it off. "It seems to me that you have fallen under this guy's influence." Anger boils inside of me as he continues. "You're young and shouldn't have to wait around day in and day out for this guy to figure out what he wants to do or if he wants to be with you."

"He's only a year older than me and I'm not waiting around for him. I'm in school. He's working. He'll be here soon, like really soon. And I don't understand why you think I'm under his influ—"

"Mallory," Ryan starts in again. "We've all been privy to watching you waste your life sitting around all semester daydreaming about this guy like he's the second coming of

James Dean or something. Shit, he can't be that special. Wake up! He's probably seeing girls in New York. He's a player. That was obvious when I met him. He's arroga—"

"Stop it! I will not sit here and let you trash Evan like that. He's faithful to me. He's my forever." I jump up, baffled where this is coming from and angered by the accusations and insults.

"*But are you his?* I mean, don't we go to school so we can land high paying jobs? He's already got one, so why get the degree? Why come back here... *to you* when he has every-thing he already needs there?"

All three of them look at me, a look of sympathy on Sarah's face, Will is intrigued, and Ryan self-righteous.

"I'm his FOR-EV-ER!" I grab my bag and toss *Lolita* at him. As he catches it, I say, "I think you're reading too much fiction. This is my life. It's real, not fantasy and not trickery, but with real people and emotions. This is the life I've chosen and I *am* his forever." I start to leave, but stop to add, "I think you're just jealous, Ryan, because like Will, you'll never be anything more to me than a guy I once knew in college."

I almost make it to the elevators when I'm grabbed from behind and spun around. "Mallory, don't be like this. I've been genuine in my friendship with you—"

"You had underlying motives all along. That's more than apparent now." I try to pull my arm from his tight grip, but can't free myself until our stare down ends and he releases me. "You were hurting me," I say, trying to stay calm, but losing the battle.

I don't even think he realized how tight he was holding me because regret crosses his expression. "I'm sorry. I need you to understand how much I care about you." He shoves his hands in his pockets as if he's restraining himself from touching me again.

"Ryan, we really don't know each other that well. We've hung out a few times and I've always been very clear about who my heart belongs to—"

"Yes, you have. I'm sorry. I felt a connection the first day I met you, the girl with the big green eyes and a smile that held a thousand secrets... your smart comebacks. *Oh, I don't know.* Maybe it was wishful thinking, but I thought you were worth pursuing to find out a few of those secrets." He looks over his shoulder where we both see Sarah and Will watching from a few feet away. "Did you ever sense that there could be more to us than just project partners that once went to college together?"

"Ryan." I sigh, looking down. "Please don't."

"Mallory, look at me," he says, his finger lifting my chin. "Please tell me I wasn't imagining all that. That maybe, just maybe, there was a time where you thought there could be more than just friendship." His eyes plead for reassurance.

But I can't. I can't lie to make him feel better, not at the detriment of what Evan means to me. "Listen, I don't think you're a bad guy. You're just not the guy for me. I'm sorry if that hurts your feelings. I'm not trying to do that. I just, I can't lie to you about something so important to me."

I push the elevator button and when it dings and the doors open, I shake my head. "I'm sorry, Ryan. Please understand that I've never had those feelings for you."

Stepping inside, I push the button for the first floor three times as if doing so will assist me in a faster escape. As soon as the doors close, my eyes fill with tears.

When the doors open, I run outside. The night is cold and dark. Fall is solidly in season and it feels like my emotions are captive to its surroundings. I bet winter will come early this year if fall feels this ominous.

Since Sarah drove us to the library, I'm stuck without a ride and I'm definitely not going back up to get her, so I start walking home. It's not a bad walk, I just feel frayed around the edges after that confrontation.

Needing someone on my side, someone who will make me feel better, I call Evan.

When he answers, a tear drops from my eye, rolling down my cheek and landing on the sidewalk below. A sniffle is all I can bare as I grasp for my voice to give him the happy he deserves. I fail in my attempt to put on the front and gulp down the swelling emotions in my throat. "I miss you."

"What's wrong, Mallory? Why are you crying?" he asks, his voice revealing his concern.

"Everything will be so much better when you're here. I can't take being apart anymore."

"Why are you upset?"

"I don't want to upset you. Just know I've handled things—"

"Mallory, tell me what the fuck is going on! I'm thinking the worst. Are you hurt?"

"No, I'm not hurt. You were right. You're always right, but I don't want to go through life not trusting people. I want to take them at face value. I want to—"

"Are you talking about someone in particular or is this a general philosophy you're deciding to live by?"

"Evan, I need you to be my friend right now not my boyfriend. Just please don't get mad. Okay?"

"This is about Ryan, isn't it?"

I stop, take a deep breath, and think that maybe it wasn't a good idea to call him. "Yes," I say, my voice a bit squeaky in the admission.

Silence.

"What'd he do?" he asks.

"I told you I handled it. So don't freak out on me—"

"Mallory."

"We got into an argument. He has the wrong impression of you, so I corrected him. That's all. Nothing else happened."

I can picture him running his hands over his face trying to reason himself down to a calmer level. When he comes back on, it seems to have worked. "So it's handled."

"Yes. I told him we're together."

"You told him as if he didn't know already?" he asks, his words clipped. "We both made it clear at the bar that night."

"I meant I *reminded* him. I also reminded him that your committed to making this work even though we aren't in the same state right now."

"Okay."

"Okay?" I ask, wondering if he really means this discussion is over.

"What do you want me to say? I wanted to kick his fucking ass the night of your birthday for assuming I'd fail you and trying that lame cupcake come-on with you. But I know you can handle yourself and I have faith in you. So, okay."

"Thank you for being my friend. As for my boyfriend, less than a month, babe. Then we're together again."

"I can't wait," he says, and I can picture the smile on his face. "Now, about that story..."

10

MALLORY

We hadn't sex-cammed much, but the other night was amazing. Everything was just right, it was easy, and felt good, almost like I was in the same room with Evan, as if he had been the one touching me.

But weeks passed where he seemed to be working long hours and I had to start preparing for finals. I studied relentlessly, twisting the ring around my finger, without thought. It was a part of me now and I felt naked without it.

When I did see Evan online, he looked paler, a little thinner, but still so handsome. An early winter was taking its toll on me, but this change from the tanned Hawaiian God with a cocky spark in his eyes to becoming the prodigal son living his parents dream was showing. He wasn't happy, but he tried to be when he talked with me.

The days practically ticked themselves down lately and I couldn't wait to have him here. Here with me, his vivacious spirit would return and the Evan I know would be back and happy again.

But for me, it's the second Tuesday in December that changed everything. Just getting off a most arousing sexual conversation with Evan, my phone rings. Still tingling inside, I'm hoping he wants another round when I answer, "Can't get enough of me, huh, babe?"

"Mallory Wray?"

My grip loosens and I sit up abruptly on the bed almost dropping the phone. I look at the caller ID as if it will save me somehow. I know it won't, so I do the only thing that comes to mind. I brace myself, lift my chin up in a show of bravery, and reply, "Yes."

"This is Claire Ashford..."

I KNOW Sunny would never steer me wrong, but not feeling like me, I tug at the hemline of my black dress. On unsteady legs, I walk toward the door, but stop when I reach it to take a deep breath, trying to calm my shaking hands. I don't know why I'm so nervous, but my nerves have been getting the best of me since I left Colorado. I close my eyes and pray I've made the right decision to surprise him like this. When I open them, I'm ready— ready to claim what's mine.

I knock three times and wait.

"Come in." His voice is firm, demanding even when it penetrates the thick wood of the door that separates us. Hearing him makes my heart race and I smile.

The door is barely open, but with the knob still in hand, my breath catches seeing him in person after all of these months. He's more man now than the boy from the beach last summer and still breathtakingly handsome.

He continues reading something on his desk that captures his complete attention and responds without looking up, "Yes?"

I use my girly wiles, putting it all out there for him. "I thought you might want some company."

His eyes flash up to meet mine and a smile lightly plays at the corner of his mouth. The spark in his eyes that I've been missing dominates the blue, my attention captured now. Leaning back in his chair, he rests his ankle on top of his opposite knee, and says, "What made you think that?" The end of the pen is tapped against his chin, then he runs it along his bottom lip several times, teasing me.

Pressing my shoulder against the door frame, I quirk an eyebrow up and run my finger across the door plague that reads *Evan Ashford*. "Oh," I say, toying with him. "I don't know... maybe because you're the only one not enjoying the *gala* in the ballroom upstairs." There's nothing natural in the way I say *'Gala'*, the word not a part of my every day vernacular.

He leans forward, his smile gone. "Fuck, Mallory, you're beautiful." I see him gripping the arms of the chair, resisting what he really wants to do. He may be restraining himself, but I don't.

Pushing off, I shut the door and walk toward him— wanting to run into his arms, but I steady my pace. I slide around his desk dragging my finger along the wood on the way, needing to be near him, needing to touch him, needing him.

Evan grabs my hand suddenly, and pulls me to his lap. I fall onto him, with a surprised giggle. Taking advantage of the angle, he runs his nose along the shell of my ear, slow and sensual, and whispers, "Marry me."

"What?" I ask, sitting straight up, completely taken off guard.

"You heard me." He readjusts as he sits up with me on his lap. One hand holds me while the fingers of the other rub my thigh. Turning my head, he kisses me and everything else, like always, fades away. I'm with Evan, *my Evan* again, and this kiss is long overdue.

He gives me life through every breath exchanged and I take it all while pushing for more. Desperate moans float between us and he pulls me even closer, his fingers winding into my pinned up hair, loosening my up-do until my hair comes tumbling down over my shoulders.

Our reunion morphs into a sexual frenzy when caresses become gropes, squeezes are followed by nips, and squirming turns to gyrating. He presses his lips to my neck, drawing them down to my collarbone, my strapless dress inching lower from the pressure of his upper body against mine.

I'm worked up, but even I have enough sense to remember we're still in his office. Pressing my hands against his chest, I ask, "Should we stop?"

His eyes searching mine, then he replies, "We're not stopping."

"I hoped you would say that." Patience is not a virtue that either of us possesses when it comes to the other. "What do you suggest we do about that then?"

He spins us around in the chair, stands up holding me by the ass, and sets me on the credenza behind his desk. With no care, he pushes some files out of the way, but picks up a framed picture of us from Hawaii and sets it carefully down on his desk.

When he turns back to me, the businessman is gone and my fuckhot surfer is back. "Spread your legs for me," he commands and I eagerly obey. His hands slide up my thighs slowly, but purposefully, setting every single cell on fire. It's been too long since I've been this turned on, my anticipation starting to peak and we haven't even started.

He reaches the top of my tights, but pauses. Moving closer to my mouth, he takes me in visually before he kisses me. The sweet and passion-filled kiss is calming after the rush of seeing him again. But I'm jolted as my tights are ripped from between my legs.

Shocked, I lean back so I can get a good look at him... surprised, but so fucking turned on.

He smirks, unapologetic. "They were in my way."

"Totally in your way."

We make out, his tongue on a mission to seduce mine as we swirl and taste. The metal of his belt buckle clangs as his pants are unzipped. "I need you. I need to be inside of you."

He pulls me forward, pushing my legs apart so his pelvis is against mine. He's been all talk and sexy action, but now I can feel how much he's affected by me. I'm surprised when he stops and takes my face gently in his hands.

Evan looks me in the eyes, his smirk replaced by a soft smile when he says, "I love you. I'll always love you." Just as his lips meet mine, he pushes into me achingly slow and though I'm ready for him, it's been a while.

I lean my forehead against his and take a deep breath. The feel of him completing all that's been missing and I sigh in contentment. Our bodies still except for his hand that massages through my hair—reassuring and appreciating.

The door opens. "I was sent down to get you," Zach says, "and I guess you know about the girls coming—"

Evan pulls me protectively against his chest, trying to hide me. Over his shoulder, he says, "Not now, Zach."

"Sunny is gonna be really fucking mad if I—" He doesn't finish the sentence. "Evan?"

I sneak a peek to the side of Evan's arm and catch Zach's eyes move from Evan's face to mine. "Oh fuck, I'm so sorry. Um, I'm going now." The door slams shut, but quickly reopens. Both Evan and I watch Zach's hand slip through the crack and turn the lock on the inside of the doorknob before shutting it tightly closed again.

"Are you okay?" Evan asks, sincerity filling his tone.

"Yes."

Good with that answer, he kisses me while backing his hips until he's almost out before tilting forward and filling me again.

My head drops back, sensations overwhelming me, our bond intensified through our emotional link as much as our physical connection. Yanking my legs, he lowers my back down flat onto the credenza and weaves his arms under my knees, lifting up.

His eyes close and when he picks up the pace, he loses himself into the same depth that has my body giving into his demands.

With faster and harder thrusts, I focus on the feeling and close my eyes. My back arches up off the solid surface, my body begging for more. As soon as he gives me everything I need, I tighten around him, my orgasm hitting me hard and I call his name. "Evan."

He follows fast, working against my body as it squeezes tightly around him. "Oh fuck! Mother of fucking fuck!"

The last of the vibrations subside and he drops on top of me, his weight feeling heavy but comforting as he pins me down against wood furniture. "Marry me," he whispers through recovering breaths that warm my neck.

"Are you trying to take advantage of my orgasmic bliss," I tease, giggling. It feels so good to feel this relaxed.

"Abso-fucking-lutely, baby."

Not entirely sure how serious he is about this marriage thing, I still want enjoy the romantic gesture. My heart does pirouettes from the thought of him asking for real one day.

Taking his hand in mine, I place a kiss on his palm. That's when I see the ring already adorning his hand. My heart begins to pound, anxiety replacing the bliss I felt just seconds earlier. "It seems you're already married. You want to explain the ring?" I ask.

"Oh," he says with a short chuckle. "Yeah, that's my deterrent."

"Mmhmm." I nod, listening. "Go on."

"Simply put, I got sick of being hit on."

"And you thought wearing what looks to me like a wedding ring would turn women off?"

"It has for the most part. I guess I should've told you about it, but I didn't want you to think I was weird or anything."

"I wear the ring you gave me on my married finger."

"But yours doesn't look like a wedding band." He looks into my eyes and states, "I'm going to keep asking, just so you know."

"I hope you do." And I really do hope he does.

After cleaning up in the restroom near his office, I slide the torn tights off my legs and slip my stiletto's back on.

"Sorry about the hose." Evan looks shy, maybe embarrassed as he sits on the counter watching me.

"I think the dress looks way better without them anyway."

My hair's a mess and there's no fixing the damage done to my up-do, so I straighten my hair as much as I can while looking at my reflection in the mirror. I'm going to have to get Sunny or Kate to help me salvage it into some presentable style, but for now, it looks sextastically sexy.

While walking to the elevator to go to the gala, Evan takes my hand in his, and says, "You're here in New York. You're really here."

I stop inside the elevator, admiring his handsome face as I stroke his cheek. "I love you."

We exit the elevator on the top floor of the building and walk toward the double doors that lead to the party, but he stops this time. "Before we go in there, I want to tell you how stunning you are, Mallory."

"Thank you," I say, blushing from his sweetness. "You don't look so bad yourself there."

I straighten his bow tie and give him a full once-over, appreciating how good my man looks in his tuxedo.

The doors open and we enter the gala, hand-in-hand as a couple for all to see.

11

MALLORY

"Holy shit, Mal! What happened to your hair? Do you know how much Larn gets paid for those up-do's? And you just go and get it carelessly messed up during sex." I couldn't tell if Kate was asking me a question or simply venting her frustration.

I try my best to acknowledge her irritation and calm her down, but I don't want her mad at me either, so I point at her brother. "Evan will pay you back since he messed it up." When I look at Evan, he's chuckling.

"It's not about the money." She looks away, annoyed. "Seriously, there are ways to have sex and still look like you didn't just have sex in your office. So I hear," she says with her own wry smirk. She touches her hair to punctuate her point.

By the time we all catch onto what she's really saying, Sunny grabs my hand and yanks me out the double doors again. "It's not that bad. I can fix it."

When I steal a glance back, Evan is glaring at Murphy and his sister. "Real classy, Kate."

Before Sunny and I are out of earshot, I hear Kate say,

"You should really learn to control your libido, baby bro. This is the Ashford Gala. A little respect."

Sunny points to the restrooms in the lobby. "In here, missy." She directs me to a cushioned stool and gets busy. A few minutes later, she says, "Bend over and let me fluff."

"Fluff?"

"Trust me and bend over."

Tossing my long hair over my head, her fingers rub my scalp, which feels quite nice actually. I should let her fluff more often.

Her tone is strict as if fixing my hair is the most important thing ever. "Flip back up."

When I flip back up, she takes a can of hairspray from the counter and sprays me while shielding my eyes with her other hand. "Perfect. Look," she says, pointing toward the mirror.

"Holy Hair, Sunny. I love it!"

She beams with pride. "And you look hot."

"I totally look hot." I turn to the side to take it in over my shoulder.

"Very sex kittenish I think."

"Glamorous. Thank you."

"You're welcome," she says proudly. Her gaze travel south. "And don't think I didn't notice your tights are missing."

"They were sacrificed for the greater good, if that makes a difference."

She laughs and sits down on the stool. "Did you even have time to say hello before you went at it?"

While I go into the first stall, I burst out laughing. "That *is* how we say hello."

"That was rhetorical by the way." The giggle in her delivery keeps the fun going.

When I walk back into the sitting lounge, I step right into a cloud of perfume. It fills my throat and I start to cough while waving my arm furiously in front of me. "Trying to kill me, Sunny?"

"No, just trying to cover up the sex smell."

My mouth drops open and I freeze in place. "You're kidding, right?"

She shrugs. "Kind of."

I chase the last bit of the perfume before it dissipates into the air. The last thing I need to be smelling like is sex when I'm seeing his mother for the first time since last summer. I reapply my lipstick and head for the door, but Sunny stops me. With a sweet smile on her face and her hand on my arm, she says, "You look good in love."

"Thanks," I say, and hug her. "Evan's a great guy and..." I lower my voice, "...I'm in so deep."

"Yeah you are, but the good part is, so is he."

As soon as the doors to the gala open, I feel all eyes on us. Guys are smiling, even winking, girls are frowning and gossiping. The weight of being an outsider is heavy on my bare shoulders as I search the room for the only set of eyes I want to see—Evan's.

Murphy, Kate, and Zach are near the dance floor, waving us over, but Evan off to the right is like a beacon straight to my heart. The light around Evan draws me in like a moth to a flame and once again, I knowingly go to him, ready to feel the burn. He smiles that sextastically perfect smile and my knees go weak.

When I reach him, he grabs me around the waist, spins me onto the dance floor, and says, "You shouldn't be alone, Miss Wray." He signals his head toward the crowded ballroom. "It's dangerous out there."

"I noticed," I say, unable to look away from his deep blues.

"And yet, you tempt fate."

"I like living dangerously."

"All those men," he says, pulling me against him, leading me, and spinning me around as the big band plays up on the stage. "They want you and all those women..." He dips me, dragging his nose down my neck, breathing me in. "They want to be you." He flips me up so we're face-to-face, and says, "Marry me, baby."

I slide my cheek against his, which is already forming an eight o'clock shadow. I press my mouth to his ear, and whisper, "No, Mr. Ashford."

He sighs. "I'm willing to wait you out. I know what I want and I want you."

"How do you want me?" I tease, remaining cheek-to-cheek with him, slowly swaying, though the music is upbeat.

I feel his cheek rise into that familiar smirk as he says, "You've put all kinds of dirty thoughts into my mind." His breath is hot against my skin and covers me in goosebumps. "But what I really want is to go to bed with you every night and to wake up to you every morning. I want to make love to you and I want to fuck you. I want to see you blush like you're doing now. I want to feel the way you make me feel every day for the rest of my life. This time apart has made me realize what I want and I want to be with you. I never want to be away from you again. I need to be tied to you and need you to be tied to me." He turns his face and looks into my eyes. With less than an inch between us, we stop dancing. "I like wearing this ring because it makes me feel closer to you and I want to spend my life making you happy forever and a day. Marry me, Mallory."

The surrounding air stills as I listen to him say what I know must be the most romantic words ever spoken to another person. The blue of his eyes sparkle in the dim lights, equally playful and lustful. It's a lethal combination and I'm mesmerized.

"Okay."

His eyes crinkle at the outside corners as his smile shows every emotion I've ever desired. "Okay?" he questions.

"Yes, Evan, I'll marry you." I've never felt more certain about anything in my life as I do right now. "I'll marry you."

In an instant, his lips are pressed firmly against mine, consuming my words as if hearing them isn't enough. Desire turns to need as he tastes and savors every syllable ever spoken from my heart to his.

The doorman opens the door and we walk outside into the chilly night air to catch a cab. Mallory's hand is safely tucked in mine. I hope I'm not hurting her, but I feel like if I loosen it, she'll somehow slip away, as if she's just a figment of my imagination.

When the cab pulls to the curb, I reach forward and open the door. She crosses in front of me with a smile and wink, looking breathtakingly beautiful. I follow quickly, slipping inside the warm cab of the car, and she asks, "Where are we going?"

"I don't know. I just didn't want to be in there anymore. I want you all to myself."

"Where to?" The cabbie shouts from the front, eyeing us up in the rearview mirror.

Whispering to Mallory, I say, "We're all dressed up. I should take you somewhere nice."

"I don't want to go anywhere fancy. I just want to be with you," she says, sliding across the ripped, cheap vinyl seat. I should've called for the car.

I lean forward and give our destination, "Fifth and 34th please."

"You got it." The cab pulls into traffic as I reach over grabbing Mallory's seatbelt and buckling her in before attaching my own. This driver is crazy.

She squeezes my hand when the cab takes a sharp corner, holding onto the door with the other. "Whoa!"

"Hang tight."

"No joke." She glances out the window then back to me with her smile back where it should be. "I'm glad it's just the two of us. I spent the day with Sunny and Kate and we had a good time getting ready for the gala together, but all I wanted to do was see you."

"I didn't even ask if you wanted to stay—"

"I didn't."

"Even though you haven't seen Sunny in months?"

"We had today and she'll be home for Christmas. We'll spend time together then. This weekend is about us, babe."

The taxi comes to an abrupt halt and shockingly we make it to our destination in one piece. After I pay the fare, I join Mallory on the sidewalk. She signals over her shoulder with a big smile on her face. "The Empire State Building?"

Taking possession of her hand again, I shrug. "I heard there's a great view at night."

"Are you romancing me, Evan Ashford?"

I open the door for her and as she walks past, I slap her ass. "You could say that?"

She stops, and with a telling grin says, "You know, despite what you may think, I'm actually not an easy lay."

I can't stop the laugh. Trust me, I try. "Don't worry. I won't tell anyone how fast you jumped my bones."

"Jumped your bones? I did not jump your bones. You

have clearly forgotten how the events of our first date went down."

"Well," I say, rubbing my chin. "It wasn't really a date from what I recall and you still ended up in my bed... under me one time..." I close my eyes remembering how fucking sexy she was that day. "... on top of me another. Oh, and I can't forget how hot your ass looks from behind. I clearly remember three different times."

"I thought it was two."

"I haven't even mentioned the pool action, so definitely three... at least, and I wore you out, Miss I'm-Not-An-Easy-La—Ouch!" I rub my arm where she knuckles me, then laugh. "You're feisty, Miss Wray."

"It's one of the reasons you fell in love with me."

"It's one of the *many* reasons I fell in love with you. Being easy was a bonus."

She jerks me to a stop in the middle of the lobby. "Oh my God, Evan, you make me sound like a slut."

Wrapping my arms around her neck, I pull her close, and whisper, "Do you regret being with me that first day?"

"No, none of it."

"You're not a slut." I kiss her on the nose. "You're not easy. We both knew there was something more between us, something different. We did what we wanted and what felt right, and it doesn't matter now anyway. Here we are thousands of miles away from where we started—"

"Starting a new life."

"Our new beginning starts today."

With a heavy sigh, she says, "Oh no." Her smile falls away. "I let you have sex with me right when we first met. I *am* a total whore."

"Only for me, baby."

She rolls her eyes. "You've turned me into a very bad girl, Mr. Ashford."

"I like bad girls. Now c'mon and let's do all this romantic stuff so I can take you home and fuck you properly."

Laughing, she rolls her eyes again. "You're terrible."

"You love it."

"I love you, so yeah, I guess I do love it."

"Are you cold?" I ask, looking down at her bare legs as we walk around the observation deck.

Mallory wraps her arms around herself as if I've reminded her that it's winter. "No, my coat is keeping me warm."

"Sorry again about your hose."

She pats me on the chest. The lights from atop the building reflect in her eyes, making them sparkle. "It was worth the sacrifice. Now stop worrying about me. I'm good. I'm actually better than good. I'm great."

We enjoy the walk around the deck, stopping briefly on each side to enjoy the view. Our earlier declarations seem more real now that it's just the two of us, the reality that she said yes sinking in. Maybe it's just the holiday spirit creeping in. Standing behind her, I wrap my arms around her waist, and rest my chin on her shoulder. Her right hand comes up, her fingers sliding into my hair, holding me close.

She whispers, "I love you."

I nuzzle my nose behind her ear and plant a small kiss near her hairline. Peace quells the New York nerves that I live with day in and day out. It's freezing, but being with her comforts my soul and when I close my eyes, we're in paradise again. The warm sun shines on us, the sound of the ocean crashes before us, and sand is gritty under my feet. I sigh, momentarily losing myself.

"Come back to me," she says, a hint of concern lacing her words.

"I never left you."

She turns in my arms and looks me in the eyes. I can feel her chest rise and drop with each breath. Lifting up on her toes, she kisses me. My eyes close and my embrace tightens around her, never wanting to let her go again.

When we part, she tucks her head under my chin and we snuggle, quietly looking out at the city.

"You're the best surprise I've ever had," I say, cupping her face while trying to protect her from the wind.

"I can't believe you didn't know, that Zach didn't tell you. You looked really stunned when I walked into your office, but you pulled yourself together quickly." She laughs lightly and so do I.

I take her hands in mine and rub them trying to warm her. "You were like an angel or apparition. I didn't want to wake up if I was dreaming. I still feel that way."

"I'm really here," she says, looking up at me under long lashes.

"Yes, you are and we need to make the most of every minute. It's too cold out here. Let's go eat."

Twenty minutes later, we walk into the restaurant I always told myself I would bring her if she was here. "Une table pour deux s'il-vous-plaît, de préférence privée," I say, holding Mallory's hand. I swing her around in front of me as we follow the maitre d' to the table. We're seated in the corner of the cozy French restaurant I discovered a few months ago. I come here when I need a change of scenery. It's authentic in detail and food.

I reach across the table for her hand as our waiter arrives with a small baguette and asks, "Que voulez-vous boire?"

"Champagne. La meilleure. Nous celebrons. Cette belle femme a accepte d'etre ma femme."

"Ah, les felicitations sont de l'ordre."

"Merci."

Mallory leans forward, lowering her voice and says, "You speaking French does very unexpected things to me. Why have you been hiding this talent from me?"

"I thought I'd mentioned I spoke other languages."

"You did, but hearing you say you speak French and hearing you speak French is two very different things." She whispers, "You've got me all bothered and I only understood the word champagne."

"Then watch out when we get back to my place because I'm going to teach you the real language of love."

Her cheeks flush as she readjusts in her chair. She's subtle, but I catch it.

"What do you think?" I ask, raising my arms out.

Mallory slowly turns, taking in my apartment then says, "I think your money's showing, Ashford."

"My parents own it—"

"Your parents bought you and Kate this fancy apartment in a fancy building in an even fancier part of town?"

"They live next door."

Her eyes go wide and she points at the door. "Like across the hall next door?"

"Yep."

"So your family owns both apartments on this floor?"

"Yep."

"Enough with the yeps," she jokes, walking to the window and looking out, seeming to need time to think this through. "Nice view." She turns abruptly. "We should talk about where you want to live once you graduate." She crosses her arms and I can tell she's starting to stress. Her tapping foot might be giving that away as well.

I walk to her, unfurl her arms, and hold her hands between us. "Wherever you are. That's where I want to be."

"But where do *you* want to live, Evan? I want to know. I can't be your aspiration in life. I know you have dreams and goals and I don't want to hold you back from achieving all that. You're smart and sexy and you spoke French tonight and asked me to marry you and I'm worried that I can't fulfill all your dreams, so I need you to—"

"Shhh!" I say, putting a finger to her mouth. "We have time, baby."

"I just don't—"

"You know my current goals. As for where to live, I don't honestly know. You may land a job somewhere and that's where we'll go. I may end up somewhere and I know you'll come with me."

"I realize the sacrifice you're making by coming to Colorado, so I need you to know that I'll follow you anywhere after that."

"It's not a sacrifice. I was bumming around Hawaii. I'm coming to college to accomplish something. Colorado's a great school. It's not a sacrifice."

I take her jacket from her shoulders, slip mine off, and toss them over the back of a chair. Giving her the grand tour, I lead her by the hand. "This apartment may look big , especially by New York standards, but it's only a quarter of the size of my parents."

"I can't believe your parents live across the hall. Why did I not know this?"

"Discussing my parents is not really a priority when we

talk." I end the tour in my bedroom just as planned. After she explores the room, we end up on opposite sides of the bed, looking at each other, and I ask, "So what do you feel like doing?"

"You mentioned something earlier about teaching me about the language of love." She lifts an eyebrow, challenging me, and I harden instantly.

I kick my shoes off and get on the bed. On my knees, I cover the distance that divides us and grab her by the hips, pulling her down onto the mattress beneath me. "I'm fluent in that language and more than happy to teach you everything I know, baby."

13

MALLORY

I've never been a contortionist, but with my head thrown back, hanging off the edge of the bed, my back arched up, and my legs draped over his shoulders, I'm starting to feel like one along with every deep, hard thrust.

Evan sets my legs down on the bed and stands, offering me a hand up. "Let's move to the couch."

As soon as my feet touch the ground, I scurry to the couch, standing next to it. His hands take my hips as his lips steal a kiss. I'm spun around and Evan's fingers drag lightly down my spine. He's in me, the sound of us together filling the quiet apartment making me thankful that Kate is spending the weekend with Murphy at a hotel.

His hand is in my hair as his other squeezes my hip tightly. "Mallory. Mallory. Mallory," he chants over and over again. I can tell by his erratic movements that he's close. I tilt up just as he takes hold of both my hips, taking all of me.

Fingers apply pressure, kneading my ass. He moves his hand between my legs, teasing me, taunting the most wanton part of my body. I quickly succumb and constrict around him sending him into his own orgasm.

The weight of his body drops down onto my back as his hands caress my waist, rubbing soft circles up my sides. He places three soft kisses on my back as we both try to regulate our breathing.

A few minutes later, we're both in the shower, exhausted, and using it for its intended purpose. I hop out after hogging the hot water. When Evan steps out, he's wet, droplets gliding over his chest and the muscles of his abs. His towel hangs too low to be legal and I sigh contented. I missed this, the freedom to ogle him whenever I want.

Legal? Making no sense, my thoughts get jumbled when I'm around his hotness. He really is too good looking for his own good... and apparently mine. I giggle at my ridiculousness.

A loud knock on the front door brings me out of my personal Evan fantasy, and my eyes meet his in the mirror. "Someone's at the door," I say. I'm drier than he is, so I walk into the bedroom looking for something to pull on.

"It's probably just Kate," he says, "Sometimes she forgets her keys. Let her wait."

"Your love for your sister is obvious," I say sarcastically. "I'll let her in."

I grab the closest article of clothing I can find, which is the T-shirt he wore tonight under his tux. I inhale his scent as it drops down over my head. *Damn, he smells good.* Bending over, I twist the towel around my hair and flip it back up before hurrying down the hall to answer the door.

When I lift up on my tiptoes and look through the peephole, my heart stops. *Oh shit!* I duck down, hoping his mother didn't see me.

"Hello, Evan? Mallory?"

Shit, shit, fuck, shit, fuckity, shit, shit! I remain frozen, tucked beneath the peephole. In through the nose, out through the mouth. I repeat and then stand, put on a brave face and open the door, *slowly*, but I open it.

"Ah, Mallor... Oh, am I interrupting?" She looks at my attire, or lack thereof, should I say. "My apologies. I can come back."

"No, Mrs. Ashford, it's fine. You're here," I say, shifting uncomfortably in front of her. "Evan just got out of the shower." Looking down at my bare legs and having my hair up in a towel, I think it's pretty obvious I also just got out of it. What must she think of me? *Ugh.* "Would you like to wait for him?" *Please say no.*

"Actually, I'm here to see you."

What? "Oh," I respond blankly though my insides are turning, twisting into one large knot, making me feel sick to my stomach. I wasn't prepared for a showdown. I don't know if I ever will be, but especially not standing here practically naked. "Please come in. I should change. I'll change." I begin to walk backwards. "Yes, I'll get dressed and be right back."

She stares at me, judging or what feels like judging. "No, please," she says, her hand landing on my forearm to stop my escape. "I don't mean to intrude on your reunion." As she talks, she remains holding my arm, keeping me near. "I'm so glad you decided to come to New York. I saw Evan with you on the dance floor tonight. I saw how much you care for each other."

She pauses and then looks me straight in the eyes as she speaks. "I've done you a great disservice," she sighs, disappointment evident. "And an even greater one to my son. I wanted to give him what he needed instead of what he wanted, only to discover tonight, that what he wanted was really what he needed." She laughs at herself, but there's no humor as she finally releases my arm. "I owe you an apology, Mallory. I'm sorry for how I treated you in Hawaii. And I apologize for calling on your birthday."

"What call?" Evan asks, walking toward us in pajama pants while rubbing his hair dry with a towel. We must look so domestic to his mother right now and I love it.

Mrs. Ashford's eyes flash from his to mine and back. I can't say I feel the relief or the smugness that I thought I would feel when I imagined her apologizing. I've always wanted her to accept me in Evan's life, but now I actually feel bad for her, knowing Evan will flip if he finds out the full details what she said on that call.

I turn around and smile, reassuring him. "Your mother is apologizing."

"For what?" His suspicions are getting the best of him.

I touch his bicep, and say, "She's being very kind. I say we give her the floor to finish what she came here to say."

"Mother," he starts again, ignoring my request. "You said something about a phone call on Mallory's birthday. Why'd you call her?"

"I'm sorry. I know I shouldn't have, but—"

He turns to me, getting madder by the second. "I knew something happened and then that call on the night of the Mayoral award. You mentioned my mother, but you didn't tell me what she said."

"I'm not on trial here, Evan. Yes, she called. Yes, what she said affected my mood, but it made me think too. I only wanted what was best for yo—"

"You're best for me!" He raises his voice as he backs away, leaning against the couch. Looking down, he runs his hands through his hair. "You tried to act normal, but I could hear your doubts about us." With a sharp glare to his mother, he accuses. "You did that. Whatever you said to her made her doubt us. All the good we had was questioned because of you."

"Evan," I reply, going to him. I stand between his legs, caressing his face in my hands. "I never doubted us. I just didn't want to be the one who kept you from being—"

"Bullshit!" He yells, making me jump. "You will not do that anymore. I don't give a fuck about a degree or a job or anything if I don't have you." He grabs me by the wrists, pulling me close then takes my face in his hands. "It's meaningless without you. Don't you see that?"

"I was trying to protect your future and my heart."

"That's my job. I will never hurt you. I'm only here to protect and take care of you. Please believe me when I tell you that you make my life worth living." He kisses me, one hand flipping the towel off of my head and weaving into the wet strands while the other wraps around my lower back. I think he's forgotten, or doesn't care, that his mother is standing five feet away from him.

A gentle cough, clearing of the throat, is all I manage in a weak attempt to stop him from going further. I nod in the direction of his mother—an unsubtle reminder of her presence.

With his lips still against mine, he asks, "Do you believe me?"

"Yes," I say against the plush of his mouth and with my eyes still closed. "Yes, Evan, I believe you."

He turns his head and when I open my eyes, his eyes narrow on his mom. "Mother, you can support us—"

"Evan," I try and stop him before he says anything more.

"Not now. I need to say this—"

"No, just listen. Please," I beg.

"One minute. Mother, you can support us or fuck off. I don't give a damn about appearances or the social BS—"

"Evan! Stop!" I yell which startles him.

"I thought you'd appreciate me standing up for us."

I throw my hands onto his bare chest to calm him down. "I do. I really do," I say, hoping he lets me say what I need to say. "But your mother is the one who flew me to New York. She *does* support us... now." I glance at her quickly before turning back to Evan. "That's why she's here tonight. You missed all the stuff about what you want versus what she thought you needed, blah, blah, blah... *oh sorry*. No offense, Mrs. Ashford."

She waves her hand in the air as if it's no big deal. I turn back to Evan whose mouth has dropped open.

"I am thoroughly fucking confused," he says.

"I know. That's why I'm trying to explain. Yes, she was horrible to me in Hawaii and even downright cruel when she called me during your visit in September. But she also called me last week asking me to visit you. She bought me a plane ticket because I couldn't afford it. She wants you to be happy and she told me she realized that *I* make you happy."

"Why didn't you tell me this before?" His gaze flows from me to his mother and back again.

"Well," I whisper, "I was going to when I surprised you in your office, but we didn't get around to discussing much. And like you, I wanted it to only be about us after that."

"I'm glad it was." He looks at me with a soft smile before turning to his mother and asking, "You really came here to apologize to Mallory?"

"Yes, I wanted to do it in person and I owe you one as well. Our talk at that bar got me thinking. I haven't given Mallory a fair chance. I could give you a million reasons why I didn't, but none of them matter because you do matter and I'm happier when you're happy and she's what makes you happy." She looks at me and says, "Mallory, as I said before, I apologize for my behavior. I think you're exactly what my son needs."

My heart softens toward my former arch-nemesis, now my future mother-in-law. "Thank you, Mrs. Ashford. That means more to me than you know."

"Please call me Claire," she says, smiling at me.

"Thank you. I will, Claire." Remembering I have only a T-shirt on and nothing underneath, I stay close to Evan. "I would hug you, but—" I start to say, pointing at my shirt.

Evan tucks me behind him. "Mallory has a problem with answering the door half-naked."

"Not helping, honey," I say, hitting him on the back.

Claire turns to open the door. "I should leave you two. I didn't mean to interrupt your night, but you disappeared from the gala so fast I didn't have a chance to speak with you."

"I appreciate you coming by," I say, smiling while peeking around Evan. Why I'm bothering with hiding now I have no idea.

His mother opens the door and steps into the hallway. Before she closes it, she says, "I know we have some work to do to repair the damage I've done to our relationships, but I'm willing to try and I hope you are too."

"Hey Mom, thanks. What you said means a lot to me."

She focuses on him for a second and I can see the hope in her eyes. "Goodnight."

"Goodnight," we say in unison as the door shuts behind her. The weight that has dragged us down for so long now gone and disappeared with the gesture of his mother's support.

Evan turns around and smirks. "Now that we have that settled, what do you say about breaking in the leather sofa out here?"

"You, sir, are incorrigible." I feign annoyance then laugh while hopping up on the arm of the couch. "Now drop your drawers and let's christen this sofa."

His smile gives him away, but with a nod of his head and raised eyebrows, I can tell he's totally turned on. "Like I always say, ladies first."

"Since I don't have any underwear on, I guess I'll take the shirt off."

He licks his lips watching as I remove the shirt over my head and toss it across the room. His pants drop to the floor and without another word, we christen the couch... and the kitchen counter... and the shower.

What can I say, I missed my surfer.

14

EVAN

"I don't want to," I say, standing firm.

"Evan?" Mallory pouts, which makes her puckered lips quite a distraction. She puts her hands on her hips, and demands, "Do it."

"No."

"Honey, *please*."

"Fine." I give in because it makes her happy, which makes me happy. Also, because when she's happy I get sex and I like sex, so it benefits us both.

"Wow! That was easy."

"You can be very persuasive when you stick that bottom lip out like that," I say, toying with it.

"Good to know. I'll pocket that information away to use at a later date." She winks at me.

"I bet you will. C'mon on. Shake a leg, lady."

"Oh, who's all showy and shit now?"

"I am." I laugh as I push off with the tip of my ice skate leaving her in my icy dust.

"Just so you know, I used to skate competitively when I was little," she announces, chasing me.

"Prove it."

"Are you really challenging a girl from Colorado when it comes to ice skating?"

She skates by me, slapping my ass in the process. Moving ahead, she spins backwards and ends with a little flourish of her arms and a bow.

"Okay," I say, clearly losing to the ice skating queen when it comes to the rink. "You win."

She comes to a skidding stop in front of me, chest-to-chest. Grasping my shirt tightly with her gloved hands, she asks, "What'd I win?"

"You're looking at it, baby."

She pulls me down by my sweater so my lips meet hers and kisses me. "Well, that's better than an Olympic medal."

We start skating again and I get a good, solid grope of her ass. "I should think so."

She bursts out laughing. "No one will ever mistake you for humble. That's for sure."

"Sarcasm is a defense mechanism. Do I make you feel defensive?"

She moves to skate next to me, slowing her speed to adjust to mine, and says, "You said that to me the first day we met and I thought you were so full of BS."

"I was."

She laughs, but looks away, her smile fading. "Sometimes I do use sarcasm to hide some uncomfortable feelings. God, now I sound like a feminine product commercial."

I give her hand a little squeeze. "Hey, everyone does that. The sarcasm part not the feminine product commercial part."

A smile graces her pretty face, bringing my own back to mine.

As we round a corner, she says, "You're going to make a

great Psychologist one day. You know that?" With a little hip bump, she pushes off, skating ahead.

I watch her, my girl unknowingly captivating everyone's attention. My gaze slides down the curves of her body from behind, from her shoulders down lower to the small of her waist and over her hips to her ass. She's changing. I see the woman she's becoming. I don't think she does yet, but I do. She's incredibly sexy. I already had a problem with guys checking her out, but looking at her now, I can tell I'm gonna have some serious jealousy issues to deal. Mallory is stunning and that much is obvious to everyone, except maybe her.

We skate until I wipe out and accidentally take her down with me. I'm finished after that and by the way she's rubbing her ass, she is too.

We grab a bite to eat near Central Park West and decide to take a stroll since we're here. She's never been to New York and enjoys the sightseeing. It's a whole new city when seen through her eyes, maybe even un-tainting it a bit for me along the way. I hold her hand, pressing her forearm under my arm as we walk. The quiet moments don't need filling. Instead, the time is used to let our thoughts wander.

Sometimes I wonder if my need to consume Mallory the way I do is healthy. *Sometimes*. But really, I just don't give a fuck because feeling like this is air for me. I come alive just being near her. So to say that I'm happy about her saying yes to marrying me is a gross understatement. It's more like giving a pardon to a dead man walking. Relief, love, happiness, and every other emotion I thought was beyond the realm of possibility floods my senses.

The funny part is that I didn't plan to ask her. Well... not yet anyway. I wasn't planning on proposing, but when I saw her standing there in my office so unexpectedly, she took my breath away. My only clear thought was that I need to be tied to her and she to me. That thought replayed over and over in my head, so by the time I had her scent filling me and her body pressing against mine, the words 'Marry me' rolled off my tongue. It may have surprised her, but I just left it there, floating between us.

Her 'No' didn't sting. She knew I'd said it unintentionally, so that made it a bullshit proposal and she deserves more than that. But when she came back into the gala, my chest tightened, my entire future wrapped up in her. Out on the dance floor, with that gleam in her eyes, I knew it was right to ask again.

This time, 'Okay,' flowed from her lips without missing a beat, but her confident 'Yes' made me the happiest man alive. I still owe her a proper proposal though.

She sits down on a park bench and I sit next to her. "You're different here," she says, looking me over.

"Good different or bad different?" I ask with a sideways glance, shoulders hunched forward, tucking my hands into my pockets.

Her eyes focus forward, observing the park surroundings. "Well, beyond the obvious—"

"*The obvious?* That doesn't sound good."

"It's not bad. Nothing I haven't told you already. You're leaner. Not skinny, just leaner muscles from the running and you really need some sun."

"I miss surfing and climbing the cliffs. I miss Hawaii." I steal of glimpse of her. She looks cold, but relaxed. "There are a few places that get decent swells this time of year a few hours from here, but I haven't had the time to go."

"You're also calmer," she states, admiring the park in front of us.

Not sure what she means, so I ask, "Is that good or bad?"

"Both."

"Hmm."

She slides closer and leans her head on my shoulder. "You smell different here too."

We continue with our game of questions. "Is that good or bad?"

"You always smell good. You just smell different. You use different soap and cologne—"

"I didn't really use cologne in Hawaii."

"I know. Back on the island, you were all sweat and ocean and sex. Also, I might say this all wrong, and I don't mean to offend you, but you've grown up a lot." She smiles at me and adds, "And it's not good or bad, it's just who you are. I love all these new and old sides of you."

I wrap my arm around her shoulders. I can tell she's getting cold. "Let's go. I want to take you shopping."

"Shopping?"

"Just c'mon."

I flag a cab and have him drop us off at the corner of Fifth and 56th Street. Taking her by the hand, I pull her reluctant body toward the door. She's resisting the forward motion with every step.

"What is this place?" She asks nervously.

"Harry Winston."

"It's a jewelry store." She isn't asking.

But I decide to confirm it. "Yes. The best."

"Like where the stars get their jewelry for the Oscars and stuff? That Harry Winston?"

"I don't know about all that. I just know they're the best." I finally manage to get her inside the door, feeling her grip tighten in my hand. Facing her, a panicky tone comes out as I whisper, "I know we haven't really talked about the proposal much since last night, but I was—"

"I still want to marry you, Evan. It's just... I'm no good at this kind of stuff. I don't know anything about rings or expensive things."

"You know what you like and I want you to have a ring you like, or even better, love. It's forever, remember?"

"Yes, forever." She nods. "Okay, show me what you were thinking." She angles behind me as if forcing me to be the brave one and go first.

A salesperson approaches, greeting us after thoroughly eyeing us both up and down twice. He leads us to a large, intricately carved wooden desk. We sit and after introductions and a quick discussion of what we're here for, he asks, "Price range?"

"Um..." I hadn't given much thought to it, but I'm willing to drop some cash on quality jewelry, especially on a ring that my girl's gonna wear for the rest of her life.

"I don't want to know," she says, nudging me from the side.

The man pushes a pad of paper and pen across the desk and I scribble what I think is acceptable. Guess we'll see what that gets us.

As he takes the paper, he smiles. "Very nice." He glances at Mallory, who's hiding her face against my shoulder. "Do you have a certain diamond cut in mind already?"

When she doesn't answer, I do. "I think she would like a more classic cut."

"Please excuse me. I'll be right back," he says, leaving us to seek out rings in the case on our own while we wait.

"I don't feel comfortable doing this," Mallory says.

"Listen, baby, I could've just surprised you, but I want you to have what you want—"

"I can't be wearing a ring without telling our friends and family first."

"So let's tell them."

"Are we ready for that? Are we ready for the scrutiny and the lectures about how young we are?"

"I'm not pushing marriage tomorrow or anything like that, but this means a lot to me and if I have to defend my actions, then I will. So yes, I'm ready for the lectures and the scrutiny. I say bring it on."

She sighs then smiles. "I just feel wrong doing all of this behind my parents back, you know. My mom has always said it's not official until you have a ring and a date. Silly, but I feel we need to be prepared when we drop this bombshell on them."

"Look." I turn my body toward her, our knees pressing against each other. "Spend Christmas with your family. Then—"

"I won't see you?"

"I think you should be with your family and I with mine. I'll come see you on the 29th. We can spend New Year's together that way, but it will give me time to pack up my shit and get it moved to Colorado. And this may be our last Christmas being our parents' children. Does that make sense?"

"Yeah." She nods, understanding. "You're right. I'll still be in Denver on the 29th."

"Good. I'd like to visit you there. I'll hold the ring until after I ask for your father's blessing."

"What? You're gonna ask—"

"It's the right thing to do and I want to do right by you."

She leans forward and kisses me softly, a gentle sigh slipping from her lips. "I have two requests," she says, smiling.

"Shoot."

"I'll help narrow down the rings to two or three choices and then I want you to pick your favorite and surprise me."

"Done. And the second?"

"I don't want a diamond that's ostentatious. I know how excited you get throwing your money around, but this is me, Evan. I don't need the biggest ring in Manhattan. I just want something pretty, something that represents us. Keep that in mind, Daddy Warbucks."

I don't know what she's talking about with this Daddy Warbucks business, but I get what she's saying. "Okay, fine. I'll keep it tasteful."

"And by tasteful you mean tasteful by my definition not yours, right?"

Laughing, I say, "Right."

We walk out just over an hour later, both of us satisfied. She doesn't know the final ring choice though it's a no brainer. I could see in her eyes and the huge smile which ring was her favorite. The sales guy also pulled me aside briefly to look at the diamonds I'd like to add to the ring since we were there. I think she'll love it and though it's not as small or nonexistent like she thinks she wants, it's not outrageous either. I think she'll be happy.

When we get back to my place, I ask her, "You have finals in a week. Did you want to study tonight? We can stay in if you prefer?"

"I don't want to study. I should study, but I did some on the plane and I'll do more on the flight back tomorrow. I don't want to waste any of our time together."

"In that case, you wanna go catch a flick?"

Her nose is scrunched up, amused. "Catch a flick? What is this 1955?"

"Stop making fun of me."

"It's fun though. I like seeing you get all worked up."

"You want to see me worked up? I'll show you worked up."

I start tickling her causing her to fall onto the couch in a giggle fit. "Shit! Please! Stop!"

When I give her a momentary reprieve from the tickling torture, she says, "Is this one of those moments like in the movies where you tickle me and then suddenly we're all heated and kissing?"

"Do you want it to be?" I hover over her, ready to attack, with tickles or kisses, depending on her answer.

"I'm hoping it is."

I kiss her.

Her hands wind around my shoulders, encouraging me down on top of her. I toe-off my shoes and work hers off before pressing my mouth against hers. The taste of her drawing me in for seconds, thirds, fourths, fifths... fuck, I want all her kisses forever—each and every damn one of them.

I bolt upright and lift her into my arms as I stand to my full height and race to my room down the hall. I set her down on the bed and our mouths rejoin exactly where they left off. She stands and we both strip our own clothes off not wanting to waste a second on the tedious task.

Dropping my head down onto the pillow beneath her head, I enter her slowly, too slow, painfully cautious. I'm not sure why I'm so cautious either, but the moment seems to call for it.

Minutes of agonizingly slow lovemaking leaves us both teetering, verging on the edge of being dragged under a wave of spinning pleasure. I move faster and my world comes zooming into focus as she throws her head back and "Evan" drips from her lips.

Heat. *Soft*. Wet. *Heat*. "Fuck, baby," I moan.

A few thrusts later, I give into the tightening, seeing

stars, blackness and Mallory all around me. She tremors below me, right there with me, sharing in depths of sexual inebriation.

As we lay there in the aftermath of our love, all feels right in my world.

15

MALLORY

"Evan, you awake?"

"Mmmhmm."

"We fell asleep," I whisper, then place a kiss on his chin.

"Mmmhmm."

Lifting up, I look at the clock on his nightstand. 1:53 a.m. I roll onto my side and press against his back, spooning him. When I drape my arm over his waist, he takes my hand and holds it to his chest.

"MALLORY, YOU AWAKE?" I feel something bump into me.

"Uh uh."

"We fell asleep." He bumps me in the bottom again.

"Uh uh."

I feel him rub small circles against my bottom with his hard-on as I peek at the clock. 4:17 a.m. "Go back to sleep, babe. I'm too tired."

He whispers into my ear, "You sure?"

"Uh huh."

"Okay."

"Love you."

"Love you too," he croons softly into the back of my head.

❀

"PASS THE SALT, PLEASE," I ask, sitting in front of my breakfast platter ready to devour it.

Evan slides it across the gold-speckled, laminate table top.

"The Tabasco too," I ask, smiling at him. "Please."

"You got it." The hot sauce comes sailing my way. "You're happy," he states.

With a mouth full of scrambled eggs, I smile, trying not to be gross. But I am happy and I can't hide it. I chew quickly and swallow. "Yes. I am. This has been an amazing trip."

"Yes, it has been." He reaches across the table and takes my hand. "Thanks for flying out. I know it's bad timing with your finals. I didn't want to pressure you, but I'm glad you came. This," he says as his hand sways between us, "is different. Know what I mean?"

"Yeah, it's calmer or we're calmer now. Do you think the visit or the engagement did that?"

"Probably both," he says, chuckling. "Everything feels settled, more at peace. It's kind of weird."

I laugh, knowing exactly what he means. "The war is over. It's gonna take some getting used to, but it feels good."

He eats his breakfast and I watch when he's not looking. His strong jaw, his shorter hair that seems to work just as well as his longer locks did, and his muscles. Watching them alternate and work so fluidly, another thing I remember being so fascinated by the first time I ever rode with him in his Maserati.

"I'll see you in three weeks?" he asks.

"Three weeks," I repeat, nodding. The thought depresses me.

"We just did over three months. It'll be okay. It's only three weeks."

"It's too long." I reach across the table, rubbing my fingertips over the top of his hand. "Definitely too long."

"After this, never again, baby," he says, sensing I need the reassurance.

"I like that sound of that."

"I like the sound of forever."

"Surferboy, you're getting soft on me."

"That's where you're wrong. I'm never soft on you, around you, near you."

We both laugh, but I stop so I can hear his laughter without mine obscuring it.

"What?" he asks, smiling at me.

"Your laugh. I haven't heard you laugh like that in a long time." I nod, grinning at how sentimental I've gotten. "Lately, everything seems to remind me of when we first met. I'm feeling nostalgic, I guess."

"You remember my laugh from back then?"

"I can never forget it. I thought it was so genuine, unlike you at the time."

"Hey," he says with pouty lips. "Don't pick on me."

"Not picking, just sharing. There was such an honesty to your laugh that it sounded as if it was reserved for only the most special moments in life." His cheeks tinge just barely, but I catch it. When he looks down with a small smile gracing his face, I ask, "Does that embarrass you?"

"Not embarrassed, just flattered that you would

remember something like that. This weekend was a good reminder of all the things we've been missing since we've been apart."

I walk around to his side of the booth and slide in next to him, bumping into him with my hip. Leaning my head on his shoulder, our fingers entwine on the table in front of us. "Yes, it has."

He kisses me on the top of my head and tosses some bills on the table to cover the meal. "We need to get going."

"Don't make me go." I pretend to resist, but he's right. We do need to leave.

"We promised."

"I know, but I just want more time with you."

"Three weeks, baby."

"Three weeks."

"Hey, Evan?"

"Yes, Mallory?"

I tap him playfully on the shoulder. "Don't mock me, mister."

He looks over, laughing, and says, "Okay. What is it, oh love of my life, Soon-to-be-Wife?"

I roll my eyes and giggle. "You're ridiculous, you know that?"

"I've been called many things, I can't say ridiculous has been one of them."

"There's a first time for everything."

"Yep, there sure is."

I start swinging our clasped hands between us, and ask, "This is all real, right? I didn't dream up this whole weekend, did I? Ow!" My hand flies to rub my ass where he just pinched me.

"Nope." A sly grin slides across his face. "See, you're totally awake."

"Ass."

"I can make it all better," he says, rubbing my ass with his hand.

"You're in a silly mood."

"Haven't you heard? I'm getting married."

"Awww, I love ya, babe."

He kisses me on the nose then taps it. "I love you, too."

We start walking again, but I stop him this time. "I'm nervous."

Evan tilts his head in understanding, then pulls me closer. "Don't be. I'm right here with you."

Turning a corner, I see a park and ask, "Do we have time to go in?"

Checking his watch, he says, "A few minutes."

After finding a dry spot in the grass, we sit, eventually lying down, staring up at the sky and cuddling.

While stroking my arm, he asks, "Do you trust her? Do you think my mother meant what she said?"

His body feels tense while waits for me to answer. I say, "I want to trust her. I think we should, but I'm nervous."

"I told her how I felt about you last week." I look up at him when he pauses, watching him close his eyes. "I want to believe she's being sincere. Her organizing this trip, flying you out here, backs what she said about making amends, but I wanted your take on it."

I laugh—it's light, but an amusing thought that makes me giggle. "I don't think we're going to be besties or anything, but I do think she's taken the first step to fixing her relationship with both of us." I watch a white, puffy cloud float by that seems more fitting for a Hawaiian sky in June than a Manhattan skyline in December. "How do you think she'll react to our engagement?"

He sits up on his elbows and looks down at me. "It's happening, so it doesn't matter what she thinks. Anyway, we have a little time. I still think your dad's blessing needs to come first."

"I'm cold," I say, sitting up. "Let's go. They'll be expecting us soon and I need time to freshen up."

"Evan! This must be your Mallory. So nice to meet you. I'm Helga, the Ashford's House Keeper."

I take her hand. "It's very nice to meet you, too."

"Let me take you back. Your sister and friends are in the dining room already." She leads us through the large apartment and I steal glances around the place trying to imagine Evan as a boy growing up in such a pristine and expensive looking home. Helga continues talking, "I don't know what the kids did all weekend, but they said they were famished and keep asking when dinner is being served."

Mine and Evan's eyes connect and we laugh, knowing exactly why everyone is starving. When I blush, Evan smiles, and sends a wink my way.

"Miss Mallory Wray and Mr. Evan Ashford," Helga announces to the gathered group in the large and very formal dining room. *Holy shit! Did she just announce our arrival?* I look at Evan shocked by the formality. He just rolls his eyes.

"Nice, baby bro. You actually made Helga announce you?" Kate says sarcastically. "That's quite the ego you got there. Are you showing off for Mallory?"

"Calm the fuck down, Kate. I forgot she was going to do that. You're such a hard ass these days."

"Hey brah, she's always had a hard ass," Murphy adds with a proud smile and a nod.

"Gross! Not cool man," Evan says, making gagging noises before he turns to Helga. "Sorry about that. I forgot about the 'protocol' of the house. You know you never have to announce me."

"I know you don't care, but your mother likes the tradition," she replies with a shrug, winning me over completely.

Evan nods.

"C'mon over here, Evan." Kate stands up and hugs him. "Since you're going to be leaving soon, promise me we can hang out and I'll promise no work talk."

"We will. Don't worry. And I'll be here for Christmas now. Will you?"

"You are?" she replies surprised and steals a glance in my direction.

"I'll explain later," he says, "but yes. So if you're here, we'll have some down time then."

They continue talking as I walk over to Sunny and we hug. "Hey," she says, "you guys seem to have disappeared the whole weekend. I don't blame you though. Guess the surprise worked?"

"More than you know."

"Zach said he walked in on you two 'reuniting.'" She giggles while doing air quotes.

I can feel my face heat. "Yeah, he did. I would normally want to die over that, but I was too distracted to care."

"All is good?" She looks into my eyes, like the true friend she is waiting for my honest answer.

I take her hand and lean toward her ear and whisper,

"It's just been perfect. A dream come true and more than I could've wished for."

We hug again, and she says, "I'm happy for you. Zach told me how hard it's been on Evan being here in New York. Sarah's kept me posted on you when you wouldn't talk about it. You're quite the pair. You two are made for each other."

Watching Evan joke with his friends and sister, it all feels so real now. He's mine and I'm his. Forever. "In three weeks we'll be together for good."

"Three weeks and Evan's going to Denver?" She laughs. "I think he'll go into culture shock."

"Ha ha. He had a good time when he visited. Well, for the most part." No need to drag the whole Ryan-Will mess up again. "Anyway, we're only staying in Denver for a few days and then he's going to head to school and get his place set up."

"Mr. and Mrs. Hugh Ashford," Helga announces, drawing our attention to the large arched doorway.

Claire walks straight to Kate and Murphy and hugs them as Hugh follows behind, hugging or shaking hands when appropriate. They move to Evan where I watch as she smiles lovingly at him, then embraces him as if she'll never get the chance again. Her gaze lands on me as she whispers a secret to him.

She approaches me and Sunny a little more cautiously. "Sunny, Zach, thank you for joining us."

"Thank you for having us, Mrs. Ashford," Sunny replies with a handshake.

"Mallory." His mother smiles, seeming to seek an assurance as she approaches.

"Hello, Mrs. Ashford."

"Claire, please."

"Of course. Thank you for inviting me, Claire." The name doesn't feel natural to me when I say it.

She smiles in relief. "I'm so glad you could make it. I know you have a flight this afternoon and probably want to spend that time with Evan, so thank you for joining us." She takes my hand and does a little squeeze before walking back to the buffet. "Come, let's eat. I'm sure you kids have lots of plans for the day."

Hugh greets me and says, "Mallory, I know you haven't had the easiest time since dating Evan." He stops and looks down as if he's screwing this all up. "I guess I should clarify. I know you haven't been given an easy time by my family and I hope you accept my sincerest apologies. I hear that a bridge is being built and I appreciate that you would consider giving us a second chance."

"Evan is worth it, and yes, a bridge has now been built."

Hugh takes my hand between both of his, and says, "I wanted to take this opportunity to thank you for giving Evan direction. He needs a strong support system with all the changes in his life and I think you're one of the strongest people I've met. You're a great match for our son."

"Thank you, sir."

"Please call me Hugh."

"Thank you, Hugh."

"You're welcome. Now," he says, clasping his hands together. "Shall we?"

"Yes. It looks wonderful," I say, referring to the spread.

Lunch is pleasantly polite. It's funny to see all of us together in such a formal setting when the last time we were together was on the island in cut-offs and swimsuits. We get teased for sneaking out of the gala early, but even Claire smiles when Evan confesses he wanted me all to himself. She then went on to say how she and Hugh used to sneak out of the galas they were forced to go to when they were in their twenties.

I'm liking this new Claire.

The Ashford's walk us to the door and Claire takes me by the elbow. When I turn, she hugs me. "I hope we'll see you soon, Mallory. I'd like to get to know you better."

I'm taken aback again by her touching words, but trapped in the somewhat awkward embrace. "Thank you. I'd like that, too." I'm undecided if that is the complete truth, but it feels like it right now.

She releases me with a smile, and Hugh says, "Good luck with your studies and have a safe flight."

"Thank you." We say our goodbyes, leaving only enough time to grab my suitcase and head to the airport.

My personal goodbye to Evan is tear-filled, but I manage to hold them back from falling. All the heavy emotions of our goodbye back in Hawaii a distant relative to today's pain. Today my heart can handle this goodbye because even though it's never easy leaving him or him leaving me, this time is different. This time I know that once we're reunited, we won't be separated again.

Leaving the dream world behind, I get back to reality and open my textbook on the plane, setting it on the tray in front of me, and start preparing for my finals.

16

MALLORY

I scan down the group names until I find ours and scroll across to see the grade: A.

Stepping away from the door and out from the crowd of students, I make my way to a nearby bench. I close my eyes, enjoying the fact that I made straight A's despite the emotional roller coaster I've been on this semester.

A cleared throat and someone saying, "Congratulations," grabs my attention.

My eyes pop open though I know who it is already —*Ryan*. "Congratulations," I reply to be polite. Gathering my backpack, I swing it over my shoulder as I stand up to leave, my short moment of satisfaction ruined.

"Mallory, please," Ryan says to my back, a distinctive plea to his tone.

I turn around, and exhale, exhausted by everything to do with him: Will, the project, his attentions. "Please what, Ryan? What do you want from me?"

"Can I apologize?" He doesn't wait for a response and I wasn't going to give him one anyway. "I was an ass. You were upfront about your boyfriend all along and uh, I don't know." He runs his hand through his hair, once again reminding me of Evan. "I'm sorry. Look, I didn't mean to be such a dick. It's just the whole long distance thing didn't work for me and I figured it wouldn't work for you."

"Because you don't know us."

"You're right. I got to know *you* though and I liked you. Simple as that. I wanted to be the one to pick you up when you were feeling down—"

"You mean when I was dumped?"

He shrugs. "Yeah, something like that."

"Well, I wasn't dumped. Actually, we're better than ever." I refuse to have Ryan be the first person I share my engagement with, even if I am feeling defensive.

"I'm glad to hear it. I'm glad you're happy."

"I don't think you're a bad guy, but you need stop all of this. You need to move on."

"I can appreciate what you're saying, but if—"

"There are no if's for us. There will never be an 'us' at all." I look down the hall, feeling bad, but I won't prove Evan right and be the one to fuck us up trying to spare Ryan's feelings. Evan comes first. "We can't be friends either. I'm just not the girl for you, but hope you find someone special." I turn around and walk away.

It's over, even before he says, "I'm sorry, Mallory."

That afternoon, I load up the trunk of the car with suitcases and hop in the driver's seat ready to head to my parent's house for Christmas break. When I turn the key to start the car, nothing happens, nothing but a few engine clicks. That doesn't sound good.

"C'mooonnn, you can do it. C'mon. I'll get you a nice oil change when we get home if you just run for me now. I promise," I say, stroking the dashboard.

Closing my eyes, I scrunch my face up as I turn the key

again. Nothing happens, not even the clicking this time. "Shit!" I yell, hitting the steering wheel.

Two hours later, Sarah pulls into my parent's driveway and my dad rushes out to help while I hug Sarah goodbye. "Thanks for the ride."

My dad grabs the suitcase and two other bags I brought home, including one full of dirty laundry. "I'll head up after the holiday and work on the car."

"Thanks, Dad."

Sarah hops back into the driver's seat, and says, "Let's get together while we're home, okay? Sunny said she'll be back on Friday."

Leaning in through the passenger door, I reply, "Yeah, for sure. And Merry Christmas."

"You too, Mal."

I settle into my girlie little bedroom, attempting to keep my stuff organized, but it's tough. I've outgrown the room in more ways than one.

On Christmas morning, I watch my parents open the last of their gifts and sit back to enjoy our time together. Evan was right, because being here this time is different. I'm not a child anymore and my relationship with my parents has changed. I'm trying to appreciate every moment because our lives are about to change, but I'm still the only one privy to those changes.

The day after Christmas, a car comes squealing into the driveway making me jump. I run to the door to look and find Sunny and Zach running toward the house, trying to avoid the light rain that I know will turn the snow into muddy slush later.

I throw the door wide open and tackle her with a hug that almost knocks her over.

"Geez, Mallory, it's only been two weeks," she says, with a loud laugh. "I appreciate the love though."

"I know, but we didn't get much time together in New York and—"

"Been kind of bored, huh?" she asks, winking, knowing me too well.

"It hasn't been too bad. Hey, Zach," I say, giving him a hug.

"Hey there, Mal," he says. "You doing okay?"

"I'm good." I shrug. "Come inside."

I introduce Zach to my parents and Sunny hugs both of them immediately making herself at home like she always does. They consider her the other daughter they never had.

We hang out for a while, catching up on the latest gossip, before making plans to meet later for a night out.

By nine that night, Sunny, Zach, and I walk into Main Street Bar and Grill. Sarah and Josh are already there saving a table in the corner.

We order a few pitchers, grab extra chairs for all of us to squeeze around the table, and chat. Zach fits right into the mix since he's his usual friendly self and Sarah tells them about Ryan and Will 'wanting' me and how the project turned out. It's all still too fresh, my emotions twisted by the memories of the trouble it caused.

"Bet Evan freaked when he found out about this Ryan dude," Zach adds in, laughing. We all look at him and his smile disappears. "What... Oh! Oh shit is more like it, I guess. What happened?"

"Put it this way," Sarah explains, "one guy ended the night with a bloody nose and the other with a broken ego and neither of them was Evan."

Josh smiles, joining in the conversation. "He became my hero after that night. He doesn't take crap from anyone."

"Not when comes to his toys or his women," Zach adds, then sips his beer.

"Women? As in plural?" I ask, turning to Zach. I'm joking with him... mostly.

"No, not plural. Woman. Only you, Mallory. He won't take any shit when it comes to you. He tends to get protective over his..." Zach doesn't finish that sentence, but with his eyes on me, I have a feeling he was going to say Evan's possessions. My stronger side would take offense to it. My softer heart swoons. Damn romantic heart.

Zach clears his throat and looks at the others. "Since I've known Evan, he never cared enough about any other girls to want to fight for them."

Sunny rubs his shoulder. "Mallory's special."

He leans over and kisses her on the cheek. "I feel the same about you."

"Awww, honey, that's so sweet."

"Well, I think he'll fit in fine at Boulder." Josh turns to Zach and they start talking. "So how do you know, Evan?"

Zach sits up straighter. "We've known each other for years. We both grew up in New York, for the most part. Our families traveled a lot, but New York was our home base, same social circles and all that. We ran into each other again when he moved out to Hawaii a few years ago and basically had each other's back ever since." Zach looks at me. "He's a good guy, but he's lucky to have Mallory."

"Here, here," Sunny chimes in, holding her glass up in the air to toast.

The rest of the night is laid-back, and easy-going. It's fun to hang out with my friends again. The more beer I drink the harder it is to keep my secret, especially with my best friends here. Evan and I promised to wait until after he got my dad's blessing, *if* he gets his blessing, but I feel guilty for keeping such a huge secret from them.

The more I drink, the more the night feels incomplete or maybe it's that *I* feel incomplete. I miss Evan and each day that passes magnifies that feeling. Doubts creep in that his mother will change her mind and try to keep us apart again. I take another two gulps and push those dark feelings down.

The night was fun, but I'm glad to be home. It's the wee hours of the morning when my phone chirps, letting me know I have a text. Sunny dropped me off hours ago, so I know the only other person it can be. I touch the message icon and read: *Open your front door.*

"Shit!" I scurry out of bed and run down the stairs. My hands are shaking with excitement, the deadbolt and chain becoming a nuisance while I roll my eyes in annoyance at my dad's overprotective nature. When I finally get the locks undone, I throw the door open.

My breath catches as my gaze lands on Evan. He's standing in front of me with snow in his hair, a sexy smirk on his face, and a bag in hand.

He drops the duffle bag, his own hands going into his pockets as if he's holding himself back. "You really should get dressed before you answer the door. You've developed a bad habit."

"I knew it was you," I say, all smart-ass, putting my hands on my hips and pretending to be irritated.

"Well, in that case," he says, taking a large step forward. One hand cups my cheek and the other weaves into my hair. His nose rubs slowly against mine as he takes in the features of my face at this close range. Closing his eyes and taking a deep breath, his lips press lightly to mine, kissing me once, twice, three times, before murmuring, "God, I missed you, baby."

"Babe, it's two in the morning. How? Wha—"

"I couldn't stay away any longer."

I throw my arms around his neck, not caring that my chest gets a little wet from the snow on his clothes that melts between us. Closing my eyes, I inhale him into my system. Cold and shivering, I turn around, grabbing his hand tightly, and say, "Come inside."

"Yeah, I don't like you being outside in your skivvies when it's cold like this. Get your sexy ass in there." He smacks my ass when I turn toward the house.

I laugh as he follows me inside, but as soon as we're inside the house, I put my finger in front of my mouth, silently telling him to be quiet. He looks at me and then whispers, "Should I get a hotel?"

Shaking my head, I point at the couch.

His shoulders fall in disappointment and he mouths, "Really? The couch?"

After setting his bag down, he turns back to me and a sweet smile appears. I go to him, unable to resist him. "I'll tell you what," I whisper, lifting up on my toes. "Leave your stuff here and come with me." Taking him by the hand, I lead him up the stairs to my room, stopping to grab a towel out of the hall closet on the way. Carefully and quietly closing the door behind him, I turn my back to it and lean against the wood while locking it.

"Are you allowed to have boys in your room?" Evan looks at me and teases.

"Stop it." I throw the towel and hit him on the chest.

He dries his hair, then tosses it on the bed. Taking two steps, closing the gap, Evan takes hold of my wrists with a tight grip and an intense gaze aimed at me. "I missed you."

The words are rushed, but the same sentiment meant. "I

missed you." My breath comes heavily, my chest starting to rise slowly and fall deeply from the sexual tension.

Leaning down to my ear, he murmurs, his words just breaths shared between us. "I want you." He releases my wrists and I wrap my arms around his neck and kiss him, holding him close.

I pull him toward the bed, wanting him just as much. But he stops. Looking over my shoulder, he asks, "What is that?"

"What is what?" I ask, following his gaze.

"Seriously, is that a twin-sized bed?"

"This is the room I grew up in—"

"Okay, but weren't you a teenager in this room at one time? Do teenagers sleep in twin beds?"

Releasing him, turned on and a little annoyed that we're not already on that bed taking care of business, I look down at my body and sway my hands in the air. "I'm not exactly a giant here."

"Good point."

To get things back on track, I pull my shirt off and over my head. He takes his clothes off and I remove my shorts and stand there admiring his physique until he catches me, his eyes scanning over my body.

The bed creaks when we lay down. I switch off my lamp and we roll over to face each other trying to ignore the springs as they bear the brunt of our weight.

He wiggles his legs and says, "My feet hang off."

"*Shhh*. I just want to look at you." I caress his cheek.

He leans forward and places a kiss on my forehead. "My eyes haven't adjusted to the dark yet."

"*Shhh*, babe. Keep your voice down. I'm so happy you're here, so just let me appreciate the moment, Mr. Complainey-Pants."

Thirty seconds or less. That's all he gives me. His hand slides up my bare thigh and then onto my hip. "Are you done appreciating me yet? Can I talk now?" He chuckles.

"You're hopeless, you know that?"

His hand slides up my ribs as his fingers play them like a piano. "Absolutely. I'm hopelessly in love with you. That's why you love me, baby."

I can tell he's grinning even in the dark. Placing my hand on his arm, I squeeze his bicep, because I can. He tightens it, showing off because *he* can. His lips are suddenly on my lips and his body leans onto the side of mine. The weight of him is heavenly and I sigh in contentment.

Time doesn't exist when we're like this—all of our worries becoming obsolete. Our tongues touch, and as if by memory, they move in harmony, feeling at peace, feeling at home. He rolls all the way on top of me, creaky springs in full effect, as he settles on top of me.

His breath is hot against my skin, awakening each nerve in my body. But then he says, "I don't think we're gonna be able to do this," and I open my eyes, confused by his change of mind.

"Please, babe. I need you."

"I need you too, so much. But this bed is too small and loud. Your parents are just down the hall."

"It'll be fun, like a challenge—"

"From what I remember you're kind of noisy, too." He nods to back his words.

"You're right. *How about the floor?*" I wiggle my middle, feeling how ready he is for me, wanting him to feel how much I want him.

"The floor solves the bed issue, but what about you?"

"I promise to be quiet."

"I really don't want to wake Clay Wray up because you're screaming, 'Oh, Evan,' at the top of your lungs."

I hit him on the chest. "You sure are confident. Now, hurry up alright already. My dad will be up in four hours to go bird-watching and guess who's going with him."

"I'm sorry, did you just say bird-watching with your dad?"

I can feel him losing interest with all this talk of parents... and birds.

"It's me, Evan. You're with me." I touch his face, making him focus on my eyes. "I want to feel you, all of you. We'll move to the floor and I promise to be quiet."

Getting up, he takes my hand and kisses my palm. I drag the comforter from the bed and we situate ourselves on the floor, assuming the same position from a minute earlier.

As we kiss, his fingers dance across my chest and then straight down. "Hey?"

"Mmhmm," I mumble, enjoying his gentle touch and soft kisses.

His fingers tighten—a pressure surging as he strokes my body. "You're mine."

We stop kissing and I pull back just enough to see his eyes. "I'm yours, always." He owns me body and soul.

We spend time, hours pass, rediscovering, though it's not been three weeks since we last saw each other. But somehow this reunion is different—our dream of being together finally a reality.

"We need to get you downstairs," I say, breathing against his chest while resting my head so I can hear his heart beat, which always seems to calm me.

"Do I have to?"

I'm tired and could fall asleep like this, but my parents would flip out and I don't want to deal with that, so I say,

"I'm sorry. It sucks, but it's either you or me down there and I think I'll stick with my tiny bed. Your feet hang off of it, remember?"

"Yeah, yeah, yeah. Use my own words against me, why don't ya."

After we get dressed, Evan covers up in blankets that I pull down from the coat closet. I also grab a pillow and we go downstairs. I tuck him in, then go into the kitchen to write my parents a note, so they're not completely freaked out when they wake up and find him sleeping on the couch.

When I pass back through the living room, Evan is already asleep. I take a seat in my dad's recliner and watch him. He has a look of contentment on his face. Before I leave, I kiss him on the forehead and softly on his lips. I sneak back upstairs and pull the covers up to my chin. I can't stop the smile that takes over my face, my own feeling of contentment filling my soul.

17

EVAN

Poke

Swat

Poke

Swat

"Evan!"

"Yes!" I startle awake, sitting straight up. My eyes are unfocused, but I can tell I'm not home. "Where the fuck am I?"

"Son, I suggest you watch your mouth in my house and around my daughter."

"Shit, I'm sorry." I shake my head to clear the fogginess. "My apologies, Sir. I traveled all night and I'm kind of out of it."

Mr. Wray sets a thermos on the coffee table in front of me, and says, "You've got ten minutes and then we're leaving."

I nod like I actually want to go on this outing. Stretching, I hear my back pop from sleeping on this uncomfortable couch. A flannel shirt is laid out on top of my duffle bag, and I get the hint. I take the shirt and my other clothes into the bathroom and get dressed. When I return, Mr. Wray is standing by the front door, and says, "I've got your gear. Meet me at the truck." He walks out without another word and I realize that Mallory gets her chatty side from her mother.

I glance at the time as I put my watch on. 5:38 a.m. *Is it really necessary to leave this early in the morning?* I grumble, but I get my ass up because this is what I have to do, three hours of sleep or not.

Coat, gloves, and a hat are slipped on over my clothes and I grab my thermos before walking out to the truck. The truck is okay, but I'd rather be in the nice SUV parked in the driveway. But the truck has the small fishing boat hooked up to it and I briefly wonder what kind of bird watching requires a fishing boat. Guess I'm about to find out.

We talk about my middle of the night arrival which somehow leads him to say, "Seems you've been in a bit of trouble here and there."

It may be freezing outside, but I'm sweating inside the cab of his truck now. I'm wondering how he knows, but it seems he does, so I think it best to be upfront with him. "I've, uh, gotten a few tickets and had a few minor arrests for—"

"Listen, I get it, the arrests. You were boys blowing off steam. But my daughter seems pretty intent on keeping you around, so I need to know that all of that is in the past. I don't want her to be involved with anything illegal."

"Neither do I, Sir. I would never put Mallory in danger."

"I hope not."

That's all that's said on the remaining forty-five minute drive to the lake. The silence is appreciated because it gives me time to wake up.

Once we're on the boat in the middle of the water, the

sun rises and he smiles. "Now that is worth getting up early for."

The sky is lighter, but my nerves are too strong for me to appreciate a sunrise in the middle of a lake in Colorado. I'm supposed to be bonding with Mallory's father and get him on my side, so I clear my throat and start with small talk. "I bet there's great fishing here."

Looking around with binoculars stuck to his face, he whispers, "Keep your voice down or you'll scare the birds away." Then he pauses, lowering the binoculars. "It's a great place to fish. I've caught a few eight pounders out here. But this time of year, if we're really lucky, a Hooded Merganser might be out. They're usually spotted in the South Platte River area, but we've had two recorded sightings of the bird in this area. I'm hoping to be the third." This is the most animated I've seen him. "Check your gear pack. There's a pair of binoculars in there."

By nine, he sets his binoculars down and reclines the cushion of his padded chair back. "I don't think it's gonna happen today." A couple of sandwiches are pulled from the small ice chest and two beers, and he hands one of each to me. He's not said much this morning, but I guess I just needed to give it some time. He cracks the beer open and says, "This whole bird watching thing started as an excuse. I never really got into fishing, but I needed a reason to get out of the house, so bird watching it was. Living with women, a man needs something for himself other than tea parties and dolls, shopping and boy talk."

I nod in understanding, not sure what I should say to that.

Sitting up and pointing his sandwich at me, he adds, "Don't get me wrong. I'm all for marriage and kids, working hard, but it's nice to get away for a few hours a month." He relaxes back again, looking off into the distance. "I think Elise likes the time just as much." He laughs to himself.

Clay Wray is an interesting man. It's funny how normal he is—just a guy who works hard and loves his family. It's not about money or the power climb to the top. He's content in life and though his home isn't huge, he seems to be happy. That's a rich man if I've ever seen one. I sit back in my chair and look out over the water to the far shore.

Looking back at me, holding steady with the eye contact, he says, "I don't usually wake up to find my daughters' boyfriend asleep on my couch. Since you arrived so late, seems to me that you're a man on a mission. I'd like to talk about your plans for my daughter." He leans forward, resting his forearms on his knees.

"I care about your daughter, but I want you to know it's more than that, Sir," I say, then clear my throat. "I'm in love with Mallory. I think she's a pretty spectacular girl." I gulp hard, a lump suddenly replacing the cough. "And I think I want to marry her."

"You *think* you want to marry her?"

"I know I do. I want to marry her."

"Hmmm."

Silence.

With a furrowed brow, he takes me by surprise. "Where does your money come from? Your family?"

"Yes. I'm given a monthly stipend that covers most everything I might need or want."

"So how long does this 'allowance' continue?"

I look down, feeling uncomfortable with the direction this conversation has taken. I rarely talk about money with anyone and it makes me defensive.

"Forever. It comes from an inheritance from my grandparents on my mother's side and started when I was eighteen."

"So the bottom line is that you'll always be rich?"

"Yes, Sir."

"Why work? Why go to school? Why not stay in New York City and work for your dad's company?"

This line of questioning is still easier than talking about my emotions, so I find my footing with him, and respond, "I have my own goals and I don't want to be a financial consultant or broker and I'm not that fond of New York. I want to be a Psychologist and that means schooling."

"How does Mallory play into all of this?"

"I've given that a lot of thought. I love her and want what makes her happy. I want to help support her dreams no matter what they are. I think she'll benefit greatly from not having to worry about money. It's the top reason for divorce in this country and a common stress factor—a factor we won't be faced with."

"Does she know about this inheritance? 'Cause you know she's not the kind of girl who cares about all the fancy stuff. She likes to shop, but she's level-headed."

"She doesn't know the extent of my wealth, no, and I know that one of her best qualities is that she's happy with simple things. But I have the ability to give her more, like taking away the concerns of paying bills. And we can travel, which I know she likes to do."

"Let me guess where this is going. You already bought the ring." He narrows his eyes, seeing right through me.

"Yes."

"I thought as much. So is this conversation," he asks, swinging his arm between us, "just a formality?"

"No, it's out of respect for you, your wife, and Mallory." I sit up straighter. "I would be honored if you would give us your blessing. I love her and want to be with her the rest of my life."

"You're both too young, but I don't come from a position to argue against age considering Elise and I were young as well. But I do know my daughter and she's going to do what she wants to do anyway, so I'll give you my blessing. But I'm asking two things of you, Evan, and I'm gonna need you to look me in the eyes when you answer. First, I need you to promise me you'll always take care of her."

I don't rush my answer, but it's heartfelt. "Yes, I promise."

"Secondly, I want you to always love her the way she deserves to be loved, making her your priority."

"Absolutely. I will."

He sticks his hand forward and says, "Then you've got my blessing. Make me proud."

"Yes, Sir."

He chuckles. "I should really threaten you like any good father would do, but I'm not going to. I think you're a decent guy. I just want to make sure that you'll be a decent man to my daughter. Oh and if you ever hurt Mallory, my face will be the last one you see before you blackout." He picks up his beer and holds it in the air. "On that note, a toast is in order. Cheers to a happy life that always starts with a happy wife."

"Cheers!" I drink though it seems odd to be drinking beer at 9:30 in the morning. With the hard part now over, I smile, feeling the relief.

"Wipe that goofy grin off your face and grab your binoculars," he says, lowering his voice. "I see some ducks in the distance."

Grabbing my binoculars, I follow the direction he's already set in. "Is it the Merganser?"

When he doesn't answer, I turn back to him, a small smile tugging at the corners of his mouth. He picks up his camera and takes pictures with the long, zoom lens attached. "It sure is. Evan, I think you may be good luck for this family."

"That's not such a bad thing." I've definitely had it a lot easier with her family than she has with mine.

"Nope, not a bad thing at all."

It rains on the way back to the house. I get wet helping to hook the boat up to the truck, so I'm cold. I'm ready for coffee, a warm house, and snuggles with my girlfri... *my fiancée*. But I guess I have some business to attend to with Mallory before that title is official.

Because of the unusually bad weather, the drive home takes even longer. I'm getting anxious, but also still curious about an earlier conversation I had with her dad. I want to clear things up before we reach the house, so I ask, "How'd you know I'd been arrested?"

Clay keeps his eyes on the road and says, "I work with a lot of connected people down at the courthouse. All it took was Elise's homemade pound cake to get the information."

"You bribed government employees with cake to hand over my records? That's illegal, you know."

He laughs. "Come see me when some punk wants to date your daughter and we'll talk."

I may not relate to the comment, but I can respect that he cares enough to protect his daughter.

This unseasonal rain storm is pissing me off. That and every stoplight in Denver is conspiring to keep me away from Mallory. I just want to get to my girl and put this ring on her finger once and for all. This time, I'm going to do this right.

The front door opens as soon as we pull into the driveway. My mouth drops open when Mallory walks to the railing on the porch in a fitted T-shirt and cut-offs—perfect for Hawaii, but all wrong for a Colorado winter.

Clay, in his puffy, insulated coat, grabs his gear and dashes for the house. I pull my hood up to protect my face, grab my gear and race to the front porch. Clay is standing there under the cover of the roof and offers his hand to me. I shake it, a silent understanding exchanged between us.

To me, her father says, "Don't forget the ice chest." He turns to Mallory, leans down and holds his daughter, tightly, as if his life depends on it. He knows the importance of this moment and a flash of sympathy kind of stabs me in the chest. With a quick turn, he goes inside, leaving us alone on the porch.

Her smile eases my racing heart, but I'm still not ready to do this, so I run down the steps and hop in the truck. I collect myself as I grab the ice chest, but before I brave the rain again, I dig deep into my coat pocket and pull the ring out. When I look up, I see her. Our eyes connect and we tilt our heads, a knowing smile creasing both our mouths. I get out, slam the door shut, and start walking toward the house, not carrying about the rain anymore. I can't rush this even in inclement weather. But Mallory sees it differently and runs out to meet me half-way.

Standing in the yard, my heart clenches seeing her beauty in such close proximity and knowing I'm the luckiest fucking guy in the world. She throws her arms around me, knocking the hood off my head, and kisses me. It's too late to keep her dry. She's soaked already, so I kiss her with all that I am, dropping the ice chest and pushing the wet dark strands of her hair away from her face.

Her tongue is warm and welcoming despite the frigid temperatures. My hands roam freely up her sides, over her shoulders, her neck, into her hair, landing on her face. My body begins to succumb to the depths of this kiss. Then I remember that it's freezing out here and she's half naked.

"Baby," I start to say between kisses, "we need to get you inside. You'll get sick."

Kiss.

Kiss.

Tongue.

Deeper.

Fuck.

I want her.

Kiss.

Kiss.

She takes a step back just as I take a step forward, but she slips on an icy mud patch. Suddenly, she's falling backwards, grappling for anything to keep her upright as she screams. I grab her flailing hands, but the ground is too slippery and I start to go down with her. Desperately trying to fall to the side of her so I don't crush her, I reach out to break our fall, but she grabs a hold of my coat and pulls me straight down on top of her.

I land in a push-up position over her with one hand under her head. She looks up at me dazed before she bursts out laughing. She lifts up and I laugh, but my muscles are straining from the fall.

Mallory pulls me down on top of her and kisses me again. She's got mud splattered all over her body and in her hair and even some on her face, but I don't think I've ever seen her look more beautiful. The rain drenches us and I kiss her just not caring anymore. I need her and she needs me.

Whispering against her lips, I say, "C'mon on. Let's get inside."

"But this is so much more fun and soooo romantic, don't

ya think?" Her eyes twinkle with delight like the cold can't catch her.

"Not if you end up in the hospital with pneumonia."

I roll off and stand up. Bending back down, I take her hands in mine and lift her to her feet. She's laughing and enjoying this so much that I have to smile at my beautiful, messy woman.

As soon as she's up, I take my coat off and throw it around her shoulders. Feeling every bit of the joy in this moment, with her left hand still in mine, I bend down on one knee and look up at her.

"Mallory, my love," I start and she gasps. "You captured my attention from the moment I saw you and my heart the very first time you called me out on my bullshit. You showed me kindness and gave me love when I didn't deserve it. And you never asked for anything but loyalty *and a note* in return. I wholeheartedly give you that and all that I am without hesitation. You aren't my match, you're my inspiration. If you'll have me, I'll spend the rest of my life showing you the man you make me want to be."

"Oh, Evan," she says, wiping a tear from her face. Somehow her tears treading their own path down her cheek separately than the rain, making them stand apart almost sparkling against her flawless skin.

"Will you marry me?"

"Yes, yes, of course." She drops to her knees, down to my level. "Partners, not inspiration. Always partners. You inspire me with your courage and love every day." She sniffles. "*Please*, equals, alright?"

I shake my head, a poor attempt to hold back my own tears. "Equals." I take the ring out of my pocket. I know she doesn't care about size, cut, clarity, or any of that, but I hope she likes it. Hell, I hope she loves it since she's gonna wear it forever.

I slide it onto her ring finger officially binding us together, and she gasps again. "It's perfect." Throwing her arms around my neck, I tuck my nose against her wet hair and skin, inhaling her before releasing a long held breath as relief settles over me. Contentment. Though we're both soaked and frozen to the bone, shivering and muddy, life is perfect.

Not gonna lie. I want her with me. I understand she made a promise to her friend. I understand she's contractually obligated to finish out her lease, but damn it, I want her with me. This shuffling back and forth is bullshit. I want her stuff over at my place. Shit, I want to call it *our* place. I mean, we're engaged for crying out loud. I toss my textbook onto the coffee table, totally pissed off.

Mallory eyes the textbook and then me. "I'll be back later, okay," she says, kissing me on the cheek.

Just as she gets up from the couch, I grab her hand. "No. I want you to stay."

She sighs. I know she's sick of this back and forth stuff just as much as I am, and it's only been two weeks. "Babe," she whispers and closes her eyes.

"I've talked to Josh," I say.

Her eyes open and she waits for me to say more.

"He said he wants to live with Sarah. That he's been trying to talk her into it for over a year."

"I feel pulled here, Evan. I pay for an apartment because I committed to it."

I stand up and take her by the waist. "Sublet it."

"They don't allow that. I already checked."

"I don't want to stay over there anymore. I like Sarah and Josh, but sometimes I just want us to have privacy. Is it too much to want to have sex with you whenever and wherever we want without someone potentially walking in on us? It puts a real damper on things." She nods while looking down, tapping my shoe with hers. "Twelve hundred square feet all to ourselves as opposed to six hundred shared. Sounds tempting, you have to admit."

"You're more than tempting, my handsome fiancé."

"I've got one last idea. Hear me out, okay?"

She sucks in her bottom lip and looks up at me under her lashes. Damn, she's distracting. I feel my cock harden and readjust while trying to stay focused on the topic at hand.

"Okay, I'm listening," she says softly, resting her palms flat on my chest.

"Let's pay to end the lease. It's not much and it would be worth it to have you here all the time. You know once school starts back up in a few days it's going to be hard to find time with our busy schedules. At least this way, we'll always go to bed together."

"Let me guess, you already know how much it costs to buy out the lease?" she asks, knowing the answer already.

"Yep."

"If," she says, pointing her finger at me. "If this is an actual option, is there any way I can afford to buy it out? Or is it too expensive?"

"It's two month's rent."

She huffs and I see the disappointment in her eyes. When she looks down, I lift her chin back up. "It's our money. What does it matter if it comes from your bank account or mine when it's both of ours anyway?"

"It's hard for me to be taken care of. You know this about me."

I squat down until I'm eye-level with her, and say, "I love you. Please, let's do this."

"I love you too." Her smile is soft, but I know it well. She's gonna say yes.

I pull her into an embrace and she whispers, "Alright."

"Really?" I search her eyes for the lie, but find none.

"Really. I want to be with you and you're right. Once school starts it is gonna be hard to squeeze in time together." Lifting up, she gives me a quick kiss. She turns and walks to the door, but before she leaves, she says, "Let me talk to Sarah and make sure everything is good with her first."

I nod, not saying another word. I don't want to push my luck when I'm ahead.

"EVAN, no complaining. You wanted me over here, so you have to help."

"I didn't realize how much crap you had crammed into that small room at your apartment."

"Shush it and move!"

She's sexy when she's bossy. *Fuck*, does that mean I like a dominant woman? I shake my head and watch her ass in front of me sashaying into the elevator. If she keeps that up, I'm gonna have my way with her when we get upstairs.

She sets the box on the floor in the bedroom, turns and says, "I think we'll be finished after two more trips to the car."

I grab her by the waist, and flip her onto the bed. "Give

me some action now, woman, or I'm gonna tickle you into submission," I say, holding her wrists above her head. "You can't just walk around looking like this. These very short-shorts are driving me mad and I'm pretty damn positive that you're not wearing a bra under that sweatshirt either. You're torturing me."

She pretends to be irritated between giggles, but I see through her act. She loves getting me all worked up like this. "Evan, you know I don't take kindly to threats," she says, hitting me on the chest while I attack her neck with my mouth.

"Oh," I say then kiss her on the throat and smirk. "And this isn't a threat. This is a promise, baby." I move down to kiss, tugging the collar of her sweatshirt down to suck on the skin of her collarbone.

Her body relaxes under mine. Yeah, she wants me. In a soft voice, she whispers, "Just two more boxes... oh God, that feels good."

"You can call me babe, baby, or Evan, but God is a bit formal, don't ya think?" I snicker then return to sucking on her neck, her natural taste so sweet.

"Just keep doing... yes, oh Evan, yes, that. Right there."

Ever since we left Denver, we haven't been able to keep our hands off each other, but somehow it's different.

Her life surrounds us in boxes. She's here and she's mine—the thought intoxicating. A desperate desire builds inside of me. My hands slide down under the waistband of her shorts and she sighs. She starts tugging at my shirt and I lift one arm at a time so she can remove it.

She tosses it off into the room somewhere, then runs her nails lightly down my chest sending shivers through my body.

My voice is gruff, my desire taking over, my patience

gone. "I want these off. Now." I lift up, and she scrambles beneath me to remove her shorts. I smile, and ask, "No underwear, Mallory?"

"Nope," she says, cocking an eyebrow and grinning.

"Fuck, I love you."

She laughs. I untie the drawstring of my pants, but she pushes them down with her hands before jumping off the bed to pull them the rest of the way off.

After she takes her sweatshirt off, I climb back on top of her, positioning myself. "I was right. No bra, you tease."

"It's called motivation. I thought it would be a good reward for helping me move."

"You know me too well. By the way, welcome home, baby."

Her lids close when I push into her. My own lids close in sync with the forward motion. Biting my lower lip, I enjoy the slow pace of our bodies moving together.

When I open my eyes, her hands are rubbing across her chest and I see her ring, *my ring*, on her finger, two and a half carats for the world to see our commitment to each other. She opens her eyes as her hand reaches up stroking my face gently. "I love you." I'll never get enough of hearing those words from her lips.

She moves against me, encouraging me to speed up, so I do and we both moan in pleasure.

I slip my arm under her leg, lifting her up by the knee and getting closer—moving deeper, thrusting harder. Her hands grab my shoulders, holding on until her head falls back and her mouth falls open. "Fuck, keep going, babe. Keep going."

Pushing up with my hips, I know I'll hit her sweet spot. She bucks beneath me, not able to contain herself. She swears, calling out my name one more time as she tenses, then tremors.

My orgasm hits me just after hearing her dirty words—both hitting fast and hard. I collapse on top of her trying to catch my breath and slow my racing heart. But when I try to move off her, our bodies slick with sweat, she holds me tighter and whispers, "Stay."

"Am I hurting you?"

"No," she says with a sigh. "I love this part."

I smile. "Mallory?"

"Yes," she answers, rubbing my shoulder gently.

"Promise me it will always be like this."

"I promise you it will always be like this."

I roll off and we move to our sides, then I pull her even closer and kiss the tender spot behind her ear. "Sweet dreams."

"Sweet dreams."

"You excited or nervous?" Mallory asks, sitting across from me and eating a bowl of cereal.

"Both." I stand up, my anxiety over the first day of school showing by the full bowl of cereal on the table. "I've lost my appetite." Walking into the kitchen, I grab a bottle of water from the fridge.

After looking at her watch, she announces, "Time to go, hot stuff."

Dropping the bottle inside my back pack, I swing it onto my shoulder and stand near the door, waiting on her.

I hear a huff as she grabs her backpack from the floor next to the table. "Hey, there isn't maid service here. Bowl. Sink."

"Remind me to find a cleaning service soon then because this cleaning stuff you're obsessed with sucks."

She giggles. "Call Ms. Chart to come for a visit. I'm sure she'd be happy to help you interview housekeepers."

That gives me an idea. "I could ask her to move in here with us. We have the extra bedroom."

Mallory looks at me, eyes narrows, frown on her face.

"I'm just playing with ya," I say, teasing. "Why would she leave Hawaii or even New York for the cold and snow of Colorado?"

"Why indeed."

I take the bowl to the sink and we leave.

While walking to school, I can tell Mallory is lost in thought. I stay quiet and let her think. One thing I've learned about her is when she's ready to talk, she will.

She kisses me in front of the English building before disappearing inside after a quick goodbye. I walk down to the Psychology building and find the auditorium of my first class.

Shifting uncomfortably in my chair, I look around, feeling much older than most of the other students. Maybe I'm feeling the toll life has taken, aged by experience. Makes me feel lucky that most of my credits transferred and I tested out of the other basics or I'd be with a bunch of eighteen-year-olds instead of kids who can at least buy beer.

Thankfully my morning passes by uneventfully. School is just how I remember. I meet Mallory for lunch at a deli near campus. When I walk in, I see her sitting in a corner. Tossing my bag across the seat, I slide in. "Hey there."

"Hi," she says, smiling. "How were your first classes?"

"So far so good. No surprises."

"That's good. Are they interesting?"

"Yeah, I like them."

"What about girls?"

"What about girls?" I ask.

She briefly glances out the window then back to me. By the way she's fidgeting, I think she's nervous. "Any girls you find interesting?"

"Only one," I say, reaching across the table and taking

hold of her hand, stilling it. "You're the only girl I've got eyes for."

"Sorry," she says, looking at our hands.

"For what?"

"For, you know, being ridiculous."

"I like when you're ridiculous. Means you think I'm hot."

That makes her laugh. "I do think you're hot."

"Good. Because I think you're really hot."

"Okay, silly boy, let's get back to your day and classes."

I lean back in the booth. "They're going to be a lot of work. I can tell."

"Well, knowing you, you'll get straight A's." She slips out of the booth and stands. "We should go up and order our food. We don't have a ton of time."

We go through the line then sit back down.

"Sooo," she starts, looking down at her sandwich. I set mine down because I can tell whatever she's about to say is important. "I wanted to talk to about some things I've been thinking about."

"Alright." I clasp my hands together under the table and lean forward to listen.

"I know you just got here and all, but I was wondering what you thought about—"

"The food?"

"No, um," she says, chuckling. "What do you think of Colorado since you've been here?"

I sit back, my heart starts racing, and I brace myself, suddenly nervous for some reason. I drag my sweating palms up and down my thighs as my eyes travel to her left hand to make sure her ring is still there. *It is.*

"I'm applying for the graduate program here, but I'd also like to apply to the University of Hawaii. They have a great program and it would be warm and I don't know where we could live or anything, but I'm sure we could figure that out. Sunny and Zach are staying there after graduation and I could work on campus or maybe even at Big Kehones to make mone—"

"Whoa, whoa, whoa. Wait a minute. Back up." I hold up my hands, stopping her. "Let me get this straight. You might be moving to Hawaii?"

"Well, I wouldn't do anything without talking to you. It's a big decision that we have to make together now." She wiggles her ring finger at me. "I'm happy to stay here if you prefer. I know—"

"That's not what I'm saying. It's probably not the best idea for me to change again, but I want to go back to Hawaii. My car is there."

"You only want to go back for your car?"

"No, but I'd have a car. We could live at the house."

"That brings me to part two of what I've been thinking about—the wedding."

"Did you pick a date?"

"I picked a location. I want to get married in Hawaii. We said after my graduation, so I was thinking this summer. June, if that's not too soon."

I get up and slide across the booth next to her. Wrapping my arm around her shoulder, I say, "June sounds perfect. I thought I was gonna have to wait until after my graduation, which is a lot longer than June." I kiss her and she kisses me back not caring that we're in public.

"You're not mad?"

"Why would I be mad?"

"Moving here and then maybe, possibly moving again." She crinkles her nose in worry. "You have an apartment with stuff now."

"I'm in my major now, but the classes I'm taking this

semester will transfer. I'd go back to Hawaii in a heartbeat. And I can sell the furniture and other stuff we don't want. June, huh?"

She looks down shyly, twisting the ring around her finger. "I'm ready to be married, to be tied to you permanently."

"You can't say things like that to me in public. Words like that make me want to bend you over this table and have my way with you."

Her green eyes lock on mine, all tempting lust and challenging. "I like your wicked ways. So what's stopping you?"

"Hot damn, woman," I say, lifting up to adjust my jeans, hoping to find some extra room for my erection. "I'm trying to be a gentleman. I'm trying to control the primal urges that tell me to fuck you right here and now."

"Well, if you ever want to *not* 'control' those urges, you know where to find me," she says, knowing she owns my ass.

She's just about to take a bite of her sandwich when I ask, "How much time do you have until your next class?"

Setting her food down, she looks at her phone to check. "Forty-five minutes."

I grab the food, toss it on the tray and dump it in the garbage bin before grabbing both of our backpacks, her hand, and pull her out the door.

"Evan?"

"Yep?" I answer, trying to figure out how I can shorten the ten minute walk back to the apartment.

"Are you taking me home to have sex? In the middle of the day?"

"No, I'm taking you home to fuck in the middle of the day."

"It's the first day of classes," she says, double-timing to keep up with my pace.

"We're setting a precedence. This is how all first days should be," I reply proudly.

LAYING NEXT TO ME, her eyes heavy, her body covered in a light layer of sweat. "Holy fuck, babe."

"I promised a solid fuck."

Mallory rolls on top of me, wiggling her sweet ass as she straddles my middle. I hold her by the hips, looking up at my sexy girl. Leaning forward, she drops her arms on either side of my head. Her hair tickles my ears and she looks into my eyes. "You sure did and you delivered. Since the day you asked if I needed a ride from the airport with all your cocky attitude and swagger, you've delivered on your promises." Leaning all the way down, she plants her lips on my mouth, her tongue finding mine, and with sensual caresses, her body begins slowly rocking against me, seeking more.

I roll her over so I'm on top, my body recovering and reacting. "We're gonna miss our classes if we do this, but I'm game if you are."

A smile slides onto her face and she sighs. "I could spend an eternity in bed with you and never get enough."

"You have my soul wrapped around your finger, so I'm counting on longer." I kiss her again.

We're only twenty minutes late to our next classes... I have no regrets.

20

MALLORY

He's so happy. The heaviness lifted from his eyes replaced with pure joy. Evan's complexion already looks more golden and we just landed in Oahu.

"I missed you," he says, gingerly rubbing his dashboard and placing a kiss there.

"Are you seriously kissing your car?"

"Don't be jealous, baby, you own my heart." He laughs, then reaches across the console and rubs my thigh. "Always, remember?"

"I'll try not to be jealous of the car as long as you don't forget who delivers the goods." I lean my head back and look out the window at the beach and ocean beyond, remembering the very first time I sat next to him in this car.

"No worries there. I love your goods," he says with a wink.

The wind blows through our hair, the scent of Hawaiian flowers fill the air, and the ocean captures my attention as we drive toward what I now call the Ashford compound.

After parking in the driveway, we walk down the path to his guesthouse, but stop when we see Ms. Chart running toward us. "Mallory!" She wraps her arms around me and I embrace her back, smiling from ear-to-ear. When she leans back, she holds my arms out and says, "You are just as beautiful as ever. Now, let me see that ring."

Evan clears his throat... loudly.

"You should probably say hi to him before he gets even more jealous," I say, giggling.

Turning to him like a doting mother, she cups his face and smiles. "Evan, I've missed you so much." She looks him over. "You look too skinny. I'm going to cook for you tonight. Okay?"

I see him smile, a bit embarrassed and hugs her again. "I missed you too, Ms. Chart."

An hour later, I'm lying on the bed, the time change catching up with me, when Sunny and Zach barge in. Startled, I jump and yell, "What the—"

"Happy Spring Break!" Sunny squeals and jumps on the bed, tackling me down into the covers.

Evan walks out from the bathroom. "Zach. Dude. How goes it?"

"Shhh! Look," Zach replies.

Both Sunny and I look up to find the guys watching us, sort of mesmerized.

"Shit, don't stop on our account," Zach says, sounding disappointed we're not goofing around on the bed any longer.

We both grab a pillow and throw it at them. "Pervs," I shout.

"It's been too long, brother," Evan says, turning to Zach and they do their boy club handshake as if nothing happened.

I'm just glad I was dressed. Sunny and I fall back on the bed in a fit of giggles. "I missed you, Mal."

"I missed you, too. What do you have planned for us?"

"More like what are your plans? Do you even have time to do anything other than wedding stuff?"

"I hope so."

"Do I get to come along with you? I wanna eat cake and try fancy food. Oh, oh, and what about the dresses? You said I could be a bridesmaid, and I'm totally holding you to that."

I throw a pillow over her face and roll off the bed. Evan grabs me by the hand and tucks me under his arm. After a quick kiss on the head, he says, "We're hitting the waves. What're you gonna do?"

"I'm taking Mallory with me. We're going shopping and then heading to Big Kehones." Sunny says, climbing off the bed and scrunching up her face. "This bed smells of sex by the way. Gross."

Bursting out laughing, I poke Evan in the ribs. "Guess we've been busted."

"Geez, Mallory, you guys couldn't survive a few hours." She rolls her eyes, and adds, "Didn't you just land like three hours ago?"

Smiling up at Evan, I answer for us both, "We're on vacation. We had to celebrate."

Shaking her head, she flops down on the couch. "I don't know how you two have time for school with all the celebrating you do."

"And on that note, go have fun, babe. We'll see you later." I push Evan toward the door with Zach.

"I'm going. I'm going," he says. "Don't miss me too much." He leans back quickly and kisses me before I smack him on the ass. "Later."

Sunny and I go to a bridal store in Waikiki and I try on a few dresses. Normally I appreciate the challenge of the hunt. But today, shopping for my dress is different, this is special and I feel the importance of finding the *right* dress.

Sunny smiles when I come out dressed in a flowing chiffon layered white gown. "Oh my God, Mallory." She clasps her hand over her heart. "You look so beautiful and it's very beachy."

"I kind of like it."

"Then that's not the dress. You should *love* the dress you wear on your wedding day not just kind of like it." As I spin in front of the mirror, taking in all angles, she asks, "So everything's still good with you and Evan since you moved in together?"

In the reflection of the mirror, my eyes meet hers. "Better than good. I wasn't sure how this whole living together thing would go, but now I can't imagine living without him."

"You won't ever have to imagine that. That's the beauty of marrying young. You have your whole lives to spend together."

"Don't make me cry, okay? I've become quite sentimental and cry easily these days."

Glassy tears fill her eyes, but she looks away and wipes them. "Well, we can't have the bride crying or anything."

Turning back to look at the dress, I spot tears filling my own eyes despite my best efforts. The sales lady is there with a tissue ready in hand, probably used to seeing a lot of tears in here. A good laugh shared by all lightens the mood.

After I try on a few more dresses, we head over to visit Johnny and Alana at Big Kehones.

"You look great, Mallory," Johnny says, taking me in. "Life's treating you good."

"Thanks," I return the compliment while hugging him. "You don't look so bad yourself."

When we part, he says, "You remember Lorelei."

"Yes, from the booth at the surf contest."

"It's good to see you again," she says with a little wave, sitting on a barstool.

"Likewise," I say, smiling between the pair.

Lorelei looks at me, her gaze dropping down to my hand and I'm sure the ring. "Evan Ashford, huh?" she asks.

"Yep. Evan Ashford."

"Johnny tells me he's a good guy and not to listen to the rumors."

I laugh. "I was told something very similar when I first started working here. I discovered he's right. They're only rumors, not who he really is... okay, maybe there's a little truth to some of the rumors, but in my book, he's a keeper."

After chatting with them for awhile, Lorelei takes off and Sunny goes to get her paycheck from the office. I lean over the bar and ask in a hushed tone, "How are things between you and Sunny?"

Johnny looks over his shoulder and says, "We're good. I'm happy with Lorelei and Sunny's happy with Zach. I realized what I had with Sunny was a crush. What I have with Lorelei is much more."

"That's good." Johnny's gaze drifts over my shoulder to somebody entering the restaurant.

And then I hear, "Mallory?"

I spin on my barstool and see Noah standing there. My mouth drops open, too stunned to speak. My pounding heart brings me back to the reality that Noah is standing there waiting for me to say something.

"I didn't know you were back on the island," he says, walking toward me, hesitant but moving closer, his posse heading behind him to grab a table on the other side of the restaurant.

"Noah," I start to say, "I don't think it's such a go—Oh!

Um..." He squeezes me tight, effectively trapping me in his grip and lifts me completely off the stool. Wriggling, I tell him to put me down after the awkward embrace. "I don't have anything to say to you. Not after what happened."

"You're not still mad, are you?"

"Mad? What would I possibly have to be mad at? Hmmm... let me think here." I roll my eyes. "Would it be that you kissed me without my permission and probably would've done more if you hadn't been stopped?"

"How's your hand? That was one helluva slap," he says, mocking.

I stand up, crossing my arms over my chest. I'm trying to think of a witty comeback when I'm cut off by Johnny, "Noah, go join your friends. Mallory just stopped by to say hi. Don't ruin her visit. No one's looking for trouble or wants to deal with your shit today." Johnny walks around the bar and stands next to me.

"Look who's finally grown a pair," Noah says, eyeing him before looking back at me. "C'mon, give me a minute to explain. Let's settle this."

"Settle this? This was settled a long time ago at the luau. You showed your true colors. I just feel stupid for falling for your lies."

Noah crosses his arms defensively. "Mallory, don't be such a bitch."

My hand tingles with anticipation, but I resist this time. "I should slap you, asshole, but you're not worth the trouble," I say, waving my left hand in front of him shooing him away like an irritating gnat.

"What the fuck is that?" I'm about to sit down when he grabs my wrist, spinning me around to face him. With my hand held up high, he asks, "Is that a wedding ring?"

Normally, I would deck him for grabbing me like that

and sounding so disgusted by my engagement. But seeing the look of disbelief on his face is sort of fun. His distress playing out before my eyes is quite amusing. I smile, proud as I turn my hand to let the light hit the perfect and large diamond. "It's an engagement ring."

A smug smile appears on his face like it all makes sense now. "I knew Ashford couldn't keep you... satisfied. He's always been a haole chump. And, Mallory, don't you know that your anger is a fucking turn on."

"Ashford couldn't *keep* me happy? First of all, no guy needs to *keep* me anything. Secondly, Ashford is—"

"Man, that's awesome you found someone else," he says, gloating. "I bet Ashford was fucking devastated. God, I love that image."

"Noah, I'm marrying Evan." I wait for it. It's coming, but there's a long pause as he processes what I just said.

Anger flashes across his face, an eerie calm eventually settling over him "Then I guess, best of luck is in order because you're gonna need it with him." He starts to walk away, but stops to add, "I used to think you were a smart girl, but you're just like the rest of them." He shakes his head in disappointment. "You don't want a good guy. You just want a guy with money."

"You know nothing about me, or Evan, so shut your mouth." I finish speaking right as Sunny walks out of the office. She stops, seeing the confrontation escalate, and hurries to stand next to me. "What's going on, guys?" She tries to lessen the tension by sounding chipper.

"Or what, Mallory? What are you gonna do if I don't shut my mouth?" Noah asks, emphasizing the Mallory with a hard edge as if my name pisses him off just to say it.

"Or I'll kick your fucking ass," a very familiar male voice threatens.

I peek behind Noah. Standing in the doorway is Evan and Zach.

Noah turns around and spits as if disgusted. "Fuck, Ashford, I don't give two shits about you. You're nothing around here, but a bad fucking memory."

"A bad memory is better than a washed up surfer who was sent home in shame. Now that's gotta be embarrassing." Evan crosses his arms over his chest, his stance steady and strong. Zach's at his side.

I walk to Evan when I see Noah's crew stand up in case a fight breaks out. "Hey babe." I lean up on my tiptoes and kiss him on the cheek.

"Sunny texted us to join you," Evan says, a wry grin on his face. "I guess we got here just in time."

"I guess you did," I reply, glancing back at Noah.

Noah's shaking his head, looking down at his feet when he says, "I don't care enough about either of you to let your stupid insults affect me."

Evan takes my hand, his fingers entwining with mine, and glares at Noah. "I think you care more than you're letting on and I'm willing to bet money when you're lying in bed all alone that this moment will repeat over and over again in your head. Mallory was never stupid enough to fall for your bullshit and that's going to bother you for a long time to come. But you know what will haunt you even longer?" He pauses and I know it's only for dramatic effect. "That I got the girl."

"Fuck you, Ashford."

I latch onto Evan's arm, nervous a fight is about to break out. "I want to go," I say, moving in front of him, with my hands purposely placed on his chest, I look up at him. "Can we go? Please, Evan?"

The hard stare he has on Noah softens when he looks

down at me. "Come on, baby. We've got a wedding to plan." He takes my hand and with the other gives Johnny and Sunny a two finger salute before we head out. Without looking back, Evan calls over his shoulder, "Hey Zach, tomorrow, okay?"

"Yep, I'll be there in the morning," Zach says and I can hear the relief in his voice that the situation didn't go any further.

When we walk outside, Evan turns to me and says, "I'm gonna have to keep my eye on you, Miss Wray. You've got quite the temper and mouth on you." He laughs as he opens the car door for me.

"You just keep that in mind," I joke.

"Oh, I will, but for now, there's only one thing on my mind and that includes you, me, a bed, and some pineapple."

Holy shit! "That does sound good."

We get back to the guesthouse and Evan disappears into the main house looking for 'supplies.'

A small knock draws my attention to the door just as it opens. I look up and my heart starts racing. Claire Ashford and I have settled things between us, but I guess my heart hasn't caught up with my brain.

"Mallory, I hope I'm not intruding," she says, staying close to the door.

I tug at my T-shirt, trying to look more presentable. "No, it's fine. Come in." As soon as I sit on the edge of the bed, my foot starts bouncing, my anxiety of the surprise meeting showing. "I didn't know you were here on the island?"

"Yes, well, it was last minute. We thought we should make a trip to help with some of the wedding details since it's taking place here. We—Hugh and I—were also hoping to spend some time with you and Evan." She shuts the door quietly behind her and walks over to the kitchen bar. "We haven't seen him since December and three months is a long time to go without seeing your children. Situating herself on one of the barstools, she asks, "I would like you and Evan to join us for dinner tonight if you don't have plans already?"

"Oh. Um." I say, fumbling over my words thinking about the plans we did have that I can't tell Evan's mother about without sounding like a complete whore. "I'm not sure. I'll speak with Evan when he gets back. I don't think we do, but I should check with him first."

"I also wanted to come by and say congratulations. I know we sent a card and flowers, but I haven't seen you since the big announcement."

I press my hand against my bouncing leg, but the other one starts right up. "Thank you, Claire. It really," I say, looking up and meeting her eyes, "means a lot to hear you say that."

"I brought you something."

"You did?" I ask, my voice going higher, once again, she surprises me.

With a smile, she holds out a small jewelry box. "A gift for you."

I get up, cautiously, and walk to her, taking the box in hand. When I open it, my breath catches and I instantly look at her. "I can't accept these earrings," I say, nodding my head.

She puts her hands under mine, and says, "Yes, you can. I want you to have them."

Staring at the sapphire and diamond earrings, I say, "They're stunning, but too much."

"I wore those when I married Evan's father. Hugh's mother handed them down to me. She wore them on her wedding day. So you see, you're carrying on a tradition—from future mother-in-law to future daughter-in-law. One day, if you have a son, you can hand them down to your daughter-in-law."

My heart is filled with love over this sweet sentiment. "What about Kate? She should get these."

Claire scoffs, waving her hand. "Pfft. Kate has so much jewelry and even more once I die. She's not lacking in the jewels department. Anyway, that's not the tradition. I have something special set aside for her that my mother gave me. So don't worry about Kate."

She stands up and straightens her skirt. "I should get going. You don't have to wear them on your wedding day, but I do hope you decide to keep them. It would make me very happy if you did." Cupping my hands between hers, she smiles, then walks to the door.

"Claire?" Her eyes flash to meet mine, hopeful, but she remains silent. "Thank you. They're beautiful and I'll always cherish them."

"You're welcome. And, Mallory? I'm so glad Evan's found someone that will fill his life with love and his future with hope." And then she does something remarkable—she hugs me and I hug her back. It's a real embrace, not one for show, but with meaning felt within her arms.

When I release her, she looks at my hand and asks, "Oh, I almost forgot to ask. May I see the ring?"

"Sure." I hold my hand out for her to see.

Taking my hand in hers, she looks at it. "It's very beautiful." She looks back at me and says, "Beautiful and classic. Very much like you."

To say I don't want to burst into tears when she says that would be a complete and utter lie. But I resist from grabbing her into a ridiculously silly hug as joy overwhelms me. Instead, I say, "Thank you. That means a lot to me."

She takes a deep breath, and as if the air between us has finally cleared, she says, "I should let you get back to whatever you..." Her eyes glance to the bed. "Well, I'll leave you to it."

As she walks to the door, she says, "Thank you again for being so kind."

I nod as she walks out, closing my eyes and exhaling loudly. "Shit." I take a deep breath and hold it in momentarily, before exhaling the air, my nerves, and all my fears out once and for all.

"Hey? Everything alright in here?" Evan asks, walking back in. "I saw my mother. She looked like she'd been crying."

I lift my head and open my eyes. "Yes. Everything is better than alright."

"Okay, if you're sure. Oh, and she told me about dinner tonight. Thoughts?"

"I think we should go."

His eyebrows shoot up and he starts nodding. "I think that would be good." Coming closer, his hands grace my face and he says, "So maybe we should postpone our plans until later. You seem a bit distracted."

"Not distracted. Just surprised how everything has turned out. Maybe even a little overwhelmed with all that has happened today. I could just be tired from traveling though."

He leads me to the bed and we sit down. "You should take a nap. You'll feel better and you know we need all the energy we can muster for dessert tonight."

"Dessert? Why do we need..." I stop mid sentence, realizing he's talking dirty to me and I play along. "Yes, we do because I have a sweet tooth that only you can satisfy."

He laughs which makes me smile. I lay back on the bed and he kisses me on the temple. "Happy napping." He leaves it at that, walking out the back door. I fall asleep to the sound of him scrubbing old wax off one of his surfboards in the grass.

21

MALLORY

I lift my head, cracking my eyes open to find Evan doing God only knows what with his tongue on my leg. I clear my throat and he pops up. "Oh, good, you're awake," he says with a big smile. "We need to be at dinner soon. I thought you might want to get dressed."

I look down at my body. I'm only wearing my bra and panties. "How'd I get undressed?" He looks around and whistles. "And what were you doing to my leg?"

"I was trying to wake you without scaring you."

"By licking me?"

"That was only once. You obviously didn't feel the twenty kisses all over your face, so I had to resort to a new tactic."

I shake my head, smiling at him. "This conversation is too weird for my sleepy brain. I'm gonna shower."

"I'll join you."

"No! Nope. If you come in there we'll never make it to dinner and I want to make a good impression on your parents."

"You already have, baby."

"No!" I point at him. "You keep your sexiness out here and away from my nakedness." He crosses his arms... and then comes that sexy smile. "See, that's exactly what I'm talking about right there." I rush into the bathroom and lock the door before I get caught up in fantastic sex with my fiancé. As the water warms, I start questioning why exactly I'm resisting fantastic sex with him. *Dinner.* That's right. We must make it to dinner with his parents. Yeah, all horniness I had is gone with that thought.

Forty minutes later, Evan and I are walking hand-in-hand to the main house. Butterflies attack the inside of my stomach as soon as we walk in the door. Ms. Chart, Hugh, and Claire are all in the kitchen laughing together. Claire sits at the bar while Hugh mixes drinks and Ms. Chart cuts vegetables.

"Hi, can we help?" Evan asks, smiling while taking in the scene before him. It's all very Norman Rockwell and something I'm sure Evan's not accustomed to. The joy of the setting also makes me happy, especially for Evan.

"Son," his dad says, walking around the counter to greet him. They hug each other. "It's been a few months. You're looking good. Colorado seems to be treating you well." Hugh turns to me. "Mallory." He takes my hand and gives it a gentle squeeze. "You look lovelier than ever. Congratulations on the engagement. I know from speaking with Evan that he's very excited. We're happy to have you joining our family."

He's always so warm and welcoming. "Thank you," I reply, "I'm just as excited."

"Hi, Mallory," Claire says, touching my arm. "Nice rest?"

"It was good. Thank you. I love being here. It's Heaven on earth."

"We think so too," she says with a light laugh. "I just

wish we could visit more, but work and Manhattan keep us busier than ever these days."

I sit down next to her. "Have you ever considered moving here or is that not an option?"

Hugh sets down what looks to be Margarita in front of each of us. "Tonight we have lots to celebrate." He holds up his drink and all of us hold our glasses up for his toast. "Happy engagement."

After the toast, Claire turns back to me and says, "Maybe in retirement one day, but not now."

Hugh laughs. "I don't think I could get Claire out of New York. She'd get island fever."

"I like to read. I could learn to relax," she says, looking from him to me. "Maybe."

Evan is grabbing carrot bites off of the cutting board and getting his hand smacked when I offer, "Ms. Chart, I'd love to help. Put me to work."

"No, no," she says, admonishing. "You're a guest. Enjoy."

Walking around the counter, I stand next to her. "I'd rather help. Maybe I can finish the salad and you can work on the main course."

She smiles and rubs my back. "You're a dear. Thank you." I'm handed the knife and she goes to peek inside the oven. "The chicken is almost ready."

I finish cutting the carrots Ms. Chart started and start on the cucumber while Evan dilly dallies around the kitchen. Obviously this is all new to him, so I help him out. "Hey, babe, do you mind making a dressing?"

"A salad dressing?" he asks, leaning against the counter. "Like make one from scratch?"

"Yes," I answer with a chuckle. "It's easy. We'll do it together."

The silence in the room makes me look over my shoulder, wondering if everyone has left the kitchen. Nope, they're all here. Hugh and Claire are watching us with puzzled faces. I think it was the suggestion that we make a dressing that threw them off. I look the other way and Ms. Chart has a sweet smile on her face.

Evan laughs. "We're new to this. Ms. Chart has spoiled us. So, this dressing. How do I make it?"

"We'll start with an easy one—Italian dressing. You'll need..." I go on to explain, helping him measure then mix the liquids and spices.

"That's impressive, Mallory," Hugh says, stepping in to help to shake the mixture.

"I always helped my mom in the kitchen," I say, feeling a little shy with all their attention on me. "I've picked up a few basics along the way."

Evan takes the dressing back in hand, holding it in front of him, proud as a peacock for his contribution, and says, "Let's eat."

Dinner is served and we all take a seat except for Ms. Chart. "Are you joining us," I ask.

"You go ahead. It will be good for you all to be together. I'm sure you have plenty to talk about and I'm missing my favorite show, so I'll eat in my room tonight."

"What's your favorite show," Evan asks, calling to her as she slips out of the kitchen.

"Wheel of Fortune." Peeking back in, she adds, "I have a crush on Pat Sajak."

I giggle, but no one else does. I have a feeling they don't know who Pat Sajak is.

Hugh opens a bottle of white wine and serves us. We each help ourselves to dinner and start eating.

There's a moment of silence that makes me look up. My eyes meet Hugh's and he smiles. "I'm sure this is a very busy time for you with your school work and now planning a wedding. I wanted to thank you for all you've done for our family and for Evan."

"We wouldn't have our son back if it weren't for you," Claire says, setting her fork down.

Hugh says, "I should have told Evan this in New York, but he's really grown tremendously over the last year and I think Mallory has had a hand in that. You've turned into a fine man, Son."

"Thank you," he says. "And Mallory does deserve some credit."

"I don't need and I definitely don't deserve any credit when it comes to Evan. He's made his own choices. I've just supported them." I want to be open with my feelings, even with his parents. "I worried I was ruining Evan's life some days. Other days, I convinced myself I wasn't. But my life is better because he's in it and that's because I held onto the hope that his life is also better because I'm in it."

"*It is.*" Evan leans over and kisses the side of my head. His hand slips down between us, grasping mine securely.

"After seeing your work for the company last fall." Hugh turns to Evan, and says, "You'll always have a position at Ashford Holdings if you want it. I won't pressure you to come back, Evan. You have a brilliant mind and as long as you're not wasting it, I don't mind what career you choose." He leans forward. "He's also a very smart man to snag you while you're both young. I think you'll have a long and happy life together."

"So do I." I feel more at ease as the conversation winds down.

He chuckles. "Don't be afraid to kick his ass every now and then to keep him in line though."

Now that makes me laugh. "No worries there."

Claire smiles. "You're a great girl and my son's a lucky man."

"Thank you and if he wants to work for your company, I'll support that decision. If that's not his dream, then I fully support that too."

With a small nod, Hugh smiles. "Thank you."

During the rest of dinner, the conversation is friendly, but I can't shake the feeling that something else underlies the tone of the evening.

My instincts are proven right when Claire turns to me and asks, "How are the wedding plans, Mallory?"

Ding. Ding. Ding. Bingo.

"We just arrived today, but it's been a full day and we've made some progress. We decided we want an intimate affair down on the beach." I look at Evan. "Maybe even a picnic. I'm hoping to secure the caterer while we're here."

"A picnic? *For a wedding?*" Claire asks astonished, holding her hand against her chest as if those words pain her.

"I like the picnic idea—" Evan starts to say before a fork crashes onto a china plate.

We both jump and look at Claire who is furiously sipping her wine. She closes her eyes and as if she's counting to ten, takes a deep breath, opens her eyes again and smiles. "Excuse me. My fork must have slipped. Mallory, would you consider a catered affair if we compromise on the beach part?"

"Oh, um... I don't know. I'll definitely think about tha—"

"Mother, how many people do you have on your guest list?" Evan cuts me off, sounding irritated.

"I was just making an informal list in my head—"

"The number, Mother," Evan gets short, his tone clipped with impatience.

"Five Hundred."

"What!" I spit out, shocked and glad my mouth is empty or I would have spewed food or wine everywhere. My head is already shaking when I say, "I'm not having five hundred people at my wedding. Evan, I'm not. I, I, I can't walk down the aisle in front of that many strangers and—"

"It's okay, I'll handle this," he says, rubbing my thigh and reassuring me. He looks back at his mother sitting across the table from him. "That number is too high."

"Four hundred," Claire bargains.

"No." Evan is firm.

Claire turns to Hugh who looks resigned to losing this battle. He shrugs and she rolls her eyes, finally caving in. "Fine. How many can we invite?"

Evan puts on his most winning smile then looks at me, redirecting the attention. "I'll let my fiancée answer that."

All eyes are on me. I look down at the cloth napkin I been twisting violently in my lap and mumble, "Ten."

"What, dear? Speak up." I look up to meet Claire's hopeful eyes.

I repeat, "I was thinking more along the lines of ten, maybe fifteen guests for your side."

"Ten?" She coughs, having a slight choking attack, which is odd since she hasn't been eating. "I don't comprehend... um, hmmm," she stutters, then gulps the rest of her wine, emptying the glass. "Ten. That's ridiculous. *Ten?* Only ten people? That's impossible. Tell them, Hugh. Impossible."

Evan leans forward and clarifies for her. "Ten. So," he says, clasping his hands together to break the tension. "Mallory's graduation is coming up and we'd like to personally invite you to Colorado."

We all stare at him in a dead silence.

22

MALLORY

"Dinner with your parents went better than expected," I say, relieved to be back in the guest house.

"How'd you expect it to go?" Evan asks, flopping down on the bed next to me.

"I don't know. I'm still not sure what to expect from your family at this point."

He rolls over and rests his head on my stomach. Running my fingers through his hair lazily, I smile, loving the calmness of moments like this with him. He laughs and my body reverberates from the movement.

"What's so funny?" I ask.

"Just remembering when we told them we got engaged."

"Ahhh, the good times of frazzled nerves and stumbling words. I was nervous, but you were a mess," I tease him and tug on his earlobe.

"Nervous is an understatement." He chuckles.

"It all worked out... eventually. " I remember the relief I felt last December after Evan called them.

Mother, Dad," He says then clears his throat. "I want to talk to you about something important." I press my ear against his hand, so I can hear the other side of the call.

"Evan, what is it?" his mother asks.

"I know a lot has changed this past year. Fuck, just in the last seven months—"

"Please don't swear," she admonishes. "It's unbecoming."

"Okay," Evan stops, gulping heavily. I can tell he's losing his train of thought, so I use my hands to wave, making signals and hoping it helps to keep him on track. "Oh! Yeah, so, I was saying that at times I can't believe the changes either. My life is so different now and for the better. I think you can both agree with me here."

"Well, son, I do agree," his dad responds. "I think you've gone through a lot of bad and you seem to finally be getting some good back into your life."

"Thanks, dad. I couldn't agree with you more."

"Honey, what is this about?" His mother is losing patience. "I need to leave for a meeting."

"I want you to know that I'm taking a leap of faith. Well, not exactly a leap of faith. More like a leap of certainty," he starts to explain, looking to me while nodding his head like he's impressed with himself. "Yes, certainty. A leap of guaranteed happiness. A leap of... well, now that I think of it, maybe it's not even a leap, but more like a jump?" He looks at me for reassurance.

I roll my eyes at my sweet man as he stumbles through this. After taking a deep breath, he announces, "Mallory and I are engaged. It happened officially last night." I hold my breath and wait for the rapture.

Silence.

Silence.

Mallory gives me two thumbs up, and I hear a shuffling noise from the other end of the line. "Son, it's Dad. Don't you think this is too fast?"

"No. I love her," Evan says, squeezing my hand. "Why put off what we know we want. I don't want to waste time being away from her in order to make everyone else more comfortable with our decision."

"Evan..." His mother sighs into the phone. "You're just starting back to school. Your focus should be there. You seem to be making a lot of big decisions lately. Are you ready to have this dramatic of a change at this stage in your life?"

When Evan exhales I back away from the phone to look at him. I don't want to be a burden on him. I never wanted that. He closes his eyes and a sadness takes over his expression. Quietly, he responds, "Yes." That's all. No further explanation.

Rubbing his back, I try to give him the comfort and support he needs. When he opens his eyes, a gentle smile appears, just for me. I remind him, "It's okay, babe. We're in this together." I squeeze his hand to comfort him, like he did for me earlier.

"Maybe there's not any more to say except for congratulations," his mother says.

I watch as Evan's smile grows. "Really? Do you mean that?"

"You weren't asking us permission, were you?" Hugh says, "You're old enough to know what you want."

"I am and that's being married to Mallory," Evan replies, looking right into my eyes. "I love her."

"I think both of your hormones are in overdrive, but I can tell your minds are made up, so we'll be there to support your union," his dad says, sounding happier.

"I love you, Evan," his mother says. "Give our congratulations to Mallory as well."

"Thank you and I will. I love you, too, Mom." I notice he uses the word mom instead of mother. I like it. I think those old emotional wounds are beginning to heal.

The sheet tighten around his body when Evan moves

closer. As we lay there stuffed from dinner, he whispers, "Baby?"

"Yeah?"

"I'm tired."

"I'm exhausted," I say. "This day was draining."

"So you won't be mad if we don't... you know?"

"Sleep sounds erotic to me right now. I'm that tired, mentally and physically exhausted. I think I can forgive you this one time as long as it doesn't become a habit."

"I think you're too sexy to let this become a habit." He slides up the bed and rests his head on the pillow.

I reach next to me and turn off the lamp. I don't know how long we lay there in the moonlight of the room until we fall asleep—knees touching, holding hands, and together—but together is all that matters.

"I was kind of thinking something a little more tropical," I say, holding the napkin up to the party planner.

"Tropical?" The planner and Claire ask in unison as if they misheard me.

"Something floral would be pretty," my mom adds from the laptop. We have her on video chat. I thought it only fair since Evan's mother was going to be here and I felt I might need the back-up support.

"Yes, a floral with pinks and greens. Like a hibiscus flower on it or something," I say.

The planner looks at Claire and then leans down toward me and explains, "We usually save those types of linens for luau's or other tourist events—"

"But that's what I see in my mind. I don't want an overly formal setting. I want people to feel relaxed and welcome."

She disappears across the room and starts pulling more samples. When she returns, I see the one I like instantly and hold it up for my mother to see. She agrees. That's the one.

Claire says, "This would be lovely on a white cloth and we can get flowers for the centerpieces to match."

I'm shocked by her willingness to go along with this, *with my vision*. "I think that would be beautiful," I tell her. She smiles and I feel bonded in that moment like she has finally accepted mine and Evan's union.

After letting her coordinate the china and silverware with the crystal, she takes my hand and says, "This is so exciting. It's going to be glorious, Mallory, just glorious."

When I hug her, she seems surprised at first, but takes the opportunity to return the embrace. "Thank you, Claire."

"You're welcome, dear."

We leave the planners accomplishing a lot. Claire drives me to a coffee shop and we sit out on their lanai enjoying our drinks. Our conversations have come relatively easy and painless so far today, so I like to think we're moving in a positive direction with our relationship.

"So Mallory, I was wondering if there is any way you might be flexible on the number of guests?" Claire asks, eyes wide, hopeful, then sips her coffee.

I swallow, hard; the sip I took hot as it goes down. "Um, maybe. How many more guests would you like to invite?"

"Just a few more. I was thinking," she says, looking up at the blue, cloudless sky in thought. "Maybe four hundred or so. Yes, four hundred maximum." She looks right at me and smiles politely.

"Oh." Not a great reaction, but I'm too stunned to react differently. I feel my head shaking from the idea before I even know what I'm going to say to her. "Claire, I know—"

"It would mean a lot to the Ashford family and when I

was speaking with your mother the other day she was saying that there were people she had always hoped she'd be able to invite. And since the wedding is in Hawaii, a lot of our friends won't be able to make it anyway, so there wouldn't be any harm in inviting them, but they'll take great offense if they aren't. Do you understand the difficult position I'm in?"

While listening to her plead her case, my anxiety heightens knowing this decision is ultimately up to me. Evan will support me either way. I lean forward, tactfully place my hand on top of hers, and say, "Claire, I understand what you're saying and I wouldn't want to offend any of your friends. I know I'm in the minority here, but I never dreamed of a huge wedding. I just dream of being with Evan, surrounded by an intimate group of our family and friends—"

"These *are* our friends, Mallory. Most have known Evan from the time he started school or since he was a baby. They've celebrated his birthdays and we spent holidays with them." She leans closer, her free hand covering mine. "It would mean a lot to me. *Please?*"

Does it really matter if their friends are there? She's probably right and they won't come anyway. And she did say Evan knows them and that they've watched him grow up. Maybe he'd like them there too, but doesn't want to pressure me. My family is so small that I never imagined anything big. Plus, I would never ask my parents to spend their life savings on a wedding, but since Evan and his family are footing the bill maybe I should give in on this request. Claire has been supportive of my ideas... I look up and see the hope in her eyes and I decide to compromise. "You can invite two hundred, but that's it."

She jumps up from her seat, claps her hands together

then comes over and hugs me. "Thank you, Mallory. Thank you so much. I'll call the planner and give her the new guest list. Everything will be taken care of. I promise. Thank you."

She hugs me again, and I must admit it feels good to see her so happy.

With most of the details of the wedding now decided or taken care of by others, Evan and I get to spend the next three days enjoying our spring break properly: sleeping in, sunbathing, surfing, hanging out with our friends, making love in the middle of the day because we can, and partying. Time flies, and before we know it, we're back on a plane to Colorado.

23

MALLORY

I shake the Dean's hand on stage at graduation, stop, pose for the photo and scan the crowd to locate where the cheering is coming from. As I walk across the stage, I spot Evan standing nearby clapping. He looks proud and handsome as ever, which makes me blush and smile.

I go to him instead of my seat. Screw the rules. I've already graduated and I'm headed to the University of Hawaii for graduate school anyway. What can they possibly do to me now?

He takes my hand and swings it gently between us. "Congratulations, baby."

"Thank you..." I say, looking down at our shoes, feeling shy. "...for everything." When I look back up his head is tilted to the side and he's smiling.

"I'm proud of you. You've accomplished so much—"

"We have so much more to accomplish together."

"Yes, we do, a lifetime of creating memories to add to the ones we've already lived."

"You're so poignant, Mr. Ashford."

"You graduating is bringing out my philosophical side, Miss Wray."

"Well, philosophize away, my love." After a short kiss, we return to our seats.

When the ceremony ends, I hurry in the direction of where my family is sitting.

"Mallory?"

I turn toward the sound of my name and see Claire, Hugh, Kate and Murphy rushing to me. "Mallory, were so proud of you," Claire says, grabbing me into a tight hug. I'm kind of dumbfounded by the outpouring of love and still shocked they came to Boulder just for my graduation.

"Congratulations, Mallory," Hugh says, smiling.

"Thank you for being here," I add, not able to contain my smile.

"Let me at that girl," Murphy cuts in, grabbing a hold of me as soon as Claire lets go. My feet leave the ground as he squeezes and swings me. "Congrats, Mal."

"Put her down, Liam," Kate says, swatting him on the back.

"Congratulations, girl," Kate smiles and hugs me. "We haven't seen Evan since this morning. I know he sat with your parents. Do you know where he is?"

"I saw him after I got my diploma, but not where they were sitting."

"Mallory, honey." I would know my mom's voice anywhere even in a dense crowd like this.

Turning around, I see her waving her arm in the air to get my attention. I run to her, almost tackling her to the ground, I'm so excited.

She hugs me so tight that I lose my breath. "Our princess is a college graduate now. Congratulations, honey," she whispers.

I roll my eyes at the princess endearment, but smile because her hug makes me feel loved. Her pride is felt through this embrace and reminds me of my impending move and how these hugs won't be as close as I want when I need.

"Okay, okay, I played a little part of bringing her into this world too. Maybe I can get a little face time with her, Elise?"

"I'm not ready to give her up yet," my mom says not relenting one bit.

My dad peers over her shoulder, making me laugh. Just beyond him, I see Evan standing, patiently waiting for them to have their turn, so he can have his. I smile and he smiles back. There's a sparkle to his eyes that lights up his whole face and then he mouths 'I love you,' I close my eyes savoring his words while appreciating my mom's hug. I'm the luckiest girl in the world.

When I release my mom, my dad takes my hands. "Hey Sweetheart." Tears form in his eyes when he says, "You've done good, babygirl. You've made us very proud."

"Thanks, Dad." I move forward and wrap my arms around his middle, his arms holding me tight around my shoulders. "Congrats, graduate." I smile against his chest when he says, "I love you."

"Ah, daddy, I love you, too."

His hand strokes my hair and memories of standing on his feet as he danced around the living room rush through my thoughts. He whispers, "You promised me when you were five you would stay my little girl forever, but you went and grew up anyway."

I giggle, tears now in the corners of my eyes. "I'm sorry about that, but I'll always be your little girl."

"Yes, you will be and that reminds me. I guess this guy behind me might like a chance to say something too," my dad says, using his thumb to gesture to Evan over his shoulder.

Laughing again, a tear streams down my face and my dad walks around, wrapping his arm around my mom's shoulders this time and kissing her on the head, reminding me of how Evan treats me. Though I know it wasn't meant for my ears, I hear him tell her, "You did a great job, Elise." And they hug.

Evan takes my left hand, his thumb sliding back and forth over my ring, and he says, "I'm kind of at a loss for the right words here. I'm proud of you, Congrats, and all that, but seeing you today up on that stage... it was... I'm just so... *I love you, Mallory*."

I grab him, pulling him to me. "I love you, too."

His hands caress my chin, bringing my lips to his. A sweet, soft kiss is placed on my mouth as his nose slides down mine. He holds me to him for a moment, our foreheads pressing against each others. When I open my eyes, I see his are still closed, caught up in the kiss or the moment or both. I slide my hands over his broad, strong shoulders, up his neck and into his hair, messing it without care. Our mouths open and our tongues meet tentatively like the act itself is forbidden. But like all things forbidden, we crave more. This kiss is delicious and needy, ravenous and sensual. It's perfect just like Evan, just like we are together.

When we part, our eyes slowly open. Our families stare at us— eyes wide and mouths agape. Apparently this kiss is completely inappropriate for the setting and the company surrounding us by looking at their faces. I twirl under his arm into the safety of his side. "Well, that's embarrassing."

Evan chuckles as he kisses the top of my head. "It's all good. Should we celebrate now?" he asks, smiling to everyone else.

"Seems you two already are. That was *so* gross, baby bro," Kate mocks, turning around and dragging Murphy with her.

My dad gives Evan a disapproving look, Evan shrugs it off and we follow the group, trying to keep our hands and lips to ourselves. But I'll be honest, it's a struggle.

Graduation lunch—I sit back, enjoying the two families interacting in such a casual way, all getting along so well. My mom and Claire haven't stopped talking about the wedding, so we end up seating them at the other end of the table to chat.

"What made you choose Hawaii for graduate school?" Hugh asks me from a few seats away.

Glancing at Evan, I say, "A couple of reasons, but one is that Evan's college credits will transfer and we miss the island. It's where we want to start our married life."

"I miss the ocean," Evan adds, to a table full of smiles and laughs.

After a toast in my honor, Evan leans forward and slips an envelope in front of me. "Happy Graduation, baby."

The table stops and everyone looks at me. My cheeks heat from the attention and Evan pushes it closer and says, "Open it."

Picking up the envelope, I gulp, wondering what it might be. I'm not the best with surprises and I have a feeling, knowing Evan so well, that this is more than just a card. Looking up, Evan's eyes shine with happiness. "I'm nervous," I say, ripping the purple envelope open. He waits, watching, with a sly grin on his face.

I pull out a card that says 'Congrats Grad' on the cover, but when I open the card a photograph falls onto my lap. My eyes flicker between the picture and Evans several times.

I'm speechless. "This... what... *Evan?* Wait, *you didn't...* Did you?"

"I did. You need a convertible in Hawaii and to ship your car over would cost more than the car is worth. So I bought you a new one."

"You can't do that. This is too much."

He leans over and I tilt my head, my face hidden from the table. He whispers, "Too much for what?"

"Just too much," I start. "You shouldn't be buying me expensive gifts like this. You gave me the ring and the wedding."

Evan takes my hand in his and kisses my knuckles. "You're going to be my wife, Mallory. You need a car in Hawaii and I can afford to give you one. *We* can afford this, so please stop worrying about money."

I look down at the photo again and smile, running my finger across it as if I can touch the car itself. "It is really pretty."

Evan smiles and says, "I knew you'd like it."

"There's no *liking* about it. I love this car and it's just a picture. Is it this color?"

"It's that very car unless you don't like the color then we can get a different color. It's called Lunar Blue Metallic," he says, his voice filled with uncertainty.

"I love the color. It's gorgeous. Is it a Mercedes Roadster?"

"How'd you know that?"

"Always admired them from afar." I don't bother telling him I went to a couple car shows with Will.

"I know you like safe and practical, but it's Hawaii, so I had to get you the convertible. And then one thing led to the next and led to the SLK55 AMG Roadster. That car is fucking loaded. It's so badass." I listen as he goes on, his expression showing his excitement. "It has this really awesome sound-system and 4.5 second acceleration from zero to sixty. It's not a Maserati, but I'm impressed and thought you'd like it." He's so animated it's fun to watch.

After lunch, we all take a stroll from the restaurant down the block, stuffed from our meal. Evan holds my hand, bringing it to his lips to kiss several times.

"I don't think I've ever felt happier than I do right now," I say, glancing up at him.

"Me either. The sky is the limit once we're married."

"Forever is ours," I add, leaning my head on his shoulder.

"Mallory?"

Evan's tone catches me off-guard and I look up. "Yeah?"

"Speaking of the sky being the limit, we should talk about our money situation. I mean I should've told you sooner, but I didn't really think about it and you never asked."

"It's your money, Evan. We don't have to talk about it right now. We can wait until some other time if you want."

"No, we should. I think you should know." We cross the street and enter a small park on the corner, letting our families walk ahead of us. He holds onto my left hand and looks at the ring. "I talked to your dad about it briefly when I asked for his blessing, but I haven't talked to you. You know my grandparents left me an inheritance, but I need you to know it's millions. I don't have the exact figures memorized because a lot of it is invested and there have been big gains. It's substantial. Substantial enough that neither of us would ever need to work again. I'll get the lawyers to send over the figures so you know everything."

"Evan, I want to work."

"I know you do, but know if at a later date, say when we have a family, you decide you want to stay home, you can."

I nod. "Okay."

"I trust you, Mallory, and I want you to know everything about me."

"Son," Hugh says, suddenly appearing, the rest of the group up ahead near a fountain. "This might be poor timing with the celebration, but we leave for New York tonight and I'm supposed to give this letter to you. The lawyers drew it up and I verified the information to be accurate on your behalf, but I would suggest both you and Mallory review it before signing." Hugh hands Evan a white envelope that he pulls from inside his jacket pocket and turns back to rejoin the rest of the group who are now window shopping across the street.

Evan opens the envelope and pulls out the thick, folded papers. I want to ask what they are, but I don't, worrying that it would be intrusive. When I look at him, he frowns then his jaw tenses as his eyes narrow while reading.

He's upset, so I put a hand on his arm and ask, "Is everything alright?" Although I'm dying to know what the papers say, they look business like and private.

Evan's eyes meet mine, and he shakes the papers in the air. "I need you to know that I'm not making you sign these." He folds them up and stuffs the papers back into the envelope. Taking me by the hand again, he pulls me behind him as he storms back toward the group.

I know what the papers are without him having to tell me. It's kind of obvious it's a pre-nuptial agreement. I stop him before he crosses the street. "Evan. Wait." He looks back at me and I smile, trying to calm him. "I don't mind. I'll sign them. Just please let's not make a scene right now. It's not a big deal—"

He looks confused as his eyes search mine trying to understand. "Mallory—"

"Listen to me." I pull him closer so the whole world doesn't hear our conversation. "Those papers don't change how I feel about you. I didn't get together with you because you had money. Honestly, I didn't even know you had your own money until much later and by then I was already a victim to your charm and sexy ways." I giggle, hoping my fun lightens his mood.

"That's why this is bullshit. I know you don't care about this, but I do. My grandparents would've wanted me to marry for love not status. I'm doing that and I don't want anything coming between us or shaking the foundation we've built."

"It won't," I try to reason. "Your parents are only trying to protect you. That's not a bad thing."

"I'm in this for life, not for five or ten years. For. Life." He emphasizes each word. "So it doesn't matter if you have access to the money. Fuck, I want you to. I want to share everything with you."

"It's security and your parents want you to be secure—"

"I couldn't live with myself if you signed these papers. This isn't us. We weren't built on contracts and financial statements."

I take his hands, rubbing my thumb over his knuckles. "We're built on love and trust."

"Which is exactly how I want us to stay. Mallory, everything I have is yours now."

"Oh, Evan." I put my hand on his cheek. "Everything I have is yours as well. Just know I love you no matter what. If they demand we sign, I will if it means being with you."

He leans down and kisses me. When our lips part, he says, "I'm sure the pre-nup is fair by legal standings, but money is just money. You have my heart so you already own me. I'm going to tell my parents to destroy this contract."

"You do whatever feels right for you, but please talk to your parents about this later. Okay? If my family sees you arguing with your parents, they'll get worried and I don't want them to stress about us. They do enough of that already with me moving away."

He smiles and agrees. "Okay, but know the matter is already settled in my mind."

The next few weeks are crazy with packing up everything, selling the stuff we won't need, and making final arrangements in Hawaii with school, the wedding, and the move.

My mom comes to visit one weekend to help me look for my wedding dress. Even though it's a nice break from packing, I'm still concerned about the cost and my parents have offered to buy the dress for me. Three stores into our shopping excursion, I find it—the dress and it's beyond perfect.

My mom sits when she sees me then bursts into tears. Through sobs she confirms this is the one, which makes me start to cry. I don't even know why I'm crying. It's been an emotional day I guess and the realities of me actually getting married and moving away is starting to affect us both.

As she's paying for the dress, she brushes my hair over my shoulder, and says, "You've become a beautiful woman, inside and out, Mallory. Dad and I are proud of the person you are and all that you've accomplished." She smiles, soft and kind, the one I always see her wearing when I picture her. "Go into your marriage with an open mind and a forgiving and loving heart. There is nothing the two of you can't work through as long as you stay a team." I feel a tear forming and my eyes get glassy. She wipes my cheek as it cascades down my face. "You're going to have a wonderful life, honey. Cherish every moment."

"Thank you, mom." I hug her.

She whispers, "And this dress is going to knock Evan's socks off and just might kill your father. So let's keep it a secret until the ceremony." Her smile turns devious and I laugh, which eases the worry of my upcoming departure from my family.

The matter of the pre-nup is never brought up again, even though I overhear a heated conversation when I come home early after visiting Sarah one afternoon. Evan is pacing in the guest bedroom, his tone terse when I hear several: no's, never, and unacceptable. He finds me reading a magazine in the living room when he walks out. He doesn't say anything, but seems pleased.

I visit my parents one last time before we leave just wanting to spend time with them. We hang out, go to the grocery store, and do completely uneventful stuff, but I love every minute of it. My dad rearranges his schedule, so he can spend the day with us too. I'll see them in less than a month for the wedding, but that visit will be different and we all know it.

When I return to the apartment after the weekend, Evan's made a lot of progress on the packing. Win for me, I silently cheer. On our final day there, we make sure to christen every room as ours—making love and fucking everywhere. I can't get enough of him, the feeling of him against me, on me, inside of me. I love it all. Though the wedding is the legal part of our union, our souls are already married, bonded by something greater, bonded together forever.

On the plane, Evan grabs the backpack from the overhead compartment and then my hand with his other. As we hurry off and through the airport, we make it to the baggage claim area in record time. I'm huffing behind him as we approach a man who's holding a sign that reads "The Future Mr. and Mrs. Ashford."

I giggle as we approach. "Did you do this?"

Evan looks at me and smiles. "You like?"

"I love," I answer, feeling light and happy.

The man places a lei around each of our necks, and says, "Welcome to paradise."

24

MALLORY

It was suggested we stay apart the night before the wedding so we get proper sleep. I'm not sleeping at all without him, so I use the back stairs and go to Evan. I tap lightly on the door, but he doesn't answer. It's not that late, so I doubt he's sleeping. I try the knob and it's locked. Walking around to the back door, I round the corner and see him sitting on the step, staring out into the ocean.

"Hey there, want some company?"

The moon reflects in his eyes, when he sees me. "I'd love some."

Quietly I settle in next to me and look into the far distance. "The moon is huge tonight."

"It's a thinking moon," he says. I bring my knees to chest and listen as he continues. "I used to paddle out on nights like this and just sit on my board. You'd be amazed how quiet it is out there, the rest of the world left back on land with your worries."

His foot nudges mine. "I haven't done that in a year. Strange how you fall out of old habits when you fall into new ones."

"Was I a new habit?" I lean my head on his shoulder.

With a soft chuckle, he replies, "You were habit forming, that's for sure." He kisses the top of my head. "So what brings you here? I thought you were supposed to be able to rest better when I'm not around."

"I rest much better with you around."

"Me too."

I stand, taking his hand and pull him up. "Can we go to bed?"

"Yeah, big day tomorrow and all."

"Yep, big day." He doesn't know, but I have no intention of getting real sleep, which is how I ended up with my head hanging off the end of the bed and the room thick with sexual tension as we make love. Correction, we start off making love, but our desires and impatience win out. I start to slip off with each thrust until Evan stops. He pulls me back by the hips until my body is supported again and realigns himself. "You okay," he asks, his tone soft while his body remains hard.

"I'm more than okay," I reply, rubbing his neck and encouraging him to continue. When he's inside of me, my head goes back, my mouth drops open, and I gasp from the pleasure.

My body moves of its own volition and I watch my earth-bound Hawaiian God. There's just something about watching his body, the muscles moving together for my gratification and his. All his arrogance is captured and put to use in his seductive ways. He's sex personified and lust come to life. He makes me feel things I never have and crave things I'm not sure I should. He makes me want him in all ways and punctuates every encounter by sending me into a cliff-diving pool of ecstasy. "Evan!"

A loud knock on the door startles us. Our bodies still

and we look at each other, both silently hoping whoever it is goes away. When another knock sounds, Evan says, "For fuck's sake." He climbs out of bed and slips on a pair of boxers before he answers the door. "What?"

I can't see her, but I hear Kate embarrassed. "Soooo,.. Ummm, This is really awkward with you know Mallory yelling your name out like that, making it obvious what you guys are doing in there, but her mom sent me down to find her. She's worried about her."

Evan looks back at me over his shoulder and releases a heavy sigh. His words aren't hurried and disappointment is written all over his face. "Guess I'll get a rain-check?"

While Kate waits outside, I slip out of bed and start gathering my clothes. "I'm sorry. I should go see her. I don't want her worried." I finish getting dressed and lift up and kiss him. I whisper, "I definitely owe you a rain-check."

After a kiss goodbye, he says, "See you at the altar. I'll be the one with the goofy looking grin."

With a smile and a small wave over my shoulder, I walk out the door, and say, "There's nothing goofy about you or your grins. Trust me on that." When I see Kate, I stop and look back. "Oh, and I'll be the one in the white dress just in case you forget what I look like overnight."

"You're unforgettable. You can trust me on that."

"C'mon, Mal," Kate says, taking me by the arm and pulling me toward the main house. "You're lovey dovey-ness is just so... um, sooo—"

"Romantic?"

"I wouldn't exactly say romantic. I was leaning toward stomach turning."

I hit her on the arm. "You don't mean that. I've heard how you and Murphy talk to each other. You're not a stranger to the love-dovey stuff."

I see a small smile and point. "See! Right there. I knew it."

"Whatever," she says, nudging me. "It's still my brother you're doing that with and you should be glad it was me who heard that sex-screaming and not your mother." I wait, knowing she'll come around. She stops at the backdoor and turns to me. "Fine. You two are adorable and I'm glad you turned my brother into a romantic. Are you happy now?"

"Yep. I am."

"You're ridiculous."

"I'm a bride. I get to be ridiculous."

She laughs. "True."

Kate and I walk inside the main house and she says, "And about what I heard right before I knocked on the door, we shall never speak of that again."

"Okay," I reply, laughing.

Working my way back upstairs, I tiptoe down the hall to the bedroom again. I find my mom sitting in my room. She looks up when I enter, and says, "Getting fresh air?" I can tell by her expression she knows exactly where I was.

"Something like that."

She stands and hugs me. "I'm going to bed. Your dad is already asleep. I just wanted to check on you. How are you doing?"

"I'm good. Really good."

"I can tell you're good. Really good." She mimics me with a little laugh. When I release her, she asks, "And how is Evan?"

"He's good. Really good." I laugh this time.

"Good to hear everyone is good tonight." She heads to the door. "And you should probably take a shower before you come down for breakfast."

And I'm mortified now.

"Thanks."

"Goodnight, dear daughter."

"Goodnight, dear Mom."

EVERYTHING APPEARS PERFECT... *to the outside world*, but it doesn't feel perfect on the inside. I should have listened to my instinct more, put my foot down, and been stronger. I wanted Claire to like me... and that meant giving into her demands. Now she likes me, but I'm caught in the middle of a wedding that feels so upscale New York and not me at all.

I should have said something when she begged for more guests, or she told me she ordered the favors without asking for my opinion, or even when a sample bouquet showed up in Colorado, Claire insisting all the fashionable brides were carrying peonies this season, even though my wedding is in Hawaii. But I didn't want to burst the cloud nine bubble she's been floating on the last couple of months. I really only have myself to blame for not speaking up sooner. What's done is done and I'll walk down that aisle with a smile on my face. But I would anyway since Evan's waiting at the other end.

Sunny's been keeping tabs on the guys all morning, but I have no fears about being left at the altar. She relays a message from Zach that Evan's in a great mood. Kate stands at the window watching the guests arrive. My mom is on the other side of the room pinning a flower into Sunny's hair, and I'm sitting at the vanity waiting for the ceremony to begin.

"I'm really nervous," I say quietly, not feeling in control of my voice. Clasping my hands in my lap, I look down to avoid the mirror in front of me. My dress is beautiful.

Spaghetti straps hold up the lace top, a deep dip in the lace leads to a full skirt that falls naturally instead of being held out by an uncomfortable hoop skirt underneath. The dress is sexy and pretty. I chose it with Evan in mind. My mom said it was very 'us' and fitting for a beach wedding. The earrings Claire gave me are on and stunning. So all the pieces are in place for a great day, and as much as I want to suck it up, something still feels off.

"*Awww*, there's nothing to be nervous about, honey," my mom says, glancing over at me as she holds the flower in place waiting for Sunny's approval.

"I think this whole day is dreamy," Sunny says, seemingly lost in her own dreams of a fantasy wedding.

Kate turns from her spot by the window and walks up behind me. Placing both hands on my shoulders, our eyes meet in the mirror. She says, "My brother is the luckiest man in the world. I've never seen him so happy and in love." Leaning down, she presses her cheek against mine, her eyes still searching mine in the reflection. "Don't be nervous. He'll be there waiting to hold your hand."

"Thanks, Kate."

A knock at the door draws our attention. I stand, needing to pull myself out of this weird wedding day funk I've fallen into. My mom answers, "Come in."

"Honey," my dad starts saying, but stops in his tracks when he sees me. He looks down quickly to collect himself before he moves closer. "You look like a princess, like in the fairytales you used to act out when you were little."

"Thanks, dad." I wrap my arms around him tightly, resting my cheek to his chest.

"Whoa there," he whispers, rubbing my back, "you okay?"

I don't say anything for fear I might start crying and I just really don't want to cry and mess up my makeup.

Since I can't see Evan right now, my dad is the only person I want to be with. With him it's not about hair, shoes, dresses, or makeup. With him, I can be me and I can be honest without ruining the dream world the girls are living in, so I hold him close just for a minute more, hoping all my heavy emotions lighten.

"Maybe you ladies could excuse us for a moment. I'd like to have a minute alone with my daughter if that's alright."

When they leave the room, my mom stops and smiles at us on her way out. "Don't be long. We have a few last minute details to attend to."

She walks out, closing the door behind her. My dad leans back, taking me by the shoulders. "Hey there. What's really going on? You got a case of wedding day jitters?"

"It feels like more than jitters." I turn away from him ashamed that I can't pretend to be the blissful bride, even for show. "It feels like someone else's wedding."

"Maybe Claire's?" I hear a lowly chuckle from behind me. But then he sounds concerned. "Sorry. Bad joke. Tell me what's going on, Mallory."

"It was funny." I smile and walk to the window that overlooks the pool and ocean, taking over Kate's spot. The guests are making their way down the stone steps to the beach where the ceremony will take place. "The joke is pretty spot on. This is not *my* dream. This is hers, maybe Mom's too."

"The wedding? I thought you wanted it on the beach—"

"I did." I shake my head to correct myself. "I do. I do want it on the beach, but I don't know most of these people. I wanted to know everyone who was at my wedding. I wanted each of those people to hold a special place in mine and Evan's heart mutually, but these... there's a lot of people

I've never met down there and I'm sure some that Evan doesn't even know."

"Eh, forget about them. Those people being here doesn't take away from what you and Evan share."

"I know, but I can't help it. I just wish I had Evan to talk to about this. He'd know what to say to make it better."

"Then we should get Evan."

"We can't. It's bad luck, remember?"

"Seems to me that going into a marriage with bad feelings is bad luck, but that's just my opinion. What do I know?"

I smile, then roll my eyes. "You're sneaky. You know that?"

"Not sneaky, just all-knowing as all fathers are."

"So when Evan becomes a dad, he'll be all-knowing, too?" I say with a wry grin plastered on my face.

"Whoa. Whoa. Whoa. Don't give your dad a heart attack, okay. Let's take this one step at a time. Enjoy marriage first." He walks to the door, but stops with his hand on the knob and turns around. "Luck is what you make it, Mallory. I'll go get Evan, and you can decide if you want to see him or talk to him through the door. But do you have a jacket or something to cover up a little?"

"Dad," I say with a laugh. "Nope, this is pretty much it."

"Your mother and I will be having words." Shaking his head, he walks out, shutting the door behind him.

Not five minutes later, a soft knock lets me know Evan's here. "Mal?" He walks in with his hands shielding his eyes.

Before the door shuts, I hear my dad tell him, "Keep your eyes above the neck, son."

The door closes and Evan calls my name, flying blind in this situation. "Mallory?"

"You can look. I don't really believe in all that superstitious stuff."

"I'm kind of scared to look because you're dad just threatened me."

"Just open your eyes, Evan."

"Okay," he says, slowly lowering his hands. "Wow! You look... I mean, you're so... Wow! You're breathtaking."

"Thank you," I say, feeling my cheeks heat from his sweet reaction. "You look pretty wow yourself."

He comes to me and holds me by the waist. "Now I see why your dad was so worried. You look incredible, even edible." He sways my hips back and forth, and says, "Since we don't believe in all that silly superstitious stuff..." He kisses me, deep with passion.

With my eyes still closed, I whisper against his lips, "That's what I've been missing."

A contented sigh is returned. "Yes, I missed these lips." He leans back and runs his index finger over my bottom lip. "And these soulful eyes." Leaning forward, he places sweet, soft kisses on each eyelid. "Nothing's felt right all day," he says, tugging at his collar. "Until now."

"That's how I've been feeling too. Something's just been off."

"You felt it too?" he asks, surprised. "It's so weird. Until I saw you, the whole morning just wasn't right."

"Sunny said you were in a good mood."

"I was, I am. I mean, I'm marrying you. Of course I'm in a good mood, but inside... I think I just missed you." He moves to peek out the window, pulling the sheer drape back just a bit. "How did a simple wedding on the beach turn into the spectacle down there?"

When he looks back at me, I say, "And about people we

don't know, and canapés, and petals, and engraved, silver picture frame favors?"

He stares at me, his eyes sparking from within. "That's it."

"What's it?"

"We can take it back."

"Take what back? You're making me nervous, Evan, and I'm already full of anxiety."

"The wedding," he says, rushing to me and taking me by the shoulders. "Just you and me, baby. None of this." He waves his arm toward the window. "We can elope."

"What?" I say a little too loud while shaking my head, shocked by what he's suggesting. "Sorry. That came out a lot harsher than I meant, but what? What are you talking about?"

With a raised eyebrow, he says, "We can do this. We should do this. For you. For me. I love you so fucking much and want to do this. Will you elope with me?"

"I want that. I would love to do that, but we can't just leave. Our families, our friends—"

"These strangers, and canapés, and petals, and engraved, silver picture frame favors. Fuck'em! This day is not about them. It's about us." He wraps his hands around me again, pulling me close, and says, "All of that out there doesn't matter. It's about what *we* want and this is not how I imagined our day. So let's do this."

"Where will we go?"

"Wherever we want."

"On the island or are we leaving? I can't just leave my parents. What about Sarah, and Sunny and Kate, Zach—"

"I've got an idea. How about we get married just the two of us and then come back for the reception. What do you think about that?"

"Like a private ceremony with just us?"

"Exactly like that."

My heart swells and I think I fall more in love with this man, which is technically pretty impossible to do because my love for him already holds no bounds. "That sounds perfect."

"You deserve perfect." His hand caresses my cheek and he kisses me on the forehead.

"We should tell someone, so they don't freak out."

A loud triple knock makes us jump and we watch the handle as it turns and opens. My dad pops his head inside, and says, "I'll handle the guests." He holds his hand up and Evan's keys are dangling from his fingers. "Your car is waiting out front. You should probably leave soon so you don't get blocked in."

"You're not mad?" I ask my dad.

"Mallory, if your heart is telling you to marry Evan, what does it matter if it's in front of a minister, a JP, or 200 guests. I know your mom will be disappointed, but everyone will get over it. Go follow your heart."

"Thank you, Sir." Evan reaches forward taking the keys from him and shakes his hand with the other.

When Evan turns back to me, he asks, "You sure you want to do this?"

"Abso-fucking-lutely, surferboy." I jump with excitement. Rushing around, I grab the marriage certificate, my purse, and my veil and we run out the door.

Sneaking down the back stairs to the hallway by Ms. Chart's room, we make our way down the corridor and run for the front door. Fortunately, the guests are using the side path today. While we hide behind the protection of a large Bird of Paradise potted plant, Evan says, "If anything happens, know I love you."

I eye him, now worried. "What's gonna happen that you feel the need to declare your love to me one last time?"

"I'm just playing with ya," he says, chuckling. "Okay, see that palm two cars over, nine o'clock position?"

"Yes."

"If we can get to that palm, we're home free. On the count of three, go. Okay?"

"Okay."

"Three." He takes off running while pulling me behind him. Although, I stumble slightly while lifting my dress off the ground, I keep up.

We dash behind the palm, our hearts racing, and Evan's face bright with unadulterated happiness. When he turns back to me, I hit him on the chest. "You said on the *count* of three, not just three."

"Sorry." He cowers playfully as I swat his ass, which is looking really good in the tux pants. "Can't resist my ass, eh?"

"I never could. That's what got us into this mess to begin with."

He smirks. "And here I always thought it was my smooth lines and charming personality that you couldn't resist."

"Nope, it's your ass."

Turning serious, he says, "Duck."

I do, but then complain. "You do realize I'm in heels and a wedding dress, right?"

Kissing my temple, he says, "And you look beautiful, but if we want make it out of here alive than we have to work with what we've got."

"I think the 'Alive' part is a bit dramatic." There's no reasoning with him though. He's on a mission. His determination was another quality of his that attracted me from the beginning... *along with his ass.*

"I'm gonna open the door on your side of the car. I want you to run and get in, but wait here until I give the signal." He takes off running, leaving me there questioning the signal.

I yell, just above a whisper, "Evan, what's the signal?" He really is shit at game-plans. Luckily for him, he's marrying me—the ultimate planner.

Holding the passenger door wide open, he whistles The Wedding March—which is apparently the signal—at the top of his lungs. *Well that won't draw any attention, now will it?* I laugh as I jog toward him. This is so ridiculous and even more fun. I give him a quick peck on the lips, then slip down into the seat. He shuts the door then runs around and hops in. After revving the engine twice, he asks, "You ready, sexy girl?"

"I'm always ready for you."

"That's what I like to hear." When he floors the car, we burst out laughing. "Holy shit! My mother is going to flip."

"She's going to blame me for ruining her wedding." I can't help smiling, feeling carefree, because today became *her* wedding, not mine.

"It doesn't matter what she thinks and I'll take the heat. I'll tell everyone that I corrupted your innocence and this was the last ploy in my plan." He laughs evilly. "Hey, let's take the top down." He looks over at me. "Oh, sorry, I forgot about your hair. It looks really lovely like that."

"Lovely?" I repeat taken aback, disgust on my face.

"All up like that," he says, making motions in the air with his fingers like my hair resembles a bird's nest. "Yeah, looks lovely."

"Well, we can't have that. Your mother does 'lovely.'" I start stripping the bobby pins from my hair and add, "I'm going for hot, so let's take the top down."

He pulls over to the side of the road and lowers the top before hitting the gas again. I continue removing pins from my hair and ask, "Do you know where you're going?"

"I know exactly where I'm going. You just sit back and enjoy the ride, baby. I need to make a call."

He pulls his phone out and calls someone. At the same time, my phone starts ringing and the name 'Kate' flashes on the screen. No way am I answering her call. Evan can handle her and her temper. After four rings it goes silent. Then my mom's name pops up. *Hmm....* my dad can handle her. After a few more rings, my phone goes quiet in my hand. I take a deep breath just as it starts ringing again —*Sunny*. I really should answer, but she'll convince me to invite all of them and I want it to be only us.

I pull the last pins from my hair when my phone rings again—Sarah. I have no good reason not to answer her call, so I do. "Hello?"

"Mallory?"

"Oh hi, Sarah."

"Hey, so whatcha doing?" I like her casual approach.

I can play that game. "Not much. What are you doing?"

"I'm at your wedding wondering where the hell the bride and groom disappeared to." *There goes casual.* "Mallory, you need to come back." She whispers, "Your mom is upset, Kate is pacing, Sunny is practically in tears over letting you out of her sight, Zach is trying to calm her down, Murphy is... well, Murphy is handing out shots. Your dad made a quick exit after announcing to us that the two of you left. That leaves me sitting here wondering why I'm *here* if you're *there*. I thought I was in Hawaii to witness this marriage."

"Sarah, I'm so sorry. It's hard to explain, but it didn't feel right. It's beautiful and what most little girls dream about, but it wasn't what I dreamed about. I don't need all that. I just want to be married to Evan."

"So why do all of this if you didn't want it?"

"The moms."

"*Ohhhh,* I see." She sighs into the phone. "Your wedding day should be perfect, so tell me what we're supposed to do and I'll do it."

"We're going to get married and we'll come back to celebrate with everyone. Evan's on the phone right now, setting things up."

"Listen, I'll keep everyone under control and you two get married. This day is supposed to be about the union, not the production. By the way, his mother doesn't know yet."

"That could be a problem and a good reason to drink that shot Murph's handing out."

"We love you, Mallory, and if this is what makes you happy, we're happy too."

"Thank you. You've always been there for me and..." I feel the tears filling my eyes, verging on falling. "I love all of you so much. I'll see you later, okay?"

"Good luck."

"I don't need luck. I've got Evan."

As soon as I hang up, Evan puts his hand on my thigh, rubbing gently, and asks, "Word's gotten out and it's complete nuts there?"

"Something like that."

"Excellent." He watches me a second longer and smiles before his eyes flash quickly back to the road. He glances at me again and I see the slightest blush in his cheeks.

"What?" I ask, feeling self-conscious.

"Nothing." He shakes his head and keeps smiling.

"C'mon, spill it. You're making me paranoid."

"I'm liking your hair like that."

My hair flies loose, soft waves of crazy chaos in the air. "Is it too wild because of the wind?" I ask, attempting, and failing, to tame the fly-aways back into place.

"It's beautiful, like you."

Rubbing my hand through the back of his hair, he keeps his eyes focused on the road and a smile on his face.

"I think you're pretty darn handsome yourself, you know," I say without hoopla, just stating how I feel.

"Do you have any regrets, baby?"

"Yeah, but none where you're concerned. Oh wait, maybe one. If I could change one thing in our past, it would be that 4th of July party. I would have fought harder to stay there with you, but I also worry that if done differently it would change the whole order of our future, including you finding out the truth about Rachel. Does that make sense?"

"And if that did change things?"

"Then I wouldn't change anything because I like where we are now." I look around as he pulls into a gravel lot near the water. "Where are we?"

He runs around to help me out of the car. "Look down there." He points down a grassy knoll to a little, white chapel sitting on a cliff near the water. The cliff rises about ten feet above the ocean, but it seems to provide enough protection from the waves crashing below.

The stunning view before me causes me to go speechless. One word. Only word comes to me. "Evan."

With a tilt of his head, he looks down at my high heels and back to the hill in front of us. "I'll take my shoes off if you take yours off."

There's no way of me making it down that hill in these shoes. The spike of the heel will sink into the ground and I'll probably break an ankle. "Deal."

Bending down, he kneels in front of me, and slips one

then the other shoe off me. He kicks his shoes off and tosses his socks. He steadies me by tucking my arm under his and leads me down the grassy slope. There isn't anything traditional about what we're doing, but everything feels real and it feels right.

As we're walking, a minister appears in the doorway of the chapel and waves. Evan says, "You remember Harold from Big Kehones?"

"Every Tuesday he ordered a burger, rare, with fried onions on top. He's a minister?"

"In his former life. He's retired now."

"I guess I should have watched my language around him."

"For a religious man, he's not very judgmental, which is why he tolerates me." He laughs.

Harold's nature is calming, grandfatherly. When we reach him, he takes both my hands in his, and says, "It's nice to see you again, Mallory." He turns to Evan and motions with his head. "So how'd you get *her*?"

"I dunno, Sir. I ask myself that question every day." They share a laugh as Harold pats Evan on the back.

"You two want to get married, huh?"

"Yes, Sir," Evan's tone changes. "We're hoping you'll perform the ceremony."

"I see you're dressed for the occasion. And you don't have to be so formal. Harold still works fine for me." He turns and walks inside. "Welcome to Chapel by the Bay. This is my old church. She treated me very well for almost forty years."

"It's—"

"Perfect," I add, looking at Evan.

"Yes, perfect," Evan says, gently squeezing my hand.

"I hear there are people waiting for your arrival as a

newly married couple. Should we get to our purpose? Evan, do you have the certificate?"

"It's in the car," he replies as we follow him to the front of the church.

"Good. We'll need that after the ceremony. Mallory, Evan mentioned you both might want to say your own vows?"

The sun is starting to set, filling the tiny chapel with a warm glow. "Okay. We say what we feel? I can do that."

"Yes, just speak from the heart," Harold says, smiling at the two of us. "I can tell this will be a long and fruitful partnership. Your presence has filled this chapel with light, love, and life today."

"Thank you," Evan says, nodding to him.

"Time to start. Face me please." We reluctantly drop each others' hands and stiffen as we turn toward the minister. He laughs. "You can still hold hands if you want."

Stifling a giggle, we smile while taking the others' hand again.

Evan whispers, "Sorry, we're both kind of new to this."

"No worries. I'll walk you through it. What are your full names?"

Harold looks at me and I reply then Evan responds as well.

He clears his throat, then begins. "Evan, Mallory, you've come here today to proclaim your love in front of God and with Nellie as your witness..." We both turn as he acknowledges the older lady sitting in the back corner of the chapel. We hadn't noticed her at all. "That's my wife. You have to have a witness other than myself and God in the state of Hawaii for this marriage to be legal. Only a formality. I hope you don't mind that I brought her."

"Not at all," I say, smiling at both of them before leaning my arm against Evan with our hands still clasped together.

"Well, we're all here to bear witness to the union of Mallory Elise Wray and Evan Theodore Monroe Ashford. Face each other, and Mallory you may begin your vows."

I take a deep breath while turn to Evan. He takes my other hand. "Evan," I say, trying to calm my nerves. "There's a sparkle in your eyes that has always meant life to me. When you wake up—" Oh no, I realize I just admitted, in church, that we're sleeping together. I glance at Harold, but he smiles, non-judgmentally, like Evan said about him earlier, which eases me.

I take another deep breath and see a small smile on Evan's face, encouraging me. "You're the sun that brightens my day. When we go to bed, you're the moon that comforts me at night. I vow to keep that light, that sparkle in your eye and to always be there for you. I'll be there to support your dreams, your goals, through failure and success, sickness and health, richer or poorer. I'll always be there for you, my love. Your light has given me life and I willingly go forth into marriage with you to spend my days showing you how much you mean to me. I love you, Evan." Tears fills my eyes again, one slipping down my cheek.

Suddenly, a handkerchief is handed to me by Nellie. I thank her while dabbing my eyes carefully.

When I look up, Evan's eyes are full of tears as well, the moment overwhelming us both. When he blinks, they run over his lids and roll down his cheeks. I wipe each cheek, gently drying them.

"Evan, your vows," Harold says, a gentle reminder.

"Mallory, you are beauty—your soul and entire being—inside and out. I'm not a perfect man, but I'll spend my life striving to be what you deserve. I vow to treat your heart with care and fill it with love. The light you see in my eyes is only a reflection of the love you show in yours. I promise to treasure every day you give me and every night that you're next to me. I promise to spend my life bringing you happiness."

He brushes some hair from my shoulder with care. "Mallory, when I look at you, I see the woman who will be my wife, my lover," Evan says, pausing when he looks down at our joined hands. He gulps then continues. "And the mother of our children." When his eyes look directly into mine there's a confidence in his words. "I see a lifetime of laughter, love, meaningful touches, and many years of heaven on earth. I used to think the day I met you was the best day of my life, but it pales in comparison to today. I'm honored to be your husband, your biggest supporter, and your partner in this lifetime and the next. Thank you for loving me as much as I love you."

I wipe my eyes again, fully aware I must look a mess after all the tears I've shed from his sweet words.

Harold's voice cracks, the emotion in the chapel affecting him as well. "Evan, Mallory, do you have rings?"

"I do," he says, reaching into his inside pocket. He pulls the simple platinum bands out and the minister takes them.

He tells us how the circle represents eternity and how our love will go beyond this life. Then I slide Evan's ring onto his finger and he does the same to me.

"It's my pleasure to announce you as husband and wife. I know you're not waiting for me to give the word. Get in there and kiss your wife, son."

Evan caresses my face while I grab a hold of his arms, bringing him closer. Our gazes lock and I can see forever in his eyes. Our lips touch, the kiss slow and tender, and like every kiss he's ever given me, my world shifts on its axis and I get lost in all that is him.

I watch as he slowly opens his eyes, aware for the first

time that he feels the same all-consuming way I do. I can't stop the smile that covers my face and it appears he can't either.

Harold is already waiting at the chapel doors with his wife when we turn, hand-in-hand, and start walking toward them, both of us beaming with happiness. Flashes of a camera burst as we walk back down the aisle as husband and wife.

"Congratulations. You make a beautiful couple," Nellie says, shaking both our hands. "I'll send you the pictures."

"Congratulations," Harold adds. "I'll get the certificate from the car and give you a few minutes alone while I fill out that paperwork. There's a gazebo right out these doors with a bench that catches a nice breeze and the best sunset on the island."

"Thank you." Evan hands him the car keys then tucks my arm under his and we walk over to the white gazebo.

"Congratulations, Mrs. Ashford."

"Congratulations, yourself, Mr. Ashford."

He sits on the bench and I wrap my arms around his neck. Leaning down, I kiss him because I can't resist him any longer.

"You taste so good that you make me want to do very un-church like things to you," I say, feeling light and relaxed now that we're married.

"You always make me want to do un-church like things to you. You sure you want to go to this party? We could just skip it and go straight to the honeymoon." He puts his hands in front of his chest, pressed together like he's praying, and begs, "Please."

"We're already gonna get wrath for skipping the ceremony. We can't skip the reception too."

"What about a detour then?"

Making myself at home on his lap, I drape over my husband. "Hmm... that might work."

"That's a yes in my book."

Right when we're about to get a lot friendlier, Harold walks in. "Here you go. I need you both to sign the certificate. Nellie and I have already signed." After we sign, he says, "Your hearts have committed to each other for eternity and that doesn't require a piece of paper to bind you. Your hearts are already bound. I'll mail this in for you, so you won't have to worry about this detail." He starts to walk away, but stops. "Stay here as long as you'd like."

Reaching for his wallet, Evan asks, "What's the fee for the service?"

"The church would appreciate a donation. Whatever you want to give."

I already know the chapel will receive a hefty donation when it comes to Evan getting to choose.

"Thank you again," he says, "And please join us at the reception. We'd be honored to have you both there."

Harold smiles. "We'll see you there then."

When we're alone, Evan's finger slides down my bare arm, a sexual suggestion as it goes lower. "So where were we?"

25

EVAN

I take Mallory by the hand and we walk back up the hill to the car. Spinning her around until her back is against the Maserati, I lean forward, trapping her between my arms. Taking her mouth with mine, I don't waste time with sweetness. I want *my wife* to feel how much I fucking want her, hoping to convince her to see things my way.

Our lips part and I watch as she seems to float back to earth before my very eyes. Her eyes slowly open—the green, a deep emerald like the pool of Manoa Falls in winter—and she sighs sweetly. I smile. "So I was thinking..." I drag my thumb over her lower lip, "...that we could make a detour on the way back to the reception."

"You want to keep people waiting even longer?" she asks.

"We can fast forward straight to the consummating part of the night." I kiss the side of her mouth, my tongue dipping out just enough to taste her as my breath fills her parted lips.

She smiles and says, "That does sound quite enticing, but..."

Turning her head, she tries to kiss me, but I pull just out of reach. "*But?*"

"But we just ditched a large gathering of people in lieu of doing things our way. Most of the guests flew to Hawaii just to come to the wedding. I think we owe them an appearance at the reception."

Damn. She's not going for it. "You're right. We should do the responsible thing and go to the party," I say with a heavy sigh. "But just know that every minute we're there, I'll be thinking about what I'm going to be doing to you later."

"Doing to me, huh?" She leans in again and kisses me. "Well, I have some things I want to do to you too... but later. Let's go do this reception thing so we can get to the later part of the night's festivities."

With the top still down, we drive back to the reception, the weather nice, making for the perfect sunset tonight. She tousles my hair and out of nowhere laughs, really laughs. I don't think I've ever seen her more happy. The wind is blowing her hair around and her eyes shine as the ocean in the background frames her gorgeous face. "What's so funny?"

"Not funny. Happy. We're married, Evan," she says, a trace of astonishment found in her words.

"We are married," I reply, punctuating with my big, happy grin.

Her hand slides between us and she rests it on my thigh. With a small smile lingering on her lips, she adds, "Life is perfect."

Covering her hand with mine, I feel it too, and repeat, "Life is perfect."

When I pull into the driveway, I can hear the music out back and the chatter of the crowd. Looking at Mallory, she says, "I need to freshen up when we get there."

"We can detour upstairs."

She nods, a lot on her mind by her quietness.

"Want to talk about it?" I ask.

That makes her smile. "Just hoping they aren't too mad."

"They'll be mad, but they'll get over it."

"Yeah." She pauses. "I guess. I don't regret it though."

"Good," I say, stroking her shoulder. "I don't either."

I put the car in park and cut the engine. After tossing the keys to the valet attendant, I run around to help my bride out of the car. We grab our shoes and make a beeline straight for the front door and inside the house unseen. Holding hands, I pull her quickly up the stairs and around the corner.

"Ah!" We yell along with Sunny and Zach as we all run right into them.

"You scared us," Sunny says, holding her hand to her chest.

"You scared us," Mallory replies. "What are you doing here?"

They look at each other with guilt written all over their faces and Sunny starts to straighten her hair.

"Oh my. Don't even answer that," Mallory adds, rolling her eyes. I know what that look is about and I'm glad not to have it aimed at me.

Right when she starts telling them she can't believe they were having sex during our reception, I cut her off when I hear people talking downstairs. "Shhh," I whisper, putting my finger to my mouth. "Come with us."

We scurry down the hall single file to my old room and I shut the door behind us.

"Are you married?" Zach asks, curious.

I look at Mallory just as she looks at me. She answers, "Yes."

"Congratulations!" Sunny squeals, throwing her arms around Mallory's neck.

"Keep it down," I whisper.

"Congratulations, man," Zach says, pulling me into a hug. "You skipped out on your own wedding. That's so badass." He claps me on the back.

"Thanks," I answer with a chuckle. With Zach it's always been easy. We don't have to use words, just looks we learned from being friends for so long. He likes Mallory and he told me back in New York he'd support my decision to marry young. He sees how much my life has changed and knows Mallory is to thank for it. He had to put up with a lot of shit from me over the years, yeah, good and some really fucking crazy times too, but my life is better than ever. I'm just glad he's here today to celebrate with me as my best man.

"Let's go to the reception and do a toast," Sunny suggests, fluffing the skirt of Mallory's dress.

"Actually..." Mallory says, touching her hair. "I should really fix my hair."

Sunny looks at Mallory. "I can help you, if you like."

"I want to pull the front of my hair back? I think it will be prettier for the party that way."

Sunny's smile softens, and she says, "Yes, I think that will be very pretty."

"I can wait here for you," I say.

Zach hits me on the arm, "Beer?"

When I look back at Mallory, she says, "Go. We'll meet you downstairs."

"Awesome. Don't mind if I do have a beer then. I'll be waiting."

The girls disappear into the bedroom and we head downstairs to raid the fridge.

26

MALLORY

We rejoin the boys ten minutes later. Sunny has taken the front of my hair and carefully spun it in two sections on either side of my face then rubber-banded them together at the back. She tucked three small Plumeria flowers from her hair into the rubber band to hide it, leaving most of my long hair down and wavy in the back.

Evan is waiting for me at the bottom of the stairs. When I'm almost all the way down, he steps up one to meet me. Standing eye level now, he grabs both my hands, and says, "You've never looked more incredible than you do right now."

"Mahalo."

Leaning forward, he kisses me lightly. "I love you, Mallory." His lips are against mine and his words are just a whisper between us.

He takes my breath away every time he says those three magical words. I rub his shoulders and whisper, "I love you, too. So much."

When he pulls back, his eyes linger indulgently on my lips and then slowly looks up to meet mine as that half smirk appears—the one that creates a current of desire throughout my body. He proudly extends his elbow and I take hold just as proud to be his—legally and eternally. "Mrs. Ashford, it's show time."

We walk into the kitchen, which is bustling with caterers and waiters, and Zach stands up from a chair and makes his way to the door, taking hold of the handle.

"Are we all good here?" Sunny asks, eyeing us both and smiling.

"All good," I reply, straightening my skirt.

"You ready?" Zach asks when we stop in front of them.

With a glance and a nod, we go.

"You ready to do this?"

"Absolutely."

Sunny rushes outside with Zach following behind, but instructs us first, "Wait here until you're announced."

My palms start to sweat, but I'm not alone with the nerves. Evan shifts on his feet and takes a long pull from the beer. I laugh to myself that our introduction as husband and wife is what makes us nervous. Not that we eloped. Not the vows that we made up on the spot. *The introduction.* Go figure.

From just outside the back door, a man on a microphone announces, "Ladies and gentlemen, I would like to introduce for the very first time, Mr. and Mrs. Evan Ashford."

I step forward, but Evan is an immovable wall and I'm jolted back in place.

When I look at him, he says, "We're still us out there, okay?" He's more serious than I expected. "Don't let their judgments change who you are."

The meaning of his words sink in as I realize he's referring to the uppity crowd from New York. Raising my chin up, I squeeze his hand. "I promise I won't."

Nodding, he steps forward, taking charge of the situation and leading us to the door. We walk out and Evan smiles, walking with pride into the setting sunset of the reception to a huge round of applause, cheers, and whistles.

Claire rushes over, hugging me, and whispers, "Congratulations, Mallory. This may seem rushed, but the photographer needs you two on the beach right away. We only have a few minutes of sunlight left."

"Alright," I say, returning the embrace.

She hugs Evan, and I overhear their exchange. "Congratulations, Evan. You heard me tell Mallory about the photographer?"

"Yes."

"Okay, take care of the photos and we'll talk about what happened today when you're finished."

Claire whispers to the guy with the microphone and he instructs the guests to hold all personal congratulations until we return from the beach. Of course, no one does as we work our way around the pool and down the stone steps. People seem genuinely excited for us though I don't recognize anyone we pass. We give lots of thanks until we're down the step and on the beach. We kick our shoes off again and continue walking, warm sand between our toes.

Claire was right. We only have a few minutes before the sun dips into the ocean, leaving a blanket of bright stars to softly light the sky. We take a lot of pictures and then make our way back up, this time stopping to shake hands, receive hugs and lovely words of wishes for our future. Back on the pool deck, I stand on my tiptoes to scan the crowd for my parents. The congrats are great, but I want to see my family.

Sarah surprises me when she shows up at my side and says, "Your parents are over here. Follow me."

I take Evan's hand again and we weave through the party,

running into Ms. Chart. Evan hugs her tight, both of them taking the time to appreciate the special moment. "I'm so proud and happy for you, Evan," she says with tears in her eyes.

"I've never been happier. She married me. She actually married me," he says, releasing her and taking my hand back in his, holding it to his chest.

"You make a beautiful couple. Congratulations." She leans forward, hugging me. "Mallory, I've never seen a more radiant bride."

"Thank you." I'm too choked up to say anything more. Gail Chart has always been a good friend to me and I know Evan is like a son to her. She should be proud of him since she's played a big part in raising him.

"Take care of him." she whispers.

"I promise I will."

We welcome Harold and Nellie to the reception before finally spotting my dad. I rush over with Evan in tow until I reach my dad and see my mom behind him. Throwing my arms around our co-conspirator, I hug my dad tight. "Was it beautiful, sweetheart?" he asks, holding me tight. "Was it everything you wanted?"

"It was perfect, more than I could dream of. Thank you for helping us."

Releasing him, I give him a quick kiss on the cheek before hugging my mom. Swaying in each other's arms, appreciating all that's led to this day, she sniffles. "I'm sorry, Mom."

She whispers, trying to calm herself to keep from crying. "Don't be. It should be about you, not us."

My mom always knows the right thing to say. My guilt over them not being there to see me get married was starting to cloud my happiness. But the clouds have cleared and happiness returns. "I love you," I tell her.

"I love you too, honey."

When I look back at Evan, he extends a hand to my dad, which he happily accepts. With a shaky, emotional sigh, my dad abruptly and surprisingly pulls Evan into a hug. "I thought you weren't a hugger, Sir?"

"You just married my daughter. I can hug ya if I want to. We're family now and call me Clay or Dad, whichever you prefer," my dad says, holding back the tears. Evan's smile might be best described as victorious, but I don't make a big deal of it, not wanting to embarrass my dad.

After making a round through the party to say hello to everyone else, Kate finds us and leads us to Evan's parents who are waiting by the cake with champagne. Hugh hands us both a glass and Evan hugs him. "I'm really proud of you, son."

I hear that right before Claire looks at me fondly, and says, "Mallory, you make a beautiful bride. I'm happy for you both. Congratulations."

Setting my glass down on the table next to us, I hug her —not because I have to since she's officially my mother-in-law and not because I really believe she's being nice. I hug her simply because I want to hug the woman who has opened her heart to me and finally accepted me into her family. She welcomes me with open arms and returns the embrace. "Thank you."

"I'm so glad that Evan has found you. I think you'll be very happy together," she says before releasing me. When we part, Evan and Hugh are smiling, acknowledging the significance of the moment we all just shared.

Hugh hugs me, and says, "Welcome to the family,

Mallory. We couldn't have wished for a better partner for Evan."

"Thank you. I'm thrilled to be an Ashford."

When we part, Murphy hands us our champagne again and we take a sip in celebration.

Evan steps forward and hugs his mother again, trying to ease the blow when he says, "I hope you understand why we eloped."

I watch as she rubs his back, holding him close, as if she knows he's his own man now, her little boy all grown up. "I would've loved to have been there, but Clay explained, so I'm trying to understand." She hides her face against Evans shoulder and I hear a small sniffle escape her. "I love you, Evan." She leans up and kisses him on the cheek while patting a tissue to the corner of her eyes. "I'll get over it." Claire backs away, but says, "Let's celebrate and toast to the happy couple."

I move back to Evan's side, slipping my hand into his. He leans over and kisses my temple as Murphy raises his glass in our honor and starts his toast. "I couldn't have picked a better match for Evan if I'd tried. Mallory, you brought our boy back from the dead and for that, we will always be grateful. May your days together be long and the sex be plentiful. Ow!" Our tight-knit group bursts into laughter as he grabs his stomach. "Fuck, Kate. That hurt." Hugh clears his throat, giving Murphy a dirty look. "Oh, sorry for the language, Mr. Ashford."

Kate grabs Murphy by the elbow and starts to drag him away from the group, griping at him. "I can't believe you just said that in front of my parents."

Evan leans down and whispers, "Not gonna lie. I want a long and sex-filled life with you, baby."

"Me too. What about the gut punch? You don't want one

of those?" I tease, poking him in the stomach. *Damn, his abs are hard. I'm a very lucky girl.*

Laughing, he wraps his arm around my shoulder as Sunny pulls us over to see the cake. "It's cake cutting time," she adds with a wink. "We're doing things out of order, so you don't have any obligations later tonight."

She gives us a moment while she searches for the planner and photographer. "I love it," I say, leaning forward to see the details of the beach-themed cake.

"Guess what flavor it is?" I look at Evan when he asks this question, his gaze nothing less than seductive. How cake and seduction have come to be mixed together I have no idea, but I'm kind of excited to find out. "Pineapple," he says, my insides tightening just from the mere mention of the fruit. He's trained me well as images of sexy beach time fill my thoughts.

Evan's warm breath brushes across my skin as his lips touch the shell of my ear. "I requested it especially for you." He plants a sweet kiss on my cheek then laughs, knowing he's left me turned on and heated while trying to keep my composure as our picture is taken with the pineapple cake.

With a big smile on my face for the photographer, I mutter under my breath, "You play dirty, surferboy."

I'm just about to tease him some more for that pineapple stunt, but the planner with her perfectly bad timing walks up with the knife for us to cut the cake. I should make him squirm the way he has me, but that leaves us nowhere but in the middle of a party all hot and bothered, so no one wins. *And really, will I ever be able to look at a pineapple the same?* I remember more innocent thoughts of the sweet fruit, but I can admit I prefer the naughty ones I have instead these days.

He seems to notice my wiggle. "Feeling a bit tense, my

love? I know how we can relieve that discomfort you're feeling."

Pursing my lips to the side, I try to show him I'm irritated, but I'm not, so I can't hold the face and I laugh. "You're very persistent."

"I am when it comes to getting you in bed. Anyway, I have a rain-check to cash in."

"Yes, you do, so I guess we should get to cutting this cake then."

"I like the way you think."

Much to everyone's disappointment we don't smash the sweet confection into each other's face. Local favorites are served for dinner as well as a mix of delicious culinary creations.

The sun set a while ago and the landscape is lit with soft lights, setting the mood for our first dance. We're introduced and my husband offers me his hand while we stand on the dance floor beside the pool. When I take it, he spins me to his chest then wraps his arm around me, and says, "I'm never letting you go."

"I wouldn't have it any other way. I'm yours just like you're mine. Always."

27

EVAN

"May I have this dance?" I ask, holding Mallory to me.

"Yes." She nods, looking me in the eyes. I can see her vulnerability from all the attention present in the pretty green depths of her eyes. I hold her close, wanting to comfort and protect her while we dance cheek-to-cheek.

The song we chose for our first dance may not seem typical for us, but it spoke to our hearts. I agreed with Mallory when she suggested 'Embraceable You' by Nat King Cole. It was the first song we heard as an engaged couple. It was playing at the gala and then again when we were ice-skating the next day. Maybe the song is sappy and traditional, but it works for us and stuck.

I surprise her by swinging her out and bringing her back to me again. Tilting her head, she laughs, making me laugh, her happiness contagious. With our noses touching, I hold her steady in my arms and we sway to the music. Feeling the importance of the day, I say, "I'm going to give you such a good life."

Without missing a beat, she says, "Better than good. I know it's going to be the best life possible." Her lips are against my jaw, planting kisses. "I can't wait to be alone with you tonight. When we're together, it feels like home."

"You are my home, Mallory. Forever."

We continue dancing to the rest of the song, holding each other close, her head on my shoulder as we move together to the music. Another song starts playing and the dance floor fills up as other couples join in around us.

"May I have this dance with my daughter," her father asks, tapping me on the shoulder.

"Of course." I place her hand in his, and leave to walk to the bar. Just as I order a whiskey and Coke, Zach joins me, ordering the same. He leans his elbows back on the bar, his own girl hanging out with Kate near the dance floor. "So what now?" he asks.

We drink in silence for a minute before I glance over at him. He seems genuinely interested, not like the small talk I've had to make with my parent's friends tonight. I shrug, "School, I guess."

"I heard your parents talking to Kate about Murphy."

"What'd Kate say?"

"She said he was moving to New York."

Shocked, I turn to him. "Really?"

Zach clinks his glass against mine. "Really. He's graduated. Guess he's leaving the island."

"I've been too caught up in school and all of this. Guess I missed the little detail that he's moving across an ocean and the country to be with my sister." I take another sip of my drink, and smile. "But good for them." When I look at Kate, she waves and I raise a glass in silent toast to her. I'm proud of her for letting love into her life. She can be a hardass in business, but she's a softie when it comes to matters of the heart. "So what about you?" I ask Zach. "What's next for you?"

"Sunny and I have graduated," Zach says, looking up at the moon hanging over the water. "Do you think she'll think I'm selfish if I ask her to move in with me without asking her to get married first?"

"I think you should do what works for you guys. It's not a race to the end of life. It's about the journey and the life you lead. What anyone else thinks doesn't matter."

"I'll admit that I never thought you'd be the first of our friends to get married."

That makes me laugh. I rub my lower lip with my thumb, signaling my wife. I miss her and ready to have her back. I lean closer to Zach, and whisper, "I'll admit I'm just as surprised, but there just wasn't any other way my life could go." I nod toward Mallory. "That girl right there took me by surprise and changed everything. I never knew someone could come into your life with a foul mouth and such a stubborn side, and make you rethink everything about your own life, but she did. I'm just lucky that both of those same qualities were attached to a woman who is forgiving and loves harder than anyone else I've ever known."

He laughs, noting I mentioned some usually not so great traits along with the good ones. "So it's okay if she's not perfect?"

"She's perfect for me."

With a sigh, he says, "Sunny likes pink a lot."

This time I laugh, imagining how his house will be redecorated soon after he asks her to move in.

He smiles. "It drives me nuts, but I wouldn't have her any other way."

"Because you get it."

Zach nods. "I totally get it."

Mallory joins us. "Hey lover, you wanna blow this joint?"

she asks, looking up at me. She looks a little tired, but she's still stunning.

"Anything you want, baby," I say, wrapping her arm under my arm and holding her close.

Unlike our greetings to everyone when we arrived, we make our goodbyes fast. Cocktails have relaxed our parents who've spent the evening chatting. I have a feeling they'll continue the party long after we're gone.

We say our goodbyes and start to leave, but Clay catches up and pulls an envelope out of his suit jacket. "This is our gift to you. I know it's usually the bride's parents who pay for the wedding and the groom's that pays for the honeymoon, but since your family paid for the wedding, we wanted to take care of your trip."

"You didn't have to do that," I say, touched by his generosity.

"We wanted to. We did a lot of checking around with your parents and your friends and they all suggested some-where tropical where you could surf and Mallory could relax. We came up with Costa Rica."

Elise comes up behind him and leans her head on his shoulder. "We wanted you to have some time together, just the two of you before diving back into your studies and work."

Mallory's eyes fill with tears again, the weight of the evening hitting her. "I've always wanted to go to Costa Rica. Thank you. Thank you very much." Mallory's voice cracks at the end. I wrap my arm around her shoulder and hold her tightly to me as a single tear escapes and rolls down her cheek.

"Oh, honey, don't cry. Focus on this husband of yours and it'll be just fine," Elise says, taking her daughter into her arms. "We love you."

I know the move to Hawaii will be hard on Mallory because she won't get to see her family as much as she likes, but I'll do everything I can to make her happy here with me. This is where we should be right now, which reminds me that I need to give her my present when we're alone tonight. I feel a pang of excitement rush through my body, a smile showing as I imagine her face when I give it to her.

Our friends are nearby, patiently waiting as we take the time to say goodbye to each of them.

"Brother," I say, slapping my palm against Murphy's.

"Brothers," he replies with a shoulder bump and a smile.

It blows my mind that one of my best friends might actually seal the deal with my sister and be my brother for real one day. I love the guy to death, but still don't like to think of my sister being with anyone... in *that* way. But when Murphy pulls me into a congratulatory hug, I realize I'm fortunate to have him as my friend and I'd be damn fucking lucky to have him as my brother-in-law.

One chest bump later, I ask, "So I hear Manhattan's in your future?"

Murphy easily replies, "Yep, but I'll be here a bit longer."

"Take care of my sister."

He nods, knowing I mean he *will* treat her well or I'll kick his ass, and responds accordingly, "Of course."

After a fist bump, I turn to my other side where Zach stands. Extending my hand, we do our brah-hood handshake—it comes automatically since we've done the same one for at least four years now. He looks down, wiping at his eyes. When he looks up, he sees me watching him and quickly says, "Damn sand."

I roll my eyes at the cover story to hide his emotions, but I get it. "Yeah, the wind has really picked up," I say, humoring him. "I'm married now."

"Yes, you are." Both of us knowing no matter how much we try to stay the same, things are going to change. Not that it will be bad. No, not bad, I expect better, but it does change the dynamic of the group. I'm responsible for two now and Mallory's my priority. "Brahs."

"No doubt, man," I say, pulling him in for a man hug. When we step back, we straighten our jackets and try to maintain our usual cool, going for unaffected. I ask, "You still up for surfing even though I'm a married man?"

"Totally. You were never my type anyway and I'm kind of taken myself." He looks over at Sunny who's hugging Mallory. "We need a surf schedule to keep the tradition alive."

"Fuck, we sound old," I say, joking.

"I'm thinking you get your class schedule worked out and I'll get my job sorted and we'll make the time."

"Sounds good."

Shaking my hand one more time, he says, "Congratulations. You've done good, Evan."

"Thanks."

"My baby bro is now married making me look like some old spinster at twenty-six. Go figure." Kate's words sound tough, but I know inside she's feeling sentimental.

I start to speak, "Kate..." but a lump forms in my throat preventing anymore words from coming out. I look at her and her eyes fill with tears. We've always had a normal bond like siblings do, but the last couple of years, it felt like she was the only one in my family on my side. Knowing she was there for me through all the bad... I gulp hard. Maybe I'm feeling a little sentimental myself.

Wrapping her arms around me, I hear her sniffle against my shoulder. "It's okay. I know. This is enough."

Murphy comes over and rubs her back. She turns

around and leans against him. "I love you," she mouths quietly just between the two of us.

"I love you too, big sis."

I turn and take my bride's hand and tug a little to wrap up the goodbyes. I'm becoming a mess and if I stay here any longer, I'll be no good to my wife on our wedding night. Mallory wipes at her eyes, trying not to make a mess of her makeup. It doesn't matter, she looks amazing without all that anyway.

Sunny starts organizing the guests to line the path that leads to the driveway as I take Mallory to overlook the beach down below. "Do you regret eloping?" I ask, admiring her in the moonlight.

"Not at all. Everything was just how it should be. We had the wedding we wanted and our family and friends had the party they wanted. It was the best of both worlds."

"Yes, it was. Now c'mon, I can hear some excitement over there."

"Here come the flowers," she says in a sing-songy voice.

"Flowers for what?"

"Just get ready to get pelted with petals."

We walk to the head of the path and see the guests lined up on both sides waiting. The photographer is at the other end, and yells, "Run!"

After a quick glance at each other, we take off, hand-in-hand, running up the pathway. At the other end, we pass the spot where I made love... okay, I *fucked* Mallory in the rain, pressing her hard against the side of the house. I don't bother stifling the smile and proud chuckle that comes from that amazing memory. Thinking back now, that's when we decided to give our relationship a fair shot—a real shot—and now here we are.

Stealing another glimpse of Mallory, she's laughing from

pure joy. I don't see the girl I thought was hot at first glance in the airport. I don't see the girl who fought every one of my bad intentions—stubborn and headstrong—protective of her heart and demanding of mine. When she looks at me, radiance reflects in her eyes, bright and happy. I see her so clearly now. She's the woman who had closed her heart off to love, but left a light on for me. The woman that gave a careless boy another chance... and another, believing him better than he believed himself. She's the woman who I thank all the ocean tides and stars in the sky for agreeing to be my wife. She's filled my life with love I didn't know existed. When our eyes meet, a simple glance exchanged, I know she understands my feelings, just like she understands me.

We run to the car that's been tagged with shoe polish and cans hanging from the bumper. Sunny tosses Mallory her bouquet which she then tosses over her head to the crowd of guests. I help her into the car and run around to the other side. When I get in, we look at each other once, sharing a smile, then turn to see a stunned Kate standing there with the bouquet in her hands. Murphy is next to her with a wide grin on his face and an arm around his woman, proudly pointing to the 'next bride-to-be' by tradition with that toss. What they've hidden for so long, sits proudly on display for everyone to see today.

Turning back to the road ahead, I hit the gas. With her fingers toying with my hair, Mallory laughs then says, "I'm in total, head over feet, in love with you, Evan Ashford."

Looking at my sweet girl, I say, "That's good to hear because I'm in total and awe-inspiring love with you, Mallory Wray."

"Ashford," she corrects. "Mrs. Evan Ashford."

"Music to my ears."

I take her hand and kiss her knuckles several times while driving to our destination. We finally pull off onto a short driveway, and I announce, "We're here."

"This is where we're staying?"

Once we park, she stands in front, staring at the little bungalow, an expression of content coming through. "I love it. It's just the two of us?" she asks, looking back at me.

"I thought it would be nice to have the privacy until we leave for Costa Rica in a few days."

"And I, for one, love the romantic gesture. This location is beautiful."

"It's dark now, but I'm quite partial to the beach view as well." I open the front door of the small house for her, but yank her back after she takes a quick step inside. "Uh, uh, uh," I gently scold.

Surprised, she looks at me perplexed and asks, "What?"

I bend down and as I start to lift her up, she says, "You're kidding me. You're carrying me over the threshold?" She kisses me on the nose. "Awww, you're such a romantic."

"I want to do things right by you and don't want you to miss anything that you might've dreamed about."

"It's been a wonderful day. Every dream come true." I set her down over the threshold, and she wanders off to explore the house. I take my jacket off and then retrieve our bags from the car. After setting down the luggage, I flop down on the couch, the day catching up.

She runs out and says, "Hey babe, the bedroom faces the ocean. We can open the windows and wake up to the sounds of the water."

Her excitement is a relief. I thought she'd prefer a place like this opposed to a resort hotel, but I wasn't sure. "Pretty awesome, huh."

She continues to explore, sliding open the large pocket

doors that lead to the patio and the beach beyond. Standing there, the wind blows her hair, the skirt of her dress rustles, and the sound of the ocean wafts in the background, I've found my own personal paradise. "This place is amazing. You did good," she says as she comes back inside and sits next to me, curling into my side.

I wrap my arm around her as she rests her head on my lap. Leaning my head back on the couch cushion, I say, "It's your present."

"You're always so thoughtful. I'm glad we came here instead a touristy hotel." She sits up and kisses me on the cheek. "We can make love and... well, whatever else you do on a honeymoon and then we get to fly off to Costa Rica."

Sitting forward, I realize she doesn't understand what I mean. She sits up, uncomfortable as I adjust. I lean in, giving her a quick kiss. "I didn't *rent* this house," I say as she looks at me. Her smile turns into confusion, but returns as she waits for me to explain. "I *bought* this house... for you and me, a home *for us*."

Her back straightens as her face shows her shock. "You *bought* this place?"

"Uh-huh. It's my gift to you. A wedding gift."

"Ummmm.... holy shit, Evan. I didn't buy you anything at all and you bought me a house?"

"You said it was amazing. You still think that, right?"

"Yes, it's amazing. I mean, you just gave me a house, on the beach, in Hawaii. That's freaking huge."

"My mother and Kate picked out the couch and mattresses since I apparently know nothing about that stuff as I was promptly told. Sunny, Sarah, and your mom chose the decorative stuff lying around, but I thought you'd like to personalize it when you have time. You know, beyond the basics."

"I think I'm still in shock right now. I need time to process this."

I lean forward resting my hand on her forearm. "Good shock or bad shock?"

She lunges, toppling me backwards onto the couch, and crawls the best she can in that big dress onto my lap. With our bodies pressed together, she says, "The best kind. I love it. I can't believe this is our home. Are you for real right now?"

"Yes. I like to tease you, but I wouldn't when it comes to something like this."

"Thank you." She kisses me with all her excitement wrapped up in it.

Holding her up by the hips, I lift onto my knees and bend so she lays down on her back. We adjust until I'm over her, my lips lingering on hers before I move to her chin and down her neck. She writhes beneath me, yearning laces her every moan, which signals my body into reaction. I continue planting wet, open mouth kisses across her chest, working my way methodically toward her breasts.

She arches her back and groans. "Evan, take me to bed and make love to me."

"My pleasure."

In the bedroom, I push her hair over her shoulder and wiggle the dress to loosen it from her body, kissing her neck and coming back up. "You are the most stunning woman I've ever laid eyes on." Her head lulls back as I squat down to make sure to hold the dress low enough so she can step out of it without falling. My body pulses from the site of her—garter intact. I kiss each of her shoulders again, then gently bite. "You're so sexy."

The dress pools around her ankles, and I lift her up and out of it. Her lacey undies removed... with my teeth, leaving her garter on while her body is displayed before me. "It's just not right. You're dressed to sin," I accuse, watching her on the bed looking way too fuckable. She licks her upper lip and then fucking teases me by running that pink tongue over her bottom lip. If I ever had a doubt before, which I didn't, I definitely don't doubt my lust *or* love for this woman.

"It's not sinful if we're married. Speaking of sinful, got any fruit?"

"Fuck the fruit. You're driving me crazy." Instead of giving her what she thinks she wants, I give her what she needs. I lower myself onto my knees and hook my hands under her legs, pulling her closer. Mallory lays flat on her back with her arms out to the sides, her head resting on the mattress and looking much more comfortable.

I plant a small kiss on the inside of each of her knees and then focus on her right thigh. I lick, kiss, and suck a trail, continuing to her other thigh repeating the performance and causing her to wiggle. She props up on her elbows and pleads, "Stop teasing me, babe."

At her demand, I kiss her there, deep and filling, my fingers and mouth working together to make her come. She falls back flat onto the bed again and I chuckle knowing she's weak to my talents. Her hands wind into my hair and she pulls hard. I maneuver up her body, positioning myself, and kiss her the same way I kissed her before—meaningful and filling.

I push forward and we're connected in the most intimate and physical way possible. I take my time, neither of us in any hurry. We've got all night. The sound of the waves crashing outside mingles with our heavy breaths as our bodies move in time together.

Her warmth enveloping me brings me close, and I

struggle to stop my impending fall. She rolls me over, demanding to be on top. I love when she's on top. She's powerful and takes what she needs. It's quite the sight to behold as she chases her own orgasm. Rocking on top of me, I hold her hips, thrusting from instinct and desire, my needs fulfilling hers as she fulfills mine.

Breathless and heated, she presses her hands down on my chest, and stops. "I can't believe you bought a house."

"I can't believe you married me."

She licks her lips then opens her mouth, taking in the air she needs to help compensate for the activity. She's pure sex and a goddess. "I'm the lucky one," she says, stroking my hair away from my forehead. Her smile is soft, her body relaxed and she begins moving again.

Closing my eyes, all the love I feel and good sensations she's causing swirl inside, quickly going lower as I let the reality that we're married sink in, increasing the feeling five-fold. I start pushing harder and faster, harder...

Clenching my teeth, I struggle to hold it together. She feels so fucking unbelievable when she comes. Her body tightens around me, encouraging my own release. I sit up and her hands slide to my back and stroke, moving to my shoulders as her body pushes against mine. With all my efforts and energy, I slam into her making her call out my name as her body responds to every thrust. Seeing her so caught up in the rapture rushes my build-up. "Baby, I'm gonna come."

"Come inside. I want to feel you."

Her words are filled with lust and are naughty when uttered from her mouth, but so fucking hot. She wants to feel me, so I give her all I've got.

Hours later, we're lying in a hammock on the beach and I'm guessing by the moon's position in the sky, it's past midnight. Mallory is asleep in my arms, her naked body snuggled around me, her head on my chest. I thought she was asleep until she says, "I'm living in a dream." She looks up at me. Her eyes tired, her expression soft. "Don't wake me if I'm dreaming. I like living in paradise."

I smile, the cool tropical breeze keeping us cool as it brushes across our bare shoulders. A blanket is under us and the sheet from our bed covering us. I kiss the top of her head and say, "Paradise is holding the girl of your dreams in your arms and watching the sunrise the morning after marrying her."

She cuddles closer, as if that's possible, and lowers her head back down. "Are we out here for the long haul tonight?"

"We're definitely in this for the long haul." I'm speaking as much about us as the night.

I don't remember falling asleep, but I do. When I open my eyes, I look around while yawning. My body is stiff, but I'm careful not to disturb Mallory as I look out at the sun rising over the water. Glancing back at the window of our bedroom, I realize I'll be able to start the day with this view for years to come. That makes me smile though it's a lazier one, not fully awake yet.

Mallory wiggles, readjusting then slides her head up enough to look out at the water. "We're married," she whispers.

"Yes, we are. How do you feel about that?"

"Am I still dreaming?"

"No, this is real," I say, not hiding my chuckle.

"Then it's a dream come true."

"You're a dream come true, Mrs. Ashford."

She lifts her head up and kisses me. "Say it again."

"You're a dream come true."

"The other part," she requests.

"Mrs. Ashford, this is the first day of our forever."

She sighs, resting her head back down on my chest and smiling. "Forever sounds good to me."

"This may be coming out of left field, but how are you feeling about kids?"

She bolts upright, flipping us both to the ground as the hammock goes spinning. Landing on top of her, the sand breaks our fall, and she says, "Kids? Evan, are you serious right now?"

"I'm talking about one day, not tomorrow."

She releases a deep breath of relief, relaxing into the sand beneath her. When she stands, she wraps the sheet around her body, and says, "Thank goodness."

Standing up, I take the other sheet and wrap it around my waist. I tug her closer by the loose ends of the wrapped sheet until she's face-to-face with me, and ask, "So what do you want to do today?"

"You've worn me out, so I'm thinking some sunbathing and a good book might be in order. If I'm lucky, there's this guy I'm hoping to see. He's really hot and a great surfer. I love watching him out there riding the waves." I smile, the right side lifting up higher impressed by how mischievous my girl is. She continues, "I'm hoping he makes an appearance today." She looks me straight in the eyes, direct and insinuating. "To be honest, he gets me all hot and bothered when I watch him surfing and don't even get me started on when he comes out of the ocean all strong and commanding. Water dripping." She shivers and bites her knuckles, seeming to get a little turned on just from talking about it.

I run my finger down her nose and over her lips where she kisses the tip, now getting me hot and bothered. "I might be able to help you out with that ogling you've got on your agenda today."

"I'd be very appreciative if you did," she replies, dragging her finger down my bare chest.

"Dude! Surfs up," Murphy calls from the side of the house, startling us.

Tightening the sheet that covers her, Mallory looks at me, makes a wonky face and rolls her eyes. My wife is not happy about the intrusion. With the boner I've got going, I can't say I am either.

Rubbing her back, I whisper, "Sorry."

She smiles and says, "It's fine. We always have later."

"I'm going to hold you to that, Mrs. Ashford."

"I'd expect nothing less, Mr. Ashford." She walks toward the open doors just as Sunny rounds the corner with Kate.

Kate says, "Sorry for barging in on your honeymoon, but Liam and I will be in New York when you guys return from Costa Rica. One last hurrah was in order."

Sunny shows up with a grocery bag in her arms, and Mallory asks, "Did you at least bring coffee?"

Sunny follows the girls inside, and I hear her say, "And orange rolls. Are you naked under that sheet?"

Before she disappears inside, my lovely wife replies without shame, "As a matter of fact, I am."

"What are orange rolls?" I ask, slipping on the pair of board shorts from the ground that I was stripped of last night before the hammock was christened and take my new board from the rack I had installed the other day.

Zach shows up with a box of pastries in one hand and his board under the other arm. "Only the best invention ever since the donut. They're like cinnamon rolls, but with this orange frosting stuff. They're insane, they're so good.

Sunny and I discovered them last week on the North Shore. They're popular on the mainland. Is that a new board?"

"Yes, sirree. I had it custom made. A present to myself," I answer, making sure the wax I put on the other day is still solid. I point to the letters on the toe of the board. "I had Mallory's initials put on it. She's my compass. Blah, blah... yeah, I sound like a total prick talking about this with you guys, so I'm gonna grab one of those sweet rolls and stuff my face instead. I'm starving." I reach into the box and pull out a pastry to start eating.

Murphy hits my arm. "You are totally whipped, man, and lucky I've gone all soft on love myself or I might not appreciate this new Evan Ashford."

"Lucky me you've gone soft," I say, rolling my eyes. "This conversation has turned all kinds of wrong." I'm not lucky he's gone soft on my sister. I'm lucky that he leaves to retrieve his board from the truck, ending this conversation.

"Man, what a view," Zach says, standing there with his arms crossed over his chest, staring at the ocean. "Check out the break. House on the beach *and* good surfing right out your back door. You're set."

When Murphy returns, he stands next to us, three pairs of eyes set on the surf ahead. "I see lots of dawn patrol happening," Zach says.

"I'd be disappointed if it didn't." I start walking and they follow. "Gentleman, it's time to pray at the church of the open sky."

With boards under our arms, Murphy takes off running while Zach and I give each other one quick glance—all bets on—then run into the ocean.

28

MALLORY

"It's just not right," I say, staring ahead.

"Not right at all," Sunny adds.

While keeping our eyes glued on the display of cocky manliness, glistening sun-kissed skin, and smooth moves in front of us, we only hear a dreamy sigh from Kate.

I stand up, not able to bear it any longer. On a mission with the girls flanking my sides, we stomp down to the water's edge, waving to the guys, who are currently floating on their boards, way past the break. I jump, hoping to entice them with... well, with my feminine wiles. *Okay, my tits.* I tempt Evan with bouncing breasts. One can't always play fair.

It's almost noon and they've been out there for hours now. I miss him. It's technically our honeymoon and I want my husband back. He grabs the next wave, stealing it from under Zach, which pisses off Zach, who has now stopped paddling and is sitting on his board swearing. We can hear him from here.

Evan cuts across the top of the wave and just as it starts to barrel over, he jumps into the air, diving into the ocean, his board dragged behind him by the leash. I stop breathing, my heart lumping in my throat until he finally pops up for air and starts swimming to shore. I'm gonna kick his ass for that move, but later because I have other plans for him first.

When he reaches the beach, I stroll over, casual in my approach, needing to sweet talk him out of anymore surfing, at least for a little while. "You must be exhausted," I say with my hands behind my back. I've brought ammunition or what I like to call a little bribe to make sure he sees things my way. But to him, he gets a little show as this position perks my breasts forward for him to appreciate all the more.

He kisses me through heavy, tired breaths, and says, "Damn, we scored. The break is epic and we live right here." His eyes are bright with excitement and possibility.

Slowly swaying my hips, I ask, "Speaking of breaks, you ready to take one? You know, for food and other stuff?"

Running his hand over his hair, rubbing roughly to shake the water out, he says, "Good idea. I'm starved. What's for lunch?"

I hold up my weapon. "I've got an idea or two."

His eyes widen, but when the smirk appears, I know I've got his complete attention. "Sex wax, huh? What do you plan on doing with that?" he asks.

I turn to walk back to the house, flipping up sand in the process. But I stop and look back at my surfer, the boy who became a man, dominating every ounce of his sex appeal and me along the way. "I've got a few ideas... and some matches." I feign innocence as I say, "Oh, and I almost forgot to tell you. A fruit platter was delivered this morning while you were out surfing." I add a little batting of the eyelashes for extra emphasis.

"You did not just go there," he teases, waggling his eyes.

Nodding, I wiggle my booty, and say, "I totally did." I

take off running as he rushes to undo the leash from his ankle. I make the mistake of looking back once, which causes me to lose my lead, but losing to him is worth it since I'll win in the end when he catches me. My hot husband runs toward me with a look in his eyes that can only be described as 'starving.'

The girls laugh and catcall as we run past them, knowing we are about to take advantage of our newlywed status with all intents and purposes that come along with that title.

With one swift move, Evan captures me, swings me over his shoulder, and smacks my ass... *hard*. Inside, he flops me onto the bed and I'm caught between his strong arms and a fit of giggles. Jumping on top of the mattress, he pins my wrists above my head. Positioned between my legs with his erection pressed against my middle, he thrusts twice, making me squirm, and asks, "Now what was this about hot wax and fruit?"

It's in that moment, looking into the deep ocean blue of his eyes, I realize I never stood a chance that day at the airport. Evan Ashford owned my heart and every breath I took thereafter from the second he asked, "Do you need the local time?"

To be continue the Playboy in Paradise journey, turn the page and keep reading the series epilogue.

EPILOGUE

EVAN

"No, no, no, no. Shhhhh. Don't cry, baby. Please don't cry." I try soothing her. I stroke Mallory's hair back from her face and hold her to my chest while placing kisses sporadically on the top of her head. I want to take her pain away. I want to take her pain away and make everything right again. Just like it used to be. Perfect in paradise. Exactly what she deserves.

But I can't.

I can't take the pain away. It cuts us both too deep, a devastation neither of us deserves. This isn't a problem I can solve or fix or make better. I can only hope she can move on from this, that I can, that we can together.

I want to disappear into the ocean for hours, days even, and when I resurface, I want to be whole again. I want to make her whole again.

"Shhhhh," I try soothing her quiet sobs. I know it's not working, but it's all I know to do for her. I hold her even tighter. "I'm sorry. I'm so sorry, baby."

29

EVAN

Six Months Later...

THE WATER REFLECTS THE SUN, making her golden skin glisten. I lick my lips and watch as she takes her hair and wrings the water from the ends. She doesn't notice me until she lifts her gaze from the sand and looks toward the house.

I stay, lying in the hammock, silently willing her to come to me. Mallory glances down and even from here I can see a slight hint of pink coloring her cheeks. When she looks back up, she starts walking toward me, making me smile.

Lying there, I wait for her. I cross my arms behind my head and enjoy the warm day under the large palm trees of our yard. But the sounds of the ocean in the backyard have nothing on her captivating voice. "Hey there," she says, casting my face under her shadow, blocking the sun from my eyes.

"Hey there."

She looks like an angel with the sunshine bursting from behind her, giving her a halo effect. Crawling very slowly on top of me in the hammock, she's careful not to send us flipping to the ground. Her wet bathing suit, though small, sends a chill where it presses against me. I wrap my arms around her, holding her tightly to me. We're pros at balancing in this contraption, so I don't have any fear of falling. We've only tumbled out of it twice—once on our wedding night when I mentioned kids and the other time was a particularly drunk sex session. I lay still as she moves to rest her head on my chest and her knee between my legs.

Knowing we're running out of time alone, I whisper, "Let's go inside for a few minutes. I want to show you something."

She looks up without moving her body, and asks, "This something you want to show me, is it something that's grown quite significantly in your trunks since I climbed up here by chance?"

I smirk, looking up at the sky. She knows me too well. I've lost all my game and have become too predictable. I chuckle, knowing she knows my tricks. "Yes, as a matter of fact, it is."

"Good, I thought you'd never ask." She carefully rolls off of me and back onto her feet. Extending her hand out to pull me up, she says, "C'mon, Surferboy, let's go see what you're packing in those board shorts."

After rinsing our feet under the outdoor faucet, she pulls me into the house and leads me straight into the bedroom. Without hesitation, she unties her bikini and lets both pieces fall to the ground. Mallory scoots on her knees across the covers until she's centered on the king-sized bed. "Evan?"

"Yeah?"

She motions her head, beckoning me to her. Without taking my eyes from her body, I let my trunks drop to the floor. I step out of them and join her on the bed. Sliding my hands under her chin, I hold her face, letting my fingers rest gently against her skin. Kissing her, my tongue enters her mouth and finds its mate. "Mmmmm," I moan, enjoying how she tastes.

I let my hands fall, gliding lightly over her soft skin, over her shoulders and then land on her breasts. Her breasts are perfection. Taking them fully in hand, I squeeze them gently. She moans into my mouth and my cock twitches against her stomach. I slide my hands further down her hour glass body, loving her curves.

As I continue rubbing along the slope where her waist and hip meets, I kiss her again, wanting to give her everything.

I kiss down her neck... lower... lower... and lower until I reach the top of her thighs, then continue. When her head drops back, I move over her, spreading her legs with my knee. There's no resistance between us and I find it such a fucking turn on that I get to be with this woman whenever I desire.

Kissing between her breasts, I swirl my tongue in her belly button where a trapped ocean droplet allows me to taste the salt as it mixes with her natural sweetness. I look up, my eyes meeting hers. She knows I'm going to move lower to taste her in other places—very sensitive, sexual places that I alone will ever get to taste.

She shakes her head, stopping me. "I want to feel you inside of me, Evan."

I smile against her thigh as she tugs me by my hair, pulling me higher. "I can't deny you anything." I align myself and push in not wanting her to ever want for anything, including myself. We both groan when my hips meet firmly against hers.

"Yes," she murmurs, lost in sensations. I start thrusting until Mallory's hands come up and press on my chest. "Roll over."

I instantly grab a hold of her hips and roll onto my back, bringing her on top of me without breaking our connection.

She stops, pushes up a little, then says, "Babe, you're so fucking deep." I can tell she's acclimating to the new angle and to me. Her face is tilted toward the ceiling, the back of her long hair brushing against the top of my thighs. She looks down, straight into my eyes, and says, "You feel so good."

Mallory creates her own rhythm as she rides me hard. Her head drops forward and her hair hides her from my view—that is just unacceptable.

Holding her in place, I sit up, attaching my lips to her neck while pushing her hair behind her shoulders. She wraps her legs around my back and with my eyes now closed, I start losing myself in the feeling of her consuming me.

She holds me so our bare chests are pressed together, and we both continue moving. As her nails scrape across my shoulders, I feel her tighten, her body squeezing me over and over again as she calls my name out. "Evan!"

My thrusting is erratic, no predictable rhythm left to be found. "I'm gonna come." I release, punctuating each thrust up with a harsh breath until my strength and energy is gone. Rolling her onto her back, I collapse on top, resting my head on her chest. I love laying on top of her like this, post orgasm.

A knock on our side door draws my attention away from her. Time passes too quickly. If I could have my way, we'd stay like this all day. I don't get my way today though. We have other obligations cutting into our time that we have to tend to.

"You should probably let 'em in, babe," she says, rubbing her fingers through my hair with comforting strokes.

"I know, but I don't wanna get up."

"They'll come in anyway."

"Let 'em."

She giggles, causing my head to bounce on her chest. I start to sit up but she pulls me back down so I'm lying next to her. We share a pillow looking into each others' eyes. I can hear Zach and Sunny talking as they make themselves at home in the kitchen.

"Can we talk for a minute?" she asks hesitantly, looking down at my chest.

She looks worried. I lift her chin up with my finger, and say, "Of course, we can. What's bothering you?"

"I'm not bothered. I just... well, I've been thinking about kids lately." She looks so nervous right now that I want to comfort her, but I wait, letting her say what she needs to say.

"Yeah?"

"Yeah. They had the cutest storytime for toddlers the other day. It's every Wednesday actually. The kids are so adorable to watch."

"So you're ready again?"

"I don't know," she replies. "I'm just kind of drawn to the group and find myself thinking about you and us and what our kids might look like and be like. If they'll have—"

"I'm worried about the pregnancy part. I mean after—"

"I know you are," she says, rubbing my cheek. "I think I'll be more prepared this time. Are you mad I brought it up?"

"Mad? Not at all, Baby. Just a little surprised since our friends just got here and we have the party to go to."

She slips off the bed and I can tell by her body language that she's hurt. I go to her when she starts shuffling through one of her dresser drawers, slamming it shut. She turns around, running right into my chest. I wrap my arms around her and whisper, "I want to talk about this. Please don't be upset."

Against my chest, she sniffles. In a muffled, tear-laced voice, she says, "I don't even know how I feel right now. I was just telling you what's going on in my head without thinking."

"I want you to always do that." I lean back so I can look her in the eyes. "Mallory, I love you and you know I want to have kids. I just want to make sure we're ready, like *really* ready, for anything that happens. I'll be honest with you here, I feel like I just got you back a few months ago. You're laughing more and you're happy again. I worry, that's all. But if you feel ready, then I am, too."

She smiles. "Thank you."

When she turns to leave, I grab her and turn her back around, to add, "Don't ever feel like you can't talk to me about what's on your mind. Okay?"

"Okay." After both of us take a deep breath, she says, "We should get out there before they burn the house down. You remember what happened the last time Zach got Sunny to light the barbeque pit."

"You take a shower and I'll go." I walk around the bed, grabbing my board shorts and slip them on before heading to the door. When I open it, I glance back. She opens her bikini drawer but stops. Her head is down and I can't quite tell her expression from here, but I can tell her mood. She's somber. She's remembering...

30

EVAN

We've been married just over three years and it's been better than I could've imagined. And I had imagined that being married to Mallory would be pretty damn good. We've both been busy with school and in the last year, Mallory was promoted to Director of Literacy for the North Shore district of public libraries. I received my Masters two months ago. Three weeks ago I started into the Ph.D. program. I was told if I apply myself, I can graduate in three years. Since I started the summer program, I'll cut another semester off that time. So, as a couple, we've worked together to get our lives where we want them to be.

To the outside world, we have no concerns at all. But to those close to us, they know the truth.

Last fall, we found out we had a little 'accident' on the way. I don't think either of us were shocked that we got pregnant on our vacation to Mexico. Mallory's luggage was lost – and never found – including her birth control pills. One margarita led to another which in turn led to our loss of better judgment and me proclaiming that the 'pull-out' method is legit birth control. Well, *whatever*, anyway, she ended up pregnant and after the shock wore off, we were thrilled.

Sure, we'd casually talked about kids to our family, but it all seemed to be future talk. So even though the news of a baby on the way was a surprise, it wasn't unwelcome. Over the first trimester, it was fun to lie in the hammock and talk about names and what he/she might look like, act like, and what bad habits of ours they would pick up. We laughed a lot just like our normal days, but each smile now held anticipation for the future.

Mallory packed up the books in one of the extra bedrooms that we had made into a library and had me move them into the other spare room. She sketched mural ideas on a pad – one for a boy and one for a girl. She laughed all the time and was the happiest I'd ever seen her. I would catch her watching me with a smile on her face when she thought I wasn't aware. She told me that she hoped the baby looked like me. I hoped the baby looked like her and had her disposition.

But unexpectedly last winter, we lost our baby. No one could explain it. No reasoning. No changing the outcome. No more smiles. No more laughter. No baby. We were left numb to the world. We didn't fight, but we didn't talk much either. I was stressed and worried.

Mallory threw the book "Nineteen-Thousand Names and Their Meanings" away. She moved the boxes from the guest room back into the bedroom and made it the library again. She worked late and ate little. She didn't smile and she didn't laugh. *She cried instead*. Hurt lived inside of her. She felt she had let me down. No matter how much I talked about it with her, comforted her, or tried to convince her otherwise, she didn't believe me. She carried the burden of loss squarely on her shoulders despite what I said.

By spring, I saw glimpses of *my* Mallory again. The sparkle slowly came back to her eyes. I started to see her smile more regularly and then I heard the best sound I had ever heard. We were making dinner and I was telling her about my car and how it sputtered that afternoon—not exactly funny if you ask me, but she seemed to think so. She burst out laughing, to the point of hysterics. She was holding her stomach, bent over, tears started filling her eyes. She kept saying things about the over-the-top love I have for my car. With a huge weight lifted from my heart just from the sound of her laughter, I burst out laughing too, her happiness contagious.

As she dabbed her eyes with a paper towel, she looked up at me with the biggest smile I'd seen in months, took a deep breath, and said, "I really needed that."

I kissed her lightly on the lips, and replied, "So did I. I love you."

It threw me off a little that she brought up the topic of kids today. I had no idea what she thought anymore in regards to having a family, so the conversation today actually relieves me. I still want what Mallory wants, and if that's kids, then we should start our family. I'm not gonna lie though. Just like before, it scares the shit out of me to have someone so tiny and helpless completely relying on me for survival. I don't want to fail as a parent. But right now, I don't want to fail as a husband. I'll give her the child she wants when she's ready.

After cleaning up in the guest bathroom, I walk out through the living room and open the doors to join Sunny and Zach who are currently messing with the pit.

"What's up, brah?" I say to Zach, laying a low five down on him. "Sunny." I hug her.

"Not too bad this fine Fourth of July. How's it hanging with you?" Zach asks, popping the top off a bottle of beer.

Sunny looks past me, and asks, "Where's Mallory?"

I thumb over my shoulder. "She's showering. She'll be out in a minute."

"That girl takes more showers than anyone else I've ever known. Seriously, Evan, your sex drive is impressive, but I'm starting to worry about my bestie's girlie parts. Give her a chance to recover from all the sex you demand." She's smiling and I know she's joking.

I wiggle my eyebrows at her and grin. "I can't help that your best friend can't keep her hands off of me."

I feel a light shove on my shoulder as Mallory comes up behind me and says, "You talking smack about me?"

"Never." I grab her arm and pull her toward me as she laughs and tries to escape. "Where do you think you're going, pretty girl?"

She laughs as I wrap around her from behind, hugging her in my arms.

I whisper, "I love you so much."

She stills, turns her head, and kisses my cheek. "I love you, too."

Turning with my back to the others, I whisper in her ear, "Are we good, Baby?"

"We were never bad," she answers, rubbing her hand on top of mine.

At that, I release her. She drags her hand across my stomach as she walks away. Mallory greets Sunny with a hug. After, Sunny grabs Mallory's hand and announces, "We're going for a walk. You guys make the burgers."

They walk around the large palms to the open beach as

Zach opens another beer and hands it to me. Just as I take a swig, he says, "We got married yesterday."

I spew my beer as I look at him shocked. "What?"

"Yeah, we did the deed and made it official."

"Why didn't you tell us? How can you be here unwrapping hamburger meat like it's no big deal when you went off and got married? That's fucking crazy."

"It's not a big deal to unwrap this meat." He laughs. "Dude, relax. Anyway, I just told you," he says, rubbing my left shoulder. "It was me, not you."

I roll my eyes. "I obviously don't have a problem with marriage," I say, pointing at my wife walking down the beach with *his* wife. "I'm just shocked. You've always said you don't need a piece of paper to show commitment. What changed your mind?"

Zach points down at the girls this time. "She did. Sunny wanted to get married and I finally realized that I want what she wants."

I would usually call him a pussy for making a statement like that, but I can't since I feel the same way about Mallory. Instead, I nod. "I know what ya mean."

We sit down and clink our bottles together. Zach says, "My parents were thrilled since they thought I'd never get married. Her parents were pissed that they weren't invited."

"How you gonna smooth that over?"

"It's already taken care of. My parents are hosting a reception. After a lot of back and forth, it will be in Denver. That way her family and friends can be there and my family and their friends can fly in from New York. All's good and the in-laws are happy."

I look over at Zach. I've always been able to talk to him and he never lays judgments on me, so I bring up a topic that we've all learned to tiptoe around. "Do you want to have kids?"

He looks at me and smiles around the lip of the bottle. After taking a swig, he says, "Yeah. Being with Sunny makes me want them. It's a win-win situation. If we have girls, they'll probably be like their mother and if we have boys..." He laughs to himself. "...Okay, maybe I drag down her gene pool a little. Either way, they'll surf."

"Is that why you stay in Hawaii? Don't your parents want you back in New York?"

"Sure. But I'm not going. I'm living the life I want, and now I'm married. Our life is here. I may not have the money you've got coming in monthly, but we've got good jobs and I've got a nice inheritance. We can have a good life here. Know what I mean?"

I nod because I do know what he means. I stand up to flip the burgers just as Zach stands up and grabs a bottle of water out of the small fridge under the grilling island.

He leans against the counter, and asks, "How's Mallory doing these days?"

Another topic we as a group tiptoe around. "She's better, more like her old self." I set the spatula down, look out to see where the girls are, then confess, "She wants to try." I don't have to say more. He knows what I mean.

"Yeah? How d'you feel about it? Last time was an accident. This time will be planned?"

I take a long pull from my bottle before grabbing a water for myself. Pacing my drinking is key tonight. "It's like you said, I want what she wants."

He nods in approval.

I look at him, roll my eyes, and ask, "What?"

"You, man. You've changed."

"Oh, it's all because of Mallory. Fuck." I shake my head.

"I hate to think what it'd be like, what *I'd* be like, if I hadn't met her."

"You'd be an asshole."

"Thanks," I say.

"Best not revisit the past. It was fun for a while..."

"Yeah, fun for a while." He pushes off the counter and we give each other a brotherly hug.

"You never could keep your hands off each other. Fuck, some things never change!" Murphy bellows from inside the house.

We turn around to see him walking out with a twelve pack under one arm and his other around a bag of groceries.

"Murphy!" We announce in unison. I take the groceries and Zach takes the beer.

Fist bumps turns into chest bumps. I ask, "Where's Caroline?"

"Resting. Long flight. You'll see her at the party."

"I know Mallory will be disappointed. I was hoping to see her sooner too."

"Trust me, dude. You do not want to see her with jetlag. It's not pretty. I've learned the hard way."

We laugh and pop open a beer for him while sitting down to enjoy some long overdue brah time, just like old times.

Thirty minutes later, the girls come back up the beach. They're laughing and having a good time. Sunny was there in ways that I couldn't be for Mallory months ago and it only strengthened their already tight bond. It's good to see them together having a good time. I sit down in a chair next to the guys. They toss me another ice cold beer straight from the cooler and we catch up.

After eating, we all horse around on the beach with a lame game of football.

"Seriously, Murph, when you come back to Hawaii, leave your fur coat at home," Zach says. "The Wildlife Department is gonna think a bear escaped from the zoo." We burst out laughing as Murphy turns in a circle trying to check out his fuzzy back like a dog chases his own tail.

Eventually, we decide to get dressed for the party, so the gang leaves. Mallory starts getting dressed while I shower. When I get out, I wrap a towel around my waist and shave.

She's putting on her makeup, but stops to look at me, watching me. I flash her a smile, which makes her laugh. "Things already feel so different, don't they?"

"What do you mean?" I ask, tapping the water from my razor.

"Sunny and Zach got married without including us and we're talking about kids again. I think we're all growing up."

"Don't say that," I joke. "I want to be young and irresponsible forever."

She laughs again. Turning her back to me, and says, "Zip me please."

"My pleasure. You look pretty."

"Thanks babe." She turns around and kisses me quickly. "Is it strange that I still get nervous going to your parents' Fourth of July party every year?"

I brush her long wavy hair over her shoulders before answering, "No, I do too. But I think we proved to everyone years ago how much we love each other, so I don't think anyone even remembers the incident anymore."

"I'm hoping you're right, but Noah calling you a murderer and all the yelling seems kind of memorable to me."

"Me too, but it pisses me off, so I try not to think about it."

"Probably best," she says, smacking my ass.

"We can be late if you want to."

She stops what she's doing and looks at me in the reflection of the mirror. "Evan, good God, you're insatiable."

"Is this news?"

She laughs. "Guess not, but the answer is no... for now." She applies lipstick and asks, "You ready?"

I laugh this time. "As I'll ever be."

31

EVAN

Taking Mallory's hand, I help her out of the car, then tip the valet guy as we pass. We smile as we walk along the path, remembering 'that' spot along the house in particular. I can hear the music before we even round the corner.

"Evan, I don't want to leave our home," Mallory says, stopping me and pulling me off the path into a hibiscus bush.

She says this every time we see my parents because they always offer me my old job, with very good benefits, if we move to New York. I look around. No one has seen us. When I turn back to her, I say, "I don't either, Baby." I squeeze her hand tighter.

She nods, reassured and we join the party that's in full swing. Gail greets us as soon as we make our way around the corner to the pool area. Yeah, I can finally call her Gail instead of Ms. Chart. "You two don't visit enough," she says, hugging Mallory.

Mallory say, "You know newlyweds..." She leaves the sentence unfinished.

"You just celebrated your third anniversary," Gail says, "Marriage is still wonderful?"

"Better with every year," Mallory responds.

As I hug Gail, I say, "It's good to see you. Where's Bill?"

"Oh, I don't know. Around here somewhere. Make sure to find him. You know how much he enjoys chatting with you."

"Yeah, I will."

Mallory leans forward and asks her, "How was the honeymoon?"

"Cold. Remind me to never leave Hawaii again," Gail laughs before excusing herself to say hi to other guests.

"I haven't seen my parents since yesterday at breakfast." Standing on her tiptoes, Mallory asks, "Do you see them?"

"Ummm." I look around. "I think that's...yep, they're by the bar. I'd recognize that Hawaiian shirt anywhere." Her dad bought it the other day when he arrived and has been wearing it ever since. Clay and Elise are visiting, our treat, for three weeks. They've been staying at my parents' house, which they love. My parents flew in almost two weeks ago and the four have been having a blast together. I never thought they would get along so well, but here they are, proving us all wrong. Mallory is thrilled.

After hugging her parents, my mom wraps her arm in Mallory's, and says, "I'm so glad you're here. Your mother and I have had so much fun. I have to tell you all about it."

When they walk off, I stay and hang with 'the Dads' and make small talk about the weather here in Hawaii compared to New York and Denver. It's riveting... not. I stay until I see my excuse to get away— Kate walks out of the house. Rescuing Mallory, I drag her with me and hug Kate being careful not to wake the baby. I glance at Mallory quickly before I ask, "Can I hold Caroline?"

"Boy, I don't even get a verbal hello anymore. It's all about the baby," Kate jokes.

"Hi, Kate," Mallory whispers, hugging her.

"Here ya go, Uncle Baby Bro. I'm gonna go find my husband—"

"Fuzzy the bear is over with Dad by the buffet table."

"Stop that. You're just jealous," Kate says, "I like his man-sweater and it keeps the other skanks away."

"Oh, I bet it does," I add, laughing. She pushes me on the shoulder then hands me my niece.

"I'm gonna find Liam. Will you be okay with her for a few minutes?"

I nod, looking down at the baby. Caroline opens her eyes and looks around. She turned one last month and I can't believe how much she's grown since we saw her at Christmas. I just hope she remembers me.

Mallory strokes the baby's hair with her finger, then kisses her lightly on the forehead. Caroline seems to remember me as she looks up and a small smile graces her face. She stretches then yawns and seems to be more awake now, but still comfortable in my arms.

"She's beautiful," Mallory says. The thing I notice most though is how happy Mallory looks. She doesn't look sad or envious, just happy. "Even more than I remember. She looks a lot like Kate and your mother." She touches her little fingers and sighs. "She has blue eyes like yours. Runs in the family."

"They've darkened in the last couple of months."

Mallory looks from me to the baby and then back up and asks, "Can I hold her?"

She's cautious, almost seems nervous. "Of course." I look down at Caroline, and she babbles. Whispering just to the baby, I say, "Your beautiful Aunt Mallory is going to hold you now, baby girl." I set her in Mallory's cradled arms and watch as my wife falls into mother mode.

She nuzzles her nose against Caroline's who then starts to giggle. Mallory walks to a nearby chair and sits down rocking the baby in her arms. When Caroline is fully awake, Mallory lifts her upright and talks to her, both enjoying their time together.

My dad comes from behind me and asks discreetly, "Evan, may I have a word with you?"

Here it comes... again. Glancing quickly back to Mallory, she gives me a pointed look. She knows. "Sure," I answer, knowing this game. I can't blame him for trying. He wants his family together.

We go to the bar and order beers. I take a few sips before he finally says, "I'm promoting Kate."

"Oh, wow!" I straighten my shoulders back and look at him surprised. "I didn't expect that."

"She's earned it and I need to start thinking about retiring. There are things I want to do in life and running Ashford Holdings is a twenty-four hour, seven day a week job. Your mother wants me home more and I'm ready to be home. With Caroline and..." He pauses in thought or reflection. "Well, I know all you kids are going to be having kids and I want to be around to enjoy them."

"I think Kate will do a fine job. Does she know?"

"Yes, I spoke to her before we left New York. She's a hard worker and dedicated, probably more than she should considering she has a one year old. But Murphy deciding to stay home, though unusual, has made it easier on her. He brings the baby up to the office often and they have lunch together, sometimes dinner up there too. I can't say I understand Murphy's decision to stay home and raise Caroline, but it works for them and that allows Kate to do the outstanding job she's been doing, so I appreciate what he's sacrificed."

I take a gulp from my beer as he continues, "Yeah, I can't say I always understand what goes through Murphy's head, but as a couple they're making things work for them and I find that admirable."

"So you've forgiven him for knocking your daughter up out of wedlock?" I laugh.

He laughs. "I don't like to revisit *that* memory."

"Yeah, I guess a father wouldn't. They've remedied it, so all's well."

My dad nods and smiles. "They're happy. That's what matters."

We toast to that.

"I'm making the announcement," my dad explains, "but I wanted to talk to you first."

"I appreciate it. Kate has earned the promotion and will make a great president one day."

He nods again then makes his way to the microphone.

I rejoin Mallory who is handing the baby to Gail who wants to show her off to some of the party guests. I tell Mallory what my dad said to me just as he announces that Kate will be the new Director of Development for North America. Her promotion puts her in direct succession to take over for him in a few years.

Mallory squeezes my hand and I squeeze back, letting her know that I'm good with that decision. My life is here with her, not in Manhattan.

She pulls me by the hand, and offers, "You wanna go for a walk down on the beach?"

"Sure."

After setting my drink on the bar, we work our way down the stone steps and onto the beach.

She holds my hand and we walk just where the water meets the sand. At home, we try to walk along the beach and just touch base with each other. It's always a nice way to wind down after our hectic day. I like that she wants to do that even here.

Looking up at me, she smiles. "We've spent so many good times here on this beach. I always enjoy being back and being alone with you."

"Yeah, I do too." I stop, taking her other hand in mine. "I don't know if I've told you lately, but I think you're even more beautiful than when I met you."

She lifts my palm to her lips and kisses it. "Thank you. I think the same about you, all the time."

"Life is busy these days."

"I love our life, Evan."

"You look happy."

"I am. I have you and a beautiful home and a job I like. I could almost say life is perfect." She turns and looks out at the ocean.

We stop and I wrap my arm around her shoulder as we face the sea and admire the setting sun.

She looks back at me and says, "I'm really proud of you and all you've accomplished."

I bend down and pick up a broken seashell and throw it, skipping it into the water. "I feel good. I think we're both in a really good place." I see an iridescent shell and pick it up. Bending over, I rinse it in the water before I give it to her. "You can add this to our collection."

She examines it. "It's beautiful. Good find."

"I have a keen eye for beautiful things." I grab her and pull her to me.

"Are you calling me a thing?"

"You missed the beautiful part."

She stands on her tiptoes and kisses my neck before she pulls me back toward the steps. "C'mon, the night is young and we still have some partying to do."

Two hours later, I'm hanging with the boys, and Caroline, watching the girls dance, including our moms. I let my eyes wander down the curves of Mallory's body thinking about how I'm going to lick, suck, and rub up against every inch of it later.

Gail takes Caroline from Murphy just as Zach nudges me. Both of us are heavy-lidded from the alcohol, but still can appreciate how sexy our girls are, even if they are taunting us. "I need to fucking go," he says, smirking. "I have some honeymoonin' to get to."

"Take a cab."

"It's already waiting out front."

"Congrats again, man." I grab him into a one-armed hug.

"Yeah, look at me, all married and shit. I fucking love that I get to take that little woman home and legit make love to her now. Who could've predicted that?"

With a chuckle, I ask, "You weren't making legit love to her before?"

"Eh, you know what I mean. I'm drunk. I'm going. Surfin' at ten, cools?" We do a very sloppy version of our handshake as I nod.

When Kate joins Murphy, I saunter over to my wife and rub against her from behind. My hands slide around her hips.

Her hands snake behind and she pulls my hips closer. I know she can feel my erection. Tilting her head back, she sighs, "Evan."

I grab one of her hands and pull her from the dance floor and we make our way up the path. Not waiting around for the fireworks, holiday toasts, or goodbyes. I need to be in her. I need to be home with her and I need to fuck her.

We hop into the waiting cab, and I give the driver directions. When I look at Mallory, she's tired and has closed her eyes. "Don't fall asleep," I whisper, "I have plans for you."

A sly grin crosses her lips and then she sits up a little straighter, opening her eyes. "Care to share?"

"Nope. Just be prepared."

She raises a challenging eyebrow up, and says, "Bring it on, Surferboy. Bring. It. On."

We're home in a flash and as soon we walk in the front door, I grab her arm and spin her around. "Here will do."

I see confusion in her eyes before clarity sets in. She stands there and looks at me as if waiting for me to make the next move... like I wouldn't. I shake my head, and smirk. "My beautiful wife, you underestimate the power I have over your body."

"Remind me then."

I scoop her up and toss her over my shoulder before she can resist. Laughter and giddiness surround us as I toss her on the bed in front of me. Her skirt flops up on her lap exposing her very skimpy, very sexy little panties. I point. "I want those off."

She lays there watching my hands as I unbutton my shirt, keeping her eyes focused on my fingers. I reach for the waistband of my pants and start unbuttoning those too, but stop. "Mallory, panties. Now!"

Pulling them off quickly, she tosses them at me. They hit my chest, then drop to my feet.

I watch her as she leans back on her elbows, tilts her head, and licks her lips. I drop my pants and kneel down at the base of the bed. "Nothing like the real thing, Baby."

Her lids seem to grow heavier as her body falls back. I

rub my nose along the inside of her thigh before kissing her clit. She encourages me by spreading her legs even further and moaning my name. My cock is hard and pressed against the side of the bed as my tongue works with precision. I know her, her body, and what gets her off. I fucking love getting her off.

When her hands find my head, she holds me tighter to her, pulling my hair. I start fucking her with my tongue, alternating with sucking. "Evan! That feels so... Fuck! I'm already so close, babe," she cries out, arching her back up and pushing herself against my mouth even harder. Her hips start moving wildly as I try to hold her steady on the bed. She tenses before the little sexual earthquakes take over, and she calls my name. As she slows, I lick her sensitivity and slide left, dragging my days' growth against her skin. She squirms again when I suck on the skin at the top of her thigh—hard and fast. I hear her gasp as she sits up to look at me. Suddenly her hands release my head, then her body drops down like a weight back to the bed.

Proud of the deep red hickey I've given her, I run my fingers over it, and then tend to my cock that is throbbing for her. I stand up quickly and command, "Mallory, move up higher on the bed."

She scrambles up with a mixture of excitement and lust in her eyes. I reach into the nightstand drawer and pull her birth control pills out. I hold the pink disc in the air and tell her, "I don't want you taking these anymore. Alright?"

I catch a glint of light in her eyes and a small smile plays on her lips.

I ask her again to make sure we're on the same page. "You understand what I'm saying, right?"

She swallows and responds, "Perfectly."

I toss the pills in the garbage pail across the room and

climb onto the bed. As I hover over her, I lean down and kiss her on the neck. When I lift up, I see she has the beginnings of tears in her eyes. I whisper, "I'm going to give you babies, Mallory. Everything is going to be perfect. I promise you we'll have a family."

She nods as her legs wrap around my waist and I make love to her.

32

MALLORY

I turn my head and see Evan deep in sleep next to me. His sweet slumbering face makes me smile. I look out the window across the room. The sun is starting to peek above the water.

Carefully and quietly, I slide out of bed. Once in the bathroom, I giggle that my dress never even came off. It came *up*, but not *off*. I use the restroom, then straighten my dress the best I can before brushing my teeth. Tiptoeing back into the bedroom, I sneak out through the large sliding glass door, not bothering to close it behind me. I settle on the double lounge chair and lean back to enjoy the beauty that surrounds me.

I'm not out here for even five minutes when I hear, "What are you doing out here when you could be in bed with me?" Evan asks, his voice groggy from sleeping. I look up over my shoulder and he yawns while scratching his stomach. He's wearing a pair of black boxer briefs like when we first met. I smile from the memory.

I scoot over on the chaise and pat next to me, hoping he'll join me. He does and then he pulls me to his side, wrapping his arm around me. His hand rubs my stomach gently. The sweet gesture gives me security, warmth, and makes me feel loved. I lean over and kiss his chest. "I love you, Evan."

"I love you too, Baby."

"You really want babies?"

His gaze is fixed on the ocean ahead when he says, "I have the most beautiful girl I've ever known, with a heart to match, wanting to have *my* babies." He looks at me. "I'm no fool, Mallory. I know I'm the luckiest fucking guy in the world, so abso-fucking-lutely, I want babies with you."

I laugh at his response. But deep in my soul, I know that *I'm* actually the luckiest girl in the world. As we sit here on the porch of our beach house holding each other and knowing we've found our soul mates, we also know that we've found our paradise – forever and always together.

33

EVAN

"Don't touch me! You will never touch me again, Evan Ashford!"

"Baby, *pleeeasssee*. I'm so sorry—"

I watch as she struggles, as she screams words that don't make any sense, words of hate and the pain I'm causing her. My hand goes to my head, my fingers weaving harshly through my hair while feeling completely helpless.

She cries, the sound breaking my heart. I would do anything to take her pain away. *Shit, I thought this is what she wanted.*

A woman shouts from behind me, "One more big push, Mallory, and your baby will be here. C'mon, you can do it. *Puuuuussssshhhh!*"

Mallory grabs my hand and pulls me to her. Her eyes lock on mine as she whispers, "I love you, Evan."

"I love you too. I'm here. It's gonna be okay. Now push."

She nods, closing her eyes tight and starts to push while grinding her teeth together. Mallory's grip on my hand feels as though she might break my fingers, but I don't care. She needs me and if this is all I can do for her right now, I'll do it.

Mallory screams and a little cry from behind me echoes hers.

"It's a boy," the doctor calls from the end of the gurney.

I stand there frozen to my spot, Mallory's hand loosening around mine. "Evan." Tears stream down her face and my hand automatically goes to her cheek. Wiping away her tears, I try to comfort my wife. "We have a son," she says, our eyes connecting. "Go to him."

As if my feet need her permission before moving, I'm instantly standing in front of my baby, my son, as he is quickly cleaned, weighed, and measured. A nurse wraps him like a burrito in a blanket and holds him out for me.

I take him in my arms, and it's the most natural thing I've ever felt, the bond already existing between us. My love for this child is overwhelming, and obvious, as a tear drops onto his forehead.

A scuffle, along with loud beeping and soft sirens breaks into my peaceful moment as a nurse brushes past me in haste to get to Mallory.

"It's dropping. We've got 68... 65... 63... 60. Still dropping."

"Prepare the defibrillator."

"I need ten more seconds."

"Stay with us, Mallory."

I'm stuck in a haze of commotion. Feeling like my life has truly just begun with this baby, when I see everyone in the room rushing to my wife, I realize my life is about to end.

A nurse stops me as I start to rush to her side. I want to show her our baby, to show her how perfect and beautiful he is and to tell her how perfect and beautiful she is. I want to save her, but the nurse says, "Stay back."

I break away and try cutting through while cradling our baby protectively to my chest. The nurse yells for me to stay put, but I can't stand back and wait. I have to get to her. Mallory has her eyes closed. She looks so peaceful, like she's in a well-deserved rest. But the words of panic surrounding her, around us, don't match the serene scene of her sleep.

"Her pulse is steady at 55."

I drop down and put my lips to her ear. "*Mallory?* Wake up, Mallory. I need you. Our son needs you. He needs his mama."

A tear hits her cheek as I listen to the sounds of the machines regulate and calm. The chaos of a moment before slows and balances around us.

"She's steady at 70 and opening her eyes."

I feel the tension release as relief settles in. I breathe, welcoming the air into my lungs, unaware I wasn't breathing before. When I glance down at our baby, his eyes are closed. He's content in my arms, oblivious to the previous drama. I reach down and take Mallory's hand as her eyes slowly open. She seems out of sorts at first, until her eyes land on me, and then him, and then a slight grin graces her perfect features.

She tries to speak, but nothing comes. She tries again. "Hi." Her voice is scratchy and jagged, but sure and strong.

I can't stop the smile that crosses my face. "Hi, pretty girl," I say, pushing the hair off her forehead to kiss her there. Her eyes go back to the baby. "I think you know this little guy." I hold my arms out as she weakly lifts hers, taking our son in her arms for the first time.

"Mrs. Ashford, how do you feel?" a nurse beside me asks.

She doesn't take her eyes off the baby. I understand. I can't take mine off of her. She replies with tears in her eyes and the sweetest of smiles, "Thankful."

34

MALLORY

In the future...

MY HAMMOCK SWAYS gently in the wind as I watch them play. I still can't believe how blessed my life is. Evan loves me with an unwavering passion and he loves our children even more than that.

He chases two sun-bleached blondes and a strawberry blonde. All boys and all look a lot like their father in coloring. All of them gifted with the true charms and features of the Ashfords with a little Wray mixed in for balance. Our little Ashford clan – they're ours—our hearts, our love, our complete lives.

Evan pretends to run as fast as he can, and yet, a three-year-old is outrunning him, dodging his grasping hands and giggling. Then he 'lets' his daddy catch him. His daddy grabs him with both hands and tosses him into the sunshine filled sky of paradise. I hold my breath until he safely returns to his daddy's arms again. I smile and laugh at my silliness. He would never drop him, but I can't help my cautious maternal instinct from coming out.

He waves his hand in my direction, our youngest copying his dad and waving too. I smile and wave back. Then he tries to wrangle the other two. A quick round-up of the kids and they come racing toward me. I should brace myself. They will barrel into me if I'm not careful. I'm always home-base, the finish line, *home*. I love it, but I should steady myself for the impact all the same.

Their daddy always loses to them... only them, sometimes me too. He loves us that much that he doesn't mind losing to us, *only* us. He has a strong competitive side that is always ever present when it comes to games and such with others.

Three kids come charging onto the patio and grab onto my legs and waist.

"I won!" our oldest son Kai exclaims.

"No, I did!" Duke whines, "I was first. Tell them, Mommy."

"It was a close call. I thought you both came in first."

"I come fwurst, Mama," Reef, my littlest, says, looking up at me after wrapping his arms around my leg.

I lean down and say, "Yes, you did, honey."

"No fair! You always tell him that and it's never true," Kai complains.

I smile at my seven and my five-year-olds. "Come on, guys. He's only three. Let's just humor him, okay?" I wink at them, my signal to let it go.

They huff and go inside as my husband wraps his arms around me and hugs me tight. I love the smell of his salty ocean skin mixing with his natural sexiness. He's all man and he's all mine. He kisses the top of my head, and asks, "Did you get to relax?"

I lean against him, molding my body to his. "I did. Thank you. Did you have fun?"

"Yeah, they really are getting fast. I held my own though," he says proudly.

I rub my palm flat against his abs, letting my fingers enjoy the feel of the sculpted muscle beneath his skin. "I just bet you did."

"I'm squmched, Dada."

We laugh and look down at Reef, who has remained wrapped around my leg the whole time.

Evan releases me and laughs. Patting Reef's head, he apologizes, "Sorry, buddy. Sometimes your Dada needs a Mama hug too."

He looks up between us as if trying to comprehend what he means but his curiosity is short lived as he gets distracted by his green Hot Wheels car that he spots on the chaise.

"You need help with dinner?" my dear husband asks.

"Wanna help me make a salad?" I give my most sincere smile, hoping to get a few minutes alone with him, even if it is just to make dinner, before the kids need us again.

"I'll help you with whatever you need, pretty girl."

He smacks my ass as he follows me inside. I yelp, but secretly I love it. The sting he left behind tells me he's feeling playful. Maybe we'll have some *real* alone time tonight... after the kids have gone to bed.

During dinner we talk about the trip that Evan and I are taking tomorrow. We remind them that Ms. Chart is in charge at all times and that we'll Skype with them every day from New York.

Since I've been pregnant and had little ones for the last eight years, Evan and I haven't had time to get away just the two of us, except for a few one-night escapes to a local resort on the island. Or we traveled with them to visit my family or his. I couldn't stand the thought of being away from the kids, but I knew it was time to do my duty as an Ashford and make an appearance at the annual company holiday party.

I went to several of the holiday parties, including the one where Evan proposed to me, before getting pregnant with Kai, but that was ten years ago. It's time to go visit and I know that Evan is looking forward to some 'us' time. I am too, but my heart hurts thinking about being away from the children for five nights.

After tucking them in, we flop down on the loveseat in our bedroom. This is where we always reconvene after a long day—a ritual we started too long ago to remember when. I look forward to it every night though.

Our hands find each other and our fingers entwine silently as we sit in reflection of the day that has faded into night.

"This will be a good trip," he says, resting his head against the arm of the couch. "They'll be okay without us for a few days. It will be good for them."

"Are you trying to reassure me or convince me?"

He chuckles. "Both."

"This will be good for all of us." I look at our connected hands. Always nervous when it comes to spending a lot of money, I say, "I bought a few things over the last couple of weeks, like shoes and stuff. And I pick up my dress for the party from the designer when we're in Manhattan."

"You can spend money, Mallory. We've got plenty of it. It's all yours, so do as you please."

"Don't say that. I don't want the responsibility."

"Welcome to my teen years."

"Not funny," I smirk.

"Kind of funny?" he smirks back, his eyes tired.

"Kind of," I agree, a relaxed smile crossing my lips as I close my eyes.

"You want to take a shower with me?" he asks casually, but I can hear the deviousness in his tone.

I roll my head to the side and see that sneaky look firmly in place in the shaded blues of his eyes, just as I suspected. My man is feeling frisky, so I play along. "A *shower* shower or a get ourselves dirty shower?"

His hand rubs lazily over his stomach. "A shower where I can worship that body of yours."

I laugh because he makes me smile and feel pretty though I lost my flat stomach after having our second child. The endless crunches couldn't save my belly, but I look good for a mother of three. The jogging leaned me out overall post-babies, but my hips are still a bit wider than before. I've always liked my breasts. He loved them before and he still loves them now. After kids and with age, they aren't as perky as they once were, but if you listen to Evan, my body is the same one I had pre-kids. He loves me as I am, whether I'm a size two or a size-ginormous. I'm not big, but I'm not a size two either. I hold steady at my current weight and feel pretty damn good about myself.

I can also still work a bikini if my husband is anything to go by as he usually eye-fucks me and becomes very handsy when we're on the beach.

With my back against the armrest, I move my feet to rest in his lap. He starts rubbing them and it feels amazing. "Inside or out?" I ask, smiling, giving into him, wanting him just as much.

"Out."

"Okay, I'll get it started. You grab the towels."

I swing my feet to the ground and head for the French doors. The house that Evan gave me for our wedding has been renovated over the years. What was once a small beach bungalow of 900 square feet has been expanded on all sides to 2800 feet with future plans for a second floor. The bungalow next to ours never went on the market, but Evan came home seven years ago with the property deed in hand. The house was a shack at best and was promptly torn down. It was xeriscaped, palm and banana trees were also planted. We now own almost an acre of beachfront property on the north side of the island. It's our personal piece of paradise.

I step outside the doors and turn on the faucet to the outdoor shower. This was added just over four years ago and we use it a couple times a week. The wall is made of large, smoothed-out lava rocks and gives us privacy while allowing us to enjoy the perfect island weather.

After pulling my shirt over my head, I toss it inside. I reach for the strings of my bathing suit, but Evan joins me and pulls me to him first. No words are exchanged as his hands roam my body, heating me up. It may be Hawaii but it's also December and we get some chilly winds sometimes at night. I feel the hot water spraying from the shower head and step forward, bringing him with me.

We sigh in unison. The warm water eases my muscles and my mind, my body relaxing against him.

Untying the strings around my neck, my top falls, then he catches it on his hands as he squeezes my breasts. The top comes completely off and he tosses it next to my shirt a few feet away.

His lips and nose slide down my neck as he continues massaging my breasts, and whispers, "You are the sexiest woman I've ever seen." I feel his arousal pressing against my back as he drags our heads under the spray, nipping and kissing my shoulder while his other hand deftly unties the bottom part of my bikini. "I want you." His breath hits my wet skin as he turns me around, rubbing his forehead against mine. "Don't ever leave me. I need you too much. You drive me so crazy."

I recognize the anguish mixed into his sexy tone. I almost died giving birth to our first child, and we've been through some tough times, like the miscarriage. So I know he means what he says.

My nails scratch his neck as I fist his hair with my other hand. "I'm not going anywhere. I'll never leave you, Evan." I try to comfort him, but find my hold on him is just as desperate as he smothers my words with kisses and moans.

He pushes me back against the wall of rocks, cushioning the blow with his hands. He slips them out from behind me and steps back, eyeing me from head to toe and back again.

My natural instinct is to cover myself, but he grabs my wrists and stops me. "Don't. You're body is fucking amazing."

The water sprays as it steams up the area around us when it hits the colder air. I sigh, dropping my eyes, "Evan."

"I love you. I love everything about you and trust me, Baby, your body is so sexy."

He sits on the built-in bench and pulls me to his lap as I roll my eyes and smile. He's such a suck-up. I straddle him without a request. I know he likes when I do this and he knows how good it feels to me. I wrap my arms around him and kiss him deeply. I can never get enough of his kisses. Our love flows freely between us when we kiss. My hips start a slow grind that builds quickly. He feels so damn good between my legs.

Evan grips my hips, pulling me down harder and making me moan. I rest my chin against the side of his head, my breath getting away from me. "I want you inside of me when I come, babe."

His hands stop, his breath stammering just before he lifts me up, my weight resting on my knees. I feel the head of his cock and balance myself with my hands on his shoulders before sliding down. I'm not slow or careful and just as it knocks the wind out of me, I cry out. "You feel amazing."

"Fuck, you feel good." With his eyes closed, he leans his head back against the rocks.

I watch him from above. My gorgeous husband has a smirk playing at the corners of his mouth, savoring the feel of our connection. Moving up and down, I use the bench as leverage.

Evan's hands roam my body then land on my nipples. Gentle pinches and soothing circles follow the way he knows I like it – not too rough, but not breakable.

I reach up and take hold of two large rocks with my hands and pull myself up to then slide back down—quicker, quicker, quicker until his voice is rough with desire as he calls to me, "Fuck me, Baby. Yes!"

His words speak to my dirty side, the side that only he brings out of me. Dropping my head down, resting my weight back down on him, I release the rocks and wrap my arms around his neck. I feel it. Deep down inside, I feel what our love twists into when we bond like this. A tightening begins and my thoughts start to spin as I chase an ecstasy that is uniquely ours. "Evan! Yes, keep going. Yes!"

He thrusts faster and faster as I tighten around him, securing myself to him and this feeling.

The fuse is lit and rushes through my body igniting every nerve, making them feel like live wires caught on fire. The pressure sends blissful sparks flying throughout my body. "Oh my God! Evan! Babe!"

Grabbing me by the hips, he slams me down mid-orgasm, his breath hot and eager against my ear. "Fuck! Mallory!!"

He falls apart as I come down, his arms wrapping under mine, his hands holding me tight. Teeth threaten to puncture my collarbone as his harsh breaths try to level. He won't hurt or scar me. He likes to see me in a bathing suit too much for that.

I rub my hand gently down the back of his head and over his shoulders before lifting off of him. I kiss the top of his head then relax back down, curling myself onto his lap.

"About that shower," he says through a sly grin, and we both laugh.

35

MALLORY

After a tearful goodbye with the kids and Ms. Chart, Evan and I catch an early morning flight to New York City. Can't say I'm thrilled with the thirteen hour flight ahead of us, but with a stop in Los Angeles to break it up a bit, it seems somewhat more bearable.

On the journey, I sleep some and read a paperback I'd been meaning to read for ages. I peek over at Evan a lot. I can't help it. I've always been so drawn to him. Obviously the flight attendants are drawn to him as well. I'd like to say I've gotten used to the attention Evan receives, but I haven't. I don't think I ever will. He handles it much better than I do and barely notices anymore, even though he's actually gotten better looking with age. His body can put a twenty-three year old to shame and he's got abs that are utterly lickable. Trust me, I have done this many, many times.

I smile as the attendant walks away rejected. Evan is rolling his eyes. He gets annoyed by the obvious flirters of the world and doesn't understand the fascination until the tables are turned. I've had a few obnoxious admirers myself. He's not been in a fight in years, but he's come close several times. The closest was one time at the grocery store. I had sent Evan, who at the time was holding eight-month- old Kai, to grab a couple of mangoes I'd forgotten to get from the fruit section. I was wearing some cut-offs that were quite short, my green bikini, and a tank top with flip flops—my usual lounge around the house and grocery store attire. I was bent over getting these cookies that Evan loves from the bottom shelf and this young haole stopped, ogled then actually whistled. I jumped up in shock, dropped the cookies, breaking them, and turned around while covering my ass in the process.

Bad timing for that guy.

I caught Evan's glare just over the guy's shoulder. He was so angry—tensed jaw and flexed arms as he gritted his teeth. His look was deadly. If not for Kai, who was sleeping comfortably in his arms, I think that guy would've ended up in the hospital. Maybe it was good timing for that haole, after all. Kai totally saved his ass.

I slide my hand under his on the armrest and curl my fingers with his. He looks over and gives me a soft, tired smile. He takes his black rimmed glasses off, setting them on the tray in front of him, the ones that drive me wild when we play Doctor and patient. I play his patient who is obsessed with her Doctor. Yeah, I make him keep the glasses on for that.

"Dr. Ashford, the Cappuccino you requested," the blonde, leggy first class cabin attendant says, handing it to him while smiling and ignoring me. *Typical.*

He takes it with a thank you and a nod thrown out. Just as she leans in to offer him her services, he turns to me. "I ordered this for you. I know you didn't get yours this morning before we left the house."

The attendant magically disappears. Funny how that happens when they discover he's taken.

"Thank you, babe. I really need it." I take a sip then ask, "You excited to see the house in the Hamptons?"

"Everything will be different this time. It's been so many years since we've been out there. Our first appearance at the party since we've been married."

A lot has changed over the last few years with the company and in the family. This will be the first time we've been back to New York to witness it firsthand.

EVAN

After settling into my old apartment in Manhattan, we shower and ready ourselves for dinner. We're meeting my family for a late reservation at a restaurant in Tribeca.

Watching Mallory, she seems to be debating what to do with her hair. She's wanted to cut it shorter for a while now, but she knows how much I like it long. It seems she lives to make me and the kids happy. I do the same, anything for them.

She settles on leaving it down, pulled forward over her right shoulder. She looks incredible. I stand in awe of her. "Wow!"

A tinge of pink colors her cheeks and it's not from her make-up. I love that she still blushes. I read somewhere once that when you start having sex with a woman they don't blush for you anymore. I'm here to tell you, that's a fucking lie. Sometimes I may have to work a little harder for those pink cheeks, but I still get them.

"You look incredible."

She grabs the end of her skirt and twirls for me. "So you like?"

"I love," I say, grabbing her by the waist and pulling her to me. "And I love you."

"Oh Evan, I love you too." She scoots out of my reach and grabs her shoes, bending over to put them on. She stands up, and declares, "These are my new shoes."

After I pick my jaw up off the floor, I shake my head. "What are you doing to me? We have to leave and all I want to do is—"

"I'm sure your mom will hate them which kind of makes me love them even more." She grabs her purse and heads for the door. "We're gonna be late if we don't leave now. C'mon."

I follow her out of the apartment, pinch her ass, and chase her playfully down the corridor to the elevators. I steal a few kisses from her once inside and on the cab ride over.

We arrive at the restaurant right on time and are led to the table by the hostess.

"Evan! Mallory! I'm so happy to see you," my mom exclaims as we approach.

We do our rounds of hugs and then sit down at the table in the corner of the crowded bistro. My mom leans toward Mallory, and says, "The food is to die for. Literally, to die for."

They start to chat about the menu as the wine is delivered and poured. "A toast in is in order," I say, getting their attention. "To my dad, congratulations on your official retirement. I hope it's fulfilling and relaxing. It's well deserved." I lean forward and lower my voice. "That means you can be lazy now if you want to be."

We all laugh and tap our glasses together.

"Fill me in on the kids."

Mallory fields this question from my mom. "Kai made the select swim team last week. He'll swim competitively starting in the spring."

"That's fantastic," my dad adds, smiling at Mallory.

She smiles, sliding her fingers between mine on top of the table. "He very much takes after his father. He's smart and a truly gifted athlete. And Duke..." She laughs to herself as if she's remembering something clever he did. "He's so much like Evan it's crazy. He wants to be an explorer and travel the world. He loves history and I think he might have a photographic memory. It's amazing what that kid remembers."

"He's also a damn good surfer," I add unabashedly.

"Yes, I can't keep him out of the water. I have to have my eyes on him at all times or he'll slip out to boogie board."

Leaning back, I feel at home, relaxing into the comfortable conversation. "I got both Duke and Kai custom boards this past summer. It's incredible watching them shred the waves."

My parents are looking between us amused by how we finish each other's thoughts. Tapping Mallory's arm, my mom says, "I'm so glad to see you both so happy. It's obvious our grandkids are gifted and take after both of their wonderful parents. Tell me about Reef. I can't believe he's almost four. We are due for a visit. Now that Hugh is retired it will be easier to spend time out there."

Mallory sips her wine, so I start, "Reef is just like his mother. He loves books and is competitive and feisty, strong-willed, so clever, and so damn cute."

"Thank you for emailing," my Mom says, "all of the photos and this new Skyping business is fun."

"Yes, I'm thankful for modern technology. I can see them

growing and changing so much every time we see them online." My dad then asks the awkward question we forgot to prepare an answer for, "Do you want to have any more kids or are you done at three?"

"I think we're done," I say just as Mallory says, "Yes, more is good."

We look at each other surprised. Okay, so maybe we don't always finish each other's sentences the same. My gut tells me to speak up and remind her of the reality of the situation. "Every time we have another is you taking a risk." I know my parents are listening. How can they not be? They're only two feet if that away from us. But I need to say this.

Mallory lowers her voice to match my tone. "I have easy pregnancies, babe. You know that. You've seen it."

"Yes, you do, but the births aren't."

"I think you're blowing this out of proportion. It only happened one time."

"You fucking died that day—"

"Evan," my dad cautions.

I turn to glare at him. "Dad, you're not a doctor. You didn't almost lose your wife right in front of you while holding your newborn."

Mallory's hand soothes over my forearm. "But I didn't die. See? I'm right here," she says, raising her hands up as if to prove her point. "I'm alive and well."

She knows me too well. Her voice is just a whisper, just for me. "Evan, you heard the doctor. It was a freak of nature type thing, unexplainable, and they never really lost me. I was just unconscious for a minute. I was always alive and with you."

Her soulful eyes pierce my soul and I feel the wetness forming in my eyes. "I don't want to take the risk."

She nods, understanding my point. Shit, I wish this hadn't happened in front of my parents. When I look back up, I see their sympathetic smiles already in place. When my eyes meet my dad's, he says, "We're sorry for touching on a raw subject like that, but Mallory's right. The doctors have given the go-ahead on the last two pregnancies. I know it scared you, but she's safe. She's here and you have three beautiful children. "

"No, it's alright, Hugh," Mallory says, flexing her fingers, trying to loosen the tight grip that I didn't realize I had on her. "We hadn't talked about another child in a while. Time keeps slipping away from us—"

"From all of us, dear. How about dessert?" my mom asks, trying to lighten the mood.

"I'd like the crème brulee," Mallory adds, helping to change the topic.

We spend the next hour finishing off another bottle of wine and our desserts. After our goodbyes, we let my parents take the first cab and wait for another. Mallory is tucked under my arm, her arms wrapped around my middle. We're freezing and yet our insides are warm from the wine, a great meal, and happiness.

"I'm so cold," she says, looking up at me.

I kiss the top of her head as the wind whips around us. Finally a taxi pulls up and we hop in. I give the driver the address, then sit back with my girl. Her right hand is running the length of my thigh and I feel the beginnings of my cock stirring to life. Her hand slides to the inside of my leg, and I warn, "Be careful."

"Or what?" she sits up, whispering into my ear before she gently sucks on my earlobe.

"Or I'm going to take advantage of your innocence."

She laughs. "Is that a threat or a promise, Dr. Ashford?"

"Both."

"Big talker."

"I'll show you big, but it's not going to be my talking."

"That's hot, Evan."

I give her the old smirk. I know it still works on her.

Her hand wanders, teasing me.

Mallory is practically purring when she pulls me by the tie down the hall. Using the door to support her back, her fingers fondle the waist of my pants as she leans forward to rub against me. I can tell the red wine has kicked in. She gets so fucking horny when she's drunk too. "I want you so bad."

"How bad?" I chuckle as I unlock the door.

She stumbles backward into the room when the door opens, but I catch her.

With a smile, she says, "I want your cock inside of my pussy right now. That's how bad, pretty boy."

I shoot an eyebrow up at her. "Pretty boy, huh?"

She taps my chin as she tries to balance in her high-as-fuck heels. "Oh, don't you play dumb, Evan Ashford. You know what you do to the ladies, so don't even play innocent."

I grab her by the waist to steady her, enjoying the show she's putting on tonight. "I don't care about other ladies, only what I do to you. Tell me." I press my lips to her neck and start sucking lightly between kisses. "Tell me what I do to you, Baby."

She exhales a deep breath and moans her pleasure as I start to lick and nibble her soft, sweet skin. "I..." She stops. "It's too much." Her eyes are half-mast, but focused. "More action, less talking."

"Okay, my love. Meet me in the bedroom. I want you naked and on the bed. Alright?"

She nods, not arguing.

Right when she's about to disappear into the room, I add my stipulation. "Hey Mallory?" She stops and looks back over her shoulder. "Leave the shoes on."

She smiles that fucking mischievous smile, one of the many reasons that drew me to her in the first place, then quietly retreats into the bedroom.

I retrieve two glasses of water from the kitchen and some Advil. Hopefully she won't have much of a hangover if she's takes these tonight. I stand in the living room and impatiently count to ten to give her enough time to undress before I enter the room. When I do, all I can manage to say is, "Holy fuck."

She's stretched across the bed on her stomach. Her legs are bent and her ankles crossed in the air, showing me the cherry red soles of her shoes. She watches as I set the ibuprofen and water down on the nightstand and reach for my belt.

Mallory rolls onto her side, propping up on her elbow, and watches me undo my belt, then my button, and finally my zipper as I slowly slide it down. I kick off my shoes and let my pants drop.

As I step out of them, I work my socks off.

"You're a naughty boy going commando at a dinner with your parents." Her voice is seductive, the words drawn out.

"I don't want to think about my parents right now. But I do want to think about fucking my wife until she screams my name."

My shirt gets tossed aside as she teases, "What would your wife think about what you're about to do with me?"

The left side of my mouth slides up, and I wink. "You're about to find out."

The way her body is presented before me makes me

possessive and crazy. I hate the way other men eye-fuck her. She doesn't realize the effect she has on them. It's insane. I'm insane for her. I gently bite her ass. I can't help it. I feel her slap me on the head. We laugh though. Sex is always amazing with her, but it's damn fun too.

"Now roll over. I need to feel these shoes hitting the back of my head as I take you."

36

MALLORY

"Slow down, Kate. I can't run in these shoes."

She stops with her hands on her hips and taps her foot. "Mallory, we're on New York time now, not Hawaiian. We can't be late because they squeezed you in."

"Fine, but these aren't exactly flip flops I'm running in."

"Welcome to my world," she says, pulling the door open.

Two hours later, we're sitting in an ultra-chic, ultra-modern café down in the Meatpacking district. I laugh to myself at that name. I'm sure Evan has gotten a kick out of that name many times too when he lived here.

"You look great, Mallory. You working out?"

"I try to run a few miles every day. Life is good."

"Liam said that Reef's gotten big."

I sip my white wine and smile, thinking of my kids. "Yes, I think he's going to be the biggest of them all one day. He's so tall already." I take a bite of my salad and chew, then add, "I think Caroline should model. She's so pretty and tall herself."

Kate glances around the restaurant before leaning forward as if she's going to share a secret. "She's such a girlie-girl. She's so into clothes and shoes and makeup and boys. Liam's freaking out over her obsession with boys. She's only ten for God's sake." She stabs some lettuce with her fork. "I think I need to get her out of the city soon, maybe to Hawaii for an extended vacation this summer."

"Why? What's going on?"

"I don't want her to grow up being some superficial shell of herself, doing mindless things like shopping all day or hanging out at the country club, or whatever. I want her to use her brain. She's an intelligent girl." She lowers her voice even more. "I caught her pretending to be dumb when she was hanging out with her friends last week. I think it's just to fit in, but they're not worth her time if they don't like her how she is."

I nod in understanding. Kate could model even though she's in her mid-thirties if she wanted to. But she runs Ashford Holdings now. She's branched out in the last two years and raised the stock value to an impressive high. Her parents couldn't be prouder. Murphy works there, overseeing the smaller Pacific/West Coast division, which sends him our way a couple of times a year.

"Being smart *and pretty* didn't work against you. Maybe you're worrying too early," I throw that out there just as a thought.

"I never got sidetracked from my goals. Kids today are so different from us. They want everything handed to them." She sets her fork down with a clang. "Well, I'm not gonna do it. I had to work my ass off to get where I am, and she will too."

"Sounds like a healthy dose of reality is about to come Caroline's way."

She laughs. "Liam thinks I'm too hard on her."

"You'll find a balance. It's tough raising kids sometimes."

"You make it look easy with three."

That makes me smile. "It's not, but I love being at home with them. I'll be honest though. It was hard to give up my job running the Literacy Program. I loved it, but I love these kids and Evan more, so it was easy to know the right path for me. I still volunteer in the library's teaching facility once a week and have a small group of students that I'm teaching to read."

"*See?* Amazing! I never had a doubt you were the one for my brother, the one that would make him happy." She sits back and relaxes as if she's stuffed off half her salad. "He deserved happiness in his life, and suddenly there you were, as if delivered right to him when he needed you most."

"SUNNY RECRUITED Zach and Murphy to build the bonfire. We have to bring the booze and Kate is bringing the food." I shout from the bathroom while shaving my legs in the tub.

Evan peeks around the corner and smiles when he sees me. "What's Sunny bringing?"

I wave my hand in the air. "You know Sunny, she's doing what she does best, delegating."

"Oh yes, that's right," he says, sarcastically. He walks over and sits on the vanity stool after moving it closer to the tub. He's barefoot and wearing a very Hampton-y outfit of khaki cargo shorts and a green Polo shirt. Of course, because it's him, the collar is popped up. Only Evan can pop a collar and get away with it. "We see them all the time in Hawaii, and here we are, in the Hamptons hanging out with them again. You'd think we'd all get sick of each other."

"They're our best friends. We can get sick of each other and still see each other all the time."

He narrows his eyes at me. "That makes no sense."

"Neither did we in the beginning, but here we are."

"I think you love that you tamed the player."

"I think you love remembering what a player you were before meeting me."

"I might, but those memories don't compare to the ones we've made."

"Suck-up."

"I was going for charming."

"Try harder next time."

"Mrs. Ashford, you're a hard ass."

"Speaking of hard asses, show me yours."

"I'll show you mine, if you show me yours."

I toss the razor in the trash can and scoot onto my knees, flashing him my ass.

"You got room for me in that tub?"

"Always."

He sits on the edge fully-clothed and kisses me gently on the lips. I feel melty inside. To my surprise, he gets up and strips down, stepping in with me. He cups my face amongst my squeals of surprise and kisses me before settling back and relaxing together.

"I'M NOT DRINKING THAT SHIT."

"Fuck, Evan, it's Jager. We can't waste it," Zach says, trying to shove the bottle in Evan's face.

Evan laughs and hits it away. "I'm not eighteen, Zach. I can afford the good shit that doesn't permanently damage my organs."

"That shit, *good shit*, bad shit. Shit, it's alcohol, E. Drink it, brah," Murphy adds his two cents.

I stand up ready to intervene. I don't mind my husband drinking, but he shouldn't be hung over at the party tomorrow. "Guys," I start, "we've still got a lot of beer. Let me get you one, Evan."

"Thanks."

"My pleasure," I say, looking over my shoulder and waggling my eyebrows at him as I bend down and dig around in the cooler.

"Actually, the pleasure is all mine, hot stuff."

"You're ogling my ass, aren't you?" I ask without turning back.

"Abso-fucking-lutely."

I laugh until I hear Kate.

"*Sttooooopp it!* I don't want to listen to your lovey-dovey sex-uendoes all night." Kate who is already half a sheet to the wind says, pouting.

Murphy gets up from the where the boys are sitting and moves over to sit next to his wife on the other side of the bonfire. "You feeling left out, Pookie?"

She plops onto his lap and snuggles against him as he holds her. Looking so young and vulnerable in the moment, she's different right now from the Fortune 500 CEO she is every other day. "I miss you all the time. We've been working too much lately," she whispers.

Murphy kisses her on the forehead, and says, "Whenever you need me, I'll be there. Okay? I promise."

She smiles. "I should go to bed soon. I can't be shit-faced for the party."

Murphy stands up still holding her in his arms. "We're heading back to the house. We shall see you tomorrow."

"I told my parents we'd be back by midnight, so they can go to bed," Zach says, looking over at Sunny. "The kids are a handful for people who don't even take care of themselves."

"Chefs, maids, butlers, drivers... yeah, when was that last time they even dressed themselves?" Sunny laughs loudest at her joke.

"We have a maid, sweetie," he says, nudging her with his elbow.

"No, we have a cleaning lady who comes twice a month, which I have to admit, I'm thrilled to have." Sunny drops her head down on Zach's shoulder and rubs his stomach with her hand.

"This is the first time since Natalie was born a year ago that I've been away from her longer than a trip to the grocery store. Is it sad to say I've been thinking about the kids since we left?" Sunny asks, sitting upright.

"Yes!" We all say in unison.

I glance over at Evan. "But I totally understand. I've been thinking about the boys since I talked to them this morning."

I feel Evan drape his arm over my shoulders. "They're fine. Gail said she and Herb are doing fine and that the boys are being good."

"Just seems like a lot to ask of her—"

"Trust me, Mallory, she loves this. If she can raise me and Kate, she can definitely handle our boys."

"Good point."

"Toast," Zach says, tossing me another beer.

They all wait for me to open my can, then Zach says, "To living life in the slow lane and enjoying every minute of it."

We spend another hour around the bonfire until we're too cold to stay any longer.

37

MALLORY

"Mallory, you look beautiful," Claire says, hugging me gently. At least she didn't give me those fake air kisses. She always gives me genuine hugs, which I'm grateful for.

"Thank you. So do you."

"Herrera," she replies, spinning to show me the full ensemble.

"Very beautiful."

She takes me by the hand, and says, "I want to introduce you to one of our newest Directors. He's from Colorado originally, just like you."

"Okay, but have you seen Evan?" I ask, following behind.

"Evan is with some of the board members. He may have found his calling in the Psychology field, but he's always been very talented in the business world."

I usually start tuning her out when she reminisces about the loss of Evan not taking over the family business.

"Kate and Evan," she says, "would make an incredible team."

"I agree, but as you know, he loves his work and he loves being in Hawaii."

She squeezes my hand. "I know. I was just saying, dear." She pulls me toward the bar. "Oh, there's Mike Marks." She whispers as we approach, "I think he's about your age. Maybe you know each other." She stops and faces me still holding my hand. "These parties can get boring. It might be nice to talk to someone about your home state."

"Sure. I just want to see Evan first before meeting everyone else."

She smiles and looks around the room. "Try to hurry. I'm excited to show you off." She points to the corner of the restaurant that was booked for the event. "Evan is over there with Zach and Liam."

"Thanks. I'll see you later."

I work my way across the room, weaving around tables and groups of people talking. When Evan sees me, our silent conversation begins. His eyes smile, crinkling at the corner. His gaze dips down my body, working its way back up to my eyes. My eyes tell him he's the most handsome man in the room and I can't wait to be back in his arms. He brushes his thumb over the side of his parted lips and angles his chin down.

I'm in his arms, closing my eyes as his comfort washes over me. "Hi," I whisper.

"Hi, my love," he says as he nuzzles into my hair.

My arms wrap around his middle without thought, just instinct. Evan's arms tighten around me.

"You look gorgeous." He leans back and tilts his head down to look at my face. "You doing alright?"

"Yes. I just missed you this afternoon when I was getting ready with the girls."

He smiles and touches my cheek, tracing the slight curve of my cheekbone. Being close like this makes me feel complete again. It's a touch that he only shares with me, one that connects us, bonding us through marriage and children and a forever love.

"I missed you too," he says.

"I miss the boys."

"I also miss them." He releases me, and asks, "Can I get you something to drink? I want you to have fun while we're away. You don't get many breaks."

"I don't need many. I'll get one in a bit. I had some champagne at the house with Kate and Sunny earlier."

He nods just as Murphy whacks him on the arm. "Dude, she gets you all the time—"

"I don't mean to steal your boyfriend away, Murph. You jealous?" I say, laughing as I poke Murphy in the ribs. "I should go. Your mom wants to introduce me to 'people.'" I do the air quotes when speaking.

"Come back and visit me when you get chance, sexy woman."

"Oh, you can count on that, babe."

He slaps my ass, making me giggle and garner a few strange looks from other guests at the party.

I look for Claire, but can't find her. I do find the bar though. Needing something to help me relax, I wait on the bartender so I can order a drink to get into the swing of things. I lean on the tall counter and order a Blood Orange Martini.

"Hello."

I turn to look at a man standing next to me. He's wearing a sharp navy blue suit, crisp white shirt, and charcoal grey tie. He looks very money.

"Hello," I reply to be polite. He's tall... and handsome. I'm guessing he's an employee of the company—most likely in the New York office by the looks of his clothes.

"Which office do you work in?" he asks. "I don't remember seeing you downtown."

My amusement shows. "That's because I don't work in the downtown office—"

"I had a feeling because I would definitely remember you. I'm Mike."

He holds his hand out to shake mine. I take it, recognizing him from when Claire pointed him out earlier. "I'm Mallory. Oh wait, you're Mike Marks?"

Now he's amused, or flattered. "Yes, you've heard of me? I hope my reputation doesn't precede me."

"If it's reputable, then you don't need to worry."

"Touché, Mallory."

I take my martini and a few sips. It's warm and sweet sliding down, but shoots straight to my knees as most alcohol does. I lean my elbows on the bar for support and continue. "Claire wanted to introduce me to you or... you to me. Whatever," I laugh. "Apparently, we have Colorado in common."

"Really? Are you from there?" He replies, "I'm from Akron."

I turn, surprised by this revelation. "I've passed through Akron before. I'm from Denver."

"No shit, really? Oh." He shakes his head. "I apologize for my crude language. It slips out more than I like."

"No worries."

"Wow, what a small world."

"Yeah, it is. You live in the city now?"

"Yes, for the last eight years. Chicago before that."

"Do you miss Colorado?"

"I miss the simple life of growing up there, living there, but I enjoy all that Manhattan has to offer." He clinks his glass against mine, eyeing me a little too intensely.

I drink, but start to feel this conversation has gotten a bit intimate for my liking. I peek over at him before making an excuse to leave. "I have to, um... use the ladies room. It was nice to meet you."

"Sure, but promise me you'll look for me later. We can talk about... stuff."

I walk away quickly, glancing back over my shoulder. He's still watching me, so I head for the bathroom to back the lie I told. I run into Kate just as I round the corner.

"Hey, I need you," she says, grabbing a hold of my forearms. "I'm nervous. I'm never nervous speaking in public, but tonight I'm nervous. I just threw up. That's how nervous I am."

I pull her down the dimly lit hallway, closer to the exit door and away from prying eyes and ears. "Snap out of it!" She looks at me stunned. "You can do this. These are your employees. You've just had the best quarter in company history and you have them, just as they have you, to thank for it. Just go out there and thank them."

She smiles, looking relieved. "You're right. I need to keep the focus on them and off of me." She suddenly looks panic stricken again. "Maybe I should do a shot or five."

"No! No shots." I lower my voice and talk her off the ledge. "Speak from your heart, Kate. Let it flow from there."

After taking a deep breath, she looks much calmer. "You're right. I think it's the champagne from earlier that made me throw up. I've been a bit queasy all day. I don't know why today of all days I developed a case of nerves."

I watch as her hand rubs over her stomach and my mouth drops open. *Holy shit!* I keep my thought to myself though. She doesn't need me making her more nervous before her speech. Taking her hand, I start to pull her. "C'mon, let's go get this over with."

But she stops me, then after a pause, says, "Let's go."

She takes another deep breath and slowly exhales.

"You're stalling. Go."

"Alright. Alright, Miss Pushy!" She turns abruptly on her heels and waltzes down the hall looking much more like her normal self, completely in charge, and in control again.

I hear the rain coming down outside and turn around to watch through the glass of the exit doors. I hear the music cease and Kate at the microphone behind me.

"It's raining pretty hard out there."

Turning around, I see Mike standing there looking over my shoulder. Then his eyes meet my slightly irritated gaze.

He leans down. He's too close to me when he says, "After being here for well over an hour, I must tell you, that not only are you the most attractive woman here, but also the most fascinating. If I don't find out more about you soon, you'll remain the most mysterious, so I hope you'll indulge me."

"I'm no mystery, and I'm married," I say, waggling my left hand in the air for him to see the rather large diamond rings placed prominently on the ring finger. "Excuse me, but I'm going to get some fresh air." I'm fast in my escape, no longer worried about niceties.

I push the door outward and step under the large awning. It's freezing out here since it's December, but I'm so annoyed that the cold air feels refreshing. Leaning against a grey shuttered wall, I close my eyes and take a deep breath.

"I can take a hint," Mike says.

Fuck! I open my eyes, shooting invisible daggers at him. "Apparently not. Let me be clear. Please leave me alone."

He takes several steps forward and I take several back. If I take one more step backward, I'm in the rain. I'm starting to feel trapped and a little scared.

"I feel something here," he says, waving between us, "a connection. I don't care that you're married—"

"Well, I *the fuck* do," Evan says. Mike turns around surprised by Evan's sudden appearance.

He tries to make nice by chuckling. "Hey Evan, I was just—"

"I know exactly what you were doing. That's my wife, asshole." Evan shoves him in the chest.

I grab onto Evan's arm. "Stop. He's not worth it. It's no big deal. Okay?"

"Mallory's your wife?" Mike asks, surprised. He knows he's fucked up big time. The look that people get when they know they've screwed themselves over... yeah, it's written all over his face. His hands go up in surrender. "I'm sorry. I didn't kn—"

"Apologize to her," Evan says, ready to fight. I stand between them, backing Evan up a few feet.

Mike turns toward me. "I'm sorry. I didn't know you were married to Evan." His words hold no worth by the tone he chooses to use. Maybe because he knows it doesn't matter at this point.

"You mean you didn't care. Isn't that what you said earlier?" I say, calling him out on his lack of respect for me and my marriage.

There's a change in his eyes, maybe alcohol taking over when Mike's gaze goes from me to Evan and then back again. "You're right," he slurs. "You're fucking hot and I didn't care that you were married to a spoiled rich kid who wastes his days working on his tan, instead of being productive in life." He turns to reach for the door.

"Fuck you! Your ass is so fired. I will fucking ruin you in this city!" Evan yells, pushing Mike's shoulder over mine before sidestepping me.

Just as Mike turns back, his own arrogance kicks in, the alcohol clouding the better judgment I know he must have to work for the company. "You're such a dick, Ashford. Since I'm fucked anyway…" He punches Evan with a strong right hook.

I gasp in horror as Evan stumbles back. Without hesitation, Evan charges him, gritting his teeth and they both fall into the street. Mike takes the brunt of the fall.

Starting to run, I'm stopped and put aside as Murphy goes to break up the fight. "Stay here," he says, passing me.

"Help him, Murphy."

Just as Murphy reaches them, Mike staggers up then falls to his knees again, but gets up and takes off running towards the main road. Murphy drags Evan back under the awning and I rush to him, my whole body shaking.

"Calm the fuck down, dude," Murphy says, squeezing his arms together behind his back. "We're not twenty-three anymore." When he feels him relax, he releases him.

"Fuck, Murph. I didn't even get a hit in."

"You don't need an assault record. You could end up losing half the company to a lawsuit, if you're not careful."

"Did you hear what he was saying to Mallory?" Evan shouts, looking back at me. His expression is torn up, as if he let me down.

Though I'm soaked and my make-up is probably running down my face, he knows the difference between the rain and my tears.

In one fail swoop, he's holding me.

I tilt my head up, my cheek pressed against him. "You scared me."

"I didn't mean to. I was trying to scare—"

"No, I mean, I was scared you'd be hurt," I start to cry again, my sobs muffled by his wet jacket.

Murphy takes his cue and leaves, mumbling something about Kate kicking his ass for getting all wet on her big night.

"I'm not that old," Evan yells over his shoulder to Murphy. "I could've easily taken him." I can hear the lightness in his tone though. He's glad his friend was there for him and he'll always be there for them. This I know.

I wipe my eyes with the back of my hand then look up at him again. "I've always caused you so much trouble. I'm sorry I ruined the party for you."

Dropping his head back, he laughs. When he looks back down at me, his eyes match the smile on his mouth. "Yeah, you're my little troublemaker." He rubs his hands down the back of my slick wet hair. "You will never understand the power you have over men, will you?"

I shake my head because I don't, and he's right, I probably never will, but I love that my husband thinks of me that way.

"You make grown men fight over you. That's powerful stuff."

I hit him playfully on the chest while a smile crosses my lips. "You just like to fight. Any excuse."

"That's where you're wrong. I'm just ready to set the injustices of the world right."

"Okay, Superman, peddle that somewhere else because I'm not buying it."

"Hey, I've got an idea," he says, "since we're already wet, let me show you this car. I'm so fucking buying this car when I get home."

I arch an eyebrow. "Are you now?"

"Yep, it can be a present to myself."

I laugh. He doesn't have to justify any purchases to me, but I kind of love when he does. I won't tell him that though because it will go straight to his head. Bracing myself around him to cover from the cold rain, I try to act pissy and say, "I'm cold, just show me the damn car."

He takes me by the hand and drags me further up the alley to where the valet parks the high-end vehicles. He proudly points at a pewter-colored sports car.

"A new Maserati?" I ask in disbelief. It looks so similar to his current car.

"Mine's like four years old. Look at her lines and curves and wait until you hear the sound system they've added. C'mon, say I can have one?"

The rain stops, but I'm still freezing as he bites his lip in anticipation of my answer, looking so adorably sexy like that. How could I really ever say no to him? Plus, he has millions, *we* have millions, stashed away for our family, for our little Ashford clan, so I definitely think he deserves his dream car, or in this case, another one. "Yes, but only on one condition."

He grabs me by the waist, twisting me gently back and forth. "Name it. Anything."

"Anything?" I challenge.

"Any.Thing."

"I've always had this one fantasy," I start, but feel myself even in the awful weather, blush with my admission. "Make love to me on the hood of it in the rain."

Evan's eyes go wide and I hear him gulp. "You've got yourself a deal."

38

MALLORY

Three months later, back in paradise...

"Is the blindfold really necessary, Evan?"

"Yes. Now hush and wait for it."

He strips the bandanna from my eyes and stands proudly in front of his new toy.

I look at the brand-spanking new black Maserati in front of me. My breath catches looking at the beautiful car. "It came."

He steps closer and says mischievously, "Speaking of coming, I think I have a condition to follow through on. And I plan to follow through over and over again."

"What about the rain?" I glance up as the sun starts to set. He looks down at his watch as I add, "The deal included rain from what I remember."

Perfectly timed, he snaps his fingers and the sprinklers kick on. I scream all giddy as the water hits us. Jumping up, I look at my man, watching me, seeming to enjoy my reaction.

"Very impressive."

"I'll show you impressive."

"Oh, I bet you will," I say, letting the water drench me. "Now it all makes sense why Sunny and Zach suddenly insisted on taking the boys to their house for dinner."

He grabs me roughly by the waist and pulls me to him, his mouth covers mine silencing my words while encouraging my moan. Evan's tongue takes control and mine starts meeting his passion equally.

We're only wearing swimsuits, so being wet doesn't matter. My nipples harden as his chest presses against mine. He's always been my adventurous man and today is no different. I'm just glad our driveway is hidden from the main road because I relish all the time I get to spend with him in carefree moments like this.

My bikini top drops with my bottoms following quickly after. His hard cock is straining in his board shorts, so I pull the string that allows him some extra room. Evan's eyes never leave mine as he backs up, pulling the Velcro closure open. Always so fucking sexy.

I take a step back, the back of my knees bumping against the fender. Naked and horny for him, I can't decide if I want him in me now or to fool around first. I lower myself carefully down onto the hood of the car, letting my body adjust to the warm steel beneath me as I stretch out, showing off my assets in the best of ways.

He licks his lips in anticipation.

Letting my eyes linger over his body, I take in his beauty, the hard lines of his jaw, and the rolling muscles of his stomach that spasm under my touch. His legs bump against mine and when he speaks, his voice backs the lust he feels. "You look so fucking amazing lying on my car like that."

I love the compliment and catch the possessive, making me smile.

Hovering over me, his hands press down on either side of my head. His pelvis is against mine and I squirm, wanting him, needing him now. "Don't tease."

My hands glide over the defined muscles of his shoulders and my fingers dance over the droplets from the water falling from above. He doesn't waste time. His fingers slide between my legs and he slowly drags them back up and down twice. Satisfied, he positions himself then pushes in without fanfare.

My eyes close as my back arches and I moan in pleasure. As he pulls back, almost all the way, and looks at me, his lids heavy like mine. Thrusting forward, he moves his hand to my right breast, making me scream, "Yes! Oh Evan."

"Fuck, you feel incredible!" He grips my hips, angling me higher to go deeper. His head goes back and he grunts through a few rough gyrates before he looks down and commands. "Hold on to the car."

The car is slippery when wet, so I slide up, feeling above my head and grab onto the lip of the hood below the windshield wipers. Evan has to lean further over the car to reach me. He thrusts again, slightly losing his balance, and a hand lands next to my head with a loud thump. I'd worry about denting the car but in this state, I don't care about it. My body is burning on the inside as my orgasm starts flickering.

Even with my eyes closed, I feel the piercing presence of his gaze on me, on my body. I dare to open them. His expression engulfs me wholly, and I fall, letting my orgasm take me alive.

"Oh Baby, yes, yes, yes." Every word hits the deepest of places—inside my soul—until he falls with me. His hands pin my wrists to the glass above, and the heaviness of his body, of his love weighs me down.

His heavy pants mix with words of adoration and

commitment, explicitness and dirty cravings. As soon as my arms are free, I wrap them around him, holding him, grounding him back to me.

"I love you," he whispers before he places the sweetest of kisses against my temple, then my ear, my chin, and finally on my lips. "I'll love you forever."

"I love you. Always, Evan."

EVAN

I stand there speechless. A girl. *A baby girl.* We have a girl. Nine months and two weeks after the arrival of my dream car, I'm holding my other dream come true, a tiny baby girl in my arms.

"She's perfect. God, I can't believe we have a girl." I look at my wife, my beautiful wife and tears fill my eyes. Her tears become mine and mine hers as I hug her to me, placing the baby in her arms. "You gave me a girl. We have a girl."

Her gentle cries of joy replace words and I know exactly how she feels. Mallory moves over and I slide down onto the hospital bed next to her. Wrapping one arm around her shoulder and one underneath the arm she cradles and cuddles our little one in.

"She's so beautiful," she whispers only for the three of us to hear as the last of the nurses leaves the room. My wife is safe. My baby is healthy. My family is complete.

"She has your hair color and heart-shaped lips," I point out. "She's a lucky girl to look so much like her mom."

I watch as Mallory smiles, admiring our daughter. "I can't believe she was conceived on the hood of your car," she says with a light laugh, making small adjustments so she doesn't wake the sleeping beauty in her arms. "And no, we aren't naming her Maserati or Grancabrio." Mallory knows me too well. Her bright eyes look to mine and she smiles. "Congratulations, Babe."

"Congratulations. You did good. You did great." I laugh before the following words even come out. "How about Masi?"

"I don't want any part of her name to come from Maserati."

I sigh. "All right. I named Duke and Kai. You gave me the name Reef, so you get to choose this little ones name. I'll go with whatever you want."

"*Really?*" She looks amused by the suggestion. "Anything?"

"Any.Thing."

"Don't say that. That's how we ended up here in the first place."

I chuckle because she's right.

"I always loved the name Emily, but Kate and Murphy claimed that one three months ago."

"That name is good for them. It's not us though."

"How about Esther?"

"Esther!" I exclaim, my voice going two octaves higher than normal.

"Shhhh. Calm down. I'm kidding. I think since the boys all have Hawaiian names we should find something fitting for her. Keeping that same vibe."

"This one is all yours. I promise. I won't fight you on it. Whatever *you* want."

Mallory looks at our little girl and smiles as she gently taps the baby's nose and lips, which match her own, and then the baby's chin, which is definitely mine. Mallory's fingers slide around the little one's ear and she remarks, "Lani. That's her name."

"Lani," I repeat, glancing up from the baby into my wife's eyes. "Means Heavenly."

"Yes, just like our life."

"Lani Ashford? I like it, but you know what I like better? Lani *Masi* Ashford?"

Mallory laughs so hard that the back of her head hits the pillow. She looks at me incredulously, then says, "I'll give you Masi only because I kind of like the flow of the name." She laughs again, looking down at the baby. "I can't believe you're being named after a car. I guess it was always meant to be."

"Destiny. Like you and me." I bend over and kiss my wife on the forehead before kissing the baby on her tiny forehead. "Welcome to the clan, Lani."

THE END

ALSO BY S.L. SCOTT

To keep up to date with her writing and more, visit her website:
www.slscottauthor.com

To receive the Scott Scoop about all of her publishing adventures, free books, giveaways, steals and more, sign up here: http://bit.ly/2TheScoop

Join S.L.'s Facebook group here: S.L. Scott Books

Audiobooks on Audible - CLICK HERE

Playboy in Paradise Series

Falling for the Playboy

Redeeming the Playboy

Loving the Playboy

Playboy in Paradise Box Set

The Crow Brothers (Stand-Alones)

Spark

Tulsa

Rivers

Ridge

The Crow Brothers Box Set

Hard to Resist Series (Stand-Alones)

The Resistance

The Reckoning

Stand-Alone Books

ABOUT THE AUTHOR

To keep up to date with her writing and more, her website is
www.slscottauthor.com to receive her newsletter with all of
her publishing adventures and giveaways, sign up for her
newsletter: http://bit.ly/2TheScoop

Instagram: S.L.Scott

To receive a free book now, TEXT "slscott" to 77948

For more information, please visit
www.slscottauthor.com

 facebook.com/slscottpage

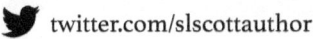 twitter.com/slscottauthor

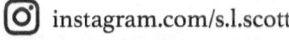 instagram.com/s.l.scott